Blind Man's Bluff

To: Richard and Judith

ENJOY!

May 31, 2014

Blind Man's Bluff

Ross S. Preston

VANTAGE PRESS
New York

This is a work of fiction.
Any similarity between the names and characters in this book and any real persons, living or dead, is purely coincidental.

FIRST EDITION

Published by Vantage Press, Inc.
419 Park Ave. South, New York, NY 10016

Manufactured in the United States of America
ISBN: 0-533-15403-0

Library of Congress Catalog Card No.: 2005910117

0 9 8 7 6 5 4 3 2 1

To my grandchildren; Devlin, Eli, and Seamus,
who I hope will never suffer
the trials and tribulations of Nomis Chester.

Contents

Acknowledgments

I began this project on New Year's Day of 2000. The events of September 11, 2001 and their aftermath substantially changed the focus of *Blind Man's Bluff*. Ann Ireland, who provided a detailed review of an early draft, convinced me that a substantial rewrite was in order. Following the rewrite, Saul Himmelfarb provided me with numerous revelations as to what the lay reader is looking for in a good tale. Victoria Bell and the editorial staff of Vantage Press provided editorial assistance during critical stages of the book's development. My son, Andrew, his wife, Julie, my daughter, Elisabeth, and her husband, Oliver, all offered ongoing support and encouragement during the entire project. Unfortunately my mother, Hazel, who had a keen interest in the project, passed away in her ninety-eighth year, before *Blind Man's Bluff* was published. Amy Preston, my aunt, who is in her ninety-seventh year, has also shown an ardent interest in the project. Bluff Island, where I spend my summers, and my grandchildren, Devlin, Eli, and Seamus, provided a respite from the project's many demands. To my wife, Judy, I owe a great deal. She supplied me with support, insight, encouragement and love during all phases of the development of *Blind Man's Bluff*.

Blind Man's Bluff

Prologue

On December 25, 1974 WPBS FM 99 in Philadelphia, Pennsylvania reported: "In the news this hour a man dressed in makeshift Arab garb and apparently wired to an explosive device crashed an automobile through a White House gate this morning and drove to the front entrance. The secret service said that he surrendered to police about four hours later."

1

The Maxim

Did you know there is an iron box located on the highest floor of one of the many pagodas that dot Kyoto, Japan's ancient capital? Nara claims that the warlords of the Kansai region, which stretches northeast from Osaka toward Kobe, Kyoto and Nagoya, in bygone days, stored the booty of their wars in the box. Nowadays, during the spring when the cherry trees are in full bloom, the schoolchildren of Kyoto flock to that pagoda, the temple at Nanzen-ji, to place the booty of their dreams, their poems, within the box. One by one, those poems reappear, with the addition of helpful comments, pinned to a corkboard at the pagoda's entrance.

Nara is Japanese and was born in Kyoto, so she ought to know. She's also the instigator of an annual spring pilgrimage to the Kansai region, a pilgrimage which includes Jessica, Doris and Liz. You might think Jessica, Nara's mother-in-law is Japanese too. Their facial features are remarkably similar. But she's not; she's Navajo and was born an ocean away in Socorro, New Mexico. Socorro is located some thirty miles northwest of Trinity Site, where the first atomic bomb was exploded. Yazzie's grave is also in Socorro. He was Jessica's husband. Manygoats, Yazzie's father, often scolded Jessica about her denial of his son's death. Jessica always resented that phrase "his son". After all, Yazzie was her husband. Manygoats isn't around anymore; he's dead too and Nara's the one who currently does the scolding. Now it's the phrase "my father-in-law" that irks Jessica.

Doris hails from Henely-on-Thames, a second ocean away. She's one of Nara's college chums. Nara always finds it difficult to pry Doris loose in the spring. Horticulture is Doris's gig and that wicked English garden of hers is the evidence. Liz, a cartoonist, lives in Ottawa, the capital of Canada. Herbert, Liz's artist husband, calls Nara's little foursome the Tijeras Quartet.

What brought them together was Nomis Chester. It's because of him that for the last twelve years the four of them, come the middle of April, find themselves some forty-two thousand feet above the northern Pacific headed for Osaka International Airport.

There's also another grave in Socorro whose headstone reads:

Doctor Nomis Chester
Dahetihhi
2001–2053

Nomis was Jessica's son. Carved beneath the dates on Nomis's headstone is a poem entitled "The Rings of Saturn," which Nomis wrote for his wife Nara. She and Jessica seldom visit Socorro. That bluff overlooking the Tijeras Arroyo seems to be where those two now go to pay their respects. Mind you, I don't blame her. There's no corpse in that second grave but . . . what Jessica and Nara suspect is on that bluff . . . well, that's something about which you'll have to make up your own mind.

To his professional colleagues, Nomis has an exceptional mind—some even call it beautiful. Sorry, I ought to be using the past tense . . . To others, he was a patriot. To those whose abilities were less than his, he was a loose cannon—one with the potential to go off in any or all directions at once. To the enemy—or evildoers as they have come to be known—he was a nightmare.

Herbert was commissioned by Nara to paint Nomis's portrait and once said that all he saw was a holy man with a gun. When that statue of Nomis was proposed by the state legislature Herbert even urged Liz to submit several caricatures of Nomis to the *Washington Post* to that effect . . . as working models no less. She didn't. Liz always felt there was more to Nomis than Herbert's holy man.

What the state of New Mexico did is proof enough. In the fall of 2064, despite the silent objections of the White House and the U.S. Congress, New Mexico finally erected the proposed statue in Montesa Park, on that bluff overlooking the Tijeras Arroyo, just outside of Albuquerque, New Mexico. You know, he was a world famous cryptographer and the father of the Quantum II computer.

At the base of the statue, there is a free form poem, a maxim, which reads:

There are some things that
One ought never tell
And other things that
One ought never be told

During his summer visits to Liz and Herbert's lakeside cottage near Ottawa, Nomis often repeated that little ditty but neither thought much about it. That is until last year when Nara told Liz what really happened during the summer of 2053. Now don't get me wrong. Nomis's maxim says it all. Some secrets are meant to be kept, but Nara had held her tongue for ten long years and the debate over that statue really irked her.

2
Code Talking

It was December of 2005, when Nomis was a little more than four years old, that his father, Yazzie, took him to the bluff for the first time. On clear evenings, after the sun became a red ball of fire and finally set, the sky filled with stars. To both Nomis and his dad, that was magic. There was a peace out there that Yazzie didn't find anywhere else. Nomis was at peace too; he was with his dad; he was so happy! They took turns counting stars. If Nomis counted ten or twenty or thirty stars in the hour they spent at the arroyo, they stopped on the way home for some soft ice cream. Even when Nomis didn't do any counting at all, they stopped for ice cream anyway.

Nomis learned early in life that the love Yazzie had for him was unconditional—there were no *ifs*, *ands* or *buts* about it. Yazzie was a man of few words with a huge potential to love, a dutiful man, determined to give his son all of his good qualities and none of his bad ones. After a stint at the ice cream parlor, Yazzie dropped Nomis off at home and headed for the Observatory of the University of New Mexico where he worked at night with his graduate students.

Sometimes Great-Grandpa Redhouse and his son, grandpa Manygoats, came along to the bluff. Redhouse had been a Navajo Code Talker. During WWII, Code Talkers were men who used the stealth of their language to confuse the enemy during many a battle fought in the Pacific. Redhouse told Nomis that the Navajo language was unique; the enemy was speechless every time he sent or received a message. Nomis thought that was weird.

Nomis's mother, Jessica, claimed Yazzie was a good teacher. The number of stars they counted always seemed about right to a four-year-old. Yazzie always sensed when Nomis was in a counting mood, or just on one of his little excursions of the mind. During those jaunts, an endless stream of questions gushed from Nomis. The bluff is also where Nomis learned to speak the Navajo language. Nomis's questions were often prompted by new words he had just learned, which he often repeated over and over. He was just trying them on for size. Sometimes when Nomis asked Redhouse to tell him about his days as a Code Talk they played a game.

∞ ∞ ∞

"What's a Code Talker?" Nomis asked.

Nomis bent forward toward Redhouse, anticipating the response that the old code talker quickly gave.

"He spoke a language that the enemy did not understand."

Nomis's response was always predictable: he sat bolt upright.

"Why? Why didn't they understand?"

Redhouse thought for a moment while rubbing his leathery chin. Then he leaned over until he was almost nose-to-nose with Nomis.

"The enemy was blind to our words," he whispered.

Imitating his great-grandpa, Nomis fingered the silky smooth skin of his own chin. His lips pursed and then loosened, forming a big smile that spread from cheek to cheek.

"Were you invisible, too?" Nomis replied.

The tone of Redhouse's voice became authoritative.

"Yes, you might say that; the enemy was blind, and I was invisible."

Nomis looked at him in disbelief, chiding him.

"I bet! You're not invisible now! Show me."

Then both Manygoats and Redhouse spoke some Navajo and Nomis responded in Navajo.

"*Neasjah*," Manygoats said.

"*Neasjah*," Nomis repeated. "What does it mean?"

"In Navajo, it means *owl*, but in Code Talk, it means *observation plane*," Redhouse replied.

"Another," Nomis begged.

"*Taschizzie*," Manygoats replied.

"In Code Talk, it means *torpedo plane*, but in Navajo, it means *swallow*," Redhouse said.

"Another," Nomis impatiently demanded.

"*Dahetihhi*," Manygoats replied.

"In Code Talk, it means *fighter plane*, but in Navajo, it means *hummingbird*," Redhouse added.

Nomis seemed pleased with his teachers and with himself. Suddenly he burst out laughing.

"*Neasjah, Taschizzie, Dahetihhi . . . Neasjah, Taschizzie, Dahetihhi . . .* " he repeated over and over again.

ıughter dwindled to a giggle and a smirk appeared.
ıean I'm a Code Talker too?" Nomis asked.
a Code Talker too," Redhouse assured him.
ınd Manygoats nodded.

ıNomis sat cross-legged for a while with his chin in the palm of his hand. He was still on one of his little escapades of the mind.

"If the enemy was blind and you were invisible . . . does that mean blind means invisible . . . like *owl* means *observation plane*, or *swallow* means *torpedo plane*?" he asked Redhouse.

Redhouse wasn't quite sure how to respond to such an innocent question.

"Well, not exactly," he replied.

Nomis's voice trailed off to a whisper. As his voice became inaudible, Nomis seemed to be mocking his own idea.

"Doesn't 'blind' mean you can't see, and if you can't see, then everything is invisible . . . including . . . yourself . . . ?"

All four sat cross-legged, gazing at the sky. Neither Manygoats nor Redhouse uttered a word in reply; nor did Yazzie.

"I want the four of us to have a secret code too, just like the Code Talkers. Daddy's code name will be *Neasjah*; Grandpa's will be *Taschizzie*; mine will be *Dahetihhi*, and yours, Great-Grandpa, will be . . ."

Nomis paused and turned toward Redhouse with a quizzical look on his face.

"Ah . . . *Jaysho*," Redhouse said. "It means *bomber* in Code Talk and . . . and . . . well . . . *buzzard* in Navajo."

Both Yazzie and Manygoats bellowed with laughter, nudging each other in full agreement.

Nomis giggled as he repeated over and over, "Daddy's *Neasjah*; Grandpa's *Taschizzie*; I'm *Dahetihhi*, and Great-Grandpa's *Jaysho* . . ."

∞ ∞ ∞

Yazzie usually arrived home at daybreak and slept most of the day, so Manygoats and Redhouse had many an occasion to practice code talking with Nomis. When they talked to each other in Navajo, some of his friends didn't understand one bit. To Nomis, code talking was magic. It used magic words like *Neasjah, Taschizzie, Dahetihhi* and *Jaysho*. Redhouse always said that only Code Talkers knew the power of those words and what they really mean and can do. It was fun, and it also made Nomis feel powerful when he and his friends played games, face-to-face at nursery school during recess and lunch period.

Nomis came to regard Redhouse as more than a Code Talker, and Yazzie and Manygoats as much more than his accomplices; they were wizards. Once when Nomis contracted a very bad case of poison ivy, Redhouse cooked up a salve from Jimson weed. Within a week Redhouse's knowledge of the healing power of plants had cured Nomis.

Manygoats was an amateur photographer and Yazzie worked with a huge telescope. In Manygoats' darkroom were lots of cameras. One was old-fashioned, almost an antique. It used film. Another used a memory chip the size of the nail on Nomis's little finger. Nomis always felt good in that darkroom. It was always night in there, like a wizard's cave. It reminded him of being with his dad.

When his grandpa used the old camera, pictures appeared from nowhere, like the stars in the sky. The camera with the memory chip was even more magical. It sent pictures through the air to a printer.

∞ ∞ ∞

"How does it work? With batteries?" Nomis asked one day.

Manygoats went a bit further than a simple yes.

"It sends a coded message to the printer through the air, using a lot of ones and zeros. Only the printer knows what it's saying," he replied. "The printer uses the message to make a picture. It even colors it."

Manygoats thought for a while. His lips became thin. He scratched the back of his head.

"Remember that coloring book I gave you for your birthday? You had to trace out a figure following the numbers and then fill in the picture you made using colors that corresponded to the numbers. The printer does the same thing. It talks to the camera to get the coded message, makes the picture and then colors it by number."

Nomis wrinkled up his nose. He was able to see the film and paper do their magic, just as he heard those Navajo words do theirs. But things that he wasn't able to see and hear were not that interesting. That new camera was too magical for him.

Sometimes Manygoats ran out of magic paper. To Nomis, the old camera without its magic paper was blind as a bat, just like his friends were to the double meaning of words like *Taschizzie* and *Neasjah* and *Dahetihhi* and *Jaysho*. Without the magic paper, the camera had lost its power; it had no eyes. But to Nomis, those magic words never failed him. They were Code Talk.

Nomis experienced the poetry of the mind or dreaming at a very young age. One night Nomis had a dream about his eyes. The images that Nomis encountered in his dream fascinated him.

a swallow
an owl
a hummingbird
a buzzard
a desert bluff at sunset
sitting cross-legged
counting stars
magic words
secret codes
eyes like little cameras
magic paper
pictures from nowhere

A few days later, while sitting cross-legged on the bluff, Nomis told Yazzie, Manygoats and Redhouse about his dream. He began in a most serious tone.

"How do we see? How do my eyes work? I had a dream about my eyes and in my eyes there was a tiny camera that took a picture using magic paper, just like Grandpa's. Inside my head was a tiny darkroom, just like the one you use, Grandpa, to make that magic paper work, but very, very small. What does it mean? Can that dream be true?"

Manygoats was not only the son of a Code Talker but also a Navajo Medicine Man, and dreaming was very important to him. As he spoke, his hands moved in a wide arc above Nomis's head. One hand came to rest on Nomis's shoulder.

"There is always some truth in your dreams," he replied. "But only you can know that truth."

Nomis began to fidget with the lace of his left shoe.

"Will my eyes ever run out of that magic paper, like your camera did yesterday? Do they work with batteries?"

Manygoats' hand reached out toward Nomis again. It crept between the folds of Nomis's shirt and came to rest near his heart.

"Even if they did, a Navajo can see with his heart if he is a good man."

"Am I a good man?" Nomis asked.

"Yes," Manygoats replied.

Yazzie and Redhouse nodded in agreement.

∞ ∞ ∞

Nomis was always full of questions. One day he asked what a flag was. Yazzie showed him the New Mexico state flag with the ZIA sun symbol in the middle—a circle with sixteen rays, four of which burst from each quadrant of the circle. Nomis thought that flag was neat, and so Yazzie gave him one for his fourth birthday. Nomis hung it in his room over his bed.

"What's time? Is time a watch?" was another of those surprise questions.

"Perhaps," Yazzie said.

Yazzie left it at that. He was a man of few words, not as willing as Manygoats to answer authoritatively the innocent questions of youth. Nomis's grandpa had a license to do that. Yazzie felt he had to be more responsible. Licenses like that only come with age.

Nomis liked watching other things in the sky, like clouds. During the day, when Manygoats or Redhouse were not around, he did this with Jessica or by himself, at home or almost anywhere. There were big clouds and little ones. It was fun. The sun was fun too. It reminded him of the flag that hung over his bed.

When Nomis was five, Yazzie took him to the observatory of the University of New Mexico to look through the big telescope. By this time, Nomis knew a lot about stars, and even planets.

Yazzie pointed the telescope at Saturn.

"That light in the sky is not a star, but a planet like Earth," Yazzie said.

Nomis stretched his legs, stood on his toes and peered into the eyepiece of the big telescope.

"Does it have people living on it?"

"No," Yazzie said, "but it has a ring."

Nomis was puzzled. He stared at the eyepiece and then placed his ear above it, cupping his right hand.

"Can you hear it?" he asked.

"No," Yazzie replied. "It's not that kind of ring."

One of Yazzie's graduate students produced a photograph of Saturn and showed it to Nomis.

"Wow!" Nomis exclaimed. "That looks like a big innertube. I'd like to float on that! Can you?"

This was one question Yazzie answered with authority.

"No, I can't, and I don't think you can either," he said.

3
The Scavenger Hunt

A scavenger hunt wasn't exactly what Manygoats had in mind when he tossed one last fistfull of dirt into Yazzie's grave, but according to Jessica that's exactly what killed Yazzie. When she let Manygoats have it that day he recoiled like a turtle might in the presence of a predator. I can well understand why. She can be mighty testy when she's tense . . . and when those two got going . . . sparks always flew. Her nasty comment about the bluff probably rang in Manygoats' ears for days. Fisticuffs seemed inevitable. At one point Jessica turned her head to one side and covered her ears. Soon afterward tears began to flow. Then her spine stiffened and out came the remark about the scavenger hunt, which made Manygoats' own eyes glisten. That's when Jessica passed the crying towel to Manygoats. Poor Nomis! The last things he saw with his own eyes were three big letters . . . a D, an E and an A. Those sorts of things aren't mentioned in police reports, but they are often the most important.

∞ ∞ ∞

"Money can sidetrack almost anybody," Manygoats muttered taking Jessica's hand in his while nudging her toward the New Mexico state policeman standing by the hearse.

"You've been a comfort to us all . . . thanks for taking the time to drive down to Socorro," Jessica trumpeted.

"It was something I wanted to do," the trooper replied.

"Not exactly what was on my shopping list," Manygoats mumbled. "The winter solstice . . . I mean an accident with Christmas only four days away . . ."

"He was such a careful driver," Jessica interrupted.

"Very tragic, very tragic," was the terse reply of the trooper. "I guess it's the wrong time to give you a copy of the accident report."

Jessica tugged on Manygoats' hand and then pointed toward the waiting limo.

"Not now . . . Please!" was Jessica's halting retort. "We're off to Albuquerque to see my son Nomis. Manygoats' father is waiting for us at the hospital."

Manygoats was quick to confront his daughter-in-law's denial.

"Redhouse can wait," Manygoats demanded. "I think you ought to have a look . . . and the sooner the better."

"Manygoats . . . you're the eye witness they all want to talk to," Jessica snapped as she filled his ear with a mélange of fact, grief and frustration. "And a lucky one at that . . . riding in the jump seat of Yazzie's truck with your seatbelt tightly fastened. You came away with only a few bumps and scratches. What remains of the father of my son is over there and my son is in the hospital. Anyway we all know it was greed that killed Yazzie Chester, and blinded Nomis. If it had been oranges or apples, the outcome might have been different. But it was money, money from the sale of drugs, which littered that highway."

"The little boy, Nomis, just turned six in September," the trooper remarked as he handed Manygoats the police report. "It's a terrible thing for a young boy that age to lose both his father and his sight at the same time."

"It was impossible for him to attend today's service," Jessica replied. "He's still in the hospital with a fractured skull, the loss of his sight and crushed ribs."

Jessica squeezed Manygoats' hand, shepherding him toward the limo's open door.

"Even if he was well enough he couldn't see his father's grave, his headstone, or the grieving face of his mother, or that of mine," Manygoats added.

"Was your mind back on that bluff . . . starry eyed?" Jessica again snapped.

"If you insist on picking at the wound which today was designed to heal, perhaps this is the right time to read that report," Manygoats shot back.

"Pardon me," was Jessica mordant reply.

"It's all in the police report," Manygoats said. "You ought to read it, Jessica. It will help bring closure. Thank God Redhouse didn't come to the bluff with us that evening!"

Jessica was quick to settle into the back seat of the limo.

"I can't bear to read it," Jessica mouthed as she slammed the door shut.

The dull thud of the limo door did not deter Manygoats from what he knew he had to do.

"Now is the time," he barked as he made his way around the back of the limo to the other door.

"No, no, no!" was Jesssica's muffled reply.

Regardless of the pain, she'll have to bear with me, Manygoats thought as he plunked himself down on the jump seat facing Jessica. "Interstate twenty-five was packed with holiday traffic," Manygoats reluctantly began. "There was a car weaving in and out of traffic fast—approaching from the rear and a second one in hot pursuit. Without warning, that first car passed on the left and then cut directly in front of us."

"Manygoats!" Jessica cried out. "No! Not now!"

"That car sideswiped an eighteen wheeler, veered sharply to the left and lurched onto the grassy median. The rig swayed but failed to jackknife. The driver of the rig didn't brake but stomped on the gas pedal. It shot ahead for a few hundred yards before the driver pulled it over. But the guy in that first car must have done the opposite. He slammed on the brakes and lost control. The car gouged a crescent-shaped skid mark in the grass. Sod flew everywhere. When the car hit the metal guardrail, there was a loud thud, lots of sparks and then the sound of crunching metal and plastic."

"Please, Manygoats, please . . . no more," Jessica pleaded.

"It rained plastic and glass as that first car bounced back onto the road, rolled over and came to rest straddling the center lane, teetering on its side. With its rear wheels spinning and its underbelly exposed it resembled a wounded beast trying to right itself. We plowed right into it."

"Manygoats, no," she begged.

"The impact propelled a jagged piece of the left front fender of Yazzie's truck through the driver's side window, imbedding it in my son's chest."

"Oh, now he's your son, not my Yazzie. Manygoats, you are so cruel," Jessica whimpered.

"The driver of the car in hot pursuit, an agent from the Drug Enforcement Agency, wasn't able to avoid plowing into the right front door of Yazzie's truck. The impact unhinged it, slamming the door into the side of Nomis' head, knocking him out cold. When the first car flipped, its trunk flew open. A case came sailing out. It broke open as it hit the asphalt, bouncing several times as it disgorged its contents: thousands of twenty-dollar bills. That's when Nomis' troubles began."

"You're right, money can sidetrack almost anybody," she interrupted. "It probably turned into a scavenger hunt."

"Traffic became snarled with people running to and fro, scooping up those twenties," Manygoats added softly. "Many of the rescue vehicles had trouble reaching the scene of the accident. It was a nightmare. I know. I was there. I saw my own son bleed to death. I'll never forget it. I'm also dreadfully sorry about Nomis, Jessica."

Jessica leaned forward and gently kissed Manygoats on the forehead, interrupting him in mid sentence.

" . . . And I'm sorry I made that comment about you and Yazzie being starry-eyed . . . I know how much those evenings on the bluff meant to Nomis, Yazzie, you and Redhouse."

"What will Nomis do without Yazzie? They were such pals," Manygoats asked.

"I don't know," Jessica muttered. "I don't even want to think about it."

But Manygoats did think about it and knew exactly what he had to do.

4

Only in My Dreams

A year after Yazzie's death, Nomis also lost Redhouse, the Code Talker. His saltus into death was more fitting. Unlike Yazzie, it was his time. Redhouse just slipped away at the end of a good life, for no other reason than his age. Jessica wasn't prepared for the double whammy that death dealt Nomis. For a six—or seven-year-old, death in any shape or form is a troublesome event . . . but a one-two punch in the space of a year . . . not good! Sometimes Nomis acted as if Yazzie and Redhouse weren't dead. He was moody, and his brooding many times turned into anger. He showed little interest in what his doctors told Jessica . . . someday, advances in medical technology might restore his sight. He was too angry about the magic paper that seemed to have run out and seeing with his heart . . . well, it just didn't happen. Deep inside, Nomis began to wonder if he was a good man.

"Was I ever a twinkle in my daddy's eye? Mom says so," was one of the questions that Nomis asked more than once of Manygoats after the car crash.

"Yes, you were, are now, and always will be a twinkle in your daddy's eye," Manygoats invariably assured Nomis.

"If I am *now*, where is he? Why isn't he here with me *now*?" Nomis demanded more than once, with tears in his eyes.

Nomis's blindness spared him from the only response Manygoats knew. In Nomis's presence, he also wept—silently. It was a secret he was compelled to keep from Nomis—that he too was dreadfully sad.

After the car crash, Jessica soon realized that bedtime was difficult for Nomis. Memories of those evenings on the bluff haunted him. To the blind Nomis it was always night and Yazzie was never there . . . bedtime just made it worse. He also became anxious when he visited Manygoats' darkroom. He felt and touched and smelled the dark of that room. The camera was there too which saw nothing without that magic paper.

It took some coaxing, but Jessica finally persuaded Nomis to visit the bluff with Manygoats at sunset once in a while. They practiced

Code Talking and Manygoats told him stories about Changing Woman, the most trusted Navajo holy person, and Black World, from which air, moisture, light and soil formed into earth and sky, or male and female, and Spruce Mountain, a Navjao holy place with a cloud world all its own. Nomis seemed to like those stories very much. When they returned from the bluff, Manygoats often stayed to tuck him into bed. He liked that too. Manygoats always said, "Sweet dreams, Nomis, and remember there is always some truth to them." Nomis always did what Manygoats told him to do. He was very dutiful, just like Yazzie.

∞ ∞ ∞

One night, Nomis found he saw all over in his dreams, but nobody saw him. Dreaming made him feel like he was floating around on a cloud, or on the rings of Saturn. Sometimes he even blocked out the sun, or just floated there in the sky, or whirled around on Saturn's rings, free from his blindness. It made him feel secure and powerful again. This newfound confidence soon shamed Jessica into accompanying him and Manygoats to the bluff. Jessica was profoundly saddened by what she heard one night.

"What's truth, Grandpa?" Nomis asked.

Manygoats sat cross-legged for the longest time, but didn't answer.

"Is that story you told me true, about seeing with my heart?" Nomis sheepishly asked. "If it isn't, why did you tell it to me?"

Manygoats replied with a few questions of his own.

"Have you tried?"

"Yes," Nomis whimpered.

"Can you see?"

"Only in my dreams," Nomis answered with a sigh.

"Remember, there is always some truth in your dreams," Manygoats quickly added.

Nomis was barely able to hold back his tears of anger. His voice began to crackle with emotion.

"But you tricked me; it was a trick; you didn't mention my dreams . . . only in my dreams does it happen."

Tears of guilt streamed silently down Manygoats' leathery face, following the wrinkles in his cheeks, crossing his chin, and silently dripping to the sand of the bluff beneath his feet.

"I'm truly sorry for that," Manygoats whispered.

Nomis reached out and touched Manygoats' face.

"You're crying," he said.

The next morning Nomis forgave Manygoats. What he had said was true; Nomis was able to see, but it only happened in his dreams.

Nomis's fingers, ears, nose and tongue became his eyes. Jessica enrolled him in a special school for the blind where he learned to read Braille with his fingers. Reading words with his fingers and attaching them to things that weren't visible was difficult. Numbers were things he had learned before the car crash, by counting stars with Yazzie. He thought about them even in his cloud world. They are a mind thing, numbers. They exist everywhere and nowhere. During his adolescence Nomis came to love them; their truth was unconditional, like the love Yazzie once had for him.

∞ ∞ ∞

Nomis became quite a celebrity after winning a math contest. His competition was the best that the University of New Mexico had to offer, but Nomis was only eleven at the time. Apparently Senator Charman from New Mexico heard about Nomis's abilities with numbers and arranged for Jessica, Manygoats, and Nomis to travel to a hospital near Washington, D.C., in Bethesda, Maryland. At Bethesda Naval Hospital, an experimental device was implanted to restore his sight. He was the first person to receive technology that duplicated nature so perfectly.

According to Jessica the first few days at Bethesda were something else. On several occasions Nomis touched and felt Dr. Welty's model of the eye, but it was difficult for Nomis to understand the medical mumbo-jumbo. The thought of some surgeon plucking out his eyes wasn't exactly comforting when Jessica described what Dr. Welty proposed. After several recurring nightmares in which a flock of black crows chased Nomis around his hospital room, intent on pecking out his old eyes, Jessica advised the psychiatric social worker assigned to Nomis's medical team to take a more familiar route. A talk with Manygoats was Jessica's suggestion. Dr. Welty did just that. Among other things, Manygoats mentioned that dream Nomis had about his eyes when he was five.

"Your new eyes are now miniature cameras, each with two tiny lenses. The cameras require thousands of minute pieces of magic paper, called pixels, which are connected to a tiny, battery-powered processing unit, and that's how your new eyes work," Dr. Welty said as he examined Nomis, just before he removed the bandages.

Now Nomis wasn't so little anymore. At eleven years old, he was also much wiser. Although Nomis's answer seemed deadly serious, Dr. Welty must not have realized that Nomis was making a joke of it all.

"Sir, did you say that my eyes have pixies in them? Now, that I don't believe!"

"Not pixies . . . pixels, or light-sensitive chips. They function like the rod-shaped structures of the retina that were damaged. Remember I explained . . . "

Nomis's reply was laced with sarcasm.

"Sir, did you connect those pixels and that processing unit to my heart, just in case the battery fails? I'm a good man, you know."

Dr. Welty finally cottoned on to Nomis's raillery.

"That you are, and a dreamer for sure, just like your grandpa told me you were," Dr. Welty replied, smiling. "Now, Nomis, I want you to keep your eyes shut as I unwrap your bandages. I'm going to leave the cotton wads in place. Don't move, please."

Slowly the gauze trailed onto the bed. Even with the cotton wads in place, Nomis began to sense light, then bright light, and then extremely bright light.

"How are we doing, Nomis?" Dr. Welty asked.

It was only light, but the sensation was wonderful. A feeling of joy paralyzed Nomis. He tried, but was unable to swallow. His larynx tightened as his Adam's apple moved up and down. His voice trembled, but he wasn't able to speak. He became apoplectic. His tongue dried up. He wept, but no tears appeared. His toes began to curl. He reached for Jessica's hand. Something must have passed between them. Jessica knew instinctively that he was free from the dark.

Jessica began to weep too; enough for both of them. Feeling faint and out of breath, she threw her head back, holding her chin high in the air, hoping to catch her breath and conceal her emotions. Her tears pooled on her cheeks. She tasted the salt as they dribbled into her mouth. She somehow managed to answer for him too.

"He's fine, I know it. I can feel it; he's fine."

Jessica's voice was very comforting. Nomis's first words were nearly inaudible and his voice was hoarse with excitement. There were a thousand things Nomis wanted to see. The room smelled of flowers. He wanted not only to smell and touch them, but see them too. He was curious about his own face. It had been five years since he had been able to see, touch and smell Jessica or Manygoats or even himself all at the same time. He wasn't able to wait, nor was Jessica or Manygoats. Shortly after Dr. Welty left, with Jessica and Manygoats looking on, he removed the cotton wad covering his left eye.

"Wow, have you got a shiner. Your eye is black as shinola," Manygoats screeched.

Nomis became disoriented and dizzy. All three let out a shriek as Nomis fell out of bed. Jessica and Manygoats rushed to his side and helped him up, or was it down? Nomis didn't seem to know. It felt like up, but it looked like down.

"Mom, you have purple hair. What happened?" he squealed with dismay.

Nomis's apoplexy waned. He became effervescent. Jessica, struck dumb, was unable to answer. Manygoats was effusive and began to dance exuberantly. Round and round Nomis's bed he went.

"Grandpa, Grandpa! I can see. I can see you! But . . . but . . . everything is crazy."

A nurse rushed into the room just as Nomis brought up his lunch all over the bed. When Dr. Welty returned, Nomis was flat on his back, lying in a pool of vomit.

"What's the problem? Oh, I see . . . " Dr. Welty said.

He picked up the cotton wad from the floor.

"No, I see . . . I see you!" Nomis said. "But you're on the ceiling, I think!"

"On the ceiling?" Dr. Welty replied in a tone of voice whose delivery gained a register.

"Everything is upside down . . . and backwards, and mom, mom has purple hair," Nomis added.

"Backwards . . . purple hair?" Jessica gasped.

Dr. Welty bent over Nomis and raised his own hand over his head to the right and asked Nomis to touch it. Nomis reached down and to the left. He performed the same test on Nomis's right eye. This time Nomis got it right.

∞ ∞ ∞

The following day, Dr. Welty and Jessica met privately. From his pocket he took a slip of paper and a gadget that looked like something used to open a car door.

"The camera and lens in each eye can be reset using this tiny handheld clicker," Dr. Welty began. "It is best that only we know of the clicker's existence. For a while, it must be our little secret. These five buttons control four options. He will never need sunglasses, and the business of being on the ceiling or seeing things backwards can be fixed with the push of a button or two. When I press this button, the one on the left, his electronic sunglasses will kick in. The second button will get him off the ceiling and onto the floor. Pressing it will rotate the tiny camera in his left eye one hundred and eighty degrees. The third and fourth, if pushed, will cause one or the other of the paired lens located in each tiny camera to move to the side. His implants will then send a mirror image of what he's looking at to his brain."

"Mirror image?" Jessica queried.

"Yes, he will see the word WAIT as TIAW."

"What on earth . . . as if he were looking into a mirror?" Jessica muttered.

"Exactly, and your purple hair can be fixed by adjusting the tint with this fifth button."

"Well, I'll be," Jessica replied.

"We weren't going to tell you about these options at this stage, but they are required for the upkeep of the implant," Dr. Welty added coldly.

What the surgeon said next rang in Jessica's ears for years.

"Remember, his new eyes aren't living tissue, but a piece of machinery. They will need maintenance, like a car. As he grows, the implants might be pushed around in his eye sockets. He might also notice what appears to be a list to one side or the other. His vision might become blurred, or things might seem out of focus. If this happens to you, your optician will suggest new glasses. When it happens to Nomis, he must return to Bethesda for a tune-up."

"And the options, can I . . . "

"We will explain the options to him at some future date," Dr. Welty interrupted. "It's better this way. He's got enough to deal with now. Oh, yes—one other thing. He has no tear ducts. We had to remove them. He can't cry."

Jessica was quite able to do just that . . . and cry she did!

5

Circles, Squares and Triangles

Dr. Welty wasn't too good at his own game of keeping secrets. He decided to have the engineers provide a clicker with only one button and before Nomis left Bethesda, Dr. Welty instructed him on the use of option one. One quick click turned his shades on, two quick clicks turned them off. Nomis thought his electronic shades were cool. Now, you know how kids like to fool around with buttons. Well, it was on his way home, while waiting for a connecting flight to the Albuquerque Sunport out of Los Angeles International that Nomis stumbled upon a programming glitch. If he held the clicker's button down long enough after one click, he was able to shut off his eyes completely. It was like being blind again. It was scary at first, but he finally concluded that the glitch gave him the best of both worlds. He even was able to go to sleep and it looked like he was awake or to summon his cloud world when and if he pleased. He decided to keep that glitch a secret, even from his mother.

There was only one problem . . . electronic dyslexia. Nomis sometimes drifted off to his world of numbers or just plain slept in English class . . . and when his eyes were powered up after having been shut down, words appeared backwards, for a short time, as if the third option was activated.

His secret became a plague on his life. Just before that car crash, his second grade teacher told Jessica and Yazzie that Nomis was better with numbers than with words. It caught up with him in eighth grade. About a year after his sight was restored, Nomis's eighth-grade English teacher suggested that he obtain extra help with his reading. So Jessica took him to a reading clinic at the University of New Mexico.

The examiner, a Ms. Vierdic, seemed more interested in how Nomis's new eyes worked than assessing his reading ability. She asked him a number of times to look through things that resembled little telescopes. It reminded Nomis of the times he visited the observatory with Yazzie and that made him feel good, but what he saw at the other end of those tubes sometimes didn't.

At one point, Ms. Vierdic asked Nomis to pretend he was in a car the same way he used to pretend he was on a cloud. She asked him to read the words on the signs he saw at the ends of those little tubes and tell her which side of the road he was on, left or right.

Later that day, the examiner quickly flashed onto a screen each letter of the alphabet, out of sequence. There was barely enough time for Nomis to record each letter before the next popped up. He didn't like the letters 'D' or 'E' or 'A' at all; he told the examiner those letters were the last things he saw with his old eyes. Nomis transformed them into something with which he seemed far more comfortable. He wrote them down as, Δ, ▯, and O and even played a mind game with them.

The "A" was a triangle, Δ with a misplaced line; the "E" was a rectangle, ▯ also with a line where it shouldnt be; and the "D" was half a circle, O with a line, | at its diameter. He had learned about those shapes when he was four and played with them in his head after the crash, just like he played with his numbers. He sometimes converted many of the shapes he knew into numbers with angles, lengths, widths, diameters, arcs and even equations, as a shorthand or code for their very essence or being.

For the O, he wrote down the general equation and demonstrated to Ms. Vierdic how the ratio of its circumference to its diameter produced an unending stream of digits after the decimal point. They might have been at the reading clinic all night, but after twenty digits, Ms. Vierdic indicated to Nomis she had had enough.

Ms. Vierdic concluded that almost everything in Nomis's world was a code: just an endless stream of numbers, letters and equations combined and organized in different ways—some forward, some backwards, some Nomis understood, but others he didn't. It was uncanny, even unnerving, like those numbers were silently waiting their turn to be combined, organized and then perhaps deciphered.

Nomis soon regarded the exercises and activities that day as juvenile and he voiced his disgust at every opportunity. At one point he finally did admit to Ms. Vierdic that he wasn't much good at reading with his new eyes yet; he still used his fingers most of the time. She made the mistake of asking Nomis if he also counted on his fingers. Nomis's reply was both cantankerous and belligerent.

"No, I read with my fingers, but I count with my head. I do it backwards!" he bellowed.

"Backwards? That's very interesting," Ms. Vierdic replied.

"The others in my class count with their fingers and read with their head," Nomis added.

"Oh, that's what you mean," Ms. Vierdic added. "Do you ever see letters or words backwards with your new eyes?"

"Never!" Nomis replied curtly.

"Now Nomis," Ms. Vierdic said skeptically. "I want you to peer into one of the telescopes; a picture will quickly flash on and off. Tell me, Nomis, what do you see?"

"It looks like the ZIA sun symbol to me," Nomis replied, smirking as he did.

"The ZIA," she replied. "How intriguing, and what was the word?"

"*Stop* with two lenses or *pots* with one; take your pick," Nomis quipped.

"Explain that to me, please. I don't understand," Ms. Vierdic added as her intrigue turned to fascination, and finally frustration.

"One mirror or lens turns things topsy-turvy; two makes them right again," Nomis indicated as he unscrewed one of the lenses from the telescope and encouraged her to take a look.

"Does that ever happen to you?" Ms Vierdic asked again.

"Never!" Nomis quickly replied.

Following that visit to the reading clinic, the recommended treatment was reading books, lots of books. So, with his numbers, and angles and arcs, his Ds and his Es and his As, his Os and his □ s and his Δ s, his dreams and his new eyes, and his secret about his clicker, Nomis came to terms with words and befriended books!

6

The Phantom of the Arc

Manygoats' car stopped by a barbed wire fence, next to a line of telegraph poles. Nomis and Jessica weren't happy with what they saw. The runway was a grassy strip swarming with swallows, not at all like that of the Albuquerque International Sunport or Los Angeles International Airport. The hangar was a shed with a rusty steel roof, and the control tower a wooden pole with a windsock attached to the top. On the side of the shed were the remnants of an almost illegible sign whose paint had long since peeled. Only one word was distinctly visible: RIDES.

Nick the pilot, a thin, balding man with an ill-kempt handlebar mustache and bowed legs, was a friend of Manygoats. He dusted crops for a living in California's San Joaquin Valley, between Modesto and Fresno. In the off-season, he took his plane south to Mexico in search of work. When he still had his hair, he followed the air shows from town to town. During the off-season, Nick settled for running sightseeing trips to make ends meet.

As they walked toward the shed, Nomis began to shake his head from side to side. Suddenly he stopped. When Nomis felt ill at ease, he became quite crotchety. If Nick had known about Nomis's little secret he might have used it as the antidote to Nomis's angst. That clicker gave Nomis control over his own personal cloud world. At his command, his blindness fled from sight and in Nomis's make-believe world, his rule was absolute: he was both sovereign and serf.

Nick's cloud world, into which Nomis was reluctant to ascend, was the real thing. In it, Nomis mightn't be the purveyor of his own stores. True, for Nomis the plane ride up into the clouds mightn't be like English class, where he was both pilot and passenger. But, up there in the clouds, if it got to him, as English class sometimes did, shutting down his eyes was an option.

Luckily, Manygoats was one of the few who were able to deal with the donkey in Nomis. Humor was his antidote of choice.

"It's a tri-plane. It has three wings: one for you, one for me and one for Nick. It also has three seats. It's very safe. Right-side-up or upside-down, it makes no difference. A harness will keep you from falling out, but it is loose enough to allow you the leeway to move from side to side. You'll be sandwiched in the middle, between Nick and me."

"Sandwiched in the middle, how about mom?" Nomis snapped.

"No room, Nomis." Jessica interrupted in a tone laced with apprehension.

"The open cockpit will permit you to see all over; just like in your dreams," Manygoats continued. "The difference is you will be doing it, not just dreaming it. What more can you ask for?"

Nomis just shook his head, while pawing the grass beneath his right foot.

"Open cockpit, upside-down? I had my fill of the ceiling in the hospital! I didn't feel good about it then, and I don't feel good about it now! My stomach is beginning to ache, Mom. It's too risky. Who knows what might happen? It only has one engine. It might conk out. We might crash! I've been there, done that. No thanks!"

Manygoats continued to jest as he placed his hand on Nick's shoulder, and, with the other, motioned toward the shed.

"Now, if you or Jessica were to pilot the plane, Nomis, I'd be the one turning around and heading for home. But my friend Nick here, the expert, knows the ins and outs of that flying machine over there."

Nick winked at Jessica as he bent over and whispered in Nomis's ear.

"And the ups and downs, too, kid."

Nomis flinched at Nick's remark, scowled at Manygoats and then tugged at Jessica's hand.

"I'd close my eyes if it got to me. I wouldn't think any less of you if you did the same," Jessica said as she gave Nomis a hug.

"Seriously, now is a good time to discover where your strengths lie. It's your choice! Are you a dreamer or a doer?" Manygoats added.

Nick twiddled with his mustache and nodded in agreement.

"Me too. I'd . . . "

The pitch of Nomis's voice rose as he finished Nick's sentence.

"Close your eyes? Yikes, count me out!"

Nick placed his hand on Nomis's shoulder, giving it a little squeeze.

"No, of course not. I wouldn't think less of you either, kid. I'd just laugh it off."

The climb to the cockpit was up an old wooden ladder with eight rungs. Nomis found himself fingering his clicker as he made his way to the top. The last rung was loose. He avoided it by grabbing hold of the seat back and wriggling into the cockpit headfirst. Once in, he had to stand up to see his mom who had taken a seat over by the old shed.

Nick again twirled the tips of his mustache between his thumb and his index finger, reached back and pushed the ladder to the ground.

"Sit down and buckle up, kid," he snorted.

The engine coughed a few times and then caught. Nick positioned the plane upwind and then revved the lone engine one last time. A wedding of swallows rose up from the field, tossing and turning as they did.

"Look, Grandpa—*taschizzie, taschizzie*!" Nomis shouted.

"Show time!" Nick announced.

The undulating mass of swallows swarmed to their seats on the telephone wires next to the grassy strip.

Once off the ground, Manygoats asked Nomis what he saw with his new eyes.

"A map," replied Nomis. "It looks like a map."

"A map?" exclaimed Manygoats with great surprise. "It's more than a map! The truth, now. What do you see?"

Nomis began to feel queasy when he heard that word *truth*. As the plane gained speed, the wind began to mess Nomis's hair, creating a vacuum as it rushed by his mouth and nose. As the plane gained altitude, the pressure mounted in his ears and then his eyes. Both began to throb. He groped for the clicker. It slipped from his grip, falling to the cockpit floor, out of reach. His knuckles whitened and the veins in his neck began to bulge as he grasped the sides of his seat with his stubbly little fingers. He opened his mouth wide to relieve the pressure. After taking a deep breath, he began to gag. He was drowning in a mixture of air and saliva. He coughed and hacked, trying, again and again, to force it from his lungs. His halting reply was barely audible.

"A map . . . well, and . . . a . . . with, ah . . . grass and trees!"

He ducked down into the cockpit, hunching over until his chest touched his knees. The clicker had become wedged beneath his seat. He pried it loose with his foot.

"That's the truth, no *ifs*, *ands*, or *buts*, Grandpa," he added with conviction as his lungs began to clear and his stomach to settle.

"Grass and trees. Truth is relative, kid," Nick added over the drone of the engine. "Let's pull some ggeezzss."

Nick flipped the plane onto its back. Up became down and down became up. The swallows took to the air.

The clicker began to rattle around the cockpit, like dice in a craps game. It hit Nomis in the temple, just above his left eyebrow. Nomis thought he had it in his grasp, but the wind snatched it away. Gravity did the rest. He was on his own now. He was terrified.

"What do you see down there now, kid? That is, if you can figure out which way is down?" Nick sung out as he pulled back hard on the stick.

Poor Jessica was aghast when the plane stood on its tail as it began a loop-the-loop. The swallows mimed every move. The engine labored. The swallows didn't.

Manygoats was just as horrified when Nick opened the throttle wide, enriching the mixture of fuel to air. The exhaust of the engine turned blue. So did Nick's face. He reached for a lever, pulling on it hard. Cool air began to flow over the cylinder heads, into the cockpit and onto their faces.

Over the whine of the engine, off and on Manygoats heard Nick chortling, and then laughing. *Taschizzie* provided his refrain. Nick laughed so hard, a rich belly laugh from deep inside, that he almost lost control of the plane.

Nick's laugh was infectious. Nomis chuckled, then laughed, then howled with delight. The swallows tossed and tumbled with joy. The finale was spectacular. They all became weightless for a few seconds as the plane nosed up and then down, trailing a great arc of purplish-blue smoke in the sky.

"Hey, look, Grandpa, I'm beginning to float," Nomis hollered over the roar of the engine.

Nomis let go of the seat. The harness was free to do its job. His knuckles and cheeks turned pink. His terror subsided.

"It's just like floating on . . . on the rings of Saturn. It's true, I can float!" Nomis shrieked.

His voice rose in pitch, seemingly determined to turn what had begun as a statement into a question, but wasn't sure it was able or ought to. It finally did.

"My dad was . . . My dad was wrong?"

Suddenly he puked. For a few seconds the vomit, shielded by the windscreen, just hung there in the air, mocking him. Then the wind carried it away. Some of it hit Manygoats right in the face.

Being both weightless and airsick in a small space at the same time was a messy business. When they returned to the grassy strip and Jessica found out what had happened she voiced her disgust. Manygoats was very apologetic and offered to pay to have the cockpit and seats steam-cleaned. Nick assured Manygoats and Jessica he had ten extra seats in the shed. Apparently it happened all the time, especially during that rollercoaster of a ride called the great arc. It made Nomis feel a bit nauseous again when he walked past the shed on the way to the car and saw no extra seats.

Manygoats' rendition of what had happened up there in the sky became stock talk at the local coffee shop. By noon the following day all of Manygoats' friends knew that Nomis had 'floated'. Floating was probably the high point for Nomis, but the absence of those ten seats was surely the low point. He didn't know if that comment by Nick about the ten seats was true, an excuse, or a little white lie. Such situations made Nomis distrustful of adults, even those close to him, like Manygoats.

Nomis loved Manygoats, just as Yazzie had loved Nomis, in an unconditional way. Manygoats, like Yazzie, was a wise and prudent adviser; a mentor. Nomis used to love going to Montesa Park at dusk with both of them. But the good times Nomis had on the bluff were diminished by the car accident.

That crash still made Nomis very angry when he thought about Yazzie. It was hard to know exactly what to do with his anger. Often his tantrums ended up in Manygoats' lap. Nomis might have easily forgiven Yazzie for those little mindless remarks made by parents, if Yazzie was still alive. He might even be able to forgive him for being wrong about floating. But, how might he forgive a dead man?

During that wild ride in the sky Nomis came to some sort of understanding as to which way was up. Most things were relative, yet death was an absolute; it periodically confined him to an empty space. Nomis's periodic bouts of nausea worsened. Although he had nothing to do with what happened to Yazzie, he secretly shouldered the blame. He developed an iron will and held his anger inside himself. Manygoats called his little problem the phantom of the arc. Nomis called it the little-white-lie syndrome—those unmentioned *ifs, ands,* or *buts.* His doctor called his repressed anger and resultant bouts of nausea "displacement".

7
George

After Nomis received his new eyes, he attended regular school. He was an eager student and a wizard at math. As for words, it was tough—like the end of the world. They weren't his forte. It was a relief when a new clicker arrived from Bethesda. Periodically he secretly returned to his cloud world and read with his fingers, but even that helped less and less. More and more he found himself drifting in that vacant space which had nothing of interest to say. Running provided some reprieve from his emptiness. However, the older Nomis got, the worse the syndrome became.

While eating lunch at a table with a group of noisy students, Nomis was quietly enjoying a peanut butter sandwich. The teacher on duty was a little man with an enormous ego. He had a chip on his shoulder which always twitched, and gigantic feet. His beastly personality reeked and so did he. Nomis claimed it was because he farted a lot. When he talked to a student or taught his class, that shoulder twitched even more often. It was no surprise that the students in Nomis's class called him Bigfoot behind his back.

But it wasn't me; it wasn't me. I didn't do anything, Nomis wanted to blurt out, just as Bigfoot reached his end of the table.

Nomis wasn't able to muster the courage to follow though. Instead, dutiful Nomis produced his pencil and made ready to sign a detention slip, even though inside himself he was writhing with anger. It was a repulsive feeling, the business of guilt by association, which for Nomis often turned into self-blame. On the outside he remained calm and collected. His iron will, not the beast within him, always won out. But on the inside Nomis became bloated with rage from head to toe.

As Bigfoot approached the noisy table, his tic was going full bore. When he glowered at Nomis, Bigfoot's arm almost jumped out of its shoulder socket.

"Well, Nomis, if you're so eager, I'll give you two detentions instead of one," growled Bigfoot.

Later in the week, the track coach asked Nomis why he hadn't been at practice. As Nomis searched for an answer, the image of the car crash shot through his head. Venom began to pump within him.

The coach put his hand on Nomis's shoulder.

"Are you OK? You look a little pale."

Nomis's voice was barely audible. His gut was writhing with anger.

"I was given two detentions. But it wasn't me. It wasn't me."

Sometimes he was barely able to control his anger. He began to salivate; dizziness and a cold sweat followed. Finally, all hell broke loose. And when that happened, he always had the urge to vomit, like he needed to rid himself of a pestilence whose location was uncertain, but whose presence was both real and terrifying.

"You might have told me. Fixing a detention is easy," the coach replied.

One teacher was eager to dole out undeserved punishment; another was willing to annul the decision of the first, Nomis thought.

Nomis felt even sicker.

On another occasion, the coach pulled a *grandpa* on him. Nomis had taken up smoking, as many students did. He didn't like it, but it was part of the culture of the crowd with which he ran. The coach was well-connected and knew lots of harriers at the University of New Mexico. Every so often one came to practice. One week, a harrier gave a talk about the way in which smoking caused reduced performance. At the end of the talk, the coach made it clear that smoking was grounds for suspension from the team.

A few days before the biggest track meet of the season, while limbering up at practice, dutiful Nomis confessed to the coach that he had been smoking, but had given it up.

The coach stood there, looking at Nomis. Then he turned away and stared into empty space.

"Have you been smoking this week?" the coach asked the empty space into which he gazed.

"No," the empty space replied.

The coach shifted his gaze toward Nomis.

"Then as far as I'm concerned, you haven't been smoking."

Again, quickly and efficiently, petulance began to consume Nomis. He tried to laugh, but it sounded more like a cough. It was hollow and came from the back of his throat.

"Are you sure you haven't been smoking this week?" the coach demanded.

"Yes," replied Nomis as he turned and tore down the track.

∞ ∞ ∞

The school basketball coach was also the man who taught Nomis ancient history. He had a bulbous chin, which supported a monstrous lower lip. A little, thin black mustache adorned his upper lip, much like the black crepe one might find on an old horse-drawn hearse. His students referred to him as The Lip.

He had taught for some forty years and was close to retirement. The year that Nomis was his student, The Lip's hearing began to fail. During the first few weeks that The Lip wore his hearing aid, the students in the back of the classroom spoke in very low, soft voices until he turned it up. Then they spoke in a normal tone of voice and he turned it down. He went along with their little game until one day, when he gave one of his crazy tests, nobody but those in the front row were able to hear what he was saying. The ones in the back rows asked him to speak up.

"Read my lips," was his surly reply. "Of late, I've become an expert in reading yours."

George, one of Nomis's best friends, turned toward the back of the class.

"They're big enough, ass brains," he silently mouthed.

The Lip had the strangest way of determining whether a student had been truthful about doing his homework. Every Friday The Lip gave one of his so-called history tests. They consisted of fifty words, which were always taken from the assigned readings of the prior week. Students were asked to spell words and names like *Thermopile* and *Agamemnon*. George, who sat in front of Nomis, was a regular wizard at spelling, but never read any of the assignments. Nomis idolized him.

However, George was lousy in math, and Nomis spent many hours tutoring him. George returned the favor and helped Nomis with English. They often kibitzed about what might happen if, on the double helix, one isolated the gene that contributed to George's natural ability with words and to Nomis's natural ability with numbers, somehow splicing them together. "Awesome" was the only word they thought of to describe the result—the marriage of math and words.

George won the first-term prize in ancient history. His test average was nine out of a hundred. Not only did The Lip give crazy tests, but he kept track of the number wrong rather than the number right. The principal's office always had to subtract The Lip's grade point submissions from 100 in order to make any sense of them.

George was also a shit disturber. When he accepted the prize, he made mention of how much he enjoyed doing history with words. The Lip was both clueless and speechless. He didn't know what to say. At a Halloween dance, George dressed up as a gorilla with enormous feet. He used duct tape to affix an old wind-up alarm clock to his shoulder and toted around behind him the waterboy's wagon used at basketball games. In it he placed a big dictionary with a false cover, on which he had written *Ancient History II: The Sequel*. Neither Bigfoot nor The Lip was amused.

During the second term, George sealed his doom. He let The Lip know in a most insulting manner what he thought of his tests. One Friday, George marked his own test before he handed it to The Lip, noting in the margin of his paper that he, George, was able to predict his score in advance. George wrote "fourteen" in the margin above his remarks and when The Lip marked it, he got the same result: fourteen. The Lip was angry and accused George of using a crib.

"Stand up, George, when I'm speaking to you! You can't predict anything, no less your score. That takes a lot of math, and you're no good at math. I suspect you used a crib. What you did is not possible," The Lip bellowed.

George's defense was simple. He was just good at doing *history with words*. He also said he was good at spelling, too; very good.

"You lock up your list and I'll demonstrate my innocence by predicting my score in advance. Anyway, I'm too old for a cri . . . " George began to reply respectfully.

"George, I don't need any more of your lip. Sit down."

The Lip was a competitive soul, so he took George on. Every Thursday, at the end of class, George, the wizard speller, went to the blackboard and wrote down his prediction; on the following Monday The Lip recorded George's test result.

By the third Monday, it was clear that either George knew the test words in advance or The Lip was a fool. The Lip was furious.

"George, no one can predict their score in advance. It's not possible," The Lip bellowed again. "I've got your number. If you can predict your score in advance, then you surely must know every word perfectly."

George's head bobbed up and down in full agreement.

The Lip's brow furrowed as he continued.

"No doubt you have somehow seen them in advance."

George's head wobbled reluctantly from side to side.

"No!" George responded.

The Lip's bulbous chin jutted out, pulling his monstrous lower lip with it and exposing his teeth. His little mustache disappeared from sight as the skin on his upper lip became deeply rutted.

"Yes," The Lip nodded. "I'm no fool. I must therefore assume that you have somehow lifted the list of words from my desk. Is that the case?"

George stood there for a minute, fumbling for his response. At first the tone of his voice was unfailing, but it soon became depleted of any certainty at all.

"Sir, I assume you kept your part of the bargain and locked up your list. So, the truth of the matter is that I haven't lifted your list, but have been able to predict my score in advance, perfectly. Therefore, I do know every word. An eighty is really a hundred; I mean, a twenty is really a zero—in fact, all of my scores are . . . umm . . . ah . . . zero. The only conclusion I can draw is . . . is . . . that I, I mean, that your test is a sham, as my only failing is I am just a wizard at spelling who is thoroughly bored . . . umm, yes . . . with your stinking tests."

The Lip turned up his hearing aid.

"What? What was that, George?" he snapped.

George covered his mouth with his hand.

"Nothing, Sir. I have the stick-ups . . . I mean, the hiccups."

Nomis reached over and slapped George on the back.

"Nomis, cut that out," the Lip hollered.

"The hiccups, Sir, George has the hiccups," Nomis replied respectfully.

Now, George was a very tall boy who was even less interested in sports than spelling words like *Mesopotamia*. Nothing much ever came of the confrontation between George and The Lip, except that George began to play basketball soon after he confessed to not reading any of his assignments. In that game George was no good at predicting the score in advance, but it made The Lip just as furious.

8
The Cloud Chamber

Periodically Nomis and George worked out at the University of New Mexico fieldhouse. Before heading for the showers, they spent time in the steam room. The cloud chamber, as Nomis and George called it, was a good place to flush the salt from their pores. If the valve, which controlled the flow of hot vapor, was opened wide enough, it got quite humid in there. Most anyone who stuck his or her head in the door gave it a pass.

It was just as well. Nomis and George preferred to sit, naked, on opposite ends of a wooden bench in the middle of the room, and let the steam do its magic. There was a cold water hose, which both were able to reach, located behind the wooden bench. In one corner of the room, against a wall of bluish-green tile, was another wooden bench. At times, only their silhouettes were discernible through the clouds of hot steam that wafted between them.

Nomis picked up the hose and drenched his back and head with the nozzle's fine spray.

"So, what's your secret? How do you remember how to spell all of The Lip's crazy words?"

George disappeared into a cloud of steam. He sat down on the other bench, resting his back against the warm, tiled wall. He clasped his ankles and brought his knees up toward his chest as far as possible.

"I know what I know," George replied.

Nomis flicked the nozzle's fine spray into the steam in George's general direction.

"You what?" Nomis said.

"Cut that out," replied George. "I always try to do my personal best. Yeah, and I know what I don't know, too."

"Your personal best?" Nomis said. "Is a game point average . . . ?"

"Bullshit on you!" George interrupted.

Nomis caught a glimpse of George's middle finger as it rose from the steam and then fell back out of sight.

"The Lip doesn't care about what you don't know; he's only interested in what you do know," Nomis replied.

George snapped his towel against the tiles. It made a crackling sound as it recoiled.

"You've got it ass-backwards," replied George. "The Lip doesn't understand the rules of his own game. He doesn't even know how to keep score. In my book, I get a perfect score on every one of his fucking tests. I'm my own coach. I mark myself. I know what I don't know, and to me that's as important as knowing what I do know. A little criticism is OK, but to make it your life's work . . . to keep a book on it . . . no way. Life without some kudos every once in a while can be depressing as shit."

George ran his fingers through his hair as he rubbed his back up and down on the warm tile.

"Oh, shit," continued George. "All that bullshit about knowing how to spell all those words because I was able to predict my score in advance was exactly that—bullshit. I was jerking The Lip's chain . . . making fun of the bastard's stupid tests. Look where it got me—a game point average of a little over two points. No. According to The Lip, my game point average is a little over twenty missed shots."

"You mean you aren't able to get a perfect score even if you chose to?" Nomis asked.

"Now you've got me going. Of course not, bonehead. That crazy business of focusing on your weaknesses rather than your strengths by recording the number wrong in his book rather than the number right is ass-backwards. If he croaked tomorrow, a substitute teacher might think most of us were flat-out failing the fucking course, with all those tens and twenties in his book. Teachers have a tendency to focus on their best students. The stragglers have to fend for themselves. I admit a substitute might end up focusing on the poorest, but . . . "

Nomis cut him off, grunting as he stood up to stretch his legs.

"My fucking calves hurt like hell. Isn't that the way it ought to be?" Nomis said.

"What do you expect after a five-mile run, dummy?" replied George.

Nomis placed his right foot on the wooden bench and bent forward, stretching his thigh and calf muscles.

"No, no, ass brain. If The Lip croaked, a new teacher might end up focusing on the worst of us, which, in my book, is the way it ought to be."

"But he hasn't croaked yet," replied George. "I don't want his recommendation. I can just imagine what he might say. 'George's test scores were in the low teens'."

George emerged from the steam with his arms outstretched, groping his way toward Nomis. His towel was wrapped around his head, covering his eyes and nose.

"I want your body," George moaned. "Hey, did you ever get your hands on anything besides your own wang when you were blind?"

"You fucking deadbeat," quipped Nomis. "I wasn't old enough."

"Liar. What's it like when you're blind? Get any good feels in your cloud world?" George asked.

Nomis didn't answer.

"You know, speaking of deadbeats," George continued, "that math teacher of ours, Mr. G, wrecked my plans for spring break with that surprise take-home test."

"Come on, George, once you figured out where he's coming from, those little puzzles of his are a piece of cake. They're Zeno's four innocent little paradoxes. They've been around for two thousand, five hundred years," Nomis said.

"And exactly where was that deadbeat coming from, with that question about the stupid turtle that Achilles never was able to beat? And the one about motion being impossible was a corker—arrows in the air that never move? Bullshit," George replied.

Nomis began to chuckle.

"Maybe old Zeno is the root of your problem.

. . . Lip's crazy tests I had not fudged,
My game point average never budged,
I shot round balls through the air,
They came to rest I cared not where . . . "

"Aw, fuck off," George replied. "I always do my personal best."

"G was just trying to get you to think about *continuity* and *infinity*," said Nomis. "Back in the days of Zeno, his opponents were hampered by the difficulty that non-mathematical language had in dealing with such ideas. Words aren't the best medium to convey thought in math. Math is itself a language. Even today some thinkers regard Zeno's paradoxes as unsolved."

"I don't have time for guys who jerk me around," George said. "I busted my butt over those puzzles."

"I did a week's worth of research before I began working on that assignment in earnest," interrupted Nomis. "You know me. I always bone up on what everybody else has to say, climbing up on their shoulders to see what I can see . . . and what I saw was no solution—yet. That was my answer."

"G's recommendation . . . probably not much better than The Lip's," George mumbled.

"Yeah, you didn't know there wasn't any solution—yet," Nomis added.

"Mr. G ought to have been a monk or a priest," George replied. "Tests without answers. Life without end. Great bed buddies! Doyee, what the hell might that mean to a college admissions officer? 'George doesn't know which way is up—yet'. I'd end up flipping burgers.

"On this one, I don't give a shit what other people know or say," George continued in a mumble. "I compete with myself. I focus on my own strengths and limitations. Others might speak of weaknesses; I prefer limitations. If others force me beyond my limit I will go—reluctantly, I admit—but I will go. Sometimes I even go willingly. But because I know myself, I am very good at predicting the outcome in advance. I always give my personal best. You spend too much time figuring out what everybody else knows. But what about yourself, Nomis? What do you really know about yourself?"

George's babbling image faded as he disappeared into the steam.

"The Lip's crazy tests are an extension of his bullshit personality, as is his butt-backward system of scoring. So is Bigfoot's tic, your track coach's tendency to converse with empty space, and Mr. G's tests that have no answers. I defend myself from bullshit behavior on the part of those around me by doing my personal best and keeping my own score. That's my secret. I get a hundred every time, as far as I'm concerned. What's your secret with math? And don't give me that blather about it being a language."

"Like I said, I know a lot about what others know about math," Nomis replied.

"Try mixing some words in with your math. Your world might be more interesting and a lot less stressful," George replied.

Nomis heard the door to the steam room open and then close.

"George?" Nomis whispered softly.

No one answered.

∞ ∞ ∞

It was some time later that Nomis stumbled upon an alternative to both the clicker and belly laughter. His first attempt was about very personal but painful things. It was an apology of sorts.

Clouds

Have you ever seen a cloud
Wallowing in the sky
Like a giant mound
Seen by the naked eye

Did you ever stop to realize
How much that cloud has seen
The countries by the tens and fives
That said cloud has been in

Did you ever see the sky, so proud
With argent sun
What must the sun think of my cloud
Who spoils all its fun

And then there is that star
So far from even sky
Who stares and glares so very hard
But never seems to meet the eye

Under the circumstances, it was the best he was able to do. Its shape on the page was that of an urn. He took it with him when, with Manygoats, he visited his father's grave at dusk one day. They sat cross-legged. His emotions poured forth as he softly read it aloud. It felt good.

∞ ∞ ∞

Nomis's English class was taught by a Mr. Potts. He was a round, playful, soft-spoken little kitten of a man, who might have rolled around the school corridors if he so chose. His nose supported a pair of spectacles whose thick lenses made his brown eyes appear like chocolate cookies, with dabs of white icing around the edge and a black jellybean in the middle. Assignments included a novel a week and some poetry, mostly modern, unstructured ditties that made little sense to Nomis.

George referred to the course as "Plots with Potts," but Nomis came to like it. Toward the end of the course, students were asked to write a poem. Nomis had forgotten about the assignment until the last minute. He was desperate. He considered using "Clouds", but that poem was too personal. Only his grandpa knew of its existence. He hadn't even shown it to Jessica.

The day before the assignment was due, a letter addressed to Nomis arrived from the Massachusetts Institute of Technology. It was Nomis's unconditional acceptance with full scholarship to MIT's mathematics program for gifted students. Nomis read and re-read the letter several times. Later that night, he wrote a new poem.

He entitled it "The Magic of Code Talk and Counting". When he finished, he printed it out. He sat for the longest time, just staring down at it. It had the appearance of an ice cream cone or an inverted pyramid; he decided it was top-heavy, both in form and content. He was afraid that it might topple over any minute. His mind wandered back in time. The words of Nick, the crop duster, rang in his ears:

What do you see down there now, kid? That is, if you can figure out which way is down . . . .

Nomis flipped the poem around so up was down and down was up, printed it out again, and stuffed it into his knapsack.

MIT.
of Saturn;
the Rings
Floating on
Maps, grass and trees;
Blind means invisible;
The ZIA, eyes and clouds;
Owl, Neasjah Observing;
Fighter, torpedo, bomber;
Taschizzie, Dahetihhi, Jaysho;
Swallow, hummingbird, buzzard;
Soft ice cream, mmm mmm good;

Code talking and counting stars;
Sitting cross-legged on a bluff;
Twinkling eyes and September 11th.

The Magic of Code Talk and Counting

Like "Clouds", he felt it was the best he was able to do.

9
The Sorcerer's Apprentice

After Nomis's bout with the reading clinic, Manygoats periodically provided him with books to read. Over the years, Nomis had come to feel like the sorcerer's apprentice. The more expeditious he was, the quicker a replacement appeared. There was only one problem: Manygoats' personal library was replete with paperbacks first published in the twentieth century. On his sixteenth birthday, Nomis had hoped for a reprieve from his grandpa's neverending supply of antiquated titles. Nevertheless, when Nomis's special day arrived, Manygoats presented Nomis with two more dog-eared, out-of-print titles. One was *The Nine Billion Names of God* by Arthur C. Clarke; the other, *The Professor and the Mad Man* by Simon Winchester.

The former played up the old theme of men searching for their nirvana. Those in Clarke's ancient kingdom were certain that if they recorded every name for god, life would enter a blissful state, time would stop, and the stars would cease to shine. The latter traced the history of the Oxford English Dictionary to the end of the twentieth century, from its beginnings a hundred or so years before. It, too, was about recording things that led to a nirvana of sorts, but the focus was on earthly words, not heavenly gods.

His grandpa also surprised Nomis with a gift of the most recent edition of The Concise Oxford Dictionary. The story of its older brother was found in Winchester's book. By itself, it was just a plotless, but very influential, book of words, some of which were for gods, like Jesus, Allah, Buddha and Jehovah. A search led Nomis to conclude that none of the words in that dictionary had Navajo roots, save one:

> Nă̦ vajō, Nă̦ vajō, (-ahō) n. (pl. ~s). (Member or language of) Amer. Ind. people in New Mexico and Arizona. *[Sp., = pueblo]*

Changing Woman, the most trusted of all Navajo holy persons or immortal beings, was nowhere to be found, nor was Black World mentioned. The word *code* made no mention of *talkers*, only of *books*, *names*, *numbers* and *symbols*. *Diné*, his people's own name for themselves, was nowhere to be found. Nomis was determined to break the sorcerer's spell. His birthday gifts were doomed to a dusty life beneath his bed. It was Mr. Potts who uncorked a scheme that saved those books from their fate. The entire class winced when Potts set down the ground rules for the assignment.

"You are to select three books, any books, read them, and then write a book report," Potts purred. "Its form isn't to be a boring regurgitation of the books' plots. Write an original tale of some four thousand words that synergistically combines some of your own thoughts with those found in the books you have chosen to read."

Potts' schema tweaked Nomis's creative juices. He framed his tale as a Navajo *story* told by an old medicine man, in the same tradition as the stories told to him by Manygoats on the bluff when he was blind and his only other source of enjoyment was his □ s, his Os and his Δ s. Nomis entitled his book report *Footprints of the Gods*.

10

Footprints of the Gods (by Nomis Chester)

Snakeless Bluffs

It was a crisp, clear winter's evening. A blind old medicine man riding a donkey and a young boy slowly made their way toward the bluff. With much difficulty, the old man's arthritis-ridden left leg finally bent at the knee, permitting him to sit cross-legged. The young boy's knees were much more cooperative. The old man turned toward the boy and placed the crooked fingers of his left hand on the boy's head, as if anointing him. The old man's eyes twinkled like the lenses of a camera in the evening twilight.

"I have made my story about words and gods no one's, since it was made mine long, long ago," the blind old medicine man said. "Now it is time to make my story yours."

The old man's crooked fingers returned to his lap.

"Why?" the boy asked.

"Winter is the right time for stories; there are no snakes on the bluff; I am old, and you are young."

"Must I be old like you when I make it someone else's?" the boy asked.

"Yes! And you must agree to use the words of the day when you do."

"Why?" the boy asked.

"Stories are timeless, but time can change the form and meaning of words. Words can mutate!"

"And if I can't find new words to replace the old ones?" the boy asked.

"Then your version of my story might have a different meaning!"

The boy nodded his agreement.

"To make your story mine, I must ask questions!" the boy asserted.

"And if I don't know the answers?"

"Then there will be two of us!" the boy replied.

As he began the old medicine man nodded his agreement.

Avoiding Enemies

"A blind old man like me dreamt that he was invisible. He used this queer idea to avoid his enemies."

"His enemies . . . you mean the things he feared the most," the boy replied.

"Yes."

"Hey! I saw that old movie *Little Big Man*," the boy exclaimed. "It was on the classic movie channel a couple of weeks ago."

"You did?"

Stars filled the boy's field of vision as he uncrossed his legs and stretched out on his back.

"Yeah! That blind old man and that other guy escaped by running straight through a raging battle, both believing they were invisible," the boy replied.

The boy's voice became skeptical.

"Hollywood has already made your story everybody's," the boy added.

The old man ignored the young boy's remarks. His crooked fingers first pointed to his eyes and then to the boy.

"In that battle, the old one and the other thought they were invisible, but the truth is the enemy saw a blind old man and a small boy as harmless."

The truth, the boy thought. *How I hate the truth.*

"You mean they really weren't invisible?" the boy asked.

"I mean the enemy had no vision."

The old medicine man paused.

"So, is that it?" the boy finally asked. "The enemy has no vision!"

"Don't be so impatient! The old man's people, your people, made their way across the ice floes from Asia to North America a long, long time ago. The queer idea of blind men being invisible was a feint repeated many times by your people. It also crossed the ice and was handed down, or, in the language of the Diné, the

Sioux, and the Navajo, *storied* from generation to generation. It never fails."

A trick, the boy thought.

"Never?" the boy asked.

"Never! But first you must dream you are invisible and you must be blind before you have your dream."

"I bet! Can any blind person make the trick work?" the boy asked. "I bet you can't do it. Show me!"

The old man smiled.

"I said it was a feint not a trick; only good men can acquire it in their dreams."

"Is there a dark side to this weapon?" the boy asked.

"Weapon? I said nothing about using blindness as a weapon. It is only a pretense your ancestors used to avoid their enemies!"

"And if this trick is used for anything else . . . what then?" the boy asked.

The old man's smile turned to a scowl as he mumbled to himself.

"Trick. it's not a trick. It's the truth!"

God Counters

"Your people came from the Himalayan plateau. On that plateau, seven thousand years ago, a wise old man, a soothsayer who claimed he was invisible but in fact was only blind, had a dream that a circle might be formed to record the names of God. He also saw in his dream a glorious sight. When the last name of God was recorded, the entire kingdom entered nirvana, time stopped and the blinding light of billions of stars filled the universe forever."

"What's nirvana?" the boy asked.

"A state where individuality and desire are extinguished, where fear has no currency."

"You mean everyone's a clone?" the boy asked.

"Not exactly."

Except for the fear bit . . . not for me! the boy thought.

"Recording the names of God was what your ancestors did for another six thousand years. The task wasn't a speedy one, using the kingdom's primitive technology of pen and paper. By the year 1955, they were just beginning the bs. It seemed that they had been at it for an aeon."

"What's an aeon?" the boy asked. "Sounds like the noise your donkey makes."

"Its predecessor was *aiōn* from the Greek, and it means a very long time."

"Aiōn to aeon. Is that what you mean by a mutation?" the boy asked.

"Yes! The God counter's goal was honorable and there were many light moments. Each time a name was recorded a new star was born."

"Is that why there are so many stars?" the boy asked.

"Perhaps! But I prefer to call them footprints."

"Footprints?" the boy replied.

"Yes, stars are the footprints of the gods," the old man said.

Star Trackers

"God counting spawned another activity which provided an estimate of how close the entire kingdom was to nirvana. Each night the new footprints, the ones not visible on the previous night, were tracked down and recorded by a second group. The star trackers, as they were called, were located all over the kingdom. Although communication was very poor, every tracker claimed he was able to see the sky."

"So the sky talked to the trackers and eventually the trackers talked to everyone else . . . just like my satellite telephone talks to me about everything under the sun . . . and the stars," the boy said.

"Yes, just like the sky talks to you and everyone else . . . if the sky's talk isn't encrypted."

"Encrypted?" the boy queried.

"In Code Talk," the old man replied.

So far, nothing's new under the sun or the stars . . . except for the dream-blind thing and those footprints! the boy thought.

Circles

"A young man whose name was Even Conrad Oxford Mazel, or Conrad as he preferred to be called, entered the outer circle of those who counted."

"The outer circle of those who counted?" the boy queried.

"In the kingdom, circles were extremely important. They made it go round. Among those who counted, those in the outer circle didn't count much; those in the inner circle counted a lot."

"So did this guy Conrad ever count at all?" the boy asked.

"About one hundred and fifty years ago, Mazel's father fled from what is now Turkey, having been accused of running a con game which fleeced millions from his business partners. He traveled to London, then to Baghdad and then finally he emigrated to the kingdom. He ended up in the shirt business and made a fortune selling his wares to the Oxford Company of London, England."

"So how did this guy's son end up with such a screwy first name?" the boy asked.

"His father wanted to name him Conrad Oxford in recognition of the good life the shirt business had provided his family. His mother insisted that Keven be the boy's first name. But the language of the kingdom was very strange. K was always silent and always dropped."

"Always?" the boy asked.

"In fact *OK* was pronounced *O*!, not to be confused with *Oh*!"

"So, Even, not Keven, became his first name," the boy replied.

"Yes, it was a crazy language. Letters like *m* and *n* were always mixed up because they were pronounced the same. The language was so crazy that those from outside the kingdom weren't able to make head or tail of it."

"Didn't the kingdom have a dictionary?" the boy asked.

"Not when Even was born."

Things Politic

"When his father died, Conrad decided to use his inheritance to support himself in things politic. It was Conrad who, in 1955, came up with the clever idea of purchasing a number of computers, which might speed up the counting process and thus compress time, by speeding it up, or perhaps saving it."

"Did anyone in the kingdom know what a computer was capable of doing . . . or not?" the boy asked.

The old man smiled.

"Regardless, because of his cleverness, Conrad was admitted to the inner circle of those who counted—those who counted a lot."

God-counting computers. What's next? the boy thought.

"Conrad was also the brains behind an electronic network which connected, via those same computers, all of the serious and deep thinkers throughout the kingdom. The majority of those who thought spent their time counting stars, both new and old, not gods."

"But aren't stars gods and didn't the god counters . . . ," the boy said.

"No, no, stars are only the footprints of the gods and the thinkers were . . . well . . . a truth squad. They kept the counters and trackers honest."

A truth squad . . . what a neat idea, the boy thought.

Mutations

"The name of the electronic network, Scholarwind, was often misspelled, as the letters *ch* in the kingdom's language were often dropped in usage."

"So Scholarwind eventually became Solarwind?" the boy added.

"Right on!"

"The God counters and the trackers must have been jealous of the thinkers' access to those computers," the boy said.

"Not at all. Conrad networked the counters and trackers, just like he networked the thinkers."

"Did productivity take a quantum leap with those who counted, all counting in unison?" the boy asked.

The old man smiled.

Word Counters

"There was another group in the kingdom, who didn't count at all. They also saw Conrad's game as useful to them."

"Let's see. We've got god counters, star trackers and the truth squad . . . not a competing god counting group!" the boy exclaimed.

The old medicine man's brow furrowed.

"Not exactly. They argued that Solarwind might also be put to work creating not only a heavenly list of gods, but also an earthly list of words—the first edition of the *Kingdom's Language Dictionary*, or the KLD, as it came to be known."

"Was Conrad a dictionary nut too?" the boy asked.

"While in London, Conrad's father became familiar with the *Oxford English Dictionary*."

"I suppose he couldn't help but do so. The same English word had many different meanings," the boy said.

"So Conrad argued that the KLD must take its cue from the OED. Based upon historical usage, anyone ought to be able to submit words and supporting quotations for consideration during its development."

"Anyone?" the boy asked.

"Even a madman . . . "

"Conrad was mad?" the boy replied.

"No, no! even a madman was able to submit . . . "

"I know that story," the boy replied. "After the first edition of the OED was complete, as new words were invented from old words through usage, they were added by way of a supplement. For example, today *wafer* or *cookie* means to us computer geeks something quite different than what was eaten at teatime, back in the late eighteen hundreds, when those word counters were building the first edition of the OED."

"With a computer and Solarwind, time might be further compressed and the job might be completed in no time at all, as those from all over the kingdom, who didn't count gods, track their footprints, or act as watchdogs were able to submit words via Solarwind."

"You mean all those who didn't count at all?" the boy asked.

"Those who were neither god counters, nor star trackers, nor thinkers."

"And the KLD, when it was finished, might provide a guide to the origin of words," the boy added.

" . . . And the very strange things that happened in common usage—that is, the business of the silent *k,* the dropped *ch, OK* which was always confused with *Oh,* the *m/n* problem and the aiōn-aeon mutation."

"Even Conrad's first name . . . Even?" the boy asked.

"Yes, even Even!"

"So now there were god counters, star trackers, a truth squad, and word counters, all vying for use of Solarwind. Did a cyber war erupt?" the boy asked.

"No, not really. Conrad was all too familiar with the crazy things that might happen for lack of a dictionary. His first name, Even, was one of them. So he was a big supporter of the KLD."

Making Wind

"The newly appointed chief of the KLD was a Mr. Wordsworth O. F. Mouth. His friends called him Word. His enemies were very polite and called him Mr. Mouth."

"I bet those who counted claimed he got the job only because of his name," the boy added.

"Yes! When the lexicographers met to choose the first editor of the KLD, many argued that any attempt to construct a dictionary of historical usage must not ignore word of mouth. When the ballots were counted, Word O. F. Mouth won."

Typical, the boy thought.

"Word wanted Solarwind to be renamed Worldwind. He expected his lexicographers to become just that when connected together—a Worldwind. He also knew that *l,* like *k,* was silent in the kingdom's language, thus, through usage, Worldwind became Wordwind. But Conrad argued that their activities weren't about making wind with words—"

Does he mean farting around with a bunch of words? the boy thought.

"—but catching things, like names of gods and definitions of words whose origin was common usage. After much to-ing and froing, Word finally came up with Solarnet, and Conrad reluctantly agreed."

"In the KLD, under the word *Solarnet*, I bet Word planned to include a lexicographic history of how all of this happened—that is, the link between Scholarwind, Solarwind, and Solarnet," the boy asserted.

"He also intended to make a brief reference to another episode. A small band of those from the inner circle who counted kept referring to the Solarnet as the *Innernet*. But through the extraordinary effort of Word, openly supported by Conrad, the word *Innernet* was never adopted in common usage. In fact, Conrad sent Word a patronizing note thanking him for putting a stop to the Innernet. It was also about that time those closest to Conrad began to use the sobriquet Con."

"So, was it Con who squelched the Innernet?" the boy asked.

"Patience, boy, patience!" the old man said as he wagged his finger.

Nicknames

"There had to be some way of keeping the gods and the words from getting all mixed up," the boy added.

"Con hit upon an easy solution. He proposed a simple way to distinguish between them. When a computer spat out a name for god, such as Jesus, it was sent across the Solarnet as Jesus.*God*; for a word like *Magdalene* it traveled the Solarnet as *Magdalene.word*."

"I might have thought that egoist, Con, would have toyed with the idea of proposing *Conrad* or maybe even *Con* as the identifier for *God*?" the boy asked.

"Yes, he did. After the world/word slight of Mouth, Con thought the use of *Con* for *God* would put the mathematicians, I mean god counters, on an equal footing with the dictionary makers."

So, the god counters were mathematicians, the boy thought.

"Word rejected Con's idea . . . that is, the substitution of *Con* for *God*. He reminded Con that what they were up to was all about words and gods. The fact that Con's words were also god's while Word's words were only words, had nothing to do with it."

"Did it make Con angry? He knew the manner in which Word had secured his job as chief of the KLD," the boy replied.

"Correct! This was the second time that Word got his kudos, just because of his name or more precisely his nickname."

"Kudos?" the boy queried.

"From the Greek—glory or renown."

"I suppose that those who set up Solarnet were amused by its dual use—counting gods and catching words," the boy remarked.

"Yes, the kingdom bubbled with joy."

Serendipity

"I also suppose some serendipity developed too. God counters and word counters easily changed jobs because the same technology was used in both activities," the boy added.

"True enough. But some counters never changed jobs because they didn't like Word's game, insisting that once defined, a word oughtn't acquire a new meaning. Some of those who didn't count never changed jobs, as they didn't like the sterile nature of Con's game."

"There were even some intermarriages between those in the Con game and those in the Word game. It was this mixing of the genome that produced Generation L, which almost saved the kingdom from its doom."

"Doom! Generation L?" the boy replied. "In the KLD the word *generation* must have taken on a new meaning when paired with the letter L."

The old man smiled.

"It did. Their offspring, or *Lateralists*, as they were called, were well-educated in the arts, the sciences and in mathematics."

"So they cut three ways?" the boy asked.

"Yes!"

"With either side of the blade and a deadly tip that was flattened and razor-sharp, I suppose," the boy added.

"Most *Lateralists* were taught by the God counters that God counting was to take much longer than word counting."

"Taught by the god counters!" the boy snorted. "What did the truth squad think about that?"

"Yes, taught by the god counters. The thinkers . . . "

"Even with those computers doing most of the work?" the boy asked.

"Yes . . . and the thinkers suspected that the KLD might be completed far in advance of the time when god-counting ended in nirvana, stopping time and any other sort of counting underway in the kingdom."

"Didn't some of those *Lateralists* question that point of view?" the boy exclaimed.

"Some did. A few began to doubt the thinker's logic. They took to writing about what the god counters might really be up to. Others began to guess when all the names of God might be written down and when Word might have the last word, and what it might be."

"Right on . . . I know I often wonder what is meant by time stopping forever!" the boy added.

The old man smiled.

Monster Slayers

"Some Navajo stories have a monster slayer. Is this when it enters the picture?" the boy asked.

"Yes . . . one of those sharp young blades knew the kingdom's history. In his youth, he had been fascinated by the suggestion that you might avoid the things you feared the most by dreaming."

"You mean dreaming was his nirvana?" the boy asked.

The old man smiled.

"But young Crazy Eyes, as he was called, came to regard this idea as the poetic thoughts of old men. The counting genome in him remained uneasy."

"I can see why," the boy added. "There were two activities—one that promised nirvana and one that promised a dictionary of historical usage. But when the last name of God was counted and time stopped, did this mean that Word's game stopped too?"

"The counting genome in Crazy Eyes struggled for the longest time with that very question. Finally he decided to follow his counting instincts. He questioned Solarnet: which might end first—Con's game or Word's game?"

"I don't need a computer to figure out that one. For a Navajo, everywhere you look there are gods," the boy replied. "As for words, there is only one I know of in the OED, and that's *Navajo*."

"The making of the KLD produced many revelations. The Solarnet's response to Crazy Eyes' query was one of them. Since the names of God were all words, but some words weren't names of God, there were more words than names of God. A debate soon broke out as to what nirvana might be like with only a half-finished dictionary."

"Wow!" the boy exclaimed. "What might happen if Con had to know the meaning of *sequideledalian* and its origin in usage? If the KLD stopped at *r,* through non-usage, that word might be lost forever. *Art* might survive, but if the dictionary stopped at *o, poetry* might not."

"This is where it gets a bit messy!"

"You mean Crazy Eyes puked when the word *write* came to mind," the boy said. "I know I would!"

"No! He consulted Solarnet to find out where Word was in building the KLD."

"What happened?" the boy asked.

"Our young blade was horrified. Word was stuck at the silent *k*s. If the dictionary stopped there, *literature* would be lost forever."

Terrorizing Word

"Crazy Eyes wanted more time on the Solarnet allocated to Word's game and less to Con's game. It wasn't that gods were more important than words; it was simply that without words, nirvana might be boring, lifeless and uninteresting."

"Did Crazy Eyes decide to get into the loop like Con did?" the boy asked.

"Yes! He made friends with those who counted, and was eventually elected to the outer circle, only to find that those who counted a lot were firmly in control."

Typical, the boy thought.

"There was more. He found that Con had set up a branch of the counters who were selling the names of God on a private network called . . . "

"Let me guess . . . the Innernet. I bet it also used the *Con* identifier exclusively," the boy added.

"And it seemed that the money derived from this activity was earmarked to fund Con's godly work in other areas."

"What godly work?" the boy asked.

"Terrorizing Word . . . on the Solarnet!"

"How so?" the boy asked.

"With his version of nirvana."

"You mean stopping time?" the boy asked.

The old medicine man's lips became thin as his head reluctantly bobbed to and fro.

"Con's failed attempt to have *Con* substituted for *God* had made him and the inner circle of counters so angry that they went ahead on their own and set up the Innernet for their exclusive use."

"Patronizing Word in that note was a clever way of covering his own tracks!" the boy replied.

"And once the Innernet was set up, a slick marketing ploy was used—the idea that each name of God offered its own version of nirvana."

Building Blocks

"Why didn't this Generation L character hack the hell out of the Innernet and expose Con?" the boy asked.

"Crazy Eyes did. Using the Innernet he immediately bid on the word *alphabet* which had been officially accepted by Word as a word, but clearly was not a name for God. He cringed when *alphabet.god* popped up."

"As a name for God?" the boy queried.

"Yes, as a name for God."

"Just an ordinary word . . . nothing to do with nirvana," the boy mused.

"Well, not that ordinary . . . the alphabet contains the building blocks for a world of words some of which are gods," the old man replied.

"Did Crazy Eyes find anything else?" the boy asked.

"Yes, he also found a calculation made by Con before he, Crazy Eyes, was born. In fact, the KLD might never, ever be finished. But there might be a time when god counting stopped, bringing any other sort of counting to an end."

"Most sinister of all, time might stop," the boy added.

"Exactly!"

"And when might that be?" the boy asked.

"When Con had learned the secret of life itself."

"You mean like making dead rocks see?" the boy asked.

The old man smiled as his eyes twinkled in the moonlight. "Perhaps."

But only God can know that, the boy thought.

"What a drag," the boy replied. "When time stopped, nothing would change. The same books might be read over and over, but no new ideas would surface, nor words emerge via common usage. No wonder Con had all those names of God, and some that weren't, up for sale on the Innernet. Did Crazy Eyes confront Con?"

"Yes, on the darkest night of the year, the winter solstice. But at first Con refused to show himself and remained in the shadows," the old man replied.

"Why?" the boy asked.

"At one time or another everybody in the kingdom had seen that film *Little Big Man*. Con was captivated by the power of the old medicine man's blindness. He saw it many times, even though the older he got, the less he was able to see. In fact, the night Crazy Eyes confronted Con, as far as Con was concerned he himself was unseen."

Unseen

"Unseen?" the boy remarked.

"Unseen!"

He must mean invisible, the boy thought.

"Even though old Con remained a silent and shadowy figure, Crazy Eyes reminded him again and again that Word was past *d*."

"Past *d*?" the boy replied.

"Yes. Words like *denouement* were already in the KLD for all to see when the kingdom arrived in nirvana."

"Did words like *denouement* have any effect on Con?" the boy asked.

"He made a mental note—some of the material on the Solarnet had been hacked and deciphered; better encryption algorithms were needed."

"You mean better Code Talk was needed, because all the light from all those new stars was making everything a little too clear," the boy said.

"I've never thought of it that way. Anyway, Con eventually emerged from the shadows and circled Crazy Eyes, going round and round, hurling insult after insult. At one point Con reminded Crazy Eyes again that, he, Con, was unseen."

"Unseen? You must mean invisible?" the boy asked.

"Con meant invisible, but it was a poor choice of words. *Unseen* can mean to move from one condition to another *without previous preparation.*"

The blind-dream thing again, the boy thought.

"Is that the truth, old man?" the boy demanded.

"Yes! Con hadn't dreamt up his *Con* game before his eyes began to dim. Con's game was ongoing for years."

"So did Con's god-counting exercise do him in, or was this criminal blindly going to go to his reward, hawking anything that sold on the Innernet as a passport to nirvana?" the boy asked.

Changing Woman

"Crazy Eyes was determined to stop the counting, at least until the KLD was complete."

"I don't blame him," the boy replied. "If you sped up time, you know, with that computer-driven god-counting exercise, some things wouldn't get done. No time would be left. When the counting was done and the kingdom arrived in nirvana, nothing would change. Life would be a bore. The ennui would be all consuming. Nirvana would be a repetitive world of sameness. Luckily the world still turns, so I suppose Con and his army of counters are still at it."

"Your world still turns."

"My world?" the boy mused.

"One day Changing Woman moaned and then roared, swallowing the entire kingdom in one gulp. Neither the word counters nor the god counters survived."

"Changing Woman?" the boy queried.

"The most trusted Navajo holy person, whose origin is the cloud world on top of Spruce Mountain."

"And the star trackers . . . and the truth squad," the boy asked.

"Gone!"

"But the gods remain," the boy said.

"You mean their footprints remain."

"No, I mean the gods . . . to be counted again?" the boy asked.

"Yes, I suppose to be counted again!"

"And what happened to the KLD?" the boy asked.

"It lives in the Black World."

"It survived?" the boy mused.

"In the company of insects."

"What were Word's last words?" the boy asked.

The old man smiled.

"They aren't in any dictionary . . . yet."

"And the fate of Crazy Eyes?" the boy added.

The old man began to chant.

"*Neasjah, Taschizzie, Dahetihhi, Jaysho . . . Neasjah, Taschizzie, Dahetihhi, Jaysho . . .* "

The boy soon found himself alone on the bluff, save for the footprints of the gods that filled the sky that night.

11
Show and Tell

It was a warm, sticky September evening in Cambridge. After the Freshman orientation dinner, the heat and humidity drove Nomis and his roommate, Alfred, out into the evening air. Alfred had been an oarsman in high school. He suggested they hike down to the MIT boathouse. As they walked along Memorial Drive, the shrill calls of crickets and cicadas abounded. The boathouse lights were still on when they arrived. A new, high-tech, eight-oared racing shell had arrived late that afternoon. From behind the new shell, a head popped up, sporting what looked like night vision goggles affixed to the brim of a baseball cap. The person belonging to the head must have been a coxswain before those high-tech shells became infested with electronics. His delicate five-foot frame was no match for his booming voice.

"What's up, son?" the head asked.

Alfred was six foot one, with the telltale physique of an oarsman—large hands, broad shoulders, and a v-shaped torso which rested on two huge thighs.

"Mind if we sit for a while on the dock and take in the evening breeze?" Alfred replied.

"Not tonight, chief. The coach's planning session is underway," the head bellowed.

"How about the new shell . . . can we take a look?" Alfred asked.

The booming voice gave Alfred the once-over. Alfred wasn't able to contain himself.

"Washington and Lee High School, U.S. Scholastic Champions, Senior Eight, Potomac Boat Club, 2017."

"Ah, sure . . . and your name?" the thundering head asked.

"Alfred."

"Say, Alfred, stop around sometime this week, and . . . ah . . . Go ahead, use the dock. Don't fall in."

Alfred ran his fingers over the shell's smooth, glassy bottom as he and Nomis walked the length of the boathouse, toward the dock.

"Seventy years ago the skin of a racing shell was made of cedar, about three-sixteenths of an inch thick. If you weren't careful a hole might be the result. Now they're made of a high-tech, carbon-based composite. It's very difficult to knock a hole in these babies," Alfred remarked.

"What was that gadget on the little guy's cap?" Nomis asked.

"Oh, they're the coxswain's high-tech eyeballs," Alfred replied.

Nomis turned away and began swaying from side to side, as if a footrace was in the offing. A few beads of perspiration formed on his upper lip. He wiped them off onto his shoulder. His voice quivered.

"High-tech . . . eyeballs," Nomis said.

"Yeah, they give the coxswain the peripheral vision of a horse. It permits him to see what's on his butt without turning his head. When an eight is at full throttle, balance counts. Like a zebra trying to outrun a hungry lioness, heads can't be rolling around. Any shift in weight will slow you down. Those things also have a readout that gives the stroke count."

Nomis and Alfred settled on a bench beneath a light to the left of the boathouse. A warm breeze was making its way toward Charlestown. Facing them was the Charles River, the surface of which was shimmering with light reflected from the Boston skyline.

Freshmen usually engaged in show and tell soon after they arrived on campus. Such palaver was always awkward for Nomis. As soon as he disclosed the untimely death of his father, the conversation became tense. It was the rule of seven which made the evening palatable for Nomis. Alfred politely moved back a generation or two when Nomis mentioned his father's death. They quickly found common ground when Alfred mentioned his Great-Grandpa Jake.

"So Jake played a role in aircraft carrier defense during WWII," Nomis remarked.

"Yeah, I think he might have been a spook," Alfred said.

"Spook? You mean spy?" Nomis asked.

"Not exactly. He was a civilian, but spent a lot of time on the big carriers. Off and on he turned up in Hawaii . . . also knew a lot about the big bombers; B-24s and B-29s, they were called. Those B-29s were regular flying battleships. One of them, the *Enola Gay*, dropped an atomic bomb on Hiroshima. Story is Jake worked on the bombsight of the *Enola*. Most of the stuff he did is still secret, or buried in the bowels of the Office of Naval Intelligence."

"Come off it, Alfred. How do you know? That's more than seventy years ago."

Alfred waved his left hand in the air as one of those fierce-looking beetles with the appearance of a rhinoceros and the determination of a kamikaze buzzed around the light above his head.

"My dad's a computer nut—works with nano technology," Alfred said. "He designed a device a few years back which can easily archive the entire, unabridged version of the *Oxford English Dictionary* one hundred times over. He used one of them to develop his own personal archive. Included are all sorts of stuff that he, my mom and my grandparents collected over the years. For me and the family it's a time capsule without a date . . . We can all add to it as time goes by."

Nomis scratched his head. His tone of voice became envious.

"Jeesuuss. It's all word of mouth in my family. I only know what my mom, grandpa and great-grandpa told me," replied Nomis. "Spooky stuff, eh . . . Say, Great-grandpa Redhouse worked with the Office of Naval Intelligence, too, at Pearl Harbor. Redhouse and Jake must have crossed paths at one time or another."

Alfred looked pensive.

"Maybe. Maybe not. Jake also spent time in White Sands, New Mexico, not far from Albuquerque. At White Sands he designed . . . "

"Albuquerque! I was born . . . " Nomis interrupted.

"Yeah, I know. The information is under your picture on that freshman orientation gizmo," Alfred replied.

Nomis nodded.

"Oh, right, your father's idea."

Alfred smiled.

"No. MIT is using old technology—a CD! As I was saying, Jake also designed feedback control systems that used radar-guided guns to shoot down attacking enemy planes during the battle for the Pacific."

Nomis sat straight-backed on the bench, extending his arms into the warm humid air, hoping to catch any breeze that floated by. The squeaks of a bat were heard as it foraged for its dinner in the cloud of insects above the light.

"Feedback control. A lot of math, eh?"

Alfred began to chuckle at what Nomis sensed was a private joke.

"Not really. That's what those bats are up to. Anyway, feedback control is nothing more than the governor on a lawnmower engine, a primitive little brain that opens the throttle when the RPMs decline or the spark weakens due to thick grass. In Jake's case, the thick grass was a bunch of incoming zeros, and the gun's brain was radar. Well, radar was the gun's eyes. Its brain was really a primitive analogue computer."

Nomis frowned. Alfred added a caveat.

"Hey, Nomis, I may sound like I know what I'm talking about, but all I really know is what's in the archives on that memory chip of my dad's."

Nomis nodded, giving Alfred the benefit of the doubt.

"After the war, Jake got a Ph.D. in psychology," Alfred continued. "His field was in optics and perception."

Optics, Nomis thought.

Nomis's heart rate jumped and his teeth began to grind. He flexed the muscles of his chest and neck, and then bent over, putting his elbows on his knees.

"As a graduate student, Jake designed a crazy room for the Franklin Institute in Philadelphia," Alfred continued. "There's a picture of it in our family archive. A comedian named Ernie Kovacs used the idea on his morning TV wake-up show. Kovacs had one of those crazy rooms built as a TV set. He dressed up as a gorilla, sat at a table, pulled out a sandwich, a carton of milk, and a mug, and proceeded to pour the milk into the mug. But when the milk flowed from the carton, it looked like it was falling at an angle onto the table, missing the mug."

Alfred's rendition of Kovacs's trickery using Jake's crazy room brought back memories of Nomis's first few minutes of sight at Bethesda Naval Hospital. Down hadn't been where it was supposed to be.

"He then moved the glass over three or four inches and poured again, hitting the mug," Alfred continued.

Nomis interrupted him.

"The camera was tilted so the tabletop looked level to the viewers at home."

"Yeah. How'd you know?" Alfred replied.

"I . . . ah . . . it seems only logical. Anyway, what a waste of talent."

"Whose, Ernie's or Jake's?" Alfred asked.

"Both," Nomis replied.

"That's only half the story. Later in life, Jake tossed optics, perception and feedback control and began to worry about both preference theory and airlines," Alfred continued.

"He became a man with two careers?" Nomis asked. "I thought that was a twenty-first century . . . "

"Yeah, yeah, uncommon back then. University professor and a board member of a big airline," Alfred said.

"A modern-day Dr. Jekyll and Mr. Hyde," Nomis replied.

Nomis got up from the bench, walked over to the edge of the dock and studied the Boston skyline.

"Sometimes I view myself as two people—the one who can see and the one who can't," he mumbled.

Alfred didn't hear Nomis's comment. He was already drumming away on the next phase of Jake's life.

"There's more. On a sabbatical from the university, rather than worry about utility theory or airlines, Jake and his wife, Lilly, went to Sicily, then Rome and Florence, and finally London. It took them four months. When he returned to the university, he began to read art history and anthropology books. When he wasn't teaching, he spent more of his time with medieval and Greek scholars and art historians, and less of his time with his psychology colleagues. His psychology books got dusty and then got tossed to make room for books on Greece and Rome and the Renaissance and anthropology."

Nomis turned and stared at Alfred in disbelief.

"You mean he abandoned the sciences for the arts?" Nomis replied.

"Don't know. Nobody ever got to ask him. He died soon after he retired from the university," Alfred replied.

∞ ∞ ∞

Nomis took to exploring the second-hand bookshops that ringed Harvard Square. One afternoon he came across a little book entitled *Hiroshima* by John Hersey. Nomis read the entire book in one sitting. That was when he learned there was a *ground zero* in New Mexico, too. Trinity Site was located just down the road from Albuquerque, northwest of the Osura Mountains, not more than forty miles from Socorro, where Redhouse had been born and Yazzie was buried. When Nomis was very young, neither Yazzie, nor Manygoats, nor Redhouse had ever mentioned Trinity Site, where the first atomic bomb was exploded. Nomis knew only of that *other ground zero*—the one where the World Trade Center had once stood in New York City.

The *other ground zero*, with its horrible scene of devastation and destruction, was the only one known to Nomis's generation. On his way to MIT, Nomis had stopped in New York City for a day to take in the sights. The quietness of that space and the memorial provided a feeling of closure to many of those whose loved ones had perished on 9/11. Yet Nomis remained in a quandary about that day. September 11, 2001, as he insisted it be called, was his day too. It was his birthday. Perhaps that was why his birthday had never seemed to be a happy time. After he read the Hersey book, the *ground zero* at Trinity Site bothered him, as did the sunburst on the flag of the state of New Mexico, which Yazzie had given him on his fourth birthday.

Just before Thanksgiving of his first year at MIT, Nomis received a letter from George. His letter brought back a lot of memories.

> Nomis, have you learned the difference between shit and shinola, or your ass from a hole in the ground, yet? In that cloud chamber at the University of New Mexico, my advice, if you remember, was to mix up a potion of words and math and take it in a public place. Daily if necessary. Any luck? If it's done any good, maybe you might bottle it and send it my way. Calculus is the pits. The stuff about the absolute value of *delta* and *epsilon* is depressing the hell out of me. I think I've reached my limit already.

George's letter arrived at an opportune time. Nomis had tried George's potion and it had given some relief from his demons. But by Thanksgiving of his freshman year, he had reached his limit too and had slipped into one of his periodic emotional ruts.

Nomis's reply to George's letter was prompt.

> Your reference to our steamy conversation and that nightmare of a remark you made in plain sight of the entire student body as to how much you enjoyed Lip's crazy tests, or doing *history with words*, as you put it, has produced a renewed ardor (great word, eh . . . look it up, ass brain) within me to do my own dreaming out loud and in plain sight of others on a regular basis. As for your limits, remember that those *deltas* and *epsilons* eventually vanish; once they do, you're rid of them forever.

To Nomis, mixing *math with words*, as George had suggested, became no laughing matter; it became serious business. A few days after George's letter arrived, Nomis went to a lecture at Harvard, which was just up the road from MIT. The subject matter dealt with the ideas and writings of Arnold Toynbee, the world-famous historian and philosopher. A resident scholar was giving a public lecture on Toynbee's notions about the existence of God. Nomis arrived late and sat in the back.

When the lecture was over he didn't leave, but just sat and thought. Only when he had written the poem "On Toynbee" did he leave.

On Toynbee

O great God
Have you lost your way
Or is it I

Oh foolish men
What is it you seek to measure now
Or do you know

Oh foolish men
Who seek to know the truth
There is no beauty in your plan

Oh lost soul
What purpose do you bare
What wisdom do you seek

You do not know

Oh foolish men
What is this truth
What is this image you create

I see no plan
no truth
no God
I see only men

∞ ∞ ∞

One evening, while browsing in one of those bookstores on Harvard Square, Nomis discovered another little book, entitled *The Immense Journey* by Loren Eiseley. Eiseley had been an anthropologist. In it, he set out his personal view about man's immense journey from the beginnings of time. As he so aptly put it, the book was about birds, bones, spiders and time. It opened with Eiseley floating, floating down an ancient stream. Nomis knew instantly that he wanted to read Eiseley's book.

The physics of the Big Bang was only a prelude to Eiseley's time. His clocks began ticking when life sprang from dead rocks or from the electro-chemical soup of swamps. Nomis felt he himself knew and understood exactly what Eiseley said and meant and felt. The life in Nomis's eyes had sprung from dead rocks, too, and they were electric. Eiseley hadn't discarded science; he had made it human and soulful, just like Nomis's eyes.

The last chapter, entitled "The Secret of Life", conjured up within Nomis mystical, Zen-like images of nature . . . rings and circles that came back on themselves in a constant cycle of renewal and rebirth. The Eiseley book so impressed Nomis that he suggested that Alfred give it a read. At coffee one afternoon, Alfred expressed his disappointment.

"I bet Eiseley's colleagues thought he was off his rocker writing such a book. What he did wasn't science; at least it wasn't the kind of science that his colleagues probably did. Reading that book was a waste of my time," Alfred said.

"Let's avoid the . . . ah . . . 'what the hell is science' question. You know my position on that one. Pure math lords it all over you guys in the hard sciences," Nomis replied.

Alfred took Eiseley's book and thumbed through the pages.

"You're so right, Nomis, but what he did wasn't math, either. There's not one of your blooming numbers in this book, save for chapter headings and page numbers," Alfred said.

Nomis winced.

"He was elected to the National Institute of Arts and Letters in the last half of the twentieth century," Nomis said.

"Sure, big deal, an honor given in the arts, not in the sciences," Alfred shot back.

"It's my gain and your loss. Eiseley's response to the bad-mouthing of his colleagues was to write ten more books just like it," Nomis replied.

"Ten, balls. Then ten times the waste," Alfred said.

Nomis's tone turned aggressive.

"Neighbors never fight with neighbors once removed; they always pick on each other. You guys in the hard sciences are always fighting with your neighbors. You're the sandwich discipline, the one in the middle, the bologna in the sandwich," Nomis replied.

At that, Alfred threw the Eiseley book down on the table and stalked out of the coffee shop.

In the months that followed, Nomis read all of Eiseley's books, one of which was entitled *Francis Bacon and the Modern Dilemma*. Eiseley, like Nomis, wrote an apology, and Nomis was sure this book was it. Nomis typed up a passage he found near the end of that book and put it in the middle of the flag of the state of New Mexico, which hung on the wall of his room at MIT. The passage covered the ZIA completely.

> A few years ago I chanced to write a book in which I had expressed some personal views and feelings upon birds, bones, spiders and time, all subjects with which I had some degree of acquaintance. Scarcely had the work been published when I was sought out in my office by a serious young colleague. Now with utter and devastating confidence he had paid me a call in order to correct my deviations and lead me back to the proper road of scholarship. He pointed out to me the time I had wasted—time which could have been more properly expended upon my own field of scientific investigation. The young man's view of science was a narrow one, but it illustrates a conviction all too common today: namely that the authority of science is absolute . . .

To Nomis, the authority of pure mathematics was the only absolute; it was unconditional. Mathematics was a language, and a very precise one at that. Science was just a humble sidekick, feeding on its precision and authority. Any other view was a sham. Just like The Lip's spelling tests or Bigfoot's tic, any wizard of a speller or a person quietly eating a peanut butter sandwich was able to deflate the authority of science.

He did have an interest in applied number theory. Cryptography fascinated him, and code-making was Nomis' *piece de resistance*. But with crypto, there was a constant battle going on between code-makers and code-breakers. Number theory was the makers' defense; computers and networks were the breakers' offense. But, in the limit, unless the marriage of number theory, computers and networks followed the laws of nature, a system that was very good at keeping secrets, there was the potential for no security at all—for no secrets to exist.

This is why he was attracted to pure mathematics—that and teaching. There was always a continuum of puzzles to solve, and the battles were purely intellectual. There were no limits to the authority of pure mathematics, and its truth was absolute. All of those *ifs*, *ands*, or *buts* were well understood beforehand. With crypto, he saw only men; with pure mathematics, he was able to glimpse God through the mist of its continuum.

So it was with his poetry . . . and his dreams. They too had come to have a certain authority over Nomis.

12
Poetry and Its Secrets

Once the snow began to fly, it became Nomis's habit, almost a Saturday ritual, to go cross-country skiing northwest of Boston. Skiing was a welcome relief from his heavy course load. His junior year wasn't the piece of cake he had expected, and Friday nights were always late ones at the library. One Friday night, when he emerged from the library, a fine snow was falling.

The trails will be in excellent shape by morning, he thought as he plodded up Massachusetts Avenue to his apartment.

The late night almost proved to be an obstacle. He nearly missed the 7:00 A.M. ski bus to Concord. The bus was crowded. He moved toward the back, looking for a seat. A gap appeared. He plunked his boots and knapsack onto the floor, and himself into the gap. It was a tight fit.

"Thanks," Nomis said.

There was a hiss as the doors of the bus closed, and another as the driver released the brakes. The diesel engine roared. The bus jerked to one side as the driver bullied his way into the traffic on Massachusetts Avenue. Sleepy heads prepared to doze during the forty-minute trip to Concord.

Nomis's seatmates couldn't help noticing the innovative method he used to hold his ski boots together.

"Duct tape?" one asked.

Nomis nodded.

"No money," he replied.

A young woman seated across the aisle from Nomis reached down and retrieved one of her boots.

"Me too," she replied.

Nomis dug into his knapsack. Ski wax, lip balm, a handful of pens and pencils, a spare ski tip, a pad of paper, a water bottle, some oranges, an O'Henry bar, a cell phone and a roll of duct tape tumbled to the floor in a pile. Nomis plucked the duct tape and the O'Henry from the pile and stuffed what remained back into his knapsack.

"Nomis Chester at your service," he announced.

The young woman smiled as she handed Nomis her boot.

"Nara, maiden in distress," she replied.

Her smile was coy. Her ski jacket, open at the neck, concealed a figure that appeared firm and full. Her eyes were dark, feminine and alluring. Her delicate, high cheekbones and long, straight black hair glistened, demanding that a lingering glance enjoy the timeless, imperial grace of her round face.

"Nara who?" Nomis asked.

There was no reply. Her silence was reminiscent of a recent bout with his bank's call center: "no last names" was the iron-fast rule, even if you wanted to call back later. For a good five minutes, Nomis occupied himself with repairing her boot. The sole was loose at the toe. He meticulously reinforced it with duct tape. As he returned the boot to her, he tried again with a less invasive question.

"Nara where?"

"MIT, chemistry," she quickly answered.

"Chemistry? I'm in math," Nomis replied.

A nerd? Nara wondered as she examined her boot. *No, a shoemaker, and not bad at that.*

"Thanks," Nara said.

Nomis unwrapped the O'Henry and bit into it. A lump emerged in his cheek and then slowly departed.

"Albuquerque," Nomis replied.

Nara looked puzzled.

"Albuquerque?"

"Albuquerque, New Mexico. That's my home town. I'm Navajo. And you're from?"

Again, there was no reply. The bus rocked from side to side as it barreled north along I-95. Nomis finished his breakfast. His eyes grew heavy. He nodded off.

His snooze ended with a series of bumps and wheezes as the bus pulled into the parking lot. It hissed one last time and then went silent. In Cambridge, Friday night's snow had already begun to turn to slush. In Concord, the snow was dry and crunchy. Conditions were excellent. Nomis was eager to get going. He was quick to lock his boots into his bindings, much quicker than Nara. As he made his way toward the trail, he caught her following his progress.

His technique seems incredibly natural. His skis seem to glide effortlessly over the fine snow. The energy of his torso makes its way to his hips, down his legs, into his calves and is then released by his foot into his ski. He just seems to float on the snow, Nara thought.

∞ ∞ ∞

The routine—skiing on Saturdays, math during the week—worked for Nomis. For Nara, that Saturday wasn't a routine, but a beginning of sorts. Albuquerque, or whatever his name was, had intrigued her.

The following Saturday, there were lots of empty seats on the bus. It hadn't snowed all week and conditions weren't the best. As Nomis climbed aboard, he heard someone calling: "Albuquerque . . . Albuquerque." It was Nara. She motioned for him to join her.

"Hey, Albuquerque, how's the boot repair business?" Nara quipped.

He ignored her query, sat down in the seat facing her, took an orange from his knapsack and began to peel it, offering her some.

"Nomis Chester, again at your service. Breakfast, Nara . . . whoever you are?" Nomis replied grinning.

"No thanks, Nomis . . . ah . . . Chester," she replied apologetically. "I'm sorry. I'm a very good listener but all that popped into my head when I saw you climb aboard was 'Albuquerque'."

Nomis continued, nibbling at his orange.

"Nara Moriguchi," she said.

"Pardon?" replied Nomis.

"Moriguchi; my name is Nara Moriguchi," she replied, nodding her head up and down.

Nomis's reply was matter-of-fact.

"Oh, hello, Nara Moriguchi," Nomis said. "Glad to make your acquaintance. I see. I must have passed your credit check. But aren't last names a no-no, regardless?"

Nara blushed as her foot began to tap the floor.

"I looked at Albuquerque's web site. Neat place. Not as interesting as Kyoto, though."

Nomis looked perplexed but pleased, as he had hardly been able to get a peep out of her the previous Saturday.

"Kyoto?" Nomis replied.

Nara began to paw through her knapsack.

"I know it's in here somewhere. Last night I put it—ah, here it is," Nara said.

A map appeared. She pointed to a spot near the bottom. Nomis's eyes blinked four or five times.

A map of Japan on the way to Concord . . . Interesting, he thought.

"My birthplace. Japan's ancient capital. See here, northeast of Osaka," Nara said.

"Osaka," Nomis replied.

Nara's babbling was infectious. Nomis folded his arms across his chest and leaned back against the seat, raising the soles of his shoes off the floor. Only his heels touched the rubber matting beneath the seat that faced him.

"Japan's Chicago . . . lots of industry. This area here is called the Kansai region. Kyoto is located in its heart, some thirty-six miles northeast of Osaka. For a thousand years, Kyoto was the centre of Japanese feudal society," Nara said.

Nomis's response became mechanical.

"Feudal society," he replied.

"You know . . . fiefdoms, palaces, castles, temples, chivalry, armies, wealth. Some of that still remains in Kyoto. The Imperial Palace, for one, as well as lots of Buddhist and Shinto temples. My parents' house is within walking distance of Nanzen-ji, a classic Zen temple . . . very old," Nara said.

"Shinto?" Nomis asked.

"A religion," Nara replied.

Nomis's head bobbed up and down politely as he cupped his right hand and with it rubbed his lips and chin.

"As you might suspect from my ski boots, my father, Fumikazi, is not a wealthy man."

She has no qualms about revealing personal stuff to a perfect stranger, Nomis thought.

" . . . but he's proud and of the old school. Almost imperial in his manner. My five brothers and I are his fiefdom. Growing up with them was a real challenge. My father calls them his army. I refer to them as the mob. They're all engineers," Nara continued.

"The mob?" he asked.

"Yeah, the mob. When I was much younger, they were a real bunch of thugs at times. They repaid the compliment and nicknamed me "bony", claiming that one bony little maiden per fiefdom was more than enough."

Nomis's eyes found Nara's feet and then slowly rose to her face. Nara felt his penetrating eyes as they slowly made their survey.

"Bony?" Nomis said.

Nara's coy little smile appeared momentarily as their eyes met. She raised her arm and pretended to make a muscle. Her voice became husky and thick.

"I'm one of the guys now . . . MIT and all that," she replied.

Again Nomis nodded politely.

"The mob often shunned me for hours on end, and when they did acknowledge my existence, they rarely asked me to take part in their fun," Nara continued.

Nomis wasn't able to help laughing as Nara continued to chatter away.

"What?" Nara asked.

"I guess I'm no brother of yours," Nomis replied.

Nara looked a little askance.

"It has its rewards—shunning, I mean. I'm an excellent listener, a sponge, never take notes in class, I go to a quiet place afterwards and always do a recap from memory," Nara declared.

An excellent listener, my ass. Didn't even remember my name, Nomis thought.

Nomis's tone became a mite biting.

"Albuquerque, for one, thinks you're an excellent listener!" Nomis interjected sarcastically.

Nara raised her eyebrows and squinted.

"My brothers weren't chivalrous either. And my mother called me her little nightingale," she continued.

"Nightingale? That's . . . " Nomis said.

Nara cut Nomis off again.

"I twittered and peeped and squeaked when the mob threatened me with their dirty tricks, just like the nightingale floors of the Imperial Palace. In bygone days, those noisy floors warned the emperor's guard of impending doom," she chirped.

Nomis bent forward toward Nara. As he did, he puckered his lips. Nara drew back and turned away, not knowing what to expect.

"Shhhh," he whispered. "I've changed my mind. Pretend I'm one of your brothers."

Nara was a little stunned, perhaps even offended. She began to braid her hair into loops of thick black rope. Her fingers were nervous, but nimble and quick.

Perhaps a noose, maybe a snare, but for whose neck? Nomis thought.

Silence separated them for a few minutes.

"Nightingale!" Nomis said. "My grandpa called me *Dahetihhi* when I was a kid."

"Dahetihhi?" Nara questioned.

"*Dahetihhi* is Navajo for *hummingbird*," Nomis replied. "It also means *fighter plane* in Code Talk."

Her tone of voice became inquisitive as she snapped a band around the finished braid and rolled it into a bun.

"Fighter plane . . . in Code Talk?" she queried.

Nomis realized, like Nara had done, he had just revealed something personal and private to someone who had been a perfect stranger only forty minutes ago.

The bus came to a halt in the parking lot. Nomis locked his boots into his bindings and took off toward the trail that followed Black Creek.

"Hey, Albuquerque, wait for me," Nara yelled.

∞ ∞ ∞

Skiing became a regular Saturday outing for both Nomis and Nara. They were like brother and sister. On the way up and back, Nomis did the talking and Nara did the listening. They talked about Redhouse and Albuquerque and the way Yazzie, Manygoats, Redhouse and he sat cross-legged on that bluff near the desert and how he counted stars and learned to speak Navajo. He told Nara about Yazzie's death, and his new eyes, too. Those high-tech eyes of his were so natural, the technology was so much a part of him, that Nara had no idea of his secret about his eyes until he told her. They fascinated her. Nomis was a long time in coming forth about the plane ride. It might have led to that bit about getting airsick. Likewise, Nomis didn't reveal right away his proclivity for peevishness and the demise of a good healthy belly laugh as an antidote.

Following one of those Saturday trips to Concord, they went out for dinner at the Lady Bug, a reasonably priced Thai-Chinese vegetarian restaurant with a Zen atmosphere, located off campus. As they sat down, Nara kicked off her shoes and began rubbing Nomis's shins with her toes. They got talking about George's most recent letter. George wanted to know if Nomis, the *numbers man*, was, as George so decorously put it, a *word man* yet. Nomis admitted to Nara that at first blush, poetry, or dreaming out loud, was a potent, risk-free potion for his tendency to barf. It was a substitute for a belly laugh's diminished potency. Nomis was very bad at taking his own or others' advice seriously. Nara wasn't the blaming type, but she concluded that it was Nomis's own fault he hadn't begun to follow through until late in the first semester of his freshman year. As to why, Nara almost had to drag it out of him.

"Well," Nara said, "why didn't you take the cure right then and there, when George's steam room antics put the seed in your head—daily if necessary? Why didn't you say to yourself, take a pen, keep it handy, don't hesitate to use it when your demons show their face!"

Nomis produced a pen from his shirt pocket just as the waiter arrived at their booth. He put the pen down and picked up the menu.

"Good evening."

"Yes, we'll begin with a few bean cakes, two vermicelli rolls and four spring rolls," Nomis replied.

"And to drink?"

"Tea for me," replied Nara.

"A soy shake, please, strawberry," said Nomis.

"For your main course?"

"Nomis, let's try the garlic and pepper seitan with a seaweed salad?" Nara suggested.

"Ok, and the mushroom pot, too," Nomis replied.

"Rice?" the waiter asked.

"Yes, and for dessert, the vegan cheese cake," Nomis replied.

The waiter soon returned to their booth with a pot of tea and two small cups.

Nomis picked up the pen and waved it in the air. His tone of voice firmed.

"I have a pen. I do keep it handy and I did take the cure regularly after I received George's first letter," Nomis replied.

Nara took the pen from his hand and nervously clicked it several times. She was dumbfounded as to why he hadn't understood the obvious.

"Well, what is the problem?" Nara responded.

"After those first two attempts, what I did had its downside," Nomis began slowly. "Ah, they went awry. That first poem, 'Clouds,' did make me feel good. But look, Nara, I didn't know it was the cure then, anyway. Some of my other attempts ended in unpleasant little tussles . . . with myself."

"Bean cakes, spring roll and two vermicelli rolls," the waiter said.

"Mmm. These are delicious. Try the spring rolls, Nomis," Nara said.

"On top of that, in my first year at MIT, what made my feelings, and also my dreams, lush and green or sad and grim seemed more and more out of my control," Nomis continued. "Some of my dreams were outright nightmares. Bringing my feelings and dreams out into the open was risky."

Nara tapped Nomis's shin with her shoeless foot.

"Eat while it's hot," Nara said.

"Anyway, I preferred to bury them and all my other negative feelings deep inside myself. I know how to do that. I chose to endure the pain that resulted. I know how to do that, too," Nomis said.

Nomis took a sip of his soy shake. Nara's tone of voice turned to disgust.

"You're a wimp, Nomis. What do you mean by 'risky'?"

"You're a girl. You ought to know better. In a poem, it is the words that make the math lush and green or sad and grim, and the math—you know, the rhythm and the rhymes or even their absence, and the triple meanings and all of that—well, all of that keeps the words secure and secret. Good poems, like Code Talking, don't give up their secrets easily," Nomis responded.

Nara was compelled to finish his thought on a positive note for fear he might drag her into the pit of self-pity she sensed he was digging for himself. She filled his plate with some bean cakes and the two remaining spring rolls.

"Eat!" she demanded as she put her own chopsticks down. "So? The danger of exposure can be confined and contained. And, Nomis, from what I can see, poetry has a calming effect on you; believe me, I know. It seems to rout those insidious feelings of self-doubt which often turn to anger. To you, poetry has got to be a panacea; it makes you feel much more in control of your feelings, doesn't it?"

Nomis nodded in agreement as he finished off the last of the bean cakes and started on the spring rolls. Nara poured herself some tea and continued her line of thought.

"A nightmare is nothing more than an adventure of the mind, a good mystery or even a good horror story. After all, it's like being at the movies. Behind the camera there is always a director sitting in a chair. In the case of your dreams or your poems, that's you, Nomis; you and no one else. You must have thought about it rationally, Nomis, didn't you!"

"Garlic and pepper seitan, seaweed salad, mushroom pot and rice," the waiter said. "The mushroom pot is very hot."

"It took a while . . . " Nomis began.

"Pardon?" the waiter said.

"Sorry, I didn't mean the food. The service is excellent!" Nomis replied.

"It took a while. Let me tell you, I was a mess until after Thanksgiving break," Nomis went on. "On second thought, poetry isn't rational. I don't think of it as rational. With me it just happens, like shit. My problem is others may think it just that . . . shit."

Nara furrowed her brow and her tone of voice hardened.

"Oh, come off it, Nomis. My guess is that part of you, during those early days at MIT, yearned for a medium of expression that was cloaked, one that shrouded your feelings but provided some ventilation. Let in some fresh air to get rid of that musty odor of your own breath, which I think you've been smelling for too long now."

Nara paused. Her voice softened. Her coy little smile appeared.

"I think you have been chasing your own tail for years. Give it a rest, brother! Find someone else's to chase," Nara replied.

Nomis helped himself to some rice, seitan, mushrooms and some of the seaweed salad. His tone became matter-of-fact.

"You're probably right," Nomis responded. "Sometimes I even imagine I'm back on that bluff with Yazzie, Manygoats and Redhouse."

"I didn't mean th . . . " Nara began.

Nara cut herself short. Instead, she decided to risk a frontal assault as she smothered her rice with what was left of the stewed mushrooms.

"I'm no shrink," Nara said, "but the notion that poetry is akin to a map with grass and trees, or doing math with words, perhaps has taken on the task that your little cloud world had done so effectively for you when you were blind. And if it has failed, so what? Nomis, after all, you are a budding mathematician. Your rational self surely realized that *no solution yet* or, for that matter, *no solution ever* are both very acceptable answers. They are in math, aren't they? Why not in life?"

Nomis tried to creep away from the safety of his bluff into his world of forms and shapes.

"Yes, I know. Mr. G, one of my old math teachers, taught me that. But, my world of math is an ideal world. It's not real. I'm not sure *no solution ever* is acceptable in life in the real world," Nomis replied.

"Nomis," Nara responded, "your early attempts at writing poetry must have been just like seeing in your dreams when you were blind. You were prepared to let others experience what you were seeing and feeling and touching and smelling and hearing deep inside yourself then . . . "

"Only with Manygoats," Nomis replied.

"So what if the guy on the street can't decode the messages in your poems," Nara added. "For God's sake, go back and read some of them, especially that first one on 'Clouds'—who'd ever guess it's the murmuring of a blind boy's brain about his need for his dead father's forgiveness? *You* know, and that's what counts."

"I think you've hit a sore point there. If they weren't able to decode it, they might attach their own crazy meaning to it or even chuck it as a pile of crap," Nomis replied.

"Nomis, Nomis," Nara said, "you mustn't insist others take your feelings in as their own. The importance is in the giving—out in the open—what you feel, even if it is cloaked in your own personal code talk that others think is nuts."

Nara became pensive as the waiter delivered the dessert. The vegetarian cheesecake looked irresistible. Nara ate her fill and offered what remained to Nomis. As Nomis dug into the cheesecake, Nara took a deep, deep breath.

"Your father wasn't able to hear 'Clouds' when you recited it by his grave, but it made you feel good! Right or wrong?"

Nomis's chopsticks stopped in mid-air. He slowly put them down, pouted a little, and then smiled broadly at Nara.

"This dessert is out of this world. Let's come back for more soon."

13

Nara's Loop

Once Nara had had her little talk with Nomis, it was hard to say which he was—math major or poet. Whenever he got the urge, he pulled out his pen. It happened in the strangest places, like at the ornithological gardens at the Franklin Park Zoo one Sunday afternoon. He tacked his handiwork up on a bulletin board near the entrance to the gardens for anybody to see, signing it *Dahetihhi*. Later that same week, he got the editor of MIT's student newspaper, *The Tech*, to publish it. He even dared those who read it to decipher its coded message.

The opinions of some of Nara's apartment mates weren't anything to write home about. One night, Nara found the following, scrawled across a copy of *The Tech* that had been pinned to the bathroom door: YOUR BIRD MAN IS A NUTHATCH.

Another friend of Nara's, Doris Llewellyn, a Romance language major at Harvard, was moved enough to write a letter to the editor of *The Tech*. She said the poem expressed her own views about how she felt each time she emerged from the language lab.

Now, Doris was a strange duck. Her father was from Wales, her mother was from India, and one of the languages she was studying at the time was Rumanian. She admitted that after each session at the language lab she felt like a baby bird flopping helplessly around on the ground—neither Rumanian nor Hindustani nor Welsh.

Man's Flight: By Dahetihhi

I am a man, not unlike
A bird in flight
Birds and men are much the same
Except for what we call the brain

It would be wrong to make a bird
Behave as if he were a man

For if birds did, it would not be
A natural thing for me to see

A song, a note, a sound of bird
This is the clatter of his brain
A word, a phrase, a sound of man
These are the murmurs of the same

To mix the two, if nature's way
Would be a strange result
A bird should be a force of flight
A man should watch with sheer delight

But what if birds and men were one
There would not be a single man
To hear a song so quickly sung
That he might know the truth of fun

But then again, if man and birds
Could speak on common ground
This difference found in nature's herd
Would not be part of any sound

And birds who learn to murmur thus
Would not be birds or man to us
Nor free to watch or fly on high
A lesson for the naked eye

The keeper of the ornithological gardens was a Navajo himself. He sought Nomis out the next time he came to visit the gardens. He was all smiles.

"We have no hummingbirds here who write poetry," the keeper said.

Nomis roared with laugher at his comment.

"But I am *Dahetihhi*, the hummingbird," Nomis replied.

Nomis and the keeper became very good friends during the time he spent at MIT. Years later, whenever Nomis was in Boston, he always returned to Franklin Park to visit the keeper and the swallows, and the hummingbirds and the owls and the buzzards. When he did, he felt a closeness to his past, to that bluff. It made Nomis feel good.

It was about that time he began to write poetry for Nara too—little bits of math; that's what she called Nomis's poems. Nara always said they were her private map to the lush green garden of his soul.

More often than not, Nomis's reply was an oxymoron.

"No, girls can't make any sense of maps, only poems."

She always thought the way he put it was so awfully funny—girls being unable to read maps, but being quite able to make sense of poetry in a world where poems were maps.

Nomis and Nara found that crisp snowy Saturday mornings at daybreak, when they counted on empty trails, were their favorite. It was a time when their breath frosted the air and they heard the snow crunching under their skis. There was a peace out there on those trails up near Concord that they found nowhere else.

One trail formed a loop, which they often took. It branched at a fork onto what they first thought was the main trail. It went down a gently sloping tree-lined hill, crossed Black Creek on a little wooden footbridge, made a sharp turn to the right and then went up a steep grade to the McPharlin Farm. That farm contained the remains of an old stone mill that had been built in the nineteenth century by Scottish immigrants.

When the snow fell, it had a tendency to slip through the cracks, leaving the planks of the little footbridge bare and making it unsafe to cross on skis. Once, as they approached the bridge at Black Creek, a man was shoveling snow onto the planks. His face was ruddy and red, and he wore a white and blue toque. When he spoke, his voice was high-pitched and sing-songy. The man shoveling snow removed his toque and took a little bow.

"Sometimes we go clockwise and sometimes counter-clockwise around the loop," Nomis remarked.

The man shoveling snow pointed to a hole in the ice.

"It's dangerous to go against the clock, as the counter-clockwise route brings you to a sharp turn just before the little footbridge," he sang out. "It's better to take the turn on the way up rather than on the way down. There is always a hole in the ice, with mist rising from the swirling water of Black Creek as it finds its way through the narrow little gorge below. The energy of the swirling water might carry you into that hole and under the ice if you fail to make the turn."

Nara paused and thanked him for making the bridge passable.

"If either of us fell into the mist, the other would come to the rescue," Nara said.

Nomis looked at Nara and smiled as he nodded.

Upon crossing the bridge, one proceeded up the grade with the dangerous right turn to the remains of the old mill. In the 1850s, the stone walls of the mill had housed the most modern technology of the day. Those stones were still marked by the precision of the stonecutters' science, square and smooth. But the old stone walls were rubble now, used only by skiers like Nomis and Nara as a perch while eating their lunch. As Nomis sat upon that wall, he often worried about his eyes.

"Will they become rubble some day, like the stones of the mill wall? The man shoveling snow might have been correct; going against the clock is a dangerous thing to do. Those rocks have come full circle. This little spot has also made its circle in time and hasn't suffered. It has just come back on itself," Nomis said to Nara on one of their Saturday outings.

It was then that Nara thought Nomis had also begun to think about her as his wife; she might be part of him forever. They could always circle back and talk about the things they both feared the most.

The trail then cut around to the right of the old millhouse and made a wide circle, crossing several frozen swamps. As Nomis crossed those swamps, he told Nara that he often thought of those chemical factories where Eiseley's clocks had first begun to tick, and the loop those rocks made. The trail then crossed Black Creek again and ended up back at the fork, where it all began. The whole circle was about three miles. It was called the McPharlin Loop. Taking either branch of that fork led back to where it started.

Shortly after one of those Saturday outings, Nomis had a strange dream about eyes and clouds and rings and numbers. When he awoke the next morning, he took pen in hand and put words to the strange images that had wafted from his unconscious mind. He wanted Nara to experience them too.

Eyes, Clouds, Rings and Numbers

In the beginning
the universe
had no eyes
and there was darkness
everywhere.
A cloud,
a ring,
and numbers
were the sum total
of what filled the void.
Then there was a big bang.
It was electric
and out of the cloud
poured a chemical soup
forming swamps full of numbers.
The ring made lots of paths
looping around the swamps.
As the numbers aged
they became math.
As the rings went round and round
they became the songs of birds
and the words of man.
Math and words
and the songs of birds
were finely one
and poetry and its secrets
were born . . .

"What do you think it means, Nomis?" Nara asked.

"Like poems, dreams always have many hidden meanings. In fact, I think dreams are the poetry of your subconscious. One might say that dream was about you and me, or . . . Once George and I wondered what the result might be if my abilities and his were somehow combined into one. Maybe it's about the double helix and the manner in which simple things can create and then keep such complicated but beautiful secrets, like the secret of life itself, or why birds sing and men write poems, or why life oozed from dead rocks. Who knows?" Nomis replied.

Nara smiled and cocked her head to one side.

"Or maybe your subconscious is trying to tell you to make babies," said Nara.

"Babies?" Nomis said.

"Babies!" Nara replied.

"I don't think so," said Nomis.

Some time afterward, when Nomis came to the fork in their loop, a new trail sign covered the old. It was Nara's little gift to Nomis.

Nara's Loop

It always circles back
if you don't go
against the clock

and if you do
and fall in
Nara will pull you out

It was soon after that, on one of their trips with the clock around Nara's loop, that she thought Nomis had made up his mind. It had snowed the night before. The trail was slick and Nomis had fallen on the tree-lined slope that led down to the little footbridge at Black Creek. Some of the duct tape had come loose. As he lay there, he told Nara that he was glad that they had decided not to go against the clock. Going with the flow was slippery enough.

In early March, he and Nara went for a walk all the way around Walden Pond. There was fresh, wet, heavy snow on the ground from the night before. On the northeast side of the pond, they came upon the foundations of a log house.

"Henry David Thoreau lived in the little log house that once stood here," Nomis remarked.

Nara turned and stood face to face with Nomis.

"Yes, for a year. Solitude was his elixir," Nara replied.

"Solitude," Nomis replied. "He had a cloud world too. He made reference to it in an essay entitled 'The Maine Woods'. A few years back I memorized the passage. I don't think I ever understood it, but I think my father . . . "

Nomis's voice became choked. He took Nara into his arms beneath his down-filled coat and kissed her.

"Your father what?" Nara whispered.

Nomis didn't answer her question, but recited the passage from memory.

"Thoreau's cloud world was a . . .

> cloud factory . . . where the mist was generated out of pure air as fast as it flowed away . . . It was vast, titanic and such as man never inhabits. Some part of the beholder, even some vital part, seemed to escape through the loose grating of his ribs . . . "

Nara snuggled into his shoulder and nibbled his ear.

"What did it mean to you?" Nara asked.

"When I first read the passage, memories of my own cloud world rushed into my head. I felt that Thoreau's cloud factory depicted my own misfortune—my blindness, my solitude, its cause and its consequences," Nomis whispered

Nara kissed him. His eyes became narrow. He tried but he wasn't able to openly cry.

"My grandpa told me that I was a good man and my heart would always see. But my ribs were crushed in the crash and as a child I thought, deep down inside, that my sight had leaked from my heart through my crushed ribs. Because of that I questioned what both my dad and my grandpa had told me until the night I began to see in my dreams," Nomis continued.

Nara kissed him again softly on the lips. Nomis's eyes remained dry but his heart wept openly. Tears flowed from Nara's eyes onto Nomis's cheeks.

"I'll cry for both of us," Nara whispered softly into his ear.

"I had also questioned myself, until that night you suggested I must give openly of my feelings and expect little in return—a lesson somehow misplaced or buried in the rubble of that car accident. Thoreau's cloud factory doesn't depict my misfortune, but the opposite. His mystical world isn't one of solitude but of exhilaration and elation. Of seeing and smelling and touching and feeling and hearing," Nomis said.

It was there, standing among the old foundations of Thoreau's little house, that the unconditional love which Nomis had for Nara burst forth.

"I have a little something for you. It's my personal best," Nomis whispered.

He stepped back a few paces. As he spoke, his eyes and hers became one. She saw what he saw; she felt what he felt.

What Is This I See?

What is this I see
Could it be a part of me
Could it be

What place is this
An ancient way
Perhaps an ancient courier

What message do you bear
What ancient trust you air
This is not fair
To be in such despair

Why at this time
Why at this place
What is your past
Why are you here

What is this I see
Could it be a part of me.

Nara rushed into his arms.

"Yes," Nara said. "I will be your other half."

They were married in late May.

14

Nanzen-ji

Unfortunately, Nara's mother and father, Fumikazu, didn't attend Nara's little wedding. In early May Nara's mother was taken ill and wasn't able to travel. Nevertheless, the day Nomis and Nara were married, an e-mail arrived from Nara's parents. They suggested that Nara and Nomis visit Japan in late June. Her parents even offered to pay the airfare. It was a marvelous wedding gift; a chance for them to relax, for Nomis to meet Nara's parents, and for Nara to touch base with old friends.

In Kyoto the cherry blossoms are long gone by late June; but they weren't the real attraction. Nomis and Nara expected their fourth year at MIT to be hectic and exhausting. The grind of student life by the Charles River included an endless round of seminars, stints in the library and the Friday afternoon math and chemistry colloquia. Rarely did they ever have the time to make it across the Charles to Boston. Even if it were only ephemeral, like those cherry blossoms, a trip to Japan was just what they needed—a sudden and unexpected change.

The day before they were to leave, Nomis was still packing odds and ends. He was in the bedroom, sitting on his suitcase, using his weight to force it shut so he might snap the lock. He asked Nara to push down on his shoulders, adding her weight to his effort. Instead, she sat in his lap, clasping her legs around his torso.

"Just what I need, an abrupt and radical change from the idea that one and only one line can be drawn between two points," Nomis said.

Nara grabbed him by the shoulders and shook him.

"Give it up!" Nara replied.

Then she looped her arms around his neck, apologizing for her outburst with a soft wet kiss.

"Me too, but no points and lines, please," she pleaded.

Nara snuggled into his lap.

"Where are those books I bought yesterday morning? I want to take them along on the plane," Nomis remarked.

"Some of them look a little out of character to me. No math books! I stuffed them into your carry-on knapsack," Nara said.

"Not so! I told my physicist friends that I was taking along a little light reading. They were impressed," Nomis replied.

Nara was impressed, too. She kissed him again.

"You're always so engrossed in your mathematics; you seldom have much time to read for pleasure anymore. I'm delighted to see . . ." Nara beamed.

"I'm really looking forward to that sudden, radical, even mystical change which Japan promises; so I thought why not get an early start on the plane?" Nomis interrupted.

Nara listened but, knowing Nomis, seeing was believing. She puckered her lips and looked Nomis squarely in the eyes.

"Why not start right now?"

"You know my affinity for old books. I told the bookshop to find me something different, romantic and magical," Nomis replied.

Nara's hand went looking for exactly that.

"What they gave you is out of print. Why didn't they provide you with a few of those dollar paperback love stories . . . or how about the little girl right here on your lap?" Nara said.

"I asked for literature, not a pacifier," Nomis replied. "You saw the titles: *Green Mansions* by W. H. Hudson. It's supposed to be a fantastically romantic tale with a serpentine plot, wonderful to both read and relax by. The other, *Lost Horizon* by James Hilton, is a chimerical tale about those who rely on potions or magic water, not the speed of light, to avoid the ticking of clocks. Honey, I do believe doing it on top of a suitcase will be a first for us. What do you say we just snap the lock?"

With Nomis's remark about pacifiers, ticking clocks and locks that needed snapping, Nara slid from his lap and stood up.

"My poor baby, will you ever leave your ticking clocks behind?" she begged. "And what will you do without a pacifier?"

Nomis grinned, leaned forward onto his knees and nibbled her toes.

"Very good, Nomis, you devil you," Nara whispered.

"OK, you win. I agree. That's what we both needed, to avoid the ticking of clocks by absorbing ourselves in the fantasy of a few good tales; and that's exactly what I promise you we will do," Nomis replied as he picked her up and carried her off to bed.

∞ ∞ ∞

The non-stop flight from Boston to Osaka took nearly half a day. They arrived at six oclock in the morning Osaka time after crossing the International Date Line, which killed a day. Their bodies wanted to sleep, their five senses told them not to, and their stomachs didn't know what to do.

Shuji Matsubara, an old friend of Nara's, was kind enough to meet them at the airport.

Nomis extended his hand. Shuji nodded and then bowed.

"There is no doubt that long-distance travel messes with one's internal clock," Nomis remarked.

Nomis wasn't prepared for Shuji's staccato reply.

"Hi!" Shuji replied.

Nara wagged her finger at Nomis.

"Nomis. No clocks! Remember."

Nomis's forehead became furrowed.

"Not even a concern for my poor stressed-out body clock?"

Shuji turned to Nara and struck up a conversation in Japanese. Nomis knew a little Japanese, but nowhere near enough to become part of a fast-moving exchange between old friends. He did sense, from all the bowing, hand-waving and hugging, that they were delighted to see each other. Jealousy wasn't what he felt, but it was close.

As Nomis finished loading the baggage into Shuji's car, he was relieved to find Nara tugging at his sleeve.

"*Hi* means sure, or yes, or OK. Shuji understands English, but is usually reluctant to speak it."

Nomis's reply was as dart-like as Shuji's.

"Hi."

Nara hooked Nomis's arm in hers, pulled him toward her and gave him a little peck on the cheek.

"Nomis, it feels so good to be back in Japan, especially with you, and my old friend, Shuji. I haven't seen him since last summer. Nomis, you're going to love it here."

They spent their first day and night with Shuji in Kobe. Nomis did backslide a bit that first evening. Everybody has their *ground zero.* He toyed with the idea of making a side trip to Hiroshima the next day to visit Nara's *ground zero.* She didn't want to go. She insisted they spend the extra time with Shuji before she and Nomis went on to Kyoto. As a youngster, Nara had been to Hiroshima too many times, and it hurt; it always hurt. Nomis might have hopped the Bullet train by himself, but he didn't. Instead, they visited the Osaka Castle and then went directly to the home of Nara's parents in Kyoto.

There was one maladroit moment. Kyoto hadn't been bombed during WWII; it was full of art, and history, and culture. Unlike the World Trade Center, nobody had counted there during that war. When Nomis met Nara's parents, he remarked that in Kyoto, unlike Hiroshima, art in its duel with science had apparently been victorious. Nara didn't think her parents quite understood what Nomis meant by his gauche remark.

The awkwardness of that early moment didn't detract from the joy that marked the remainder of their first day in Kyoto. Nara's mother was thrilled to have her little nightingale home, even if only for a short visit. She was just as delighted to finally meet Nomis. From Nara's letters she was aware of his acumen on skis. She apologized more than once for the lack of snow.

Her brothers gave Nomis the once-over. All but one, Isao, the oldest, were impressed. Nara told Nomis not to worry: Isao was never impressed by anything, no less his bony little sister's husband. Nara's father, Fumikazu, appeared to Nomis exactly as Nara had described him: a proud man with an imperial manner.

The Moriguchis' house was situated on the slopes of the Higashijama Mountains. It was within walking distance of the Nanzen-ji Temple, which dated back to 1291 A.D. The house had many amenities, the most novel being a toilet that doubled as a bidet. It had a button which, when pushed, caused a warm stream of fresh water to erupt from its innards. Shoes weren't worn indoors. The heated floors made a big difference on cooler days.

One of the rooms in Fumikazu's house was decorated in the traditional Japanese style. A low, square wooden table dominated the center of the room. Chairs weren't part of the decor. Natural wood had been used on the walls and much of the ceiling. Off to one side, behind a small door, was a Buddhist shrine. Above the shrine, on the ceiling, was a painting of sky and clouds.

Tea or even a meal was usually taken kneeling at the large wooden table. What stumped Nomis was the manner in which Fumikazu was able to kneel comfortably with his lower legs neatly tucked beneath his thighs for the hour or two they spent around that low wooden table during the meal that first evening. Even Nara's brothers and Nara herself had to shift their position periodically. Nomis found that his knees weren't as supple as those of Fumikazu. He ended up sitting cross-legged.

Despite the gallons of water Nomis and Nara had ingested since leaving Boston, neither had overcome their jet lag. As they snuggled in bed, Nara said something that Nomis didn't quite understand.

"I think they know and feel both your sorrow and your joy," Nara said.

"About what?" Nomis replied.

"About Hiroshima and Kyoto," Nara said.

"You mean the way science is sandwiched between art and math?" Nomis replied.

"No, simply about your sorrow and your joy," replied Nara.

"Time forgets," Nomis said. "The decision to bypass Kyoto is a forgotten footnote in a dusty history book. That war was horrible, but even in its midst, someone somewhere knew right from wrong."

"You ought to have gone!" replied Nara.

"To Hiroshima?"

"Yes, to see . . . the wrong. We'll see the right tomorrow."

"I know. I should have gone."

Nomis rolled over and kissed Nara softly on the lips.

"Nara, how can your father kneel for hours on end and not change his position?" Nomis continued.

"Oh Nomis, I thought for a moment some of your magic was about . . . " Nara said.

Nomis interrupted her.

"Tell me, how does he do it?" Nomis replied.

Nara rolled over on her tummy, kicked the quilt onto the floor, and stuck her leg out from under the sheet.

"The fact that my brothers and I can't disturbs him. That's part of his proud imperial manner. Knee joints need practice every day, but the younger generations in Japan have lost that ability. I guess we too often sit on chairs. It's sad but true," replied Nara.

"It's strange how a chair can cause culture to change," Nomis remarked.

"Think about your eyes," replied Nara.

"I'd rather not! And the sky and clouds above the shrine?" Nomis asked.

Nara giggled at the manner in which Nomis brushed aside her comment about his eyes, and then pounced on her father's closet-bound cloud world.

"A shrine must be open to the sky. There was no way that was possible, given the design of the house. So my father had the space above it declared as sky by a priest. It's a very practical religion."

"Everything must be well known in advance, including the assumptions?" Nomis asked.

Nara snuggled up to Nomis, wrapping her legs around his torso. She began to work her own magic.

"Oh, there's plenty of mystery, plenty of magic. My little loop, for one," Nara replied.

"Perhaps he keeps his own personal cloud world in that closet," Nomis added.

∞ ∞ ∞

Early the first morning in Kyoto, Nara was awakened by the muffled notes of the bells, or gongs, coming from the direction of the Temple. She poked Nomis.

"Nomis, listen to the bells. I had forgotten about them. Listen!" Nara said.

"What . . . what time is . . . " Nomis replied

"About six A.M.," Nara said. "Shhh, we mustn't wake my parents, Nomis."

Nara hopped out of bed and went to the window. As she opened it wide, the notes became crisp and pure. Nomis's curiosity was aroused by their clarity.

"Listen, Nomis. Listen to the bells coming from the Temple! In my youth I became so acclimated to those pure notes that after a while they went unnoticed. I must have tucked them away somewhere in the back of my mind," Nara said.

They were like a tuning fork or a pitch pipe used by a piano tuner or choirmaster to ensure that harmony, not discord, prevails. The notes seemed to rush toward them with long tails that eventually melted away to nothingness.

Nomis was so intent on leaving the house to find their source that he forgot to take his camera.

"I want to track them down before they evaporate into thin air. You bring the camera. Which way to the temple?" Nomis asked on his way out the door.

"I have only a vague memory of where to look for both—the camera and the temple," Nara replied. "I went to the temple many times as a child, but to worship, not to explore. I have a fuzzy recollection of a path that follows a canal or stream to the temple grounds. I have a map of Kyoto in my bag."

"Come on, let's go. Bring the map!" Nomis pleaded.

"I can't find the camera," Nara complained.

Nomis's voice became impatient. He was so eager to get going, he returned to the house and tried to shoo Nara out the door like a bird.

"Come, my little nightingale. No, today you're Rima," he begged. "Forget about the camera, let's go!"

Nara was astonished when Nomis called her Rima.

"Rima!" Nara replied. "Have I missed something? Is there another woman in your life who I somehow missed along the way?"

Nomis grinned.

Payback for that little scene at the airport with Shuji, Nomis thought.

"No, of course not, but today you're Rima," Nomis replied. "She's a character, a tree fairy, an enigma in Hudson's book, *Green Mansions.* She lived in the treetops. Her voice was melodious and alluring, but she always remained just out of reach of those who pursued her, like you are now."

Nara was a bit miffed.

"OK, but remember, Nomis Chester, I'm your wife, who is always within reach, and I'm a chemistry major, not an enigma," replied Nara.

Those gongs were so pleasantly intoxicating, Nara even left the bag with the map in it, which she usually toted around on such expeditions of discovery, sitting on the bed. Later they discovered they had forgotten their watches too.

Without a map, their guide became the sound of the bells. They rambled along a residential street, which eventually took a sharp turn toward the direction of the bells. Once around the bend the canal was visible and in the distance the San Mon Gate.

"Those books I've been reading for pleasure are about time, technology and culture. I feel like we have been drawn into a time warp, leaving our own notions about today's technology and culture firmly glued to the present," Nomis said.

The sound of the bells intensified as they walked through the gate.

"The gate was built in 1628 A.D. to console those who had died some thirteen years before, during the siege of Osaka Castle," Nara remarked.

"Another *ground zero,*" Nomis replied.

"Perhaps, but long forgotten," Nara said.

"You mean overwhelmed by technology. I can easily imagine that you and I are characters in that book, *Lost Horizon*, by Hilton. I feel we are entering a mystical place, a make-believe world where time has stopped," Nomis said.

The canal cut though the grounds of the temple. It was fed by an aqueduct, which carried water from the mountaintop. They went in search of its source, spending the better part of the morning ambling along the *philosopher's path* that accompanied the aqueduct as it made its way up the mountain. It turned abruptly at the foot of some worn, steep stone steps, which disappeared into the densely wooded mountainside. The movement of the steps was snake-like, going from left to right to left as they worked their way up into the tree canopy.

The air was damp and fresh. Sundogs made their way through the tree canopy to the steps below. The melodic songs of birds surrounded them. Nomis felt that they had stumbled upon a variation of Hudson's enigma; both seemed very comfortable as just a piece of Hudson's puzzle. All seemed to describe to their ears, noses and sense of touch the images their eyes so enjoyed. Once in a while, Nara noticed that Nomis closed his eyes. At one point, he remarked how astonished he was whenever he did.

"This morning Hudson's green mansions seem also to be ours, or is it the other way around—does it really matter, Nara?" Nomis remarked.

Nomis wanted to kiss Nara, but the temple grounds were sacred. She shied away. He squeezed her hand instead.

Nara's tone of voice became curious.

"What do you see when you close your eyes?" Nara asked.

"I can see the songs of birds," Nomis replied.

"See the . . . " Nara said.

"Look, Rima, ah, look, Nara, the birds. I think perhaps Rima's alter ego beckons us," Nomis whispered.

Both thought for a minute that what they had seen was a flock of brightly colored birds, skimming the tree canopy. But the flecks of red and orange, barely visible through the jumble of leaves and branches, were a procession of holy men dressed in bright orange tunics, some with very elegant red headpieces or cap-like crowns. They were monks, making their way from the mountaintop down the steps after morning prayer.

As the monks approached, their tenancy seemed so well-established that Nara and Nomis instinctively moved aside, delaying their own quest while they watched with envy those who seemed so sure in their own destination.

They turned and followed the procession down the mountain. Nomis paused and took one last look up the stone steps.

"The phantasms of both *Green Mansions* and *Lost Horizon* dwell here on this mountainside. The songs of birds make you want to return again and again to finish your search," Nomis remarked.

When they reached the temple, Nomis and Nara had to make their way through throngs of schoolchildren to reach the San Mon Gate and the path by the canal that led them back to Nara's parents' house. As they did, Nara gave Nomis's hand several little squeezes.

"In the Hilton novel, wasn't it the water that stopped time?" Nara quipped.

The canal disappeared beneath the ground a few hundred feet from the Moriguchi home, but the path didn't. It seemed to continue in search of its other half—the waters of the canal, or perhaps another set of stone steps that leapt up into the tree canopy.

"It needs to turn around and go the other way," Nomis mumbled.

"What?" Nara asked. "What needs to turn around?"

"The path! It needs to come full circle and go the other way, or it surely will become lost in a world it doesn't understand," Nomis replied.

They didn't find the source of the aqueduct that day as it worked its way up into the tree canopy. It was a long time before Nara understood what Nomis had meant about seeing with his ears. Nor were their watches there at the Nanzen-ji Temple, that fresh June morning, as they searched for the tails of those gongs.

∞ ∞ ∞

On the way back from Japan, Nomis quickly returned full circle to his numbers. He didn't even wait until he got back to Boston. He bought a book entitled *Fermats Enigma* by Simon Singh at Narita Airport, just before they boarded the plane. For most of the flight, his head was buried in it.

Nara bugged him only once. She felt they must deal quickly with a hole in their budget upon their return to Boston. They had taken a few more days than planned and gone to Sapporo, on the island of

Hakkaido. They had also visited the Asahi National Park for a day of hiking. Their little excursion to Hakkaido had cost them a month's rent.

"What's your solution to the rent problem?" Nara asked.

Nomis didn't want to deal with the issue. They were forty thousand feet over the Pacific and there was lots of time. He paused for a moment after putting his book down. Nara sensed that his answer might have little to do with the issue at hand.

"Honey, Fermat's Last Theorem was around for more than three hundred and fifty years, before Andrew Wiles came up with the solution in 1993 or '94. Fermat was an advocate, a lawyer. That's how he paid the rent. Apparently he only had the time or inclination to ask questions, not answer them. How might you solve the rent problem?" Nomis replied.

The muscles around Nara's mouth became tense. Her lips went thin and pale as she tried to contain her unwanted feeling of anger. She didn't respond, but instead shrugged her shoulders. Nomis shifted his position as he stretched his legs. Nara changed her mind. That coy smile appeared.

"Nomis, honey. Please don't give me any of that *no solution yet* malarkey even though this is the real world," she said.

"Now, my little nightingale," Nomis began, "it wasn't uncommon in Fermat's day to have a patron, whether it be the law, the Medici family or whatever, which permitted you to do your thing. Even early in the last century, Einstein worked as a patent clerk to support his own intellectual activities. Andrew Wiles was a professor at Princeton. That's how he paid the rent. A well-endowed university makes all the difference. In such circumstances, a man has the time to both ask and then answer his own questions."

Nara wrinkled up her nose at his little soliloquy.

"Are you trying to tell me that you have a patron, or worse, that I am your patron?" Nara replied.

"No, of course not! I'll just put my name in at the computer center. I'm not beneath solving other people's problems for treats. You know that," Nomis replied.

Nomis smiled, looked out the window at the Pacific, momentarily stuck his head back in his book and then again turned toward Nara.

"As for the rent in the long run, I have decided to make a branch of math called number theory my life's work. This book on Fermat is a real tease of my talents and I love it. I'm going to get a Ph.D. That's how we'll pay the rent in the future. The coiled tale of his enigma—Fermat's not Hudson's," Nomis said as he chuckled, "is, in part, the foundations of crypto, the science of secrecy, and that is something with which I feel very comfortable."

Nara took his hand and gave it one of her little squeezes.

"Redhouse—the Code Talker—would have been very pleased."

Nara settled back into her seat and soon fell asleep. Nomis' head again went down into his book.

∞ ∞ ∞

When Nomis and Nara returned to their apartment in Boston, there was a message on their answering machine.

"Heeeyyy, Nomis and Nara, my condolences. George here. Long time no see. Sorry I didn't make the wedding—plan to make it up to you guys in ten days or so. My partner and I—Lucy's a math major—just can't seem to stay away from it, old buddy . . . set theory drove me nuts. She wanted to do the sea-to-shining-sea thing, so we're doing Zen and the art of motorcycle maintenance—the sequel, in reverse, coming east on a BMW. Left Albuquerque right after exams for northern California, spent a few days on Vancouver Island, up around Tofino, cut across Alberta and Saskatchewan, then turned south toward Hardin, Montana. My squaw wanted to see the Little Big Horn. She regretted it. Got strip-searched at some podunk town on the border. Lost my cell phone somewhere between there and Hardin. Calling from a pay phone in Sheriden, Wyoming . . . Will be passing through Boston on our way to the Cape in about a week or ten days. Depends on whether we go back up over the big lakes or under; don't know yet, hey, buddy, we're grass eaters—don't eat our friends anymore. Plan to treat you and Nara to a tofu feast . . . Out of time . . . call you again in about a week," the message said.

"I'm really looking forward to meeting George and Lucy. We'll let them treat us to dinner at the *Lady Bug*," Nara said.

15
Avoiding Eureka

As promised, George arrived late Friday afternoon, a little after 5:00 P.M., on his BMW motorcycle with Lucy clinging to his torso. It was a hot July day. He was naked to the waist. George had shed everything above the belt when, to avoid a sudden rainsquall, he and Lucy had taken shelter under an overpass on I-90, west of Albany. Lucy had declined his invitation to do the same, even though her wet t-shirt probably caused as much rubbernecking as the rings that pierced George's nipples. A pair of suspenders that held up his pants had left two strips of lily white skin which looped over his shoulders. His shirt, which Lucy had tied around her waist, was fluttering in the breeze like a royal pennant.

George was neither anal nor oral. Being an average of the two, it was his mid-intestinal tract that usually dominated his needs. He announced they hadn't eaten since Watertown, New York. His hair suffered from its own unique problem. The hot, humid weather, that rainsquall and his helmet had given it an unwanted permanent. A clean shirt and a quick pit stop in Nomis's bathtub dealt with all but his appetite. The four of them then set off by bus to the *Lady Bug* to care for his stomach.

The late afternoon rain shower, as it made its way to the coast, had left the streets of Boston damp and steamy. Although it had sponged some of the moisture from the air, giving it a crisp, fresh feeling, the air in the bus remained hot and stale. George was tempted to disrobe again. Lucy pinched him on the butt, threatening to chain him to his BMW by the rings in his tits instead of taking him into her bed that night. An elderly couple who was privy to her remarks suddenly moved toward the front. As the bus passed by the Boston Commons, the wet, green, leafy canopy which had taken on a deeper, richer hue because of the rain, seemed to calm George down.

As they made their way to the exit, the bus driver warned them of a large puddle by the curb. Nomis, Nara, and Lucy managed to avoid it. George didn't care. He was still wearing his steel-tipped motorcycle boots. As he walked, his boots made a clanking sound that sometimes turned heads. George enjoyed the attention.

Their quick departure had left them without reservations. Nomis hoped that the late afternoon rain might reduce the size of the Friday night crowd that normally came to graze at the *Lady Bug*. He was wrong. It was a good thirty minutes before they were seated.

An endless procession of bean cakes, vermicelli rolls, spring rolls, vegan dumplings, vegetable tempura, seaweed salad, soba noodles, white rice, faux meat of several varieties—including chicken, beef, pork and lobster—stewed mushrooms, curried coconut, garlic and pepper seitan, bean and tofu shakes, vegan cheese cake and assorted teas passed by on its way to those already seated. Even after the four of them were finally settled in a booth by the window, George continued to assess the visual menu provided by those around him who had already been served.

∞ ∞ ∞

"Waiting has made it easier to choose. Sh . . . " George remarked in a rather loud voice.

Nomis whispered into George's ear.

"This place has very good acoustics."

George elbowed Nomis in the ribs and whispered back.

"Fuck off."

When the menus arrived, George confiscated all four. He insisted on ordering the meal, making short work of the waiter's questions. His choices were excellent. The meal began with green tea and an assortment of vegan appetizers. Soon the table was overflowing with entrées. There was little room left for the additional rice George ordered, and little time for talk. George and Lucy were too busy shoveling it in. Dessert was another story altogether.

"This weather reminds me of the cloud chamber at the University of New Mexico," George said. "We don't get the humidity out in the desert."

"Talking about the steam room, in your last letter you said something about taking a little of your own medicine, mixing some math in with all those history courses you've been taking," Nomis replied.

Nara shook her head slowly from right to left to right.

"Yeah, I picked set theory. I figured it didn't have anything to do with numbers. But it's driving me nuts. There're too many *ifs, ands,* or *buts,*" George said.

"But when it's over, if you've done a good job, there're no surprises," Nomis replied. "You know what's been assumed, where it all leads and where it finally ends."

"Nomis, you realize there was an *if*, an *and*, and a *but* in your answer," George said.

Nomis beamed as he nodded in agreement.

"Thanks to Mr. G."

George cracked open his fortune cookie and read the message. He crumpled the message up, deposited it on his plate and wolfed the cookie down.

"I guess I never got over those tricky tests of Mr. G, where the best answer might be *there is no answer*!" George said. "Also, those *ifs*, *ands* or *buts* aren't as cooperative as those *deltas* and *epsilons*. Like you said, they do vanish."

Lucy retrieved the crumpled fortune from George's plate, read it, began to laugh, took a pencil from her pocket, and scribbled something else on it.

"George, I lied. Those *deltas* and *epsilons* are still there, cloaked by the limit," Nomis said. "You know, George, I had forgotten about Mr. G until I bought a little paperback on my way back from Japan. Remember that thing called Fermat's Enigma which old G used to harp on?"

"Nomis, isn't that the one that Wiles finally cracked?" Lucy asked.

"Yes. Say, what did it say, the cookie?" Nomis asked.

"Originally?" Lucy asked.

"No matter," Nomis replied.

"Ah. *Don't be led by a ring in your nose*, but I changed 'nose' to 'nipple'," Lucy replied.

George turned and leered at Lucy.

"As long as it's to your bed," George added.

Nara frowned as she bit into her cookie.

"As I was saying. Yes. Find the general solution to $x^n + y^n = z^n$ for $n = 3, 4 \ldots$ For 350 years for $n=3, 4 \ldots$, the answer was *no general solution, yet*. By the time George and I got to twelfth grade, that Enigma of Fermat's had been cracked by Andrew Wiles. In fact, there was *no general solution*, none at all; just an endless stream of specific solutions. Mr. G must have been fascinated by it. I suspect he was talking about that Enigma of Fermat's long before Wiles cracked it. Can't seem to give it up, either. Story was that every year, early on, he always cautioned his students to look for the answer *no general solution, yet* for every math puzzle they might undertake to solve," Nomis said.

"I must have been asleep or sick that day," George said. "What does your fortune say, Nara?"

"It was empty," Nara replied.

"Ah, a lady without a fortune. How are we going to pay the rent?" Nomis replied.

Nara tried to bunt Nomis with her foot, but it found the leather of George's boot instead.

"Now, now, Nara," George responded. "I'm busy tonight."

"How many times have I told you, George . . . " Lucy began.

"OK, OK. I take it back," interrupted George.

"OK what? As I was saying . . . In math, *no general solution, yet* is an acceptable answer, as is the more interesting response *no general solution,* or the less useful result, *eureka, there is a general solution,*" Lucy said.

Nara turned to Nomis. Her tone was matter of fact.

"In life, I think, the second is usually not interesting. Not acceptable," Nara said. "It is always important to add the *yet* and then strive for the *eureka,* especially when it comes to the rent."

"You mean pray for the *eureka,*" George added.

"Yes, Nomis might want to do a little of that, too," replied Nara.

"In math if you get to shout *eureka,* it usually results in a publication in a prestigious journal, followed by big kudos from the code-breakers and frowns from the code-makers," Nomis said. "If you were able to discard the *yet* and avoid the *eureka,* the code-makers thank you while the code-breakers silently grimace. When that Enigma was cracked, the code-makers were ecstatic; the code-breakers mumbled something about needing faster computers to even the score."

Nara made a fist, out of which popped her thumb, pointing at the tabletop. She rotated it a full one hundred and eighty degrees as she spoke.

"I think you mathematicians have it backwards," Nara said. "Why ought the solution to a problem that is general receive thumbs-down from the code-makers, while ones that aren't receive the opposite? It always appeared to me that something with a wider rather than a narrower application ought to be the more valuable. Isn't that what you mathematicians are always trying to do? Make some other guy's results a special case of your own?"

Nomis grabbed Nara's clenched fist and wrestled it to the tabletop.

"In cryptography, which way is down isn't what you might think. Consider a town where all the locks have only one key. In such a case nothing is safe or private or secure. As long as I am in possession of the one key that fits all locks, I can enter into any space I choose," Nomis said.

"Not good," George said. "Sounds like my landlord."

"That's why *eureka* is greeted with a thumbs-down from the code-makers. A general solution," Nomis said.

"You mean a single piece of information?" George asked.

"Yes, one that gives access to many places at once," Nomis said.

Nara wriggled free from Nomis's grip. She extended her hand up behind Nomis's head, making a V with her fingers.

"Are those rabbit ears or a war bonnet?" George asked.

Nomis batted her hand down.

"V for victory!" Nara proclaimed. "George, I've heard this lecture at least a hundred times. No doubt, so have you. Think of the Navajo language. It was so specific, so different, so mysterious, so unrelated to the hundreds of other spoken languages at the time that the Japanese code-breakers were speechless every time they ran across it during the battle for the Pacific. It was this fact that made it valuable to people like Chester Nimitz and William Halsey."

George's eyelids began to droop.

"For Andrew Wiles, the man who finally solved Fermat's puzzle, it was his life's work," Nomis said. "No doubt his stock answer until the mid-1990s was *no general solution . . . yet.* It was then, and only then, that he demonstrated that the correct response was, in fact, *no general solution*. He discarded the *yet* rather than the *no* . . . and avoided the *eureka.* The code-makers breathed much easier, while the code-breakers perspired a lot more. Retaining the *no* meant that there were many, many, many specific solutions, each with its own key or starting point, which might be used to encrypt a stream of numbers or letters."

"Solutions to problems take time, and if they are good solutions, no matter what kind, they give time," Lucy said.

Nara leaned over and gave Nomis a little peck on the cheek.

"Good solutions are the sort of thing that I like. They're like a time machine; if they are really good, they can even make time, like our little side trip to Sapporo," Nara said. "Shall we go? Looks like George is asleep with his eyes open."

George suddenly came to life.

"Yeah, learned that one from Nomis," George added.

∞ ∞ ∞

In 1993 Andrew Wiles had had a hectic year, thinking he had his mind around Fermat's challenge, only to see it slip away. He finally bagged it forever in 1994. All of this taught Nomis how precious and fragile time was. During that final year at MIT, time was exactly that. They both enjoyed classical music, using what little time they had together to do things like attending the Boston Symphony at Symphony Hall. Late one night on the subway, as they were returning from a concert, they began to muse about time.

"You and your physicist friends ought to make a time machine next week with your mathematics," Nara said. "We sure can use it, with all the time you have had to spend at the computer center, solving the problems of other people."

The doors of the subway seemed to sigh as they closed, as if the subject was not a welcome one. As the car gained speed, the clickety-clack of the wheels filled their ears.

"What kind of time machine?" Nomis responded reluctantly. "Whose ticking do you want to avoid—Einstein's or Eiseley's, or the wheels of this subway?"

"All three," Nara said.

"Einstein set down the blueprints for his time machine more than a hundred years ago," Nomis replied.

"Then follow his plan!" Nara said. "Make sure there is a button for me to push. You can get anything these days just by pushing a button—if you understand the technology, that is."

"Even save on toilet tissue, like your father," Nomis replied.

"Oh, Nomis," Nara said. "Sometimes I think your brains are in your . . ."

The subway car rocked from side to side. The lights dimmed as they approached each station. Nomis yawned and interrupted Nara.

"My father once said time was like a watch," Nomis replied. "No, he said it was not exactly like a watch. My friends tell me time is more like a series of events that wind and unwind. Maybe he was right; maybe it . . ."

"I think it's more like an old-fashioned VCR," Nara interrupted.

"No, more like the vibrating strings of a lute or a tuning fork in perpetual motion," Nomis responded.

He paused. His eyes fluttered shut. For a minute, Nara thought he had drifted off to sleep. She poked him.

"No. I don't think that such a machine comes in a box with buttons; it never will!" he replied.

Nomis paused again. Nara poked him a second time.

"What? Oh, no, time was once in a little box, but it escaped into the vastness of the universe with a flash and a bang. I don't know who pushed the button the first time, or maybe it was the second or third or perhaps the last. Maybe it was God, maybe not. God knows, I don't know. Someday, just like your loop up there in Concord, it will come back on itself, carrying the rubble of a billion technologies with it, and, hopefully, the blueprints for a billion more yet to be discovered, when and if it ever escapes the boundaries of that little box again," Nomis babbled.

"Like I said, you mean a little box that rewinds time, like an old-fashioned VCR used to rewind a movie or speed it up," Nara replied.

"OK, but the plot differs each time it's replayed," said Nomis.

It was late and Nomis was tired. He nodded off again. The wheels of the subway seemed to disapprove. They screeched and whined as they rounded each turn. Nara poked him a fourth time.

"If you insist. But going against the clock takes a lot of skill and energy; remember Nara's Loop," Nomis said. "Neither I nor the universe have enough energy tonight to think about going against the clock. Even if I had the energy to go against the clock at Nara's Loop, or any other, there is always that hole in the icy dark of Black Creek to worry about."

"There is always Nanzen-ji. Remember, I think one can stop time there," Nara replied.

"Yes, I remember," Nomis responded as he nodded off to the pejorative screeching of subway wheels rumbling toward Cambridge.

16
MAIHEM

In 2022, Nomis and Nara moved to Princeton, New Jersey where he had been accepted into Princeton University's Ph.D. program in mathematics. He hadn't used his fingers to feed his intellectual appetite for some eleven years, having long since learned to read with his eyes. He had gone back to Bethesda from time to time to make sure that his eyes were functioning properly. However, neither his mother nor his grandpa nor those at Bethesda had ever told him the whole truth. It was a few years later, just before he began work on his thesis, that those people from Bethesda paid him a visit. There were some caveats, some *ifs, ands,* or *buts,* of which he was unaware. His implant was experimental, and its life was finite, not infinite. A new implant was required within a year or he would sink back into his cloud world of blindness, where his fingers would again become his eyes, along with his nose and his ears. It would be sudden. Like a lightbulb, one eye, the other, or both would go pop. There was no telling which would go first, or how long the other might function. It could happen anywhere, anytime.

To a mathematician, the word *finite* has a very different meaning than the word *infinite*. Two little letters, *i* and *n*, makes all the difference. *Finite* is characterized by a path that has a beginning and an end: ______ ; *infinite* by a path that begins but never ends, ∞. The former is linear, the latter fluid and circle-like, but it comes back on itself in a figure eight, just as Nara's loop does. Thus, to a mathematician there is more to ______ and ∞ than just the little word *in*. Nara's loop, dynamic as it is, gives one a feeling of permanence, while going from *a* to *b*—well, how would you get back to *a*, with a little box that rewinds time? That's what Nomis felt he might have to do if he was to survive another bout of blindness: rewind time, and he didn't feel he had the emotional energy to do it.

Worse still, those implants were in high demand in 2024. There would be a waiting period of about a year and a half. He might be blind for six months for the second time, at a critical period in his intellectual life. The technology had been refined and there were more features, but he was angry and depressed at the thought of having to put aside six months to a year of his life to blindness again—a cloud world of only numbers and dreams.

During a follow-up session at Bethesda Naval Hospital he learned there was a remote possibility that he might be able to avoid a repeat visit to his cloud world. COP, an organization in Boulder, Colorado, which administered Quantum I, the computer that, among other things, controlled Solarnet, might be able to help. A subsidiary of theirs, MAIHEM, which COP had recently acquired from a French high-tech firm, had become interested in these sorts of devices some years back. They were looking for a few good men to test out their most recent inventions and gimmicks. What went on in Boulder was very hush-hush, as were most high-tech breakthroughs. It was just like Los Alamos must have been in the early 1940s. Not everybody need apply, nor know what was really going on.

He hadn't even told Nara that he was going to go blind again. So, when he mentioned to Nara he was going to Boulder to interview for a possible job opening, she looked puzzled. It didn't fit.

∞ ∞ ∞

MAIHEM turned out to be another NASA. Seventy-five years ago, in order to be shot into space in one end of a can full of liquid hydrogen, you had to be a jet pilot first—small, familiar with flying machines, and always in control—but a scientist second. Those jet pilots learned to do what was asked of them early on: they had to, to survive. Anyway, it would have been difficult to stuff the six-foot-six-inch frame of someone like Ernest Rutherford into a Mercury space capsule, even if he did want to be shot into space. Like Nomis, Rutherford, who had spent most of his productive years as a professor of nuclear physics at Manchester University in the U.K., was a workaholic and needed running room. The Mercury capsule would have cramped his style. Nomis feared MAIHEM might do the same.

Rutherford even believed in swearing at his experiments when things weren't going well. He was a disciple of Mark Twain, who had once said, "In times of stress, swearing affords a relief denied even to prayer." When the only things between you and the earth or the moon were the laws of physics, the last thing NASA expected to hear was a string of expletives coming from space. *Apollo Thirteen* was a case in point. What mission control heard was, "Houston, we have a problem," not "Shiiiitttt, an oxygen tank just blew the fucking side off this bastard of a tin can." The interview blew Nomis's mind. It was all so very serious and formal, and extremely stressful. At one point he felt like swearing too—Nomis was no jet pilot. He had even puked on that upside-down plane ride.

"I see you have a solid background in number theory," the interviewer began.

"Yes, I have participated in all of the advanced seminars at Princeton," Nomis replied.

"At what age did you go blind?" he asked.

"When I was six years old. I was in a car crash," Nomis replied.

"How long was it before you received your first implant?" he asked.

"I was eleven at the time," Nomis replied.

"Did you dream much during that time?" he asked.

Seems to be weaving back and forth on a path which might rule out individuals whose blindness was recent. Only repeats need apply, Nomis thought. *Technology requires a solid background in number theory? Candidate also has to be a dreamer?*

"Do you have to be a dreaming genius to make these new models work?" Nomis blurted out.

The interviewer didn't answer but repeated his question.

"Did you dream much during that period of time?"

"Yes, and I still do," Nomis replied.

The questions about dreaming went on and on. At one point, Nomis misjudged the intentions and focus of the interviewer. Some of his questions seemed much too personal. He thought the interviewer was joking, and told him about how he and Nara always said *sweet dreams* to each other before dozing off at night.

"The problem was we always had nightmares," Nomis admitted with the candor of a little boy who had just confessed he had wet the bed.

The interviewer wasn't amused.

"Exactly what did you dream about shortly after you were blinded by the car crash?" the examiner asked.

For the first time in a long, long time, Nomis felt like he was going to vomit. He felt something was amiss; he wasn't being told the whole truth. There were conditions lurking somewhere in the background. Nomis decided two could play what he had come to believe was a ridiculous game. Even Nomis was surprised at what happened next. It seemed that some sort of beast within him had escaped from its cage. However, he remained calm and cool as the beast roamed within him.

"I am Navajo. Navajos, if they are good men, can see with their hearts. When I was in that car crash, my chest was crushed and when I went blind, I thought that my sight had leaked out from my heart through my ribs. But my grandfather assured me that I had a good heart. After that, it was only in my dreams that I could see. In fact, nobody could see me, as I was also invisible—you know, *blind* means *invisible*, just like *Dahetihhi* means *hummingbird* in the Code Talk of the Navajo. I was mad as hell when they put that first implant in my head and not my chest. I suppose that you will put the second in my ass, as that's where you must think my brains are. And by the way, what the hell does MAIHEM stand for?" Nomis snorted.

The examiner didn't flinch.

"MAIHEM stands for Machine Assisted Intelligence—Human-Enabled Matériel," the examiner replied.

Nomis's voice took on a quizzical tone.

"Human-enabled material?" Nomis replied.

"Not material, but matériel," the examiner responded.

Nomis was a little taken aback by the examiner's reply. His demeanor changed. His voice became firm and resolute.

"Doesn't matériel mean . . . ah . . . the materials and equipment of warfare?" Nomis asked.

The examiner's reply was uncharacteristically upbeat.

"You bet your life it does," he replied. "Even though the Solarnet is the world's most secure network, it's still war out there; war between the code-makers and the code-breakers. MAIHEM backs up COP with the technology needed to fight that war. With any research and development program, there are spin-offs. Your eyes are one of them. It's like kitchen cookware and rocket nose cone ceramics—your eggs don't stick because our rockets don't burn up during re-entry. We all eat and sleep a little bit better because of it."

"A comforting thought," Nomis replied skeptically.

The examiner seemed to be collecting his thoughts when he politely excused himself. He was only gone for a few minutes. When he returned, a very old gentleman accompanied him—a native American who looked as old as Manygoats.

"*Dahetihhi* means *fighter plane* in Code Talk," the old man said to Nomis as he sat down.

"What? What was that?" Nomis asked.

"You got it backwards. *Dahetihhi* means *fighter plane* in Code Talk; but it is the word for *hummingbird* in the Navajo language," the old man responded.

Nomis nearly fell off his chair. The old man was right! Nomis was so mad he had got it backward in Code Talk; it did mean *fighter plane,* not *hummingbird.* Madness can do that: get it backward. The old man was also the son of a Navajo Code Talker and he knew of Redhouse. They chatted in the Navajo language at lunch that day. It was just like old times with Manygoats; nobody had any idea what they were talking about.

∞ ∞ ∞

In early December, Nomis received a letter from COP accepting him as a participant in MAIHEM's program. However, they wanted him to return to Boulder for a final interview, and there was a catch he didn't like. When Nomis finally told Nara what was going on, she thought it was outright ruthless and cruel that he hadn't told her about the problem with his eyes.

"Nara, I didn't want to burden you," he replied. "There is a fine line here, and perhaps I crossed it and shouldn't have. I chose to bear the pain alone. I guess in times of crisis, old habits are hard to shake. I'm sorry. Truly sorry."

Tears came to her eyes as he kissed her.

"But Nomis," she replied. "You had hoped to take a teaching assistantship at Berkeley while you were working on your thesis."

"Yes, but in return for a spot in the program at Boulder, I get new eyes, no cloud world; no reading with my fingers," Nomis said.

"But you must become a full-time employee of COP," Nara replied.

There was a new resolve to Nomis's tone of voice.

"Yes," Nomis mumbled. "I hope those engineers haven't corrected that little problem with the clicker."

For the first time in a very long time, he did a little math with words for Nara.

Demons of the Mind

What are these demons of the mind
They come, they go, but never die
Why do they seem so much of me
Are they what will let me see

Must I be
Is this the part that is not me
What is this that I seek
Does this mean that I am weak

Where are you, soul, what is the key
Am I now what should not be
Is this the way you make me see
Cruel is this to those near me

To find a way, to finally be
What message should I see
Don't play this way, for goodness' sake
Or would your secret make me ache

To run, to walk, to break this knot
What method do I use
To give a bit, to find a pit
What can there be in this

A loss, a loss, to be this way
Myself is too much not
But then again, is not is not
And then again it is

Nara read his poem and afterwards said she wanted to go walking. She had resolved in her own mind her feelings about the unexpected but sudden change in events, but she felt Nomis hadn't. It was then he learned that Nara was a Code Talker of sorts too. She had a few things to say to him about the wobble of Mercury, the Balt, spinning photons and being on the edge.

It was twilight, gray and cold. Nomis donned his parka.

"The wobble of Mercury, the Balt, spinning photons, the edge. I must say, Nara, it's catching, whatever it is!" Nomis replied. "What's the connection?"

As they walked, a gentle snow began to fall. Soon, Nara hoped it would be good skiing.

"Honey," Nara began. "Did you know George Washington dated his farewell address to the Continental Army right here in Princeton?"

"Yes. He came by way of Boston, Valley Forge, Trenton and Yorketown," Nomis replied.

Their walk took them by the white clapboard house where Albert Einstein had lived, on Mercer Street.

"And then there is Albert Einstein, who landed here in 1933. He came by way of Berne, Zurich, Berlin and London," Nomis added.

Nara turned and winked at Nomis.

"Now, Nomis, I don't want to be stealing your lines, but the former helped forge the foundations of a nation; the latter hammered out a blueprint for the universe. Both were men who made immense political and scientific contributions, right?"

Nomis stopped and took Nara by the shoulders.

"Now that's good. I've been a good teacher."

Nara took Nomis by the ear and whispered.

"What those men did is a standard that all who come to Princeton, for whatever reason, look to better."

"So, that's what I feel I've been up to, in my own small way," Nomis replied.

"Nomis, honey," Nara said, "you and Einstein have a few things in common."

"Come off it, Nara," Nomis replied.

They walked for another block in silence. The newly fallen snow began to crunch under their feet. It felt and sounded good. Nomis's ego got the best of him.

"What are they?" Nomis finally asked.

Nara smiled and then tugged on his arm, pulling him closer.

"Well, for one, Einstein enjoyed sitting on hot summer days, savoring the Balt," Nara said.

Nomis's voice sputtered with surprise. It dropped a register.

"The Balt? What?" Nomis asked.

"Your father used to take you to count the stars in the desert, and afterward, if you had counted correctly, he treated you to soft ice cream. Remember!" Nara interrupted.

They turned down Nassau Street, passing by the place where the ice cream shop, the Baltimore, had stood some seventy years ago.

"Albert Einstein often sat over there, outside the Baltimore on a bench, savoring his ice cream cone," Nara continued.

"So?" Nomis replied.

"Now hear me out, Nomis. I'm new at . . . it was a cone fit for a man who dared to go to bed early because he knew his numbers would work," Nara replied.

Nomis knew the story well. In the early 1920s, when an eclipse of the sun was about to validate Einstein's predictions about the wobble of Mercury, he went to bed early, rather than wait for the telegram that would confirm his notions about how the universe worked. When he set his ideas down on paper, he had no doubts; he knew that his mind experiments were correct.

"Einstein was a theoretical physicist who worried about clocks and how they would tick if perched on top of a speeding photon," Nara continued. "His intellectual life was nothing more than one mind experiment after another. You often said that your laboratory was your mind too, and your tools were paper, pencil, chalk and a blackboard, just like Einstein used to say."

"But the foundations of his most fundamental ideas were set down in Berne, when he was a patent clerk. As you said on the way back from Japan—that's how he paid the rent! After that, he was like one of those spinning photons that occupied so much of his thought: moving back and forth between Berne, Zurich, Berlin and London, and finally he landed here in Princeton at The Institute for Advanced Studies. We all know the story," Nara continued.

"Today trillions of those spinning photons carry many more trillions of messages to the far corners of the earth, and then some. At COP you have a chance to get in on the ground floor of what began as flashes of light inside Einstein's head, some 120 years ago. It's not theoretical math at Berkeley or Princeton, but it is an application on the edge of technology," Nara said.

If anyone but Nomis had been privy to her words, they would have concluded she was already on the edge or depressed or both. Maybe she was, but Nara was in good company that evening. When they returned from their walk, they both sat for a while at the kitchen table, reticent. Nomis broke the silence, but before he could complete his thought, Nara had answered his question.

"I'll support whatever you decide to do!" she replied.

17
Skiing by Number

There was no skiing in Princeton during the Christmas holidays. The week before Christmas, the weather turned warm. Two days of rain washed away the snow that fell in early December. The year 2024 was about to end, and Nomis and Nara had no regrets. A few days before New Year's, they decided to go north. They considered both Boston and Montreal, but had friends in Ottawa they hadn't seen since their undergraduate days. There was the promise of excellent cross-country skiing across the Ottawa River in Quebec, and the Rideau Canal, as it cut through the city, claimed to be the longest ice-skating rink in the world. This intrigued them.

While searching for a bottle of champagne, Herbert Eigen, a guest at the New Year's Eve party given by the Chesters' Ottawa friends, stumbled upon Nomis and Nara in the pantry. Nara was quite relaxed. Nomis was getting there. He had bought her a box of chocolates and a rose, which she had pinned to her dress. Nara had bought him a bottle of single malt, his favorite, and had wrapped it carefully, enclosing a note which read, "candy's dandy, but liquor's quicker!"

When Herbert flipped on the light, he caught Nomis and Nara in the far corner, by the partially closed cellar door. Nomis was alternately nipping on the single malt and nibbling on Nara's well-lubricated lower lip.

"Hi. I'm Nomis, and this is my . . . ah, Nara. My wife."

A sheepish grin monopolized Nomis's lips. Nara smiled and turned away, burrowing her head into Nomis's shoulder while slowly rubbing one of her bare feet up and down the calf of his right leg.

"Nara's a little off the wagon," Nomis said.

Nara's reply was muffled but firm.

"I beg your pardon."

"Ah, yes, whatever that means. Herbert Eigen here. Sorry to intrude, old boy. I'm looking for some champagne."

"Outside, buried in the snow bank. You might have to dig."

Nara cut short Nomis's reply, smothering his mouth with a deep, wet kiss as her hand went in search of more interesting digs.

It was pretty deep; the snow bank, that is. But it took Herbert only a minute or two to locate an unopened bottle. Nara heard the cork pop as Nomis reached for the light switch.

Herbert bumped into Nomis and Nara a second time in the den early the next morning—about 2:00 A.M., or thereabouts. Nomis was hunched over what Nara hoped was his last single malt of the evening. As Herbert approached, Nara began to blush. This time the chitchat covered most things that surface during polite conversation.

Herbert was an artist. The miniature crab cake finger food was delicious. Herbert's wife was Liz and it was she who had made the delicious crab cakes. Yes, Nara and Nomis were married and house guests of the host. Nomis was a graduate student attending Princeton University enrolled in their cryptography program.

When Nomis mentioned cryptography, Herbert's remark was a touch puerile.

"I spy with my little eye?" Herbert joshed.

Nomis's hunched posture straightened. He frowned. Nara began to feel ill. As a budding Ph.D., Nomis had developed a streak that was both adversarial and verbose. Once he got going, he had a tendency to drone on and on. Familiar with the drill to come, she plunked herself down on the sofa. The chatter from the noisy little group around them died down and the circle widened as a few others joined them.

"Yes, crypto is the science of secrecy, but there is more to it than spying with my little eye," Nomis shot back. "The underpinnings of crypto are a branch of mathematics called number theory," Nomis began.

Nara knew that the rest of what Nomis was about to say might be above everybody's head. She excused herself and headed for the sack. As Nara departed number theory 101, Herbert let go with a second salvo just as infantile.

"Some of my critics have accused me, from time to time, of painting by number."

Nara had the urge to stay and pin a medal on him, but she didn't.

After Herbert's second crack, the conversation about crypto fizzled, drifted for a while, then landed on more common ground. Herbert and Liz were avid cross-country skiers.

∞ ∞ ∞

Plenty of cold water was needed the morning after to reverse the flow of blood in those little shunts in Nara's skull which cause a hangover. As the cold water ran over her scalp and down the back of her neck, she vaguely remembered Nomis telling her, as they had snuggled in bed, that Herbert had mentioned something about joining him and Liz on a ski toot in the Gatineau Park, north of Ottawa. A quick phone call to Herbert confirmed Nomis's recollection.

"It might be late morning or early afternoon, as Nomis was off the wagon," Nara said.

"Nomis. Off the wagon?" Herbert replied.

"You know. In the mid-nineteenth century, in the old west, if you were still a bit tipsy the morning after, the wagon master made you walk," Nara explained. "Once you sobered up, you were permitted to ride."

Nara and Nomis were sure that Herbert and Liz had almost given up on them. It was after lunch before they appeared on the Eigens' doorstep.

"We're sorry we're a bit late, but we walked," Nomis remarked.

A little smirk appeared on Herbert's face.

"So, who's the wagon master?" Herbert replied.

Nara winked at Herbert. Liz took it the wrong way.

On the drive to the Gatineau, Liz produced a trail map. She pointed to a place called Kingsmere, their starting point. She proposed they follow trail number three, which looped around to Ridge Road, and return by way of Ridge to Kingsmere. Herbert was quick to add his précis.

"As an artist, loops and circles have always fascinated me. They are a refuge for change from change. There is a dynamic permanence to them. On our jaunt today, you'll never see the same vista twice, but we'll end up where we started."

When they arrived, it was much colder than in Ottawa; cold enough to freeze fingers, tongues or any other sweaty body appendage to the car door handle. They were quick to buckle up. Herbert snatched the map from Liz and stuffed it into his pocket. As he did, he chuckled.

"Just in case we get lost. Today we do want to end up going in circles, you know," he remarked.

By mid-afternoon, quite a snowstorm was brewing. The sky was a steel gray, except for an icy blue patch to the west. It wasn't long before the blue patch vanished and a snow squall was upon them. It quickly passed, leaving a gentle, fine, dry snow that dusted the trail just enough to eliminate most of the friction between their skis and the well-packed base. They just seemed to float along.

A short time later, the sun appeared, casting long, late afternoon shadows on the freshly fallen snow and leaving a gray-blue hue at their edge. Midway around the loop, they stopped at a shelter. The smell of wood smoke coming from the chimney was too much to resist. The one-room log structure looked warm and inviting. Keogon was the shelter name.

"There must be a secret to it, those shades of white, blue and gray, their hue, those shadows and the way the sun and the wind can sculpture the snow," Herbert remarked as they approached the shelter. "I must confess I've never been able to translate that secret to oil on canvas."

Herbert planted the back end of his skies in a snow bank just outside the shelter door and invited the rest to do the same. Nomis preferred to put his on the ski rack to keep the tips from becoming encrusted with a hardened ball of snow. Nara followed his lead.

"You know, an anthropology friend of mine tells me that the native peoples of northern Canada have some 500 different words for the stuff. Are there 500 secrets too?" Nomis replied.

"A well-known piece of trivia for us Canadians," Herbert replied. "As to secrets, I suppose one can't generalize."

Nomis scooped up a handful of snow and playfully flung it toward Nara. She returned his mischievous advance by nuzzling him on the cheek while planting a handful of snow down the back of his sweater. As she did, a gust of wind caught the smoke from the chimney, bringing it down into both of their faces. Nara's eyes began to water profusely. No one but Nara noticed that Nomis's didn't.

"I've tried to capture the spirit and character of some of those words," Herbert said. "I'm told that watercolor is a better medium to . . ."

"Snow does contain hidden secrets; perhaps hundreds," interrupted Nomis.

Nara tugged at what turned out to be only the top half of a Dutch door at the entrance to the shelter. The interior was like an old schoolhouse, a mélange of expertise, from little kids to men in racing tights. Some looked like advertisements for Karhu skis.

As they headed for a table by the wood stove, the professor in Nomis began to emerge. Nara began to pout. Liz caught her eye and smiled sympathetically.

"Professor Chester, wizard of the world. No, Nomis, honey, my other half, enjoy your day; no lectures, please!" Nara pleaded.

Nara added a little hissing sound to the word *please* to make her point.

Nomis bent over and softly nibbled Nara's ear.

"Viper," he whispered.

Nara gave him a big, toothy smile. She flung her jacket down on one of the wooden benches next to the wood stove. Those already seated squeezed over to make room.

On a line above the stove hung an assortment of socks, toques, and gloves drenched with perspiration. Sweaters and ski jackets not needed for the moment were hung on wooden pegs by the door. Boots were strewn about the pine board floor as toes and fingers flexed in the warm dry air rising from the stovetop.

It was the perfect place to peel, rest, snack, and search for the toes of your other half. Nara, Liz and Herbert shed their boots and hung their socks while Liz rummaged through her knapsack for the mandarin oranges, trail mix and O'Henrys she had packed for snacks. Nara's toes momentarily found Herbert's. Nara winked. Liz frowned as she unlaced her boots.

Perhaps Keogon might be a northern Nanzen-ji, Nara thought, as she continued her search for Nomis's toes.

"I've been reading lately about what one can learn from ice cores taken from the glaciers of Greenland," Nomis said.

Nara's thought was short-lived. She retrieved her toes and reached for some trail mix. Nomis blew her a kiss and then bit into the skin of his orange. The warmth of Keogon wasn't able to compete with Nomis the professor. Nara began to feel like she was back in Princeton.

"They can reveal a bundle about what went on long, long ago," Nomis continued. "When you perform a spectral analysis on those cores, you enter a world of coded colors, a dreamy world of pastel blues and whites and grays filled with all sorts of secrets. I've even developed some software for my anthropologist friends at the university to help with their analysis. I'll send you some material about it on my return to Princeton."

"Perhaps, Herbert, you can do a surrealistic painting of the icy north, with images of those secrets shimmering in the blues and purples of the Aurora Borealis," Liz jested.

And sell it at the corner service station, Herbert thought.

Herbert soon discovered that Nomis was an avid reader, with a very wide set of interests. Nara knew it wasn't long before a reading list might be distributed. The assigned reading was that little book by Simon Singh, entitled *The Code Book*. Nomis assured Herbert it was a painless introduction to crypto.

"Even though it was published in the late 1990s, a few years before the Twin Towers were hit by those terrorists, it's still a useful layman's introduction to what crypto is all about and to what I'm up to at Princeton."

Nara announced she had to pee. Liz volunteered to show her the way to the outhouse. As they got up from the table, Liz made a comment that turned a few heads.

"In this weather you've got to be careful, or you'll freeze to the seat."

An image of Nomis with his penis frozen to the seat, crying out in pain, passed through Nara's head. As she pulled on her boots, Nara caught Herbert's eyes wandering about the room. Before she and Liz headed for the Dutch door, Nara whispered in Herbert's ear.

"Skiing by number must be as boring as painting by number."

When Nomis mentioned the Priory of Sion, a European secret society supposedly founded in 1099, Herbert's interest perked up. By the time Nara and Liz returned, Herbert and Nomis were well into it. They had finally found common ground.

"Leonardo da Vinci and Sir Isaac Newton had purportedly been members, along with many other leading European intellectuals," Nomis remarked.

"There's no truth to that story. But Leonardo did have a habit of leaving coded messages in the body of his paintings and frescos. To the church, Leonardo was a terrorist of a sort, promoting ideas such as men ought to be able one day to sprout wings and fly like angels, or Mary Magdalene was the wife of Christ, or, even worse, his lover," Herbert said.

"As an artist you'd be interested in the fact that those 9/11 terrorists used steganographic methods; you know, pictures or graphics, to communicate with each other by way of the Solarnet's predecessor, the Internet," Nomis replied. "And they weren't sending each other GIF files of a pair of giraffes. They broke into the home pages of many of the most prominent dotcom retailers in Germany, and hid their secret messages in the retailers' graphics. It was the cookies that gave many of them away. NSA analyzed thousands of hits pre- and post-9/11 and found a pattern."

At that, Liz and Nara motioned that they were ready to go. Nomis and Herbert pulled on their boots and retrieved their gloves. Outside, the temperature had dropped even further. Herbert took the lead, pointing himself southeast, toward Kingsmere. The rest followed in single file, as the trail was packed in both directions. Nomis brought up the rear.

A fitting honorarium for his lecture on GIF files, Nara thought as she turned and glanced at Nomis.

"Ice cores, crypto, code books, steganography, cookies, the twin towers, NSA . . . what the hell is NSA? Did he mean NASA? Leonardo da Vinci, Mary Magdalene, and Jesus Christ," Nara heard Herbert mutter as he chugged along in front of her.

18
The Real Propulsion Plant

By the time they arrived back at Kingsmere, the sun had fled over the western horizon and it had begun to snow heavily. The Eigens suggested they all return to their home for a bite to eat. Nomis wanted to pick up his car. He didn't want Herbert or Liz to be both host and chauffeur that night. They had done enough driving. Nara agreed, but kept her reasons to herself. She wanted an easy escape route if Nomis's loquacious manner continued into the evening.

When Nomis and Nara arrived at the Eigens' big old stone house, Liz put them to work. She suggested that they lay a fire in the large fireplace in their back room. She then headed for the basement freezer to retrieve some sea scallops. Herbert took on the task of organizing the wine. Soon afterwards he heard Liz bellowing from the cellar. He relayed the message to Nomis.

"Make sure you open the damper and hold a flaming newspaper up the chimney. Get the draft going in that monster or you'll smoke us all out."

There was a rustle of paper as Nomis formed the torch needed to start the draft.

Nara saw an opportunity to kiss and make up. She put her hand under his sweater and caressed his bare back.

"Look at this, Nomis; it's right up your alley," Nara said as she pecked him on the cheek. "No, not that old pitchfork of a fire poker, silly; here, in the newspaper."

Nomis wandered into the kitchen and asked Herbert if he might use his computer to send a letter to the editor at the *Ottawa Citizen*.

"About what?"

"As Nara was stuffing some of those old newspapers between the logs, a headline caught her eye: 'Memo warns Prime Minister to further tighten Solarnet security', and I thought I might make a little comment on the issue," Nomis replied.

"Sure, the machine's in the basement," Herbert said. "It's an antique, like everything else in this house. It dates the files in a funny way. Clock's on the fritz or something. It's a pain in the butt. Make sure you put the date in the subject heading, or those at the other end might think it's porting a worm."

At dinner, Nara and Nomis told Herbert and Liz a little more about themselves. Herbert's curiosity soon got the best of him.

"Nomis, pardon the intrusion," Herbert asked, "but how does a Native American end up with Chester as his surname?"

"That's an easy one," Nomis responded. "Great-Grandpa Redhouse did a stint in the U.S. Navy during WWII. He was assigned to the staff of Chester Nimitz in Hawaii after the attack on Pearl. He idolized Nimitz. Soooo, he had his last name legally changed to Chester after the war."

"But you called him Redhouse," Herbert replied.

"Habits are hard to break. I suppose his old friends weren't willing to give up his Navajo name. The same was true of Grandpa Manygoats. But legally his surname was Chester."

"What made you break with tradition?" Herbert asked.

Nomis was slow to respond.

"It wasn't me, it was my father," Nomis replied as his brow furrowed.

Although he had never thought about the issue, Nomis realized he had just given Herbert an unwanted opening. He brushed aside any further discussion about his father without revealing anything about his early death. Aside from this, Liz and Herbert weren't able to make much headway with small talk. As the wine flowed, the conversation soon drifted back to crypto.

"So, Nomis, where are you going to go with crypto as your background?" Liz asked.

"Somewhere like Berkeley or Chicago for a post-doctoral fellowship, maybe one or the other," Nomis replied. "Either will permit me to both teach and do research."

"How about Boulder?" Nara added.

Nomis was again slow to respond.

"Yes. In a few weeks I'm speaking to an outfit called COP, about which I know little," Nomis said.

Liz jumped at the chance to talk about the Bay area and Chicago, as she had lived in both places before meeting Herbert. Nomis seemed relieved that the subject of the conversation had quickly turned away from COP. Being a Canadian, from a cold climate, Herbert thought

Chicago or even Boulder was much more interesting than the Bay area, but soon he surrendered to the chatter of Liz and Nara and the contents of his wine glass.

Out of the corner of her eye, Nara caught Herbert doodling on his table napkin while he studied both her face and Nomis's. It looked like 911, or maybe 9/11. Nara had a better idea of what was on Nomis's mind. Nothing. He looked bored.

Herbert suddenly snatched the conversation from Liz and Nara.

"Those who have abilities in music or math, like Mozart or perhaps Nomis, usually shine early in life, right? Like a rocket overcoming the earth's attraction, some burn out quickly. Those that do often expend all but a small fuel reserve during the first few minutes. Once they are free, they use the forces around them—even those which they have just overcome, such as gravity—to propel themselves to their final destination. Am I right so far? Like a ballistic missile, some mid-course corrections might be needed; hence the small fuel reserve. But it is the forces around them that remain the real propulsion plant as they come slamming down on their target."

Nara's feet began to feel cold. She instinctively removed a shoe and went in search of Nomis's toes to warm her up. Her legs were too short. Nara's toes grew colder.

"The forces around them. The real propulsion plant," Herbert muttered.

Liz snickered.

"What was that all about, Herbert? Too much wine? Sunk into your nightly stupor?"

"Nothing, nothing, Liz," Herbert mumbled.

"I sympathize," Nara joked. "Perhaps Herbert's fallen off the wagon."

Liz began to laugh.

Nara replied in kind.

"The mumbling can get to you sometimes," Liz said.

Liz picked up where she had left off and continued to extol the benefits of the San Francisco Bay area and the drawbacks of the windy city. Nara's mind wandered.

What Herbert had mumbled, "the forces around them," replayed over and over in Nara's head. The cold in her feet spread to her spine. It had been a long time since she had thought much about the events of 9/11. Nara had been only an infant, half a world away, during the aftermath. The only thing she knew about that terrible event was what she had read in books.

But he's right, she thought. *It was more than steganography or the laws of physics that drove those terrorists to do what they did, and many of them were graduate students like* Nomis. *The pressures must have been horrendous on those—*

Nara's thoughts ended abruptly as the Japanese word *kamikaze* came to mind.

Herbert came charging back, catching Liz in the middle of a sentence.

"You look awfully young for a graduate student. How old are you?" he asked.

Nara answered without thinking.

"Nomis is twenty-four; he was born on the morning of 9/11."

Nomis tried to bunt her leg but hit the table leg instead, with such force that he upset his wine glass. Liz used her table napkin to mop it up, dousing it with soda water to avoid a stain.

"Isn't that the date of . . . " Liz started.

"Yes. Yes, it was," Nara interrupted.

Nara turned and looked deep into Nomis's eyes.

"I meant to say September 11, 2001, Honey. I'm sorry."

"What time?" asked Herbert.

A silence erupted around the dinner table, the likes of which Nara had experienced only once before—at the end of a piece played by the Boston Symphony. It was part of the score. The conductor's baton remained in the air for fifteen seconds. Not a sound was heard. Nara wasn't sure what was going to happen next—another movement, or what? The old timers were poised to leap to their feet. And then it happened. The baton came down and the audience went wild with applause.

Not so around that dinner table that night. Nomis didn't reply. He left the answer to Herbert's question hanging in the air.

"I guess that makes you the millennium man, Nomis," Liz said.

A hollow laugh emerged from her lips.

Herbert's question, and Liz's disquieting remark got Nomis's attention in a negative way. His boredom fled the scene. He became uneasy, aloof—even cool. Nara failed in her second attempt to reach his toes.

∞ ∞ ∞

The meal Liz produced was sumptuous: asparagus from Mexico,

sea scallops from the Texas Gulf, a lovely French baguette and, for dessert, an upside-down cake made with fresh pineapple from Thailand.

"Technology made it all possible," Liz remarked.

Herbert followed with a list that sounded like an offertory e-mail from a stockbroker hawking an initial public offering for an energy income fund that included the sun as one of its holdings.

"The natural gas was piped from Alberta and the electricity generated from an atomic pile located at Pickering on the shores of Lake Ontario," Herbert said. "The wine is an uncomplicated white—a French Muscadet. The atomic pile which had a hand in the production of the Muscadet was located some ninety-three million miles from earth —the sun."

"Like missiles in a silo to the man in the street, sitting around this table in your lovely dining room, all of that is out of sight," Nomis remarked.

"Nomis, what a silly comment," Nara said.

After the meal, Herbert offered a short guided tour of the house, followed by some cheese and port in the back room by the fire. They took a detour through Liz's new kitchen to a room filled with flowering plants and lots of windows, which, during the day, let in the southern sun. Liz called that room her Florida room. The snow bank outside the row of windows to the south formed a white backdrop for the plants standing like sentries along the window ledge. The contrast was comforting for those looking out. For those looking in, envy might be the more appropriate word. Lurking in the corner of the room was a high-tech gas fireplace poised to ward off the most brutal attacks of the Canadian winter.

"Newness does have its strong points," Nara said.

Herbert pointed to the old wood fireplace and hearth as they entered what they called the back room.

"This old stone house was built in 1831, before central heating was invented," Herbert remarked. "A Scot named William Rutherford, who emigrated from the region near the Firth of Forth, north of Edinburgh, built it, all but the Florida room. That we added a few years ago.

"This room used to be the kitchen in the days when all that technology that helped Liz produce that sumptuous meal wasn't part of the landscape," Herbert went on. "That big old fireplace you came face to face with earlier is where the cooking was done in the 1830s. See that cast-iron pot anchored to the wall over the fire? It might have been filled with a rabbit stew or cabbage soup; now it's filled with water. It keeps things from drying out."

The name Rutherford tweaked the professor in Nomis.

"Rutherford," remarked Nomis. "A fine Scottish name. Ernest Rutherford was a Scot too—a big, gruff Scot from New Zealand with a walrus mustache and a loud booming voice. He helped pioneer the science of radioactive dating of materials by determining the half-life of a substance, and thus its precise age. That technique radically changed the science of paleontology, anthropology and archaeology. Even the technique of ice core dating, which I mentioned to you while skiing, can be traced back to his work."

"Well, at one point the house had five other fireplaces," Herbert continued. "Now, two are bricked up. One lies entombed behind the plaster walls, or perhaps 'cowering' is a better word, overtaken by the technology of central heating. A second, located upstairs in our guest room, has come back as a towel cabinet built into the wall. But three remain, like old soldiers, hanging onto their past, ready to do their duty during the snowy cold winter months. We do things . . . "

Herbert paused for a minute and then finished his thought.

" . . . the old-fashioned way sometimes. It offers a personal touch that can't be beaten."

"And it's always reliable," added Liz.

"On snowy winter evenings like tonight, fireplaces do seem organic; they come alive, and add comfort and cheer," Nomis remarked.

"One can see and smell and hear and feel them," replied Herbert. "They aren't at all like our high-efficiency gas furnace, out of sight in the basement, with its electronic dust filter, automated sensors, and computerized thermostat."

"I agree. Only in a generic sense is a modern furnace able to duplicate the ambiance of a big old fireplace," Nara remarked. "I see your bloodhound also knows the difference. He isn't sleeping by the heating vents, but by the hearth."

The room also contained some of the more recent work that Herbert had completed during the summer just past—mostly portraits. He pointed out some he regarded as the more interesting.

"I try to do with pigment and brush what Yousuf Karsh used to do with his high-tech cameras," Herbert said. "But I feel I can come a little closer to what I see and smell and hear and feel about my subject using low-tech methods. It is the fireplace and hearth, not the furnace and electronic filters, which I seek out in a person."

As Herbert opened the fire screen, letting the warmth of the blaze fill the room, Nomis turned toward Herbert, nodding in agreement. The glow of the fire imparted a devilish appearance to Nomis's eyes which only Nara noticed.

"The bookcases on either side of the fireplace long ago replaced two narrow beds used by the kitchen help, who slept there during Rutherford's time," Liz said.

A huge mantle spanned the wall between the bookcases. The ceiling was beamed and the walls were paneled with elm. The boards were wide and darkened with age. A plate rail that made its way along three sides was filled with mementos, an old violin, and what looked like some native art. The windows were smaller and less numerous than those in the Florida room. The fish bowl feeling of the Florida room wasn't part of the ambiance of the back room.

"One feels wrapped in a cocoon," Nara added.

The same is true of Nomis, Herbert thought. *At dinner he seemed to be wrapped in a cocoon of sorts, too.*

The room demanded that one relax. No, it commanded that one do so. As the fire blazed away, one had little choice but to obey its unique powers of persuasion. Its warmth and power had no problem undoing Nomis's cold, tight-lipped eccentric dinner table manner.

19

Mary, Queen of Scots

Liz arrived with a tray of fine Stilton cheese and a vintage bottle of port. Over a glass of port, which quickly added additional warmth to Nomis's jaw, they got talking about the extent and manner in which today's most successful technology duplicates nature.

Nomis stooped down and scratched the nose of Sandy, the Eigens' bloodhound. Nothing moved but the dog's tail, which wagged its approval.

"For example," Nomis said, "take the nostrils of your bloodhound. They are each shaped like little *T*s, but in a lateral position. In a sense, these little holes at the end of your bloodhound's nose are the essence of your dog. When he tracks his prey, they're what he's all about."

He took his pen in his hand, and with a sweeping motion, as Nara had recently seen him do several times before, drew on his cocktail napkin: ⊣ ⊢.

"Nature was smart," Nomis continued. "When your hound inhales, those *T*s are fully open; when he exhales, the trunks of those *T*s remain open while the hats close. His ability to track his prey is controlled by a very primitive part of his brain—a part that doesn't think. That infrastructure, those little *T*s, which mindlessly open and close with each breath, is supported by a cluster of receptors located in the hound's airway, numbering thirty times what you have in your own nose. Thirty times! But tracking his prey without those little *T*s . . . "

"Why?" Liz broke in.

Nomis chuckled while placing his glass of port on the mantle.

"A bloodhound tracks his prey for the love of his master," he interrupted. "The motivation lies in his heart, not his head—well, not really: his stomach motivates him; he does it for treats. Don't we all do it for treats, when push comes to shove? Of course, it depends on what turns you on."

"You're so right, Nomis," Herbert said. "What motivates a gambler is quite different from a person who must be coaxed across the street even when the light is green."

Nomis paused, retrieved his glass, took a sip, nibbled on some Stilton, and then sank deep into a chair, which had two enormous wings that sequestered the warmth of the fire.

"Love of master, treats. What's the difference?" Nomis replied.

"No, no, no, why that shape?" Liz interrupted.

"Simple!" replied Nomis. "When the hound exhales laterally to the side, this ensures that the poor dog doesn't confuse his own breath with the scent of his prey on the trail. You might call it *lateral smelling*. It is a very specialized function—the bloodhound does it without thinking. It is nature's way of making him very good at his job."

Herbert rose to the occasion.

"Sort of like ball bearings, which are very good at their job, but seldom noticed."

"Invisible, one might say," Nomis added. "I must admit, those people at COP tell me there are mechanical sniffers that do a much better job than bloodhounds. They must know; they're in the business."

Herbert's eyes narrowed as he bent forward in his chair and rested his elbows on his knees.

"You just program them for the substance you're sniffing for and, bingo, if it's present, they buzz," Nomis continued. "They don't need any treats either. As for love of master, machines can't love. Like your ball bearings, Herbert, they just do what you ask of them, until they wear out, and then you replace them."

"So, Nomis, you do know a little bit about COP after all?" Herbert inquired.

Nomis didn't reply. He just looked at Nara. She tried her best not to crack a smile.

"How about your senses?" Herbert retorted. "Take your eyes, Nomis; now there's a complicated piece of nature's technology that's difficult to duplicate."

Nomis was totally unprepared for such a remark. His tone of voice firmed as he cut Nara off just as she was about to say something. Another one of those fifteen-second silences descended. This time it was the type that leads everyone to change their position in their chair or take another sip of port. Like a partridge protecting a nest, Nomis cleverly led the discussion away with another one of his verbose comments.

"Books, poems, scientific papers, the telephone directory, our speech, dictionaries, a web page, cookies, graphics, even your artwork, Herbert, anything we write down, say, see, smell, hear or touch is about messaging," Nomis said. "What we usually hear and see and smell and taste and touch in our everyday lives requires little effort or attention to understand. However, unlike your bloodhound, we are only equipped for a certain normality of signal which reaches our senses. Things outside our mindset, beneath the surface, the abnormal or the paranormal, we usually ignore or miss—we just aren't looking for them."

"If our senses are so mundane, why hasn't nature given us a specialization like Sandy's; say, a sixth way of messaging?" Liz questioned.

On hearing his name, Sandy got up from his place by the hearth, put his head down, raised his rump, and extended his front legs forward, as if to take a little bow. He then nuzzled Liz, plunking himself on the floor at her feet.

"It has," Nomis replied. "Take those steganographic messages on those German home pages. Did you know that during the week prior to 9/11, over one hundred thousand Germans viewed those home pages with that steganographic message containing the command to hit the Twin Towers? It was right under their collective noses. By my count, only some twenty-five people knew what it meant. Those twenty-five were the bloodhounds. They had the technology, the receptors, to understand what was right under our noses."

"More like the Hounds of the Baskervilles," Herbert muttered.

Nara wasn't able to conceal her titter.

Herbert was Nomis's homologue. Somewhere way back in time, their genealogy must have had a common ancestor, Liz thought.

"You mean we have the ability to invent, to substitute tools, or perhaps technology, when nature has come up short," Liz finally shot back.

Nomis's tone of voice thickened.

"Maybe, but let me finish! I'm no expert, but it seems to me that the human ability to think laterally or dream is our smart thing," Nomis replied. "The use of steganographic messaging and the discovery of those cookies is a case in point. No doubt the guy who proposed that they be handed over to the FBI for analysis was a dreamer."

He paused for another sip of port, cleared his throat and then continued in a more confident tone.

"Our ability to think laterally may be what you're looking for, Liz—the ability to process what seems to be unrelated pieces of information and make sense of them all. It's what we do when we dream. If we lose the ability to think laterally, or message within ourselves as we dream, so to speak, we too will soon become unworkable pieces of nature's technology."

Nara got up and put her hand over Sandy's nose. The dog sneezed, licked her hand, stood up and stared intently at the piece of cheese in her other hand.

"And unlike a bloodhound, who will quickly become an unworkable piece of nature's technology without his little *T*s, our smart thing is always there, even if we lose one or another of our five ways of messaging," Nara replied. "In fact, without one or another of our five senses, our sixth sense has to work even harder."

Nomis's lips pursed.

"Enough said, Nara! Sandy, come!" Nomis said.

The dog looked at Nomis, then at Liz. Liz snapped her fingers.

"No begging, Sandy," Liz demanded.

The dog fell to her feet, tucked his head between his paws and closed his eyes. Nomis looked at Nara, grinned and then pointed at Sandy.

Herbert got up and put another log on the fire, stoking the coals beneath the new log with that long, forked poker. The glow of the coals returned. There was a sudden puff of smoke and then flame. Nara felt the heat again.

"You're absolutely right, Nara," Herbert replied. "In that classic film *Scent of a Woman*, the main character, that old marine captain, had a real sense of smell. Although blind, he seemed very lucid about the real issues of the day. The old boys' network, which entangled that New England prep school in a messy plot of dishonor and non-truth, was blinded by self-importance. That old boys' network spent too much time smelling its own breath."

"Correct," Nara replied. "It was a man with no eyes who put the pieces together and made sense of it all. No doubt his sixth sense had to work overtime to make those old boys see what was going on around them."

Nomis slowly shook his head from side to side as his lips thinned.

"This business of smelling your own breath is a big problem," Nomis said. "It isn't uncommon for people like journalists, or whoever, to apologize for their errors once a year—just about this time, at New Year's. Those media hounds can really get it wrong sometimes, especially when they mistake their own breath for that of their prey. Once one starts doing that, one really does become an unworkable piece of technology."

Nara crossed her legs and folded her arms across her chest.

"But isn't the smell of your own breath what dreaming is all about?" Nara added. "After you have savored the aroma, the trick is to take your dreams apart, to uncook them—that's how you get to really know yourself. Isn't that what COP's sniffers do, break down the aroma, molecule by molecule?"

At that point, Nomis got up from his winged chair by the hearth, picked up the poker, stoked the fire himself a bit and then sat down on the green leather sofa beside Nara. He took her hand in his, as if to plead with her to drop the subject.

"Dreams, blind marine captains, journalists, molecule-eating sniffers. I think we have strayed from the trail here."

He returned to the winged chair by the fire.

"No mind, Nomis. Go ahead, Liz, wander a bit further afield!" Herbert suggested.

Nomis's left eye began to roll around in a most mechanical manner. Nara had never seen that happen before. It was unnerving.

"If what I do and say and write and think is known only to those whom I chose to inform, that's stealth of my being, isn't it?" Liz said.

"What do you mean, stealth of your being?" Herbert asked. "Are you talking invisible men here, or perhaps little green men?"

"Come on, you know what I mean, Herbert," Liz said. "A stranger is always an unknown—and as I understand Nomis, crypto can keep it that way. For example, Nomis, if you had a secret language that only you and Nara spoke, no one else would really get to know you, unless they were able to get inside your head. Just like those terrorists, predictions about your behavior would be very hard to make, and what happened on the 9/11 attests to that."

Nomis turned and looked directly into the fire, nursed his port and put his hand over his left eye.

"OK, I know many people who are like one-way mirrors," Herbert said. "They can see out, but rarely let others see in. In fact, I've found those subjects the most difficult to paint. They exist in their own little cocoon and are always a challenge. I don't think that's a sense like sight or touch. It's more like a part of their personal being. Is that what you mean?"

"It is their personal being," Liz insisted. "It's also a way that people collect information, like a one-way messaging process. They get to know others, but others don't really get to know them. They are like listening devices that we don't know are really there. In a sense, they have an ability to tower above us, like a falcon searching for its prey, a predator."

Towering above us like a falcon, Nara thought. *A falcon seeking its prey, a predator.*

Horrible TV images of those planes, just before the Twin Towers were hit, flashed into her head.

The stealth of those terrorists was a major weapon, Nara thought. *They were like one-way mirrors, like listening devices. And at the right moment, they gathered up the most modern technology and turned it against the U.S. It was what one might call organic stealth, organic terrorism. In hindsight, it was so natural but so ugly and it caused incredible mayhem and pain.*

"I wouldn't consider stealth of your being equivalent to stealth of your corpus; you know, taking the *I can see you, but you can't see me* thing literally," Herbert replied. "That's the ultimate in stealth, corpus stealth—no codes to break and no written record. But it's too unnatural, it isn't organic. I don't see it as duplicating nature. Invisible men. Phooey."

"Phooey on you, Herbert," Nara replied. "Not so! Plenty of insects use that ploy, literally taking on the look of their surroundings. Newts are another example. The idea isn't to stand out in the crowd."

Nomis turned to Nara. The rim of his left eye socket was red and puffy.

"*Jaysho*!"

"*J-so*? Was that *j-so* I heard you say, Nomis?" Herbert asked.

"He just called me a buzzard. *Jaysho*. It's Navajo for *buzzard*," Nara replied.

Nara stuck out her tongue at Nomis.

"You're the bomber, not me. *Jaysho* yourself," Nara replied.

Buzzard just became bomber, Herbert thought.

Nomis ignored Nara while gently nudging the conversation off course. He cupped his hand and covered his left eye again.

"The only newt I know is the one in Ezra Pound's poem, 'Winter is a-coming in, newt . . . ,' if I remember correctly," Nomis said.

"You mean, 'Winter is a-cumen in, lute sing goddamn.' " Herbert interrupted. "In that one, Pound wasn't talking about newts but lutes, you know—harps. I must say, he was right about winter in Ottawa. Both lutes and newts in Ottawa, both what you play and lizards, have been singing damn for a couple of weeks now."

"Herbert, deary, Nara's talking about real stealth," Liz added. "The kind that the military has developed to make planes invisible."

Nomis interrupted.

"It depends on the surface materials and the geometric design of the plane. Those planes have an aura about them; a technological or geometric aura that makes them selectively invisible to enemy eyes."

"If we humans can dream up that one, and if crypto can impart stealth to our being, we ought to be able to dream up personal or corpus stealth," Liz suggested. "Especially if some insect has already done it."

"Nomis used to dream—" Nara began.

Nomis's eye again began its curious roll as he cut Nara off.

"As visions of sugar plums danced in my head," Nomis said.

"We are resourceful little buggers and what nature didn't give us, we dream about, and afterward we try to invent our dreams," Herbert said. "The hell with sugar plums. I've been dreaming about another glass of port; let me invent one for you."

Herbert made the rounds, pouring everyone a second glass.

"And it seems that crypto, or the science of secrecy, sometimes plays a role in our dreams," Nara replied.

Nara tossed Nomis one of her most radiant smiles, after which she cocked her head to one side and waited for his response. Nara's comment left Liz and Herbert hanging there, like excellent port on the edge of a glass, wondering what was coming next. Nomis's eyes ceased that incessant rolling. Nara was relieved.

Nomis was forced to dig deep into his garrulous repertoire. Much to Nara's chagrin, Nomis was able to calmly and skillfully drag the conversation away with, of all things, a history lesson.

"Yes, Nara," Nomis said. "Mary, Queen of Scots, had a dream. She wanted to become Queen of England. Mary had a cipher that gave her words stealth. At first this gave Elizabeth I no evidence of Mary's treasonous activity."

Nara knew where he was going and she didn't like it.

"*Jaysho, Jaysho, Jaysho,* Nomis, you terrorist, you," Nara mumbled.

First a buzzard, then a bomber, now a terrorist, Herbert thought.

Nomis paid no attention. Herbert even helped him along. Nara felt like taking her medal back, or even accusing Herbert openly of painting by number.

After all, she thought, *he had little trouble skiing by number.*

"But Mary's code-maker wasn't careful, and her secrets finally became known to her enemies," Herbert said. "What she had to say to the French Court was treasonous as far as Queen Elizabeth I was concerned."

"Yes. As I remember, she lost her head over that little tussle," Liz said.

Nomis turned his gaze toward Nara, a gaze that was telepathic, menacing and stoic. He seemed to be preparing to do the work of an executioner.

"That little tussle between Mary and Elizabeth I, the tussle between code-makers and code-breakers, carries on to this day in all sorts of venues," Nomis replied. "But our senses sometimes don't pick up on the stealth that surrounds such activity, not even the one that thinks laterally. If Mary's cipher had suspected that the stealth of her words had been broken, he would have altered her code talk. A first principle of stealth is that you must never, never reveal yourself or your activities, for if you do, you lose your advantage. In Mary's case she lost her head, because the stealth of her words wasn't secure and her enemies didn't let it be known to her that they had broken her code."

Nomis was, by then, looking straight into Nara's eyes. He got up and gave her a little kiss on the forehead.

Nara's voice became sing-songy as she turned her eyes slowly away from Nomis's, looking out the back window at the snow building up on their car.

"Winter is a-coming in, Nara sing damn," Nara chirped. "It's a day's drive tomorrow back to Princeton. With that second glass of port and the storm that's brewing, we had better call it a night."

∞ ∞ ∞

Once in the car, Nomis leaned over and kissed Nara softly on the lips. He realized the stress of the day had taken its toll.

"Nara, you know I love you very much," Nomis whispered.

"I love you too. You assassin, you," she replied.

Nomis looked into her eyes.

"But there are secrets one should never tell. And those that one should never be told. I'm blind in my left eye!"

Nara wept as she put her fingers across his lips and kissed his eyes softly.

"I'm so sorry for you, Nomis, so very sorry. I'd better drive."

"No need. But . . . did you mention to Herbert anything about my eyes?" Nomis questioned.

"No."

"What about that comment he made about my eyes being hard to duplicate?" Nomis asked.

"Maybe a guess, or a spontaneous remark. I don't know," Nara added with a big sigh. "Let's go."

The next day, when they got to Syracuse, New York, Nomis insisted they head East on I-90 to Boston. He wanted to visit a few old friends at MIT and try his hand at Nara's Loop up near Concord. Nara was sure he was in denial, but she understood.

Her little sign was still there. It was the second time within a month that Nomis listened and Nara did the talking.

They went with the clock, and neither Nomis nor Nara fell into the mist by the little bridge at Black Creek. They both knew that if either did, the other would always come to the rescue.

Later Nomis put down on paper what he thought Nara had said to him as they skied her loop that day.

Go Back a Ways on Road in Time

A road, a trail, a fork of mind
A path of now and then
I came upon you at a time
When you were at a bend

You seem to be afraid today
Of what was once a natural way
Could progress be the final fling
That puts an end to everything

This fork could cause a subtle shift
In what has been your natural gift
To play, to sing, to be as one
In times when little can be done

This fork is only in your mind
The path lies in your soul
A choice now is not to find
The thing which is your goal

Go back a ways on road of time
To see what you now miss
There are some sights to keep in mind
Before you make your twist

On January 3, 2025, the letter that Nomis had written to the editor was published. Herbert cut it out and sent it to him.

January 3, 2025
Letter to the Editor
Ottawa Citizen

Will we take quantum leap into future?

In "Memo warns Prime Minister to Tighten Solarnet Security" [C1, December 28, 2024], the Clerk of the Privy Council advises the Prime Minister that a raft of advances in computer technology, connectivity and Solarnet usage is pushing business and governments toward total delivery of services via Solarnet.

Both might also benefit from a quick read of *The Code Book* by Simon Singh. It was written some thirty years ago, but still offers many valuable lessons. The whole book is fascinating, but the Chapter entitled "A Quantum Leap into the Future" is as relevant now as it was then. What's on page 350 (the last page of the book) is most relevant even today and I quote:

"If quantum cryptography systems can be engineered to operate over long distances, the evolution of ciphers will stop. The quest for privacy will have come to an end. The technology will be available to guarantee secure communications for governments, the military, business and the public. The only question remaining will be whether or not governments allow us to use the technology. How will governments regulate quantum cryptography, so as to enrich the Information Age, without protecting criminals?"

Well done, Mr. Singh. We took that quantum leap into the future in 2011. What hasn't been well done is the manner in which governments have solved that last problem—how to enrich the Information Age without protecting criminals?

Nomis Chester
Ph.D. student in Cryptography
Princeton, New Jersey

Some weeks later, an item caught Herbert's eye in Toronto's *The Globe and Mail.* It mentioned COP, so he cut that one out too and faxed it to Nomis.

The Globe and Mail
January 17, 2025

Tech firms form cyber-warning site; U.S.-Canadian heavyweights to share tips anonymously about Solarnet attacks.

By Seamus Somers.
Technology Reporter.

A group of high-tech heavyweights have teamed up to form a national cyber-warning center to strengthen security over the Solarnet. Modeled loosely on the American missile and air defense warning system, NORAD, the Information Sharing and Analysis Center for Information Technology (IT-ISAC) was formed yesterday by 19 companies in Canada and the United States to share tips anonymously about cyber attacks. Neither COP, located in Boulder, Colorado, or The National Security Agency in Washington, D.C., were willing to comment on their relation or involvement in this new activity.

With files from AP

∞ ∞ ∞

Despite that raucous first encounter, Nomis and Nara became very close personal friends with Herbert and Liz. Both eventually learned the full story of Nomis's eyes. They were an odd couple—a mathematician and an artist—but that was one of the reasons Nomis and Nara returned many times to Ottawa. Nomis and Herbert found they weren't really able to talk about each other's work. Nomis's sterile world of points, lines, circles, squares, triangles and numbers was of a different ilk than Herbert's, although he used all but numbers to paint portraits.

So they settled for the real world of tennis, sailing, swimming, skiing, golfing, eating good food, drinking good wine, and listened to good music.

20

Generation T

Once the Chesters had settled in Boulder, Nara enrolled as a graduate student in chemistry at the University of Colorado. The year she was awarded her Ph.D. she became pregnant. It was a shock when Nara and Nomis discovered that twins, a boy and a girl, were on their way.

More and more, Code Talking became a part of the Chesters' life. The work, the science of secrecy, was interesting and right down Nomis's alley. Nomis was lucky to have landed where he did. Those who were employed by COP often said it was like working in Houston at NASA in the late 1960s, or in Yorketown Heights, at IBM's research facility, in the early 1960s, or in Pasadena at the California Institute of Technology in the 1950s, or at what was the Research and Development Corporation in the late 1940s but later came to be known as just plain RAND, or in New Mexico at Los Alamos in the early 1940s.

The second-generation implants turned out to have a much longer life. The ones Nomis had had installed when he joined COP in 2025 were still functioning in 2045. The very first implant lasted only fourteen years. The longer life of the second implant was due to a modification that also improved his hearing. In his late twenties he had become deaf in one ear. MAIHEM blamed it on collateral damage done at the time of the crash.

There were a few drawbacks. The modification drew more power, and the power source was located behind his left ear. At airport checkpoints, the alarm buzzed every time a scanner circled his balding head. He had to carry a card that indicated he had an implant. And there was his tinnitus in the other ear, which always flared up when those buzzers went off.

Nomis insisted the modification that had improved his hearing was defective. With the first implant he claimed he was able to see sounds when he closed his eyes. His doctor said he had a touch of synaethesia. With the second he claimed he not only saw but heard the shapes and colors of things. A circle always caused his ears to ring, and red buzzed.

The technicians at MAIHEM never found anything wrong. They even failed to uncover Nomis's secret about his clicker.

When their children were young, Nomis's bedtime stories often included a tale about a man who was able to see with his ears and hear with his eyes. They caught on quickly. One night, Nomis was describing his first encounter with Yazzie's big telescope. They anticipated his remark about both seeing and hearing the Rings of Saturn. A strange feeling welled up inside Nomis when they did.

My dad was wrong about that too. I swear I can hear those rings, Nomis thought, as he tucked his daughter into bed.

Alfred, Nomis's MIT roommate, had left an impact on Nomis. He acquired a number of hobbies, including the construction of a computerized family archive. Nara and the children thought his interest in family history, especially the manner in which he encouraged his children to scan everything of interest, was rooted in Yazzie's untimely death and the big hole it had left in his visual memory. That second close call with his cloud world, just before he joined COP, was also a factor. If it ever happened again, he didn't want to miss a thing.

Nomis employed his talents as an archivist at COP too. As the years passed, he was one of the few who knew its history. He tracked down many interesting vignettes, which he drew upon in the public relation stints in which he was sometimes called upon to participate. If all he talked about was crypto his audience might fall asleep.

Once, when he was interviewed by talk show host Mort Stone of the United Broadcasting System, Stone tried to engineer the exact opposite—a real wake-up call—for his viewers. Nomis had just been appointed Chief Mathematician at COP and it was his first time in front of the harsh lights of television.

Stone was a feisty little cockney and his reputation preceded him. Those lights of Stone's were intimidating, too. They made his guests feel like they were being interrogated, not interviewed. Nara's advice was to enlist the aid of Nomis the bombastic, loquacious graduate student turned professor. Nomis's strategy was a little different. He intended to stay away from touchy areas. If push came to shove, he even contemplated keeping Stone in the dark. After introducing Nomis as the father of Quantum II and congratulating him on his appointment, Stone went right for the jugular.

"When my father was a kid, C-O-P stood for 'constable on patrol'," Mort began. "In the UK, it was short for copper. Are you people involved with law enforcement?"

"Mort, COP is all about using math, very fast computers and the physics of light to both develop and deploy what we call secure photon ciphers," Nomis responded.

Mort didn't wait long to exercise the control for which he was famous. He motioned directly to the studio camera with one hand, as if he were inviting those viewing the program to step through the lens into the studio, and with the other to Nomis.

"COP is certainly the brains behind all of that—the leader in the field. But the hardware is only the half of it, right?" Mort queried.

"The hardware? You must mean the photon ciphers," Nomis replied.

"Photon ciphers. Isn't that some sort of sci-fi gismo? Nomis, my viewers are people, not machines. Let's talk about the people at COP, like you."

"You took the words right out of my mouth, Mort," Nomis said. "On the people side, COP has the wherewithal too. Its people are the architects of stealth and secret-keeping, which a worldwide network of computers and photon ciphers must offer to its users. You know, those using COP are paying for a system that is secure from soup to nuts, not an overgrown, topsy-turvy network."

The third time Nomis mentioned photon ciphers, Mort began fidgeting with his notes.

"Well, that's a mouthful. Photon ciphers, hmm. It keeps coming back like a bad copper . . . I mean penny. What are they? Let me take a stab. They're like those metal detectors at the airport which check out one person at a time. The difference is that those gismos check out little bits of light, called photons, one at a time, frisking the little buggers to see what they're carrying by way of messaging."

Nomis was impressed.

"Yes, that's one way of putting it, but they not only read, but also write . . ."

Mort didn't wait for Nomis to finish his sentence.

"I assume that your topsy-turvy remark was aimed at the old Internet."

"Yes, in the early years many of COP's users were Internet refugees," Nomis replied.

"Internet refugees. That's a good one," Mort remarked.

Mort paused to jot down Nomis's well-chosen phrase.

"Didn't COP initially benefit from that debacle?" Mort continued.

"Yes, I think that's true, especially financial institutions. Most were victims of those vicious cyber-attacks which erupted on the Internet in 2011," Nomis said.

Mort looked down at his notes again. His tone of voice became skeptical.

"In 2011, you were just a ten-year-old kid in Albuquerque, weren't you?" Mort asked.

Red flags went up. Nomis was sure the next question might be about his eyes.

"Yes, but the demise of security on the Internet is a well-known fact," Nomis responded.

Nomis left no time for Mort's next question.

"What isn't well known today is that anyone can use photon crypto if they can get their hands on the technology, and unfortunately that is the case."

"Yes. I was going to get to that point later," Mort replied. "But since you brought it up, isn't part of COP's job to keep our highways of light, those ribbons of fiber optics out there, on the up and up?"

"Yes," Nomis replied.

"How can you, if the other side has the same technology? It sounds to me like cops with radar guns against speeders with fuzz busters."

"Not exactly," Nomis said.

"The word on the street is that some of you guys act like Georgia state troopers, hiding in the strangest places just to catch some guy who's in a hurry to get to work!" Mort stated.

"Now that's unfair." Nomis shot back. "Maintaining a worldwide network, free from bad hackers, lone criminals, malicious insiders, industrial espionage, organized crime, terrorists and infowarriors, to name just a few, requires a lot of computer power and very sophisticated algorithms."

"Algorithms?" Mort queried. "And what're algorithms, a version of the Texas two-step?"

"Oh, that's just a fancy word for software, computer software," Nomis replied.

"As I understand it, Nomis," Mort continued, "even though you were just a kid in 2011 when the Internet collapsed, you claim to be a charter member of what is called *Generation T*."

Nomis's lips tightened as he nodded his head.

"Yes. For my generation, terrorism on U.S. soil first reared its ugly head at the turn of the millennium, on 9/11."

"What about the incident at the White House which occurred on Christmas day way back in 1975?" Mort shot back.

"What incident . . . when was that?" Nomis responded.

"December 25, 1975, shortly after the first hike in the price of oil. A person dressed in Arab garb . . . " Mort replied.

"I'm not familiar with . . . anyway I repeat . . . for my generation," Nomis said.

"And your birthday is?" Mort interjected.

"Mort, most of your viewers know it's September 11, 2001. The commercial ads for your show said so. As I was saying, my generation was born to a world of both terrorism and sniffers . . . " Nomis continued.

"What time?" Mort interrupted.

Nomis was slow to reply.

"Around nine A.M."

"So, you are a charter member. Maybe the first."

"I suppose so," Nomis said.

"You were also the one who coined the idea of substituting COP's corporate logo for the *T* in *Generation T*. Not so?"

Nomis drew COP's corporate logo, ⊣ ⊢ on a pad of paper and held it up to one of the studio cameras.

"Yes," Nomis replied.

Mort pointed to Nomis's artwork as the camera zoomed in on the logo.

"Now, didn't that thing cause a little bit of a problem?" Mort asked.

Mort's reference to COP's logo as "that thing" irked Nomis.

"A problem. No," Nomis said.

"How about that student thing and the guy in L.A."

"Yes. Tens of thousands of students adopted the symbol as their own. It became a cult thing."

Nomis found himself biting his tongue. That thing had become a cult thing.

"Didn't a clever wheeler-dealer in Los Angeles try to corner the novelty shirt market simply by hot-pressing COP's corporate logo on the front of a tee shirt and 'Generation T' on the back?" Mort interrupted.

"Yes, that's what happened," Nomis replied.

"Didn't COP have to wade in and make sure its good name didn't suffer from all the commercialism which followed?" Mort replied.

Mort made a special effort to emphasize the words "good name," which again annoyed Nomis.

"Not really," Nomis replied.

"Some kids even made a religion out of it!" Mort added.

"No, not to my . . . " Nomis responded.

"Surely COP enjoyed the publicity, having been in the shadows for so long. What did all your big corporate clients have to say?" Mort continued.

Nomis's tone of voice turned defensive. He ignored Mort's last question and returned to the one about his being a charter member of Generation T.

"Needless to say, my very birth, and lots like me who were born on September 11, 2001—and that logo—they all mock those responsible for that horrible event, as do all of those shirts. You can seldom go to a mall these days without seeing some kid wearing one."

Mort Stone realized he was about to end up on the wrong side of the street. His tactic—stirring a pot which contained 9/11, Generation T, COP's logo, the wheeler dealer from Los Angeles and those shirts—was about to explode in his face. If he didn't watch out, every kid who owned one of those shirts might send an e-mail to UBS, reaming him out for his attempt to polarize his conversation with Nomis, using their beloved shirts as the catalyst.

The floor manager signaled that a commercial break was in the offing in about fifteen seconds. Mort seemed uncharacteristically eager to go to break.

"Well, folks, don't go away; I'll be back right after the break with this week's guest, Dr. Nomis Chester, who's providing us with the inside dope on COP."

Nomis found himself rubbing his eyes.

Saved by the break, Nomis thought.

Stone smiled at Nomis and then motioned to an assistant to fetch his briefcase. Nomis found himself repeating his thoughts out loud.

"Saved by . . . "

Mort cut him off.

"We still have a good fifteen minutes to go."

"Aren't they going to turn those lights off during the break?" Nomis asked.

"No," Mort replied. "Excuse me while I retrieve some things from my brief case."

21

A Voice in the Dark

Nomis felt a tinge of nausea as Mort reviewed his tactics. Stone was much more aggressive that he had expected. Nomis toyed with Nara's suggestion. In a pinch he just might have to call on his old friend, the professor.

"Thirty seconds to show time," the floor manager yelled.

The producer's choice of words brought on another tinge of nausea. When the count reached the ten-second mark, Mort Stone's assistant scurried off camera. The electronic media was a strange beast. As the count continued, its eyes became its ears. The silence in the studio roared with fingers that twitched. The ends of Nomis's fingers tingled as if to object. Nomis's hand slipped into his pocket and fingered the clicker. His cloud world beckoned. The studio lights went dead with the push of a button. Nomis's ears became his eyes as Mort became a voice in the dark.

"Dr. Nomis Chester and I have been chatting about COP," the voice in the dark began. "Let's move on to . . . "

Nomis took the initiative. He had decided to maintain Mort's focus on COP's logo. He held up his artwork in the direction of the voice and pointed to the two little *T*s resting on their sides.

"Before the break we were talking about COP's logo. These two little *T*s, now they represent the sniffers of COP, and that little alleyway between them, well, that's the little passage that light, laden with messaging, photon by photon, has to squeeze through on the Solarnet, where COP's algorithms lurk, ready to behead the enemy or attach a beacon."

Nomis was unaware that his comment had prompted Mort to raise his eyebrows, lower his head and peer out over the rim of his glasses.

"Sniffers. Beacons?" the voice replied. "Tell us about those!"

Nomis ignored his comment, realizing that he had just raised an issue that he didn't want to explore in public. He decided to take Nara's advice and go the professor route.

"Say, Mort, I'm a fan of old movies. It is interesting how symbols acquire other meanings through common usage, just like words," Nomis continued. "Those shirts now have a connotation quite different from what they did in the classic movie *On the Waterfront*, when Marlon Brando made them a fashion statement."

"Didn't Brando also play the part of the deranged, insane general in that movie *Apocalypse Now*?" the voice quickly shot back. "Let me tell you, that was no fashion statement. It was a nightmare."

"I might add that the logo reminds me, in all its beauty and simplicity, of the Twin Towers," Nomis said. "They say things do come in threes, and this is no exception—the nostrils of a bloodhound, the alleyway of a photon cipher and those Twin Towers."

"The nostrils of a bloodhound?" the voice queried.

Nomis smiled. He was now sure he was able to trap Mort in a pile of bombastic bullshit.

"Yes, bloodhounds' nostrils have that shape too," Nomis replied. "It keeps them from smelling their own breath."

Stone's face turned pinkish. Even with his eyes turned down Nomis detected a dull buzzing in his ears, and then the sensation of red. He smiled. Mort didn't.

Even with my eyes off, they must be sensitive to color, Nomis thought.

"As I understand it, to a few of those who work for COP, that logo is almost a religious symbol, trinity and all," the voice replied. "You, no doubt have read William L. Shirer's book *The Rise and Fall of the Third Reich*."

Nomis became wary as his smile faded to a frown.

"Yes. A long time ago."

"The Nazi logo was a twisted cross, a swastika," the voice replied. "COP's logo looks like a cross that has been split right down the middle! Perhaps by the crescent sword of radical Islam?"

Nomis wasn't prepared for that remark. He didn't reply. The voice in the dark continued to goad Nomis on his personal involvement.

"Nomis, more than once I have said that you're well known for your silent ways, and I guess your taciturn manner proves me right," the voice said. "Now, isn't there an ongoing political debate about secrecy, security, and freedom, in which you also refused to involve yourself? As I understand it, that dialectic is also split right down the middle. Are you a fence sitter on this one, too?"

Nomis's head tilted back. He became wide-eyed. His ears roared. A smirk appeared. He was sure his response was going to put Mort right where he wanted him.

"I feel the object of politics is like the mathematician's quest for a secure cipher, but much less rigorous," he began. "To me rarely does the dialectic of political debate produce a unique solution. When a solution is proposed, *Eureka* isn't usually the unanimous cry heard in the legislature. Things that have *no general solution, yet* usually end up with many competing solutions. Debate never seems to toss the *no*, but instead discards the *yet* and fails to add the *Eureka*."

Mort's tone became acerbic.

"Can you decipher that for my viewers, Nomis?"

"Sure. The language of debate is imprecise. The assumptions aren't clearly stated, and there is always a discontinuity contained somewhere within the debate itself. It always seems to get hung up in the air, unable to reach its target. I call it the *Zeno syndrome*."

"Zeno . . . what?" the voice said.

"The Zeno syndrome!" Nomis replied. "It's an old Greek puzzle in math that has no possibility of solution unless you change your point of view."

Mort left that one quickly. Nomis felt he was firmly in control.

"Weren't the Afghan, Iraqi, and the more recent problems in Indonesia, only the tip of the iceberg? International cyber attacks have been the follow-up to what occurred in the early part of the twenty-first century. It all came to a peak in 2011. The infowar on the Internet, and subsequently on Solarnet, has been truly a war without end, almost a crusade, and you have been right in the middle of that war for the greater part of your professional life. Right?"

Nomis ought to have avoided that one, but he didn't.

"I am their worst nightmare; what I bring to the table is mayhem, pure mayhem," Nomis replied.

Because of that comment, Nomis received several calls from MAIHEM the following day. Apparently, they didn't like his choice of words. The problem was that some viewers, including many of his colleagues, weren't quite sure if the word "their" referred to the terrorists or COP, or both.

Mort turned his attention to COP's inner workings.

"Aren't you the overseer of COP's worldwide system?" the voice asked.

"The technical end, yes," Nomis replied.

"The word on the street is that it has come to the point where every bit, every string, every message on your system is subject to real-time sniffing," the voice replied.

An answer to that question might raise the hackles of just about everybody at COP. The electronic personalities of most criminal types, and some who weren't, had been catalogued by the National Security Agency, the Federal Bureau of Investigation, the Central Intelligence Agency and the Data Enforcement Agency. COP actually stood for Crypto on Patrol. Their computers were real bloodhounds and even more so because of COP. Nomis's brainchild, Quantum II, was the alpha male.

If criminal types appeared on COP's highways of light, they were "pulled over" immediately by Quantum II. An electronic beacon—like a cookie—was attached to such strings of information, traces were run, origins and destinations were determined. In COP's War Room in Boulder, there was a mammoth computer screen (300 feet long and 100 feet high) which displayed past, present and possible future cyber attacks and the like for each and every criminal personality who had acquired a beacon. Each beacon was given a nickname. All one had to do was call them up onto that screen, using the proper cryptogram, and their travels over Solarnet were set out clear as a bell.

Many times COP didn't know the real identity of the criminal types they were tracking; they just fit a generic profile. COP called that activity ESP, or Electronic Systems Profiling. In private, Nomis was a little more poetic; he called ESP extra-sensory perception, as COP's computers processed information laterally, not linearly.

When Quantum II was hot on the trail of its prey, the lateral links between the computers at the Federal Bureau of Investigation, the National Security Agency, the Central Intelligence Agency and the Data Enforcement Agency provided unrivaled computer power, becoming one humongous brute of a computer as those at the FBI, NSA, CIA and DEA acted as four monstrous Random Access Memories.

Stealth was the modus operandi of COP. You never let the other guy know you were onto him until you were ready to take him out. Quantum II's software was fast, and also the ultimate maestro of stealth. A lone criminal or terrorist's messaging might ride around for months with one of those beacons attached to it before COP acted to shut him down for good. Strategic choices were always made to be sure that COP had sifted and sniffed out all it was able to before the shut-down. The beacon approach tied up a lot of the criminal's resources, too. The criminal element wasn't stupid, but trying to shake a beacon was like trying to find a cure for AIDS. Those beacons were insidious.

Once a take-down order was issued, Quantum II became the ultimate infowarrior. It hacked to death any file, string, bit, message or attachment, anything with a beacon attached to it, at the precise time that the DEA showed up at the guy's front door. Any or all of this might leave Mort's ears smoking.

"Nomis, exactly how much sniffing is going on?" the voice demanded.

"Mort, there are some things that one should never tell, and others that one should never be told," Nomis replied.

"You coined that little ditty, didn't you? I take it your answer is . . . -what?" the voice said.

"You have my answer," Nomis replied. "I can't answer because I don't know, and if I did, I think you would agree with me that the telling of it is a no-no."

"Well, two nos, in my book, is a yes," Mort added.

"No means no in mine," was Nomis's riposte.

"Once the war on drugs had been won, weren't you instrumental in transforming the DEA?" the voice asked. "As I understand it, the Drug Enforcement Agency just changed the word drugs to data and went merrily on its way as the Data Enforcement Agency. Wasn't that one of our big victories?"

Understandably, Nomis had a thing about the DEA. He had turned a branch of the DEA into a clearinghouse for information, which had cut out all the stove piping that had gone on in the past between the FBI, the CIA, the DEA and NSA. Nomis provided a clever answer.

"Well, Mort, it isn't at all like what happened in that classic old movie entitled *Fahrenheit 451*, the one based on Ray Bradbury's book," Nomis replied. "As I recall, Ray portrayed the fire department as a bunch of book burners. I assure you, the DEA has mutated into something positive. They aren't out there burning books."

"A lot of very slick math types and programmers work for you; some of them are even former hackers," the voice insisted. "Aren't they sometimes involved in the take-down, once COP decides to make its move? I hear they are very good at killing files from a distance. Files, books. What's the difference?"

Nomis's berth at COP was a very wide one. One of the departments he advised was the investigative branch. It was the biggest user of COP's basket of technologies, including many of COP's surveillance gismos. Some were as mundane as the sniffers used at airports, and others as sophisticated as the algorithms that sniffed COP's highways of light for the criminal element. The IB was always on the lookout for novel ways to snoop. At one point, it had even become interested in Nomis's eyes.

COP had developed very powerful parallel processing algorithms, or PPAs, as they were called. Those algorithms could do their deadly little dance step in microseconds. They could isolate and take out any network or piece of software, located anywhere in the world. They were a worm's worm.

Nomis took the low route. He lied with a smile and eyes wide shut!

"Not really," Nomis replied.

"If the perpetrator is located physically beyond the reach of COP, what happens then?" the voice asked. "There are no worldwide standards with regard to extradition or prosecution of electronic crimes. The perp's hardware, or software, might fall into the hands of others?"

Nobody, but nobody, talked about how COP dealt with a perpetrator or his hardware beyond COP's jurisdiction. What went on there was very hush-hush. At times it was the same in the TV studio. The floor manager's fingers began to speak to Mort.

"I guess you're the one who is saved by the bell this time. Time has run out. We've been chatting with Dr. Nomis Chester . . . "

As Mort droned on, Nomis slipped his hand into his pocket and fingered the clicker. Mort's image slowly reappeared. It was splotchy in places. Nomis rubbed his eyes. The spots remained.

22
The Onboards

Life was good to Nara. She taught part-time in the chemistry department for a number of years until the children entered grade school. Her area of expertise, the chemistry of global warming, eventually led to an offer from the National Center for Atmospheric Research. She jumped at the chance. The University of Colorado rarely committed a tenure-track appointment to one of its new graduates. Nomis and Nara often joked about the length of their respective curriculum vitae. Her scientific papers numbered many more than his. Hers were also in big demand, as global warming was a hot political topic. The big polluters were always getting burned by Nara's well-argued conclusions. Most of Nomis's papers were classified. In his own defense, Nomis claimed that if his papers ever made it into the public domain, the political heat generated might be of a different ilk. He might be the one who got burned. In 2047, there was one instance where he did end up on the hot seat.

The year before, a first-class passenger, a Mr. Monger, on route from Rio de Janeiro to New York, had hijacked a plane using a laptop computer via the Solarnet. He treated everyone to a wild bucking ride. Quantum II finally sniffed him out and took the necessary steps to shut him down. It took Quantum II only twenty-one seconds to do its job, but it took Nomis almost two days to explain to the tribunal exactly what happened.

The old trick of using cribs was the only way to break photon crypto. As it turned out, Monger was a maestro—a real match for Quantum II. At his trial, the man refused to reveal how he, repeatedly, had hacked Quantum II's flight guidance program, located in Boulder, Colorado. But that was only the half of it. There were also the onboard computers to deal with—the ones on the plane. How Monger had dealt with the onboards and vice versa came out at the trial.

Originally the trial was to take place in Miami, but when it was moved to Boston, Nara decided to tag along with Nomis. The trial put Nomis under a lot of pressure, but it also gave him and Nara a chance to reacquaint themselves with a few of their old Boston friends, including the keeper of the ornithological gardens at Franklin Park Zoo.

On the first day of the trial, the actions of the prosecutor revealed a nondescript man. He arrived impeccably dressed, neither late nor early, hardly ever smiled, and was always in control. Like Nomis, one characteristic of the defendant's lawyer was his stubby little fingers. Those fingers had a history. Originally he had wanted to be a surgeon, but he encountered too much trouble with his own anatomy. Next to those fingers, a scalpel looked like a bread knife, and he was just about as agile with it as a baker, too; anything left over he chucked into a can to be recycled into the next loaf. He transferred to law school when he discovered that he was able to buy a laptop with a keyboard designed for a child's hand. However, he never gave up his old habits. The prosecution often accused him of engaging in antics that had previously failed to impress the tribunal.

What Mr. Monger had done was considered both an act of fraud and an act of terrorism. He wasn't a U.S. citizen so the terrorism charge placed him in the hands of a military tribunal. There was a terrible row in the press over that decision. Monger hadn't resisted arrest, nor had he been armed with anything but a laptop, as were seventeen other passengers. Monger denied the entire caboodle, claiming the whole thing was all a big mistake.

He insisted he was just a passenger who had done nothing wrong but use his computer to complete some work in time for a meeting in New York City the next day. His software package did nothing more than enable him to electronically impersonate a number of the Dutch masters, like Rembrandt, and a few of the French Impressionists, like Van Gogh. His stubby fingered lawyer claimed his software had accidentally interfered with the messaging from the flight guidance program of Quantum II.

The press also got wind of a few procedural issues which, when reported, raised the public's rancor. The jewel among them: some of Nomis's affidavits were sealed for reasons of national security. The brouhaha continued when the defense insisted on calling both the onboard computers and Quantum II as witnesses.

The prosecution quickly countered any suggestion that the onboards might be regarded as such; even the pilots regarded them as low on the food chain. Then a long, drawn-out argument ensued over whether Quantum II was human enough to appear as a witness. The judge ruled in favor of the prosecution, claiming that Quantum II didn't have reproductive parts but relied on humans, like Nomis, to make copies of itself. The judge cited a long list of other attributes that Quantum II lacked, including the ability to dream or cry. When the judge read his ruling, there were a few titters.

∞ ∞ ∞

The pilot, a Stephan Rinkey from Rio, was the first to testify at the trial.

"You are Stephan Rinkey, correct?" the prosecutor asked.

"Yes, I am Stephan Rinkey."

"You were employed by United World Airlines as a pilot from August of 2031 through May of 2046 and, subsequent to May of 2046, as an examiner for United World Airlines, correct?" the prosecutor asked.

Mr. Rinkey nervously sipped from a glass of water as he prepared to answer the prosecutor's question.

"Yes, my status changed as a result of the incident on flight one-hundred. It was my finger."

Mr. Rinkey held up his left hand. All in the room saw that his index finger was missing. The prosecutor interrupted him.

"On March tenth, 2046, you were the pilot assigned to flight one-hundred, non-stop from Rio to New York?"

"Yes."

"Who was the first officer on that flight?" the prosecutor asked.

"The equipment for flight one-hundred was pilotless. It was one of those 797s. The first officer isn't human. In his place . . . "

"Not human. In your own words, tell us about that," interrupted the prosecutor.

Mr. Rinkey had been warned beforehand by the prosecutor to avoid, when talking about the pilotless nature of the 797, the notion that computers might be considered human. The pilot's mouth went dry. Mr. Rinkey took a big sip of water and then wiped the perspiration from his palms.

"Instead of the first officer, there are three onboards. Three computers. It's all very democratic; when they are in control, the onboards are constantly voting on what to do. A two-thirds majority settles any dispute. The system was first developed and used in cruise missiles. The first and second generation systems were primitive compared to those installed on today's 797s; the system in place today is capable of learning from its own mistakes, or those which might occur in a pre-programmed flight path, like a sudden change in the weather or the flow of the jet stream."

As Mr. Rinkey continued, the prosecutor noted that the lawyer for the defense seemed pleased with what the pilot had to say.

"Quantum II, located in Boulder, acts as backup if a majority vote fails to materialize," continued Mr. Rinkey. "The plane can fly itself, but Federal Aviation Authority rules require that a human be in charge of all flights entering U.S. air space, not a computer."

The prosecutor turned toward the defense and smiled. Mr. Rinkey continued.

"So, in the case of flight one-hundred, I was the one in charge, but most of the time my job was purely administrative. I did my job in a control room located at the airport in Rio. The computers do all the work."

The defense lawyer nodded as he whispered to his client.

"I'm just an old-fashioned pair of eyes and ears on the ground, watching for any weak spots in the flight plan or the technology," continued Mr. Rinkey. "I am there to make sure we make our targets, you know, our schedule."

The prosecutor was clearly rattled by the extent to which Mr. Rinkey had placed the computers front and center.

"Who, or, perhaps I ought to ask, what has control of the plane once airborne?" the prosecutor asked.

"Once cruising altitude is reached, I transfer control to the onboards."

"And when might you take back control?" the prosecutor asked.

"When the plane reaches a point just east of Cape Hatteras, North Carolina."

"Has there ever been a flight where you took back control prior to reaching that point?" the prosecutor asked.

"Never!"

"Now, what exactly is an onboard?" the prosecutor asked.

"Like I said, a small processor, like a personal computer, pre-programmed to fly the plane and receive information from Quantum II if needed."

A touch of frustration crept into the prosecutor's tone of voice.

"Fly the plane. Explain!" the prosecutor demanded.

"Fly the plane. Do everything a pilot, first officer and flight engineer do, monitor all functions, maintain course and speed . . . fly the plane."

"And what do you do after you pass control to the onboards?" the prosecutor asked.

"I monitor all the flight data from a flight simulator, one of those new ones designed by Flight Simulator Associates, which is compatible—totally compatible—with the 797. The technology is virtual, you know, virtual reality. It's like being there in the pilot's seat on the plane. You actually feel, see, smell and hear everything going on in the cockpit.

"The ion analyzers are state of the art. Those sniffers send their information back to the simulator and the atmosphere of the simulator is reproduced exactly as it is in the cockpit. If cabin pressure drops, so does the pressure in the simulator. If smoke appears, it appears in the simulator too. Touch is a little different. Our reach is the Solarnet. We pilots call it flying by spinning photon. I might add that the simulator I use can deal with about fifteen different aircraft. It's software-driven. You just click on the configuration you're assigned to fly. I'm told that those simulators will be able to impersonate more than a hundred aircraft by the middle of the century. I'm also . . . "

The prosecutor interrupted him again.

"When you take back control from the onboards, what is the procedure?" the prosecutor asked.

"They're not human so I just pull the plug on them by flipping a switch."

The prosecutor nodded and smiled.

"And what exactly happens when you flip that switch?" the prosecutor asked.

"You might call it a reversal of roles. I do the work and the onboards do the administrative tasks."

"Can the onboards flip that switch?" the prosecutor asked.

"You mean make an independent decision to give control back to me?"

"Precisely," replied the prosecutor.

"Yes, but this rarely happens."

"Has it ever happened to you?" the prosecutor asked.

"Once. When one of the engines ingested a high flying goose."

"Can they independently decide to take control from you?" the prosecutor asked.

"They can yell and scream at me. But no, it's impossible for them to snatch control from me!"

"Can anybody or anything else cause that to happen—that is, take control from you . . . or the onboards?" the prosecutor asked.

"Quantum II."

The lawyer for the defense again turned and whispered to Mr. Monger.

"Now, at one point during the flight, Quantum II, located in Boulder, did seize control of the plane, is that correct?" the prosecutor asked.

"Yes, it happened just as the plane left the coast of Venezuela. But I was unaware of it at the time. It was what we pilots call a stealth takeover of the onboards."

"A stealth takeover?" the prosecutor mused.

"Yes. As I understand it, when a problem crops up and Quantum II gets involved, it prefers to work on it from a position of stealth. It's the nature of the beast, I guess. At the time I thought the onboards still had control."

The prosecutor pointed to Mr. Monger, who was sitting facing Mr. Rinkey to his left.

"OK. Now, is it true that you had lost your index finger to your lawnmower some five years prior to the March tenth, 2046 incident that occurred off the coast of Venezuela, which allegedly involved Mr. Monger, the accused?" the prosecutor asked.

Mr. Rinkey again held up his hand with the missing finger.

"Yes. I was changing the oil and the thing started up when I moved the blade out of the way of the oil plug. I had failed to disconnect the wire to the spark plug."

"A year after you lost your finger, did you have any indication, any feedback from COP, that allegedly Mr. Monger had repeatedly breached the firewall of Quantum II's flight guidance program and made a number of recordings of your messaging technique during flight?" the prosecutor asked.

"No."

"Were you aware that Mr. Monger allegedly obtained your school records and found that you didn't do well in spelling because you are dyslectic?" the prosecutor asked.

Mr. Rinkey's tone of voice became defensive.

"My spelling scores aren't anybody's business but mine. Words were never my forte. Anyway, I'm an incredible map reader, even though I don't know my left from my right. That's what counts when you fly a plane, things like map reading."

"Just answer the question, please," the judge interrupted.

Mr. Rinkey became openly angry.

"Well, your honor, that missing finger of mine eventually caused me to be kicked upstairs as an exam . . . "

"Just answer the question," the judge demanded.

"No, I wasn't aware."

"On international flights, or perhaps I ought to say on the specific flight in question, Flight one-hundred on March tenth, 2046, the one from Rio to New York, before departure, were you required to simulate your method and technique using the flight simulators, the results of which are stored in Quantum II's memory, located in Boulder, Colorado?" the prosecutor asked.

"Yes. It's done using Solarnet."

"And why is this done, simulating your method and technique?" the prosecutor asked.

"Because a pilot's method or technique—the manner in which he lands, takes off, deals with turbulence and so on—are like his fingerprints or the iris of his eye. If one knows what to look for in such simulations, one can easily tell one pilot from the next. There are even computer programs that sift and sniff the telemetry from the onboards. Also once control is passed to the onboards, when decisions must be made, they are pre-programmed to duplicate the method and technique of the pilot in charge."

"You mean the onboards can impersonate a pilot's method and technique," the prosecutor summarized.

"Yes, exactly. Once the data is uploaded from Quantum II, the onboards are as good as the flight simulators of Flight Simulator Associates!"

"A pilot's method and technique are like his fingerprints. Do you believe this, that your method and technique is unique to you and you alone?" the prosecutor asked.

"Until March tenth, 2046, most definitely."

"Until March tenth, 2046. Why so?" the prosecutor asked.

"As I understand it, some sort of imitation or clone of me, of my method and technique, tried to seize control of the plane, before Quantum II did, that is."

At that point, the lawyer for the defense took exception to Mr. Rinkey's assessment of the capabilities of the technology under discussion, claiming that the pilot was only a user of the technology, not an expert in its inner workings. The prosecutor quickly returned to his original focus on the events.

"Was the pre-flight simulation downloaded to the onboards on the plane and then, when you were in control, continuously compared to your actual performance by the onboard computers during the flight?" the prosecutor asked.

"Yes, that is standard procedure. I already said that the onboards were pre-programmed. The download of the simulations done by Quantum II is part of the procedure, part of the database needed for the pre-programming."

"Did Quantum II also make independent, random spot checks during the flight from Rio to New York?" the prosecutor asked.

"Yes, that is also part of standard procedure."

"Can you give us your assessment as to what transpired once the plane was airborne?" the prosecutor asked.

"Well, I have an interest in a horse farm located not too far from Rio. Now those onboards are . . . well, they are simple-minded little buggers: they have no imagination or originality at all. They function like the old horse-and-rider thing. A horse can always sense his master by his method or technique in the saddle. And let me tell you, I'm real good in the saddle."

Sensing that Mr. Rinkey was about to go off on a tangent, the judge interrupted.

"Stick to the point, Mr. Rinkey."

"Yes, Your Honor. Well, these days, planes, like horses, won't let just anybody ride them. If a rider, er, pilot doesn't feel right, they can become cantankerous. They may even try to buck the pilot off. Those onboards are also very visceral beasts. They go with what their guts tell them and with what they have in plain view; nothing sophisticated, mind you. As we pilots say, they have no peripherals. My sense is the onboards decided that the person who was riding, piloting the thing wasn't me. I suspect Mr. Monger was the one who went on that twenty-one-second ride at the rodeo."

The lawyer for the defense objected to Rinkey's rather loose and colorful interpretation of events, including his last remark about Mr.

Monger. The judge had Mr. Rinkey's suspicion struck from the record. The prosecutor was forced to take another route.

"Were you aware that Mr. Monger had allegedly seized control of the plane at the time?" the prosecutor asked.

"No! Everything seemed normal until Dr. Nomis Chester called and informed me of a problem which COP was working on at the time."

"Did he inform you at the time that he knew what the problem was?" the prosecutor asked.

"No! He informed me that a problem existed, but offered no details."

"When Mr. Monger alledgedly seized control of the plane, do you think the onboards assumed their administrative tasks?" the prosecutor asked.

"Yes! That's what happens when the pilot takes control."

"Any pilot?" the prosecutor asked.

"Well, that's what happens when they relinquish control, so I suppose, yes, any pilot."

During cross-examination, the defense put the pilot to a test. He was asked to pick, from some one hundred pre-flight simulations, those that he had completed. The test backfired. The pilot identified three: the only three which he had completed, among the one hundred that the defense confronted him with. The defense did score some points, by focusing on the fact that COP had never informed Mr. Rinkey of the theft of his school records, nor the surreptitious recording of flight data, and by dwelling on Mr. Rinkey's lack of awareness of any problem with the flight in question until informed by Nomis. Finally, the defense confirmed that when Dr. Chester had informed Mr. Rinkey of a potential problem, Nomis didn't point to anything specific.

A smirk appeared on the face of the lawyer for the defense.

"For all you knew, it might have been those onboard computers horsing around with Quantum II in some sort of slugfest," the lawyer for the defense said. "But as far as you were concerned, the flight was routine, until Quantum informed you, via your computer screen in Rio, that it was taking control of the plane."

"No! Dr. Chester informed me by phone, and shortly after that, as I understand, Quantum II took control."

During redirect, the data associated with those three pre-flight simulations were later shown by the prosecution to have been resident on the hard disk of Mr. Monger's laptop at the time he was arrested. Mr.

Rinkey also indicated that it was well-known among pilots that once Quantum II got involved, or anyone else from COP, for that matter, pilots were kept in the dark unless they were part of the solution to the problem. In the case of Mr. Monger, the prosecution argued that Mr. Rinkey and the onboards had unknowingly played the role of decoy or bait until Quantum II was ready to come out in the open and bare its fangs. Stealth always provides an advantage in the hunt!

23
Chop, Chop, Chop

A fellow from the FBI was the next on the stand that first day.

"Your name is Carl Minsig?" the prosecutor asked.

The witness sat upright in the witness chair, his back straight as a board.

"Yes, sir, my name is Carl Minsig!"

The prosecutor pointed to a laptop, which the clerk of the tribunal had just handed him.

"Is this Mr. Monger's laptop?" the prosecutor asked.

Agent Minsig booted it up and carefully examined its configuration. "Yes, sir!"

"Your field of expertise is electronic systems profiling?" the prosecutor asked.

"Yes, sir! More to the point, my specialization is electronic cloning."

"Have you subjected the hard disk of Mr. Monger's laptop to examination and analysis?" the prosecutor asked.

"Yes, sir! My people have done exactly that."

"Now, will you tell the tribunal in plain language what you discovered in the course of your examination and analysis?" the prosecutor asked.

"Well, we determined that Mr. Monger developed software that simulates the character of his own keystrokes and the manner in which he moves his joystick or his mouse, devoid of any mistakes that might be made by a dyslectic."

"Then what did he do?" the prosecutor asked.

"He chopped off his own finger, the index finger on his left hand, with a Chinese cleaver," the agent replied.

A few expletives of disbelief, some tittering and even some laughter was heard throughout the room. The judge wasn't amused.

"He chopped off his index finger with a Chinese cleaver? You must mean a meat cleaver. That must have made a hell of a mess," the prosecutor replied.

"Yes, sir! We uncovered some hospital records to that effect and are also in possession of his pickled finger and the cleaver."

The agent paused to look at his notes and then continued.

"Oh, yes, a Chinese cleaver is used to chop vegetables, not meat. Mr. Monger is a vegetarian."

The prosecutor joined those in the room who were unable to keep from laughing.

"A Chinese cleaver is for chopping vegetables, not meat, but apparently fingers. More to the point, a pickled finger?" the prosecutor responded.

"Yes, sir! But he pickled it after he chopped it off. He kept the finger in his apartment in Rio, in plain view, on a bookshelf in a jar with hot peppers. Jalapeños, as I remember."

"How do you know the pickled finger in the jalapeños jar was Monger's finger?" the prosecutor asked.

The clerk handed the prosecutor a file folder and a jar that contained the peppers and a finger.

"DNA testing!"

"Is this the DNA report?" the prosecutor asked.

The agent carefully examined the contents of the report before he replied.

"Yes, sir!"

"Is this the jar with the finger?" the prosecutor asked.

"Yes, sir. The finger is bluish in color. The peppers are bright red."

"What did he do after he chopped his finger off and pickled it?" the prosecutor asked. "Say, did he pickle it or spice it?"

"He both pickled it and peppered it, I guess. Yes, and after the wound had healed, I suspect he set about trying to detect the difference in method used by a three-fingered man, compared to one with four fingers. And yes, devoid of dyslexia. This, I believe, provided him with the crib he was looking for."

"Crib? Please explain," the prosecutor replied.

"Something that permits you to fool the system," the pilot said.

"Such as convince a professor you know the right answers when you don't," the prosecutor asked.

An image of George welled up in Nomis's mind, causing him to laugh out loud. The judge was not amused.

"Well, more like plagiarizing someone else's work," the agent added.

"Now, you said you suspected?" the prosecutor prompted.

"Well, I know that he did this, as we found the beta test results on his laptop with file dates which postdate by three months the dates found on the hospital records. I might add that the file dates associated with that first set of simulations—the four-fingered ones—predate the chop-chop-chop episode."

"So first it was software development with four fingers and a thumb, then chop, chop, chop, off goes a finger, and then software modification to account for how the missing finger might impair Mr. Monger's use of a joystick," the prosecutor stated.

"Yes, that's what happened. That and the pickling of the finger in the jalapeños pepper jar."

"And what did he do next?" the prosecutor asked.

"Well, once he had detected those differences—three-fingered versus four-fingered manipulation of a joystick—he modified the software to analyze the differences in method between a three-fingered man who had no difficulty spelling and one who did. You know what I mean: dyslectic versus non-dyslectic. He found subtle differences and accounted for them in his own software system."

"And how did you determine all of this?" the prosecutor asked.

"Well, I already indicated that my people had access to the files on his computer, his laptop. They had all been erased, but we managed to retrieve them by doing a low-level reconfiguration of the hard disk. We found all of the files related to each step, even the blind alleys he went up during development and testing."

"I have one last question. How might you characterize Mr. Monger's final product?" the prosecutor asked.

"Electronic cloning, sir. Well, you might also call it electronic impersonation, or electronic fraud."

"Please explain to the tribunal what you mean by electronic cloning," the prosecutor responded.

"The criminal's cloning software is designed to accept input from a keyboard, a joystick, a mouse or what have you, process it, and then output a cloned electronic signal that is indistinguishable from that produced by the target individual. In this case, the target individual was the pilot assigned to fly the plane that day, Mr. Rinkey. Mr. Monger's software eliminated all of his own personal quirks, keyboard mistakes, mouse movements and so on as he went about the task of flying the plane, and in their place the software substituted those that would be made by the assigned pilot as he or the onboards went about the same task. The cloning software also managed to flip the switch."

"What switch?" the prosecutor interrupted.

"The one which takes control from the onboards. And when it did it fed to both the pilot and Quantum II a simulated flight program, designed to keep them, or perhaps I ought to say him and it, in the dark as to what was really going on. That is why to the pilot, at least, everything looked normal and routine. In a sense, the criminal assumed the electronic identity of the pilot. He went stealth by cloaking himself in the identity of another person, or, more correctly, in a stream of spinning photons on the Solarnet. It was very clever, going stealth by becoming a beam of light, wasn't it?"

"Sorry, Agent Minsig, I'm not the witness: you are! Please rephrase the last part of your answer," the prosecutor demanded.

The agent began by chopping at the air with his left hand.

"Well, it was very clever to go stealth by becoming a beam of light. Also, it is my assessment that that dyslectic missing finger was the crib the defendant needed to break the light codes used by the pilot who regularly administered the flight from Rio to New York. That three-fingered hand of the pilot produced unique and uncommon movements. It had little quirks that were idiosyncratic. The key was, in fact, the method and technique of a three-fingered man who was dyslectic. The preparation time for that attempted hijacking turned out to be about four years. It gives you an idea of how cunning and persistent the terrorist mind can be."

On cross-examination, what the agent had to say held up, although when he produced the pickled finger, one member of the tribunal claimed that it was difficult to distinguish the peppers from the finger. It turned out the member was color blind. The prosecutor quickly demonstrated that only one of the items in the jar had fingernails. He also produced the hospital records, and even used Monger's laptop in a demonstration to show how electronic cloning worked.

At the beginning of his demonstration, he selected the wrong options and drew Van Gogh's famous picture of sunflowers in a pot and then the one of haystacks. The haystacks weren't too bad, but the detail of the sunflowers was terrible. When he finally got the software to work, the defense did an about-face and proposed that all computer-related evidence be thrown out, citing the previous ruling that computers ought not to be able to testify, as they weren't human. At that point, there was a meeting in the judge's chambers. The judge subsequently ruled that the testimony that day wasn't directly obtained from a computer, but from two expert witnesses.

∞ ∞ ∞

As Nara sat cross-legged on the bed and began to walk her fingers up and down Nomis' chest, he began to rehearse his testimony.

"Theoretically, Einstein might have approved of the idea of electronic cloning," Nomis said.

"From a practical point of view, I'm sure he might also have been horrified at some of the potential consequences, especially the business of electronic cloning which went on during that flight from Rio to New York," Nara replied.

Nomis rolled over onto his stomach, took Nara's hand and placed it in the small of his back.

"It's the muscles in the small of my back. Too much sitting in hard-backed chairs. Other than that, the cloning software as a technical exercise was brilliant," Nomis said.

"Brilliant!" replied Nara. "It started with ATMs, now it's pilots! What's next, my husband?"

"Some good always comes from evil," Nomis remarked. "Remember the rib from which Adam cloned Eve."

Nara slapped him on the buttock and then snuggled up close to him, leaving her hand in the small of his back.

"Remember the apple," Nara responded.

"Of course, the software doesn't really get the pigment textures right, but it does a very good job with the colors and the content most of the time, especially with haystacks," Nomis remarked with tongue in cheek. "Someday you might be able to buy a commercial art software package, or just a computer game, which might contain two hundred or so different options; maybe more, who knows. If you want to become a Van Gogh, or a Renoir, you just point, click and draw."

"How about just plain old Nara tonight," Nara remarked.

Nara felt the muscles in his lower back tense up.

"Tomorrow it's my turn on the stand. It might be difficult to take. Are you sure you want to go?" Nomis asked.

"Well, tonight it's my turn! And I promise it won't be difficult at all," Nara replied.

Nomis's face became elastic as Nara continued to massage the small of his back. She bent over and kissed him softly on the shoulder. He coughed, scratched the back of his head, rolled over onto his back and reached for the light switch.

24

Sunflowers and Haystacks

On the second day of the trial, Nomis made a big blunder. He referred to his eyes during his testimony. When the lawyer for the defense learned about Nomis's eyes, he made a feeble attempt to convince the tribunal that Nomis was part computer and for that reason ought to be disqualified as a witness. Monger's lawyer argued Nomis's eyes were battery-powered, chip-based and driven by firmware, much like one of those onboards. The prosecutor argued that such a claim was ridiculous: "utter rubbish" were his very words. Nomis's eyes were nothing more than a high-tech prosthesis. Once the implants were in place, their functionality was impossible to alter. His eyes were good for only one thing and that was seeing.

The business about hearing colors and shapes, and the fact he couldn't cry did cross Nara's mind. But to her Nomis was a living, breathing, dreaming person, no different from one with an artificial heart or leg. Having been the mother of his children, and a partner in sin the night before his testimony, she was able to do nothing but agree with the prosecutor. He and Nara had certainly satisfied the judge's criterion. They had made two copies of themselves—the twins—the old-fashion way.

Having lost the round about Nomis's eyes, the lawyer for the defense tried to explain away the incident on Flight one-hundred as a computer slugfest. This view bordered on the broader theme, originally rejected by the judge, of machine intelligence. However, the argument was quite clever. Monger's lawyer argued that what had happened was just a big practical joke, orchestrated by the onboards and directed at Quantum II.

He took his cue from the remark made by Agent Rinkey about machines like Quantum II and the onboards being able to learn from their mistakes; "learning by doing" was the term bandied about. Monger's lawyer argued that as these machines learned, like humans, they became territorial, even passive-aggressive, unwilling to give up control when a request to do so was made by another machine, or even a human. He even cited a press report that Quantum II had bullied the onboards on a flight between Los Angeles and Miami. Apparently Quantum II had acted out of sheer boredom at the tail end of a slow day of message-sniffing in August of the previous year.

The episode on the flight from Rio to New York was payback—the little guy trying to bully the big guy. Nomis thought it was the press smelling their own breath, or perhaps the press trying to bully COP. His baby was just a machine, like his eyes—no dreaming, no crying, no emotive or possessive feeling of any sort. Quantum II just went about doing what it was told or programmed to do quietly, quickly and efficiently, and those onboards were even more docile.

In fact, in only one sense was Quantum II able to be creative. It was extremely good at parallel processing, or the sort of thinking needed for puzzle-solving, but it wasn't human. You were able to pull the plug and be done with it, if that was your fancy, and at some future date resuscitate it just by plugging it back in again. Pulling the plug on a human was a bit more difficult. With Mr. Monger, Nomis was determined to do just that. He wanted Monger put away for good. Monger had a dangerous, unfeeling, emotionless, machine-like persona. He went about his job quietly, quickly and efficiently too—a real match for Quantum II.

∞ ∞ ∞

"You are Dr. Nomis Chester, and as such have a detailed knowledge of the events in question, being an employee of COP and having worked directly in the area of the flight guidance program," the prosecutor asked.

"Yes," Nomis replied. "I might add that my area of expertise stretches beyond the FGP."

The prosecutor was overly eager and a bit nervous, as Nomis's reputation had preceded him.

"OK," the prosecutor replied. "Now, two years ago you were a guest on Mort Stone's late-night talk show. Correct?"

"Yes," Nomis replied.

The clerk handed the prosecutor a sheaf of paper.

"This transcript contains your answers to a few of the questions posed by Mort Stone. Please read the part that is in bold print into the record," the prosecutor said.

Nomis studied the transcript and then read out loud the relevant part.

CHESTER—Mort, COP's all about using math, very fast computers and the physics of light to both develop and deploy what we call secure photon ciphers.

STONE—COP is certainly the brains behind all of that— the leader in the field. But the hardware is only the half of it, right?

CHESTER—The hardware? You must mean photon ciphers.

STONE—Photon ciphers. Isn't that some sort of sci-fi gismo? Nomis, my viewers are people, not machines. Let's talk about the people at COP, like you.

CHESTER—You took the words right out of my mouth, Mort. On the people side, COP has the wherewithal too. Its people are the architects of stealth and secret-keeping, which a worldwide network of computers and photon ciphers must offer to its users. You know, those using COP are paying for a system that is secure from soup to nuts, not an overgrown, topsy-turvy network.

STONE—Well, that's a mouthful. Photon ciphers, hmm. It keeps coming back like a bad copper . . . I mean penny. What are they? Let me take a stab. They're like those metal detectors at the airport which check out one person at a time. The difference is those gismos check out little bits of light, called photons, one at a time, frisking the little buggers to see what they're carrying by way of messaging.

CHESTER—Yes, that's one way of putting it.

"Is that more or less the essence of what COP is all about today?" the prosecutor asked.

"Yes," Nomis added. "But my formal title at COP is now Chief Mathematician."

"Is your homologue the Chief Economist at a brokerage firm?" the prosecutor asked.

"No, my role is more like that of Chief Scientist at a firm like IBM, or Chief Engineer at Textron," Nomis responded.

"And when were you appointed Chief Mathematician at COP?" the prosecutor asked.

"Two years ago, shortly before I was interviewed by Mort Stone," Nomis replied.

"The Stone interview was the result of the publicity surrounding your appointment. Correct?" the prosecutor asked.

"Yes," Nomis replied.

"The Native American community made a big deal about your appointment. True?" the prosecutor asked.

"Yes," Nomis replied.

"How so?" the prosecutor asked.

Nomis's reluctance to respond was evident.

"Well . . . my great-grandfather was a Navajo Code Talker during WWII, assigned to the staff of Chester Nimitz, after Pearl . . . Is this really relevant?"

The prosecutor paused to look at his notes.

"Perhaps not," the prosecutor replied. "Now. You are a charter member of what is known as Generation T, correct?"

The prosecutor eyed the tribunal as Nomis responded.

"Yes."

"For the record, your date of birth is?" the prosecutor asked.

The prosecutors again eyed the tribunal. Nomis's eye caught Nara's. Her cheeks were wet.

"September 11, 2001," Nomis replied.

Nara was sure that Nomis too had shed a few invisible tears. The prosecutor had achieved his goal, and then some. Nomis's credentials were impeccable and . . . Nara was a nervous wreck.

"Now, on the day of the flight in question, United World Airlines One Hundred, on March 10, 2046, can you explain to the tribunal under what circumstances you became aware that something was amiss with the flight guidance program?" the prosecutor asked.

"I was in COP's War Room at the time. Quantum II got wind of a problem from its analysis of spot check data and reported its concerns via the big screen," Nomis replied.

"And Quantum II is?" the prosecutor asked.

"Oh, Quantum II, COP's main computer. I might add that the War Room is the venue where all problems with Solarnet eventually surface. Reporting occurs via a very large computer screen," Nomis replied.

"Yes, and the spot check data is?" the prosecutor interrupted.

"That data was derived from a random check on the status of Flight one-hundred undertaken by Quantum II," Nomis said. "Quantum II does hundreds of thousands of those every minute of the day and night for the many different systems it monitors. Quantum II's role is much like that little black box under the hood of your car, which tells you if all is well."

"You mean the one that turns the check engine light on when you forget to tighten the gas cap," the prosecutor replied.

"Yes, but the data I was referring to has nothing to do with gas caps. It was flight data, and the origin was telemetry from Flight one-hundred on the day in question," Nomis said.

"Telemetry?" the prosecutor queried.

"Radio signals filled with binary data—zeros and ones," Nomis replied.

"In plain language, can you give the tribunal your assessment as to how Quantum II got wind that something was amiss on Flight one-hundred, Dr. Chester?" the prosecutor asked.

"The problem was the hijacker's software package. Well, his crib was flawed," Nomis began. "It ignored the pilot's most recent personal data."

The prosecutor began nervously tapping the knuckles of his left hand with his pencil.

"Personal data?" the prosecutor queried.

"Yes, like how good a night's sleep the pilot had had prior to the flight, whether he got stuck in traffic on the way home from the grocery store the day before, whether his favorite soccer team had lost the World Cup, or whether he had recently been jilted by his lover. Little events like that can affect a person's demeanor. The impact shows up in the strangest places, like how he handles a joystick or a paint brush," Nomis responded.

The judge began tapping his own knuckles.

"Whoa—I said plain, not colorful!" the prosecutor said.

"Well, it's very plain to me," Nomis replied. "This is a case where biometrics or bio-tech as a filter almost failed. That's why electronic systems profiling was developed and put in place some years before all of this happened. ESP was designed to identify potential perpetrators and attach a beacon. Electronic fingerprinting and anything else specific to their electronic behavior was used to identify potential perps before the fact. Before they had a chance to act."

The prosecutor was unsure of the relevance of Nomis's remark about ESP.

"ESP, beacons? Please explain!"

"As you know, ESP stands for electronic systems profiling," Nomis replied, "one of Agent Rinkey's specialties. But I don't think he went into the details of ESP. Do you want me to go into the details?"

The prosecutor nodded his approval.

"The easiest way to understand ESP is to make reference to the manner in which a credit check is performed. With a credit check, data on both the spending pattern and the payment habits of an individual are employed to develop a risk profile, which is then used by lenders to establish creditworthiness. In the case of ESP, data on things like website visits, use of certain words or phrases in e-mail, or methods of encryption, like the use of steganography and so on, are employed to identify behavior on the Solarnet which might suggest criminal intent. If a user is so identified, a beacon, like that attached to a shark to study its feeding habits, or to a caribou to study its migration pattern, is appended to his messaging."

"Now, what is steno . . . er . . . steganography?" the prosecutor asked.

"It's the technique of hiding a message in a picture or image," replied Nomis.

"So beacons are electronic identifiers, and steganography is the art of hiding a message in a picture," the prosecutor replied.

"Like a picture of a haystack," Nomis added.

The prosecutor's response was one of surprise.

"A haystack?"

"Yes, electronic identifiers track suspicious messaging on Solarnet," replied Nomis. "I might add that finding a message that is hidden in a picture is just like trying to find a needle in a haystack."

Very good, thought the prosecutor as he glanced at the tribunal.

"Please continue," the prosecutor said.

"Well, to comprehend what happened that day, you must be familiar with the technology related to pilotless airplanes. Now, don't get me wrong: planes still have pilots, but pilots these days do their job from a remote location. Initially it was fly-by-wire; later on it was fly-by-joystick; now it's fly-by-spinning-photons. I believe Mr. Rinkey also used my last characterization just yesterday," Nomis continued.

"Can you be more specific?" the prosecutor asked.

"Yes," replied Nomis. "Pilotless aircraft had their debut in 2001 in Afghanistan with those drones. The CIA mounted cannons and rockets on them—the drones. At the time those drones looked and sounded like model airplanes. Then they got bigger and started to carry freight, and then, finally, people," Nomis continued.

"And what has been the outcome?" asked the prosecutor.

"Over time there has been a convergence process ongoing with the man-machine relationship. Planes have become more and more human, while pilots have become exactly the opposite: less and less human," Nomis replied.

Nomis paused. His eyes scanned the room, coming to rest on the defendant, Mr. Monger. If looks could kill, Monger might have died right then and there.

"Sort of what has been happening to my eyes. You see, these eyes of mine aren't flesh and blood; they're machines. Little machine-like computers."

The prosecutor turned a ghostly white.

"The same goes for the cockpit of an airplane," Nomis added. "You don't find any flesh and blood in there anymore. But on average, planes and pilots together seemed to do the same old job, just like my eyes and the rest of me," Nomis added.

The lawyer for the defense suddenly burst into a fit of note-taking. A mélange of titters, gasps, mumbles and laughter erupted in the room. To Nara's left was a young lady whose complexion turned as white as the shirt worn by the man to her right. Artificial hearts were passé, but eyes, the windows of the soul, they were much more personal, part of a person's being.

The prosecutor raised his eyebrows, clearly not expecting such a remark, nor knowing exactly where Nomis was headed.

God! Is he going to drive me off a cliff, the prosecutor thought.

He took the cautious route, like the bus driver's choice of the inside lane at the Ring of Kerry in southern Ireland. His tone of voice became detached and matter-of-fact.

"I have heard that such technology has been around for decades," the prosecutor said. "Please continue your history lesson, Dr. Chester."

Nomis did exactly that as he continued to stare at the defendant.

"But the less human pilots become, the easier it is to clone or impersonate them, and this is the part which really bothers me: the possibility that cells of those electronic clones might be floating around the Solarnet as beams of light, looking for trouble. That's what those beacons are all about; they are part of our defense, the code-makers' defense. As for those electronic clones, they are fast becoming part of the code-breakers' offense. To COP, they are a real nemesis of evil."

After about an hour and a half, Nomis finally admitted that no one at COP had any idea how Monger had allegedly breached the firewall of Quantum II and made those three initial recordings of Mr. Rinkey's messaging. With the pilot having been kept in the dark by COP and no explanation as to how that messaging was obtained, the prosecution's case seemed to rest solely on Agent Minsig's testimony. The defense began to smell a cover-up.

At about 11:35 A.M., the prosecutor asked for a fifteen-minute recess. The judge decided to take an early lunch break, so things didn't get going again until 2:00 P.M. Nara was left to fend for herself at lunch, as Nomis and the prosecutor went off together for a much needed tête-à-tête.

25
Soft-Boiled Eggs

At lunch, the prosecutor was rather curt with Nomis. He reminded Nomis that the focus had to be on specific events. Some of what Nomis had said might clearly be used by the defense. He warned Nomis that it might take the better part of the afternoon to untangle the mess he had created with some of his remarks, especially the one about his eyes. The failure of bio-filters, technological convergence, man-machine relationships, electronic clones and beacons wasn't exactly something the prosecution wanted the tribunal to hear about.

∞ ∞ ∞

"What was the specific event that put Quantum II onto Mr. Monger's alleged antics?" the prosecutor asked.

"If it hadn't been for the outcome of that World Cup soccer game which was played on the afternoon before that flight was to depart Rio, Monger might have got away with it," Nomis replied.

"Please continue," the prosecutor replied.

As Nomis began, he smiled and an ominous little laugh trickled from his lips. Nara had seen that combination of smile and laugh before. Visions of a minute man loading grape shot into his cannon came to mind.

"My breakfast must always include a soft-boiled egg. Yes, a soft-boiled egg. You know, averages are funny things. They are always there, but you never ever see one. They're like soft-boiled eggs in the old USSR."

The prosecutor was about to discover why those of lesser intellectual talents regarded Nomis as a loose cannon, this time loaded with eggs.

"Soft-boiled eggs," the prosecutor replied.

"Yes, soft-boiled eggs," replied Nomis. "One of my teachers, a statistician, visited the Soviet Union just before it collapsed. Like me, he wasn't able to get along without a soft-boiled egg for breakfast. In the

Soviet Union, when he ordered a soft-boiled egg, it was either runny as eggnog or hard as a rock. He often complained. The Soviets claimed that on average, his eggs were always soft-boiled. But he never saw one and he never got used to the Soviet claim. For him it was the variance that counted, not the mean."

A nervous quiver appeared in the prosecutor's voice.

"The variance, not the mean. The variance of what, Dr. Chester?"

"Well, a fixation on averages was the Soviets' big problem. However, an average isn't interesting without a measure of variability or variance. The Soviets never worried much about what was happening at the margin, at the edge of technology or the edge of culture, but it's the edge that counts. The Soviets assumed that the great bulk of the state, with its huge center of gravity, like the planet Jupiter, kept things from getting out of hand, regardless of what was happening on the edge."

The judge moved to the edge of his own chair.

"Get to the point, Dr. Chester."

"Yes, your honor, I will, and, it didn't!" replied Nomis.

"It didn't what?" the prosecutor demanded.

"Keep it from getting out of hand! Like Jupiter, there was always a storm raging just beneath the surface. I often fear the same for Solarnet. It might go the way the Internet did in 2011, when its great bulk caused it to collapse in on itself. The Internet wasn't a living, breathing system like Solarnet is now, but a topsy-turvy network in disequilibrium. Unlike the Drug Enforcement Agency, the Internet became something it oughtn't to have become—an electronic cockatrice, strutting around with a snake's tail ready to squeeze the life out of you."

Beneath the surface, Nara sensed a lot of tension. The tectonic plates of Nomis's mind were beginning to ride up, one upon the other.

Nomis, Nomis, where are you going with this monologue? Nara thought to herself. *This isn't the time nor the place for that poetic mind of yours to erupt like a volcano. On average you may think your eyes and the rest of you are in equilibrium, but I'm beginning to think not! You know as well as I that the DEA is also a cockatrice.*

It was at this point that the defense jumped into the fray.

"It appears to me that what Dr. Chester has said here isn't the least bit relevant to the issue at hand. He is wasting the tribunal's time with a lot of irrelevant gibberish."

Nomis didn't make haste slowly with his reply. He didn't dare. He had everybody in the room on the edge of their seat.

"Sir. Your Honor. From the first day I lost my sight, I have always been living on the edge. When I regained my sight, for reasons that I never understood—perhaps that crash when a car came from nowhere and killed my dad—it was my peripheral vision in which I placed my trust, not what was squarely in front of me. I am no onboard. Think of me and Quantum II as father and son."

"My god, he is the father of Quantum II!" Nara overheard someone behind her remark.

Nara turned and came to Nomis's defense.

"No, he's the father of my children!"

The judge called for order as Nomis continued.

"Nearly five years of blindness had taught me to focus on the periphery. To me the case of the three-fingered man is all about the near failure of biometrics, the potential vulnerability of my baby, or perhaps even technology in its generic form, not just about a hijacking that failed only because of the score of a soccer game."

At that point, the defense went over the edge.

"Your Honor, I must object!" the defense bellowed. "None of this is relevant. My client, Mr. Monger, is the defendant; Quantum II isn't on trial here, nor is Quantum II a witness. You, Your Honor, ruled against the latter previously.

"This man's eyes are computers, and you have already ruled that computers can't testify as a witness. Dr. Chester ought to be disqualified by reason of your previous ruling. Barring that, at least find inadmissible anything those computer eyes of his saw in COP's War Room; barring that, I respectively submit that the tribunal instruct Dr. Chester to focus on what is relevant. Finally, Dr. Chester has already confirmed that no one at COP knows the circumstances by which those pre-flight simulations found their way onto Mr. Monger's hard disk."

The judge ignored the remark about Nomis's eyes and asked the prosecution to move along. The prosecutor began again.

"Why didn't the beacon system track Mr. Monger's activities?"

"Well, my guess . . . "

The prosecutor cut Nomis off, barking like a hungry dog for his supper.

"I want more than your guess, Dr. Chester."

"Monger assumed the identity of only the pilot in Rio but not the onboards."

"Well, then, how did . . . " the prosecutor began.

Nomis didn't wait for the rest of the question.

"Once Mr. Monger got past the firewall on the day of the hijacking, the ability of that cloning software was put to a much more rigorous test. What happened next was the genesis of my remark about the commercial equivalent of the cloning software only being good with haystacks."

The prosecutor put his hand on his forehead in disbelief.

"Haystacks again?" he growled.

The prosecutor's tone of voice became a whimper.

"Explain!"

"Well," replied Nomis, "the onboard computers began to detect very small, unexplained differences in the pilot's performance. A smaller variance than expected was detected in all cases but one, and for that one case, the variance began to grow erratically."

Like a poorly trained dog, the prosecutor groped for consistency.

"Is this the point you were making a few minutes ago, Dr. Chester, with soft-boiled eggs, the Soviet Union and being on the edge?"

"Precisely!" replied Nomis. "A simple test of the null hypothesis. What I mean is, the difference between the way the plane was being flown as it left the Venezuelan coast and the way it was flown during the pre-flight simulation . . . That comparison made by the onboards began to fail more often than it ought to have as more and more data were processed. In other words, that difference, as measured by the onboards, got bigger. The onboards weren't able to say there wasn't any difference between the two readings."

"There was a double negative in the last part of your remark. Do you mean that the onboards did detect a difference?" the prosecutor asked.

Nomis was reluctant to respond. Statistical tests only reject; they don't accept. He looked at the tribunal, turned his eyes toward Mr. Monger, and then decided to bend the rules just a little.

"Well, OK," responded Nomis. "Those differences were the crib eventually used by Quantum II to figure out what was going on. Presented with the mean, you might think that all eggs were soft-boiled. Presented with the variance, the truth begins to emerge; eggs were either rocks or runny. The conclusion: something was all screwed up in the kitchen. In the Soviet Politburo I mean . . . in the control room."

With that remark, the prosecutor made ready for another intervention by the defense.

"And what, may I ask, does what you have just said have to do with haystacks?" the prosecutor asked.

"Monger's software wasn't very good with details. It got the broad brushstrokes right, but the detail, well, it lacked finesse. Some might say that of Van Gogh, but his brush strokes were his own personal style. The hijacker didn't have any leeway. He had to reproduce the persona and technical mannerism of the pilot exactly, not just his poetic impressions of them. By the way, I think the same goes for Karl Marx: to him, communism was the poetic expression of what the industrial revolution ought to have been," Nomis responded.

The prosecutor cut off Nomis's babbling. The defense didn't object. The prosecutor seemed relieved.

"OK. Please continue with your analysis of the cause of the incident," the prosecutor stated.

"The onboards were confronted by an error curve in the flight path with an almost imperceptible gradient, which was growing larger at irregular intervals," replied Nomis. "That error curve was also consistent with the one rogue variance. Fortunately the onboards were able to detect the gradient by using quick and dirty piece-wise linear approximation methods."

The prosecutor's brow furrowed and a pit developed in his stomach big enough to hold all the eggs ever produced in the Soviet Union, runny or not.

"Piece-wise linear approximation methods," the prosecutor repeated.

"Those onboards winged it, so to speak," Nomis quickly replied. "It's like stretching a rubber band and then holding it tangent to the curved surface of a water glass over and over again. If you do it enough, you can reproduce the curvature of the glass, or in the case of the flight path, the error curve. Such methods aren't tried and true. Even the onboards were unsure of their own result. They even did something that no human statistician ought never do. They bent the rules."

Nomis coughed. He took a sip of water and then continued.

"And tightened their statistical test of no difference. It was almost like they wanted to find a problem, and they did. It was luck on their part. They were right for the wrong reasons."

By this time the prosecutor's head was spinning, along with everyone else's in the room.

The prosecutor's tone of voice became timid.

"Were the onboards right or wrong? Which was it?"

"They were correct about something being amiss, but the manner in which they arrived at that conclusion was flawed," Nomis replied.

"Please continue," the prosecutor said.

Nomis glared at Mr. Monger and continued.

"Whatever or whoever was flying the plane wasn't only doing much better than expected in controlling the bumps from minor turbulence, but was also causing the plane to drift off course to the northwest. That's when that little tussle broke out between the hijacker and the plane's onboards. At one point, the plane got outright ornery and began to buck like it was going through a patch of turbulence."

"You mean screaming and yelling?" the prosecutor asked.

"Yes, like Mr. Rinkey said. Luckily Quantum II was making one of its random spot checks at the time."

Nomis came into his element at this point.

"Now, Quantum II is no onboard stuffed away in the ceiling of a 797 cockpit. Quantum II is the Big Bertha of the computer world," Nomis proudly announced. "It is able to go off in all directions at once, like a writhing pack of bloodhounds, if it is so inclined."

"Like father, like son," Nara heard someone remark on her right as the room rumbled like a freight train at a graded crossing.

"Quantum II isn't a linear processor; it can think laterally," Nomis continued. "If anything, one can view Quantum II as the 'no general solution, yet' champ of the universe. It is a computer's computer. When the onboards sensed something was amiss, it was the turbulence that pointed Quantum II right at the edge, right at the expected performance of the pilot versus his actual pre-flight performance. At that point, Quantum II told the onboards to take a walk."

The prosecutor looked over at the defense lawyer, who had again burst into a fit of copious note-taking.

"The no general solution, yet champ of the universe? Take a walk!" the prosecutor replied.

A puzzled look appeared on Nomis's face.

"Now?" Nomis responded.

"Now . . . " the prosecutor began.

Nomis got up from the witness chair.

"Just a minute," the prosecutor said. "No. Not now. Not you. Please, Dr. Chester, please be seated."

Nomis sat down.

"Now," the prosecutor began again. "Do you think that Quantum II was just flexing its muscles at this point, showing the onboards who was boss, so to speak? Is there any evidence to suggest that Quantum II manufactured the turbulence, making it appear to the onboards that something was awry?"

The prosecutor's question seemed to siphon away the power and determination of Nomis's effort to nail Monger.

"No, of course not," Nomis spluttered. "Unlike the onboards, Quantum II ignored what was staring it right in the face, what appeared to be a collection of sloppy little errors in method and technique. For they might just have been that: the tail end of the distribution of probable errors made by the pilot in Rio, all of which might have accumulated to producc a drift toward the northwest."

"How did Quantum II isolate the source of the problem?" the prosecutor asked.

"The pilot had lost a sizable bet the day before: a lot of cash went down the tubes," replied Nomis. "The team he expected to win the World Cup blew it. However, both Quantum II and the onboards knew nothing of his bad luck. All they knew was what they were able to glean from his most recent simulations in their memory banks. Luckily, the pilot had completed those simulations after he learned his team had lost. But the cloning software also didn't know that the pilot had just lost a substantial amount of money, nor did that software have access to the most recent simulations made prior to flight time. So Quantum II and the onboards had one more piece of information than the criminal."

"One more piece of information," repeated the prosecutor.

"Yes, the mannerisms or demeanor of a man who had just lost his shirt betting on the wrong team," replied Nomis.

∞ ∞ ∞

Nomis was quite candid that evening at dinner with Nara.

"Nara, in hindsight, neither Quantum II nor the onboards had determined at the time that the outcome of this game with the criminal was no longer zero sum. Quantum II did have the potential for advantage, but hadn't picked up the trump card. If Quantum II had initiated a search of the betting pool records and come across the data on the pilot's loss, it might have acted much sooner to shut that criminal down, maybe ten seconds sooner," Nomis said.

"Does the fact that Quantum II didn't ever search those records at the time worry you?" replied Nara.

"Yes," replied Nomis. "Quantum II isn't only fast, but it's also very meticulous and thorough. It can go off in one hundred directions at once, like a chess player who is bent on taking on the challenge of playing a hundred opponents simultaneously. It is very strange indeed that the betting pool wasn't one of those hundred."

26
The Betting Pool

On the third day, the prosecutor's mood turned cautious. He made a tactical decision not to dwell on what might be construed by the defense as another instance where Quantum II had failed, nor did he want to add fuel to the practical joke explanation the defense was pushing. He ignored Quantum II's failure to pick up on the betting pool issue and decided not to call one of his own witnesses a bookie. He chose instead to focus again only on what Nomis had to say.

"Let's start where we left off yesterday. So, Dr. Chester, Quantum II determined something was amiss."

"Yes," Nomis replied.

"At that point, unlike the onboards, was Quantum II right for the right reasons?" the prosecutor asked.

"Yes," Nomis responded.

"What happened next?" the prosecutor asked.

"Quantum II looked at weather patterns, engine performance, theoretically rebuilt the plane from scratch, put it in a theoretical wind tunnel, simulated expected turbulence and compared the results with data from all the onboard sensors.

"It looked at the last five pre-flight simulations and the corresponding in-flight data records of the pilot, comparing them to current performance. It found nothing wrong with the plane structurally, no unusual weather patterns, and no systems or control problems, only a difference in variance related to the bumps and thumps from minor turbulence, and a mean drift to the northwest. Quantum II looked at all of these alternatives simultaneously, in a little under twelve seconds. Every one of them but the betting pool," Nomis responded.

Everyone in the room, including the lawyer for the defense, noted the expression on the face of the prosecutor as the words 'Betting Pool' rolled from Nomis's lips. It was that of a man whose bookie had just called in his loan.

"Just a minute, Dr. Chester. Is there any reason you can think of, that is, why did Quantum II ignore the betting pool?"

"I have no idea," replied Nomis.

The prosecutor decided to go for broke.

"Might it be possible for the onboards and Quantum II to place bets without you people at COP getting wind of the fact that those computers were just horsing around?"

Nomis seemed insulted by his suggestion that Quantum II could or would want to hoodwink those at COP.

"No. I might add that the question itself is ridiculous."

A smile appeared on the face of the prosecutor, having culled from Nomis the answer he was seeking.

"I will rephrase my question," the prosecutor replied. "Do you think that Quantum II and the onboards, or, for that matter, someone at COP or perhaps some hacker on Solarnet, had booked bets as to who might win such a tussle—you know, a slugfest between computers—for control of a plane that was the victim of a manufactured crisis, for the sport of it?"

Nomis was visibly angry.

"No, that's impossible!"

The prosecutor was obviously pleased with Nomis's rock-solid resolve.

"Please continue," the prosecutor said.

"Quantum II didn't find anything but a red flag pointing to the human element—pilot performance," Nomis continued. "The great bulk of the plane and its systems seemed OK. The variance derived from the real-time flight data was in line with that of the last five simulations. But to get that result, Quantum II had to exclude the pre-flight simulation. Also, as I have already said, the plane was drifting northwest. Quantum II made a preliminary determination: it must be a computer-generated clone of the three-fingered pilot flying the plane, but the clone was configured from data that was more than a day old."

The prosecutor sat silently as Nomis continued.

"I was in the War Room, watching Quantum II plow through the analysis at the time. When Quantum II presented its results, a hush blanketed the room. I guess it was like what happened when someone steeped in Newtonian physics first got wind of what was in Einstein's teabags. He was back to square one; his ideas of how the universe worked needed retooling. An ugly thought flashed into my head. The human element, the human element cloaked in a stream of spinning photons. Good God, we're back to square one with these bastards!"

All eyes in the room followed Nomis's hand as it traced out a wide, jerky, crescent-shaped path above his head.

"During the next three seconds, Quantum II downloaded real-time telemetry from the black boxes located in the tail of the plane, and discovered that the slow, wide turn of one-sixteenth of a degree northwest was randomly spaced through time. Finally, Quantum II deduced what random number generator was being used to time the turn. Let me tell you, that was an adventure in number theory in itself, taking a stream of numbers and deducing both the key and the generating function. Luckily, the generator was an old one, first developed at RAND some twenty-five years ago. Quantum II immediately gave the northwest drift more weight than those variances that were related to other aspects of the pilot's performance. It decided that the use of the random number generator to time the turn wasn't random at all, but premeditated. It also decided that the cloning software was much better at flying the plane than the original pilot. Now this was true only in the small. That day the criminal was the norm, and the pilot was a little off."

"There are a lot of terms—words and phrases—that the tribunal will want you to define. For example, random number generator, key and generating function, to mention just a few. For the moment, let's explore what you mean by 'the criminal was the norm, and the pilot was a little off'?" the prosecutor said.

A hoarse cough beset Nomis.

"The pilot was just not himself due to his financial loss," Nomis replied.

Nomis paused to take a sip of water.

"Please go on," the prosecutor said.

Quantum II had by then done two things that were worrisome, Nomis thought as he put the half-finished glass of water down. *First, it failed to attach a beacon, and second, it continued to ignore the betting pool. The saving grace is that Quantum II is capable, like a human, of learning from its mistakes if they are exposed. But this is not something I want to do in a public arena, for obvious reasons, one of which is national security. The prosecutor must realize this and hopefully won't explore the issue of those beacons or the betting pool further.*

"Dr. Chester, the court is waiting. Please continue," the judge said.

Nomis decided to draw the dialogue away from anything that might expose more of Quantum II's weaknesses.

"I seemed to have lost my voice for a minute. Anyway, what Quantum II did in the space of the next five seconds was incredible. It immediately began to download all the most recent data from the plane's onboards, built a real-time model of its flight path, projected the slow turn and quickly came to the conclusion that the projected flight path took the plane right over the Johnson Space Center near Houston, Texas, not up the Atlantic coast as it ought to have. Quantum II quickly seized partial control, but didn't let it be known to Mr. Monger that it had done so. Stealth was the modus operandi now. Quantum II played Mr. Monger's game, slowly nudging the plane to the northeast. A complicated trace was also begun to determine the location of the criminal's computer."

"Do you have any evidence that Mr. Monger suspected at any time that he was now up against Quantum II?" the prosecutor asked.

"No! Remember he had beaten Quantum II at least twice before, but if his own computer wasn't by then telling him that his nudges to the northwest were being countered one-on-one to the northeast, I would be surprised. Let me tell you, the onboards sure did. In fact, Monger suddenly did give up his effort at the twenty-one-second mark."

"What do you mean by 'the onboards sure did'?" the prosecutor asked.

"Oh, Quantum II had only seized partial control, causing a big battle to break out between Quantum II and the onboards," replied Nomis. "Shortly afterward Quantum II bared its fangs and seized total control."

"Fangs" was a bad choice of words, and Nomis knew it the minute he had finished his sentence. Under the circumstances, Quantum II had been attacking both Monger's activities and one of its own—the onboards. The prosecutor knew it too. That comment left the door wide open for the defense to peddle his slugfest theory to the tribunal. The prosecutor quickly asked Nomis for a summary of what Quantum II had concluded.

"And finally, did Quantum II make any predictions after all of those calculations were complete?" asked the prosecutor.

"Quantum II made one final prediction," Nomis said. "It projected a high probability of finding a three-fingered man on the plane as a passenger. During its multi-dimensional search, Quantum II had also come across those hospital records in Rio. A man with the same last name as one of the passengers on the flight had received emergency treatment for a hand injury some four years prior to the now failed hijacking," replied Nomis.

∞ ∞ ∞

When the plane had arrived in the vicinity of Guantanamo Bay, Cuba, Quantum II quickly landed it and a three-fingered man was arrested, carrying a computer loaded with cloning software. Monger's system was no match for Quantum II's ability to go silently off in all directions, hide in a clutter of spinning photons and then strike like a Georgia state trooper, just like Mort Stone had alluded to a few years before.

During cross-examination, the lawyer for the defense was very cautious. He stayed away from technical issues like random number generators, generating functions and keys, accepting Nomis's sworn affidavits without question. Monger's lawyer had experienced the way in which Nomis was able to slug his way through reams of what seemed to be irrelevant dialogue, only to tie it all together at the end in a knot so tight it was extremely difficult to undo.

The defense instead put the three-fingered man on the stand. Mr. Monger claimed that he had absolutely nothing to do with the incident. It had been a kickboxing match that had got out of hand between Quantum II and the onboards, organized by an unknown party. That was why Quantum II had ignored the betting pool. No doubt it had been in on the caper. All that software on Monger's laptop had been planted by the FBI. He had been framed because COP was afraid to admit that Quantum II sometimes had a mind of its own.

Nomis thought differently. He had never been certain how the criminal had penetrated the firewall of the FGP, permitting him to collect all of that very personal data about the pilot. Neither was anybody else, because Monger didn't admit to anything. Nomis also suspected that once the hijacker had penetrated the firewall of Quantum II's FGP the second time, on the day of the flight, he had remained undetected because Quantum II thought the cloned signal was coming from Rinkey. It all stemmed from the failure of Quantum II to attach a beacon to the messaging of that criminal in the first place. The ESP system must also have been fooled by the criminal's cloning software during those very first hacks at which time Monger recorded the pilot's messaging and stole his spelling scores. All of this, especially the failure of the beacon system, kept Nomis awake at night all during the trial.

At an impromptu party celebrating Monger's incarceration, one of Nomis's physicist friends reminded him that the number of events that might require tracking during the first second of the Big Bang was mind-boggling compared to what Quantum II had done in twenty-one seconds. Twenty-one seconds after the Big Bang, the physical universe was in place. God, like Quantum II, already suspected how it might all turn out. Eiseley's clocks hadn't begun to tick, but Einstein's had. For an astrophysicist, the interesting part was over and done with by then. For an anthropologist, the wait time was a couple of billion years before it got the slightest bit interesting. For Nomis, the wait time turned out to be much shorter.

A few clone riddles circulated at that party. One mused that at the Big Bang, clocks mightn't have been clones of what they are today. As the universe expanded at lightning speed, the original second, that first one, might have been a little irregular or slow. "Time had to have some time to get started" was the punch line. Yogi Berra might have put that one right alongside his own—'it ain't over 'til it's over.' Nomis agreed wholeheartedly!

That remark of Yogi Berra described pretty well Quantum II's demeanor at about the twenty-one second mark, and perhaps God's too. Regardless, for Nomis it was a beautiful thing to watch the progress of Quantum II back in Boulder, up on the big screen in the War Room, when it was grappling with a puzzle. It was like being inside the head of a mathematician, like Andrew Wiles or John Nash, or perhaps watching the birth of the universe. Nomis was certain there was just as much poetry in Quantum II's solutions as there was math.

As one can well understand, the airlines adopted a standard that rejected any three-fingered pilot who wasn't able to spell, regardless of his map-reading abilities. This was the way they dealt with their near failure. Monger was convicted on the strength of Agent Minsig's testimony and that bit about Quantum II looking at the edge. The defense claimed that Quantum II was just a big bully and, as a result, the onboards had taken a cheap shot at it. COP never did find out how the criminal got into Quantum II in the first place or what he intended to do the second time. Monger's plug needed to be pulled for good. That was why they put him away in a deep freeze. It was the only solution. Nomis was sure that guy might just take his secrets to his grave.

The slugfest argument of the defense did cause some tribulation on the part of Nomis and COP. Both during and after the trial. Nomis felt the pressure several times from NSA, as did COP. The unfortunate business about Quantum II telling the onboards to take a walk kept the slugfest argument alive for a while, until those hospital records were produced.

Nomis admitted to Nara privately that Quantum II had also hacked the hard disk of Monger's laptop at the twenty-second mark and collected enough evidence to prove that the cloning software wasn't a plant by the FBI. Apparently, that and Quantum II's other hack of the hospital records in Rio, was what the meeting in the judge's chambers had been all about on the first day. COP didn't want to expose Quantum II's hacking abilities to public view, and the defense agreed to go along. It was in Monger's best interest to do so. NSA also put Nomis under a lot of pressure not to come forward with what happened at the twenty-second mark. Just to be on the safe side, COP also went back to the old system of no in-flight Solarnet usage.

After the trial, Nomis mounted a quiet internal campaign to convince COP to admit that what had happened was about Quantum II's vulnerability *writ large*, not just about the FGP. He claimed that some hacker lounging by his pool might do the same thing with a cloning package that was just a little more sophisticated.

There was a lot of other spin-off from the trial. The case of the three-fingered man was one of Nomis's pet examples on the lecture circuit. Almost everything was public as a result of the trial. However, the betting pool issue was a circus about which COP wanted no part. Nomis avoided it on the lecture circuit, but was fully prepared to agree with the testimony of the bookie who was never called as a witness. He suspected that, unlike himself, Quantum II abhorred the idea of profiting from the innocence of others. Thus Quantum II might have been inclined to avoid contact with such institutions, if possible.

Nomis was certain that if Quantum II had searched those records early on and found evidence of the pilot's loss, it might have taken action to seize control after only five or six seconds. To him this was a huge blunder on the part of Quantum II. It needed to be looked into, but not in the public arena of a trial, or afterward on the lecture circuit.

Much to the chagrin of COP, one outcome of the trial was akin to that which the mathematics community experienced after Fermat issued his challenge over 450 years ago. Every good and bad hacker alike tried to figure how the three-fingered man had breached the firewall of the FGP in the first place—hackers, good or bad, never took *no general solution, yet* as an acceptable answer. Nomis always worried about a reincarnated Andrew Wiles showing up on the dark side—the second coming of a three-fingered man, acting like Rome in the days when the tax man exacted his tribute under threat of mayhem. It gave him the shivers, like those cell phone antennae did which ringed the Osaka Castle, listening and looking for cracks in the warlord's armor. Technology was a triple-edged sword; it cut three ways, much like those short Roman swords did when Rome was the power of the day.

27

Perhaps . . . Never

Nomis was fumbling with the toaster in the kitchen. It was clear to Nara that he was buffaloed by more than the machine's ability to make hockey pucks from English muffins.

"Nara," Nomis remarked, "my splotchy vision is making it very difficult to see the controls of the toaster. My batteries must be going dead again."

"Are you sure it's the batteries?" Nara asked.

"No matter. MAIHEM is rumored to be working on third-generation technology that is nano-based," Nomis said. "I can't wait until production starts."

Nara came up behind him, reached over and popped his muffin from the toaster.

"What's it like?" Nara asked.

"A hockey puck," Nomis replied.

"No, honey, your vision," Nara asked. "Am I fuzzy, or perhaps feathery like a bird?"

Second-generation technology, unlike the first generation, didn't go pop like a lightbulb, leaving you stranded. Its death was more dignified. Unbeknown to Nomis, his problem had begun during the interview with Mort Stone. The harsh lights of the studio were the culprit. With his eyes turned off, he had been unaware of the glare. It had played havoc with the pixels.

"Perhaps you'll have the time to say a proper goodbye to an old friend," Nara joked.

Nomis turned around and tapped Nara on the shoulder several times, as if he was scolding her.

"Now, Nara!" Nomis replied. "This is no joking matter!"

Nara's tone of voice turned somber.

"I know, honey. I remember how depressed we both were the last time."

Nomis refused to follow Nara's cue.

"You know the saying: 'small is beautiful,' " he replied. "It's nano-driven. The components have been reduced to the size of a ganglion. The new prototype CPU looks like a little blob of brain tissue. They even devised a way to use the electro-chemical energy from the brain to power the thing. Once implanted, that's it. No batteries! I'm for that—no batteries!"

Nomis's upbeat response pleased Nara.

"Will they still set off those body scanners at the airport?"

"I'm not sure, but I think not," Nomis replied. "This time they also come with a donor card and a lifetime guarantee."

Nara voice became staid.

"Donor card, lifetime guarantee. What do you mean?"

"They're recyclable, like everything else these days," he replied. "When you die or upgrade, you can donate them to an implant bank, just like natural eyes."

Nara's half-laugh was one of disbelief.

"I suppose there's a lease/purchase plan too. What happens if you don't make your payments? Do they come with one of those wireless gadgets that some car dealers use, which foil the ignition if you miss a couple of payments, stranding you in the middle of nowhere? When I see you coming up the walk with a blind man's stick, I'll know what happened; your Solarnet payment system screwed up."

"Now, Nara, you know Solarnet never screws up," Nomis replied.

Nara changed gears. Her follow-up was very supportive.

"Wouldn't it be wonderful if you were able to rely on third-generation technology, which can't be detected at all? It might cut the hassle at the airport and at all those other meetings you go to where scanners are used at the door."

She paused. Nara wasn't as reluctant as Nomis to deal with the past. The prospect of a new implant brought back a lot of old memories. She became pensive.

"Honey, does the fact that you didn't go into teaching bother you?"

Nomis was quick to respond.

"No, not at all. I can visit key centers where crypto research is underway, attend seminars, or even give a guest lecture any time I want to. You know that!"

"With all your traveling, Nomis, this big house in Boulder is really too much for us, now that the kids are living on their own," Nara replied. "We need to think about downsizing."

"Downsizing. When and if we move, we'll have to be sure there's a big garage," Nomis replied.

"There are those new houses over near the Twin Peaks Mall," Nara said.

Nomis's voice became inquisitive.

"You've been looking."

Nara's voice firmed.

"Yes, I have, Nomis. There's even one with your big old garage. It's really an old horse stable. The agent told me . . . "

"The agent," Nomis interrupted.

"Nomis, honey. It has a big loft that was originally used to store hay, and two stalls in the rear. The rooms of the house are much smaller, which is exactly what I want. We can use the loft to store all the stuff that doesn't fit. Hopefully our children will take it off our hands someday. The agent told me that the builder wasn't going to remove the stable, but leave it for the new owners to deal with. You can turn the stalls into a study or workshop."

Except for that glitch which sometimes caused Nomis to hear colors and shapes, and his electronic macular degeneration caused by the failure of some of his pixels under Mort Stone's harsh light, his first encounter with MAIHEM's toys had worked out just fine. But, just after the big house was sold, Nomis learned that the third-generation technology, the one which was powered by the brain's low voltage and looked like a blob of brain tissue, was ready for field-testing.

Those third-generation eyes had been under development for over ten years by MAIHEM. COP was determined not to let the year 2053 slip by without bringing them into production. Nara encouraged Nomis to take the leap and volunteer. She felt she was able to handle the move to the new house if he endured whatever it might take to acquire a new set of eyes.

∞ ∞ ∞

The tall surgeon was a thin, icy-cold man with exceptionally long, slender fingers. He had been born in Chatham, Kent, southwest of London, England, but had attended Johns Hopkins Medical School in the U.S.A. and interned at Bethesda. Sedgewick was his name, Orin Sedgewick. When he entered the room, Nomis was sitting in a chair by the window, reading the Book Review section of *The New York Times*.

"Nomis—how are you, old chap? I must say you look brilliant; positively brilliant."

Nomis chuckled.

"More brain cells, I suppose. Thanks to you."

"Yes, about five hundred gigabytes more," Sedgewick replied.

His tone turned clinical as he examined Nomis's eyes.

"A yeoman's job. This technology of MAIHEM's is just super. Now, there are a number of things we must review before you leave."

"Like what?" Nomis asked.

"The ins and outs of your enhanced head."

Nomis grimaced.

"Why not phone my head and leave me a recorded message? I promise to replay it daily."

Sedgewick wasn't amused. He didn't reply, but instead began his review.

"First, the three nano computers in your head won't reboot without a boost from what MAIHEM calls 'a shot in the arm'. I rather regard it as a 'shot in the dark'."

"In the dark?" Nomis queried.

"You may not be able to see when the time comes, if it ever does," Sedgewick warned. "Second, supposedly the whole system is failsafe. But if it does fail . . ."

"Now that's comforting. 'Failsafe, but if it does fail'," Nomis interjected.

"Let's put it this way. If, for any reason, your eyes are about to shut down, the nanos will input a warning message directly to your brain," Sedgewick continued. "The warning will give you ample time to excuse yourself, head to the washroom, or any private place, and shoot up."

Nomis shook his head.

"What happens if some naive peace officer catches me in the act?" Nomis interrupted. "I'll look pretty silly, going before a judge and claiming to be an eye addict."

Orin Sedgewick's manner was acerbic and his reply was a touch sarcastic.

"And admitting to hearing voices in your head will surely land you in a psychiatric ward, too. Remember, if you do, MAIHEM can't help you. You'll be on your own."

The tone of Nomis's reply matched Sedgewick's sarcasm.

"No doubt. Or no kidding!"

Sedgewick continued.

"Third, the three nanos will be constantly voting about what you're seeing, just like the redundant guidance system of a cruise missile, or the onboards installed on one of those 797s. The warning system also provides advance notice of any malfunction, like looking directly into the sun. As was the case with the old implants, extremely bright light can seriously damage . . . "

"No electronic shades," interjected Nomis.

"Correct. The idea is to duplicate nature perfectly," replied Sedgewick. "MAIHEM determined that electronic sunglasses are a crib that might give you away. Some of the capabilities of your new eyes are hush-hush. COP wants to keep it that way. Get yourself a good pair as soon as possible."

Damn, Nomis thought. *No clicker!*

Sedgewick took a syringe from his pocket.

"Fourth, to reboot the nanos, you must inject a substance into your upper arm, using a syringe like this one. The substance will super-charge the electro-chemical activity of your brain. It will produce enough of an electrical surge to reboot the nanos. The quantity required is proportional to your body weight. If you gain or lose, the quantity must be adjusted accordingly. So watch your weight. By now you ought to have memorized the dosage function."

Nomis smirked as he repeated the formula.

"Dosage equals base weight plus or minus weight change divided by base weight times base weight dosage."

"Excellent!" Sedgewick replied. "The syringe allows for a five percent gain in weight from your current base weight of one hundred sixty three pounds. Get rid of the excess before you inject. If you aren't careful, a low-end error can produce a blackout, and a high-end error can cause an electrical storm in your head—a *petit mal* only the trained eye can detect. My advice is to sit down when booting up, just in case."

Just in case, Nomis thought.

"Fifth, as we had agreed, an experimental cell phone circuit has been installed as a peripheral to your implant. Thought commands like ON, OFF, YES, NO, E-MAIL, SEND, RECEIVE, SKIP and REPLAY are used to activate and use this option. You need only think the number and the call will go through."

As we had all agreed to, my eye. I had no choice! Nomis thought.

"Sixth, receiving a call is a little different. The calling number will be processed by the nanos. Your brain will be informed of the caller's I. D. If you want to take the call, then think YES; if not, think NO. If you don't take the call, a recording circuit kicks in."

"Does the thing reproduce my voice?" Nomis interrupted.

"Not exactly. When using this option, your voice begins as a thought process, which is then refined by the nanos and reproduced electronically as voice messaging to the caller."

Electronically, Nomis thought.

"Seventh, you can send and receive e-mail from your head by thinking E-MAIL, ON, the ramp number, what you want to say, and SEND. To receive e-mail, after thinking the ramp number, think RECEIVE, after which you must close your eyes. Only the titles will be downloaded. They will appear one by one as you blink. To read the entire message, you must access the Solarnet via your laptop. Sorry about that aspect. It's still in the development stage!"

"Is that what all that extra memory is for?" Nomis asked.

Sedgewick was slow to reply.

"Yes, but . . . "

"But what?" Nomis shot back.

"But the software that scans and sorts isn't ready for beta testing," Sedgewick replied. "It will be installed later."

"Later?"

"Yes, upgrades are possible. Your new eyes are software-driven. Firmware is a thing of the past," Sedgewick added.

Software-driven, Nomis thought.

"Eighth, to replay your messages, think REPLAY. To skip a message, think SKIP. To delete a message, think NO."

The briefing went on for another half-hour. Nomis was asked to try each of the options. Finally, Sedgewick's thin bony fingers made their way to Nomis's shoulder.

"Ninth, my friend, Nara must be kept in the dark about all of this."

A look of dismay crept across Nomis's face.

Just in case . . . cell phone implants . . . electronic voices . . . software driven . . . in the dark . . . Nomis thought.

"In the dark?"

"In the dark!" Sedgewick insisted.

"She can never know about the options?"

"Perhaps never," Sedgewick replied. "As I said before, this is top-secret stuff. NSA wants it that way."

"NSA?"

"They funded most of the development costs for the options."

I am the one with new eyes, Nomis thought, *but my new eyes have the potential to leave Nara partially blind . . . in the dark . . . perhaps forever.*

"Finally, COP will be asking you to play a more active role in the Investigative Branch," Sedgewick said. "It's just routine stuff, old boy. Part of the infowar is getting the message across in regions where Solarnet security isn't viewed as a top priority. All COP wants you to do is undertake more speaking engagements."

∞ ∞ ∞

It was a warm spring afternoon in early May. Nomis had come down with an acute case of what Nara called office fever. His condition didn't surprise her. After the new implants were installed, Nomis had spent the last week in April catching up at the office. They seemed to do nothing but wave at each other from a distance, and there was no telling when things might improve.

To remedy the situation, Nara suggested they take a drive through the Rocky Mountain National Park, northwest of Boulder. The crispness of the mountain air was an excellent antidote. Their lunch at the Alpine Visitor Center had left Nara wanting a bigger chunk of Nomis for herself than had recently been available.

"With the installation of that new implant and the move it's been a hectic spring," Nara suggested. "What do you say we take a week in mid-June and just relax? I can juggle my schedule."

Nomis reached for his Palm. He was slow to respond as he fiddled with the scheduler.

"The following week, I'm off to London and Sydney on a junket. Time is tight, but I think I can do it, too."

"You know, I think it's odd those junkets of yours are part of the IB mission statement," Nara mused. "Aren't they just a cover for IB's covert activities?"

Nomis's Palm slipped from his hand. He managed to snare it in mid-air before it hit the floor. His response was razor sharp.

"Come off it, Nara," Nomis snapped. "Those speaking engagements are part of COP's public relations effort."

"I hear you call your talks 'lectures to the infidels'," said Nara.

"Nara, Nara, Nara, my little infidel!" Nomis replied. "Perhaps I might make more mileage by staying home."

Nara wasn't able to contain that coy little smile of hers.

"Perhaps. But you might want to think of it as a romp rather than a lecture. No, I'd rather go away somewhere and romp anyway!"

∞ ∞ ∞

They had hoped to visit their friends in Ottawa, but a quick call confirmed that Herbert and Liz were out of town. Nomis spent the evening surfing the Solarnet.

"Nara, I've found a little place on Mille Lacs Lake in Minnesota," Nomis said. "It looks terrific. All one floor, right by the lake, a stone terrace facing west, a deck off the bedroom facing east. What more might you want?"

"No cell phones or laptops. Promise!" Nara replied.

Nomis's response was measured at first, but soon became adventuresome.

"You'll be happy to know I'm planning to take a couple of good novels and that cookbook the children gave me for my birthday. I intend to spend early evenings preparing sumptuous meals for you after a day of reading for pleasure."

"Reading for pleasure, yes. You cooking? I doubt it!" Nara replied.

Nomis ignored Nara's comment about his culinary acumen.

"You know, Nara, recently I've had an urge to re-read some of the books that I read shortly after my sight was first restored, and those I read for pleasure while at MIT. My gut has been telling me a re-read might help reduce the stress in my life. It might take me back to a time when my life seemed much simpler."

"Strange that you mention it," replied Nara. "I think three of them are contained in a box of old books which I earmarked for storage in the loft of the old stable. One by Winchester, one by Clarke and one by Hilton."

"How about the one by Hudson I read on the plane to Japan, shortly after we were married?"

"Sorry, wasn't in the box."

"Super. Bring the ones you found along," said Nomis.

"If there aren't too many bugs, we can eat those sumptuous meals of yours outside on the stone terrace by the lake," Nara added.

"A glass of wine as the sun sets, followed by an unhurried meal, will be my gift to you for all the hard work you've done organizing the move. It will be my pleasure . . . "

Nara cut him off with a soft, gentle kiss.

"And later, Sweetie, it will be my pleasure!"

∞ ∞ ∞

The weather that week couldn't have been better. By the fourth day, the routine of reading, cooking, retiring early and sleeping late had left them carefree and relaxed. Nomis even managed to polish off the book by Hilton and the one by Clarke.

On the fifth day, the smoke from a forest fire in northern Minnesota produced a particularly beautiful and pleasant sunset. That afternoon Nomis scolded Nara for her curiosity about the damage the fire was doing to the upper atmosphere. She had attempted to hand-calculate the tons of CO_2 which the fire had released. Nara retaliated. She sent him off to the marina to refill the barbecue's propane tank.

That evening, at Nara's request, Nomis delayed his nightly sojourn at the barbecue until the sun began to set.

"More wine," Nara said.

As Nara filled his wine glass, Nomis seemed detached and uninterested in the explosion of reds, pinks and purples that appeared in the western sky as the sun disappeared below the horizon. She felt a little uneasy about his lack of interest.

"Nomis, how can you ignore such a glorious sunset? Surely it isn't because of the tons of CO_2 that I suggested the fire has dumped into the sky?"

Nomis leaned forward in his deck chair, placing his wine glass on the little table in front of him.

"Yes, it's glorious. I talked to COP this afternoon."

Nara was puzzled. She wasn't quite sure how Boulder had got hold of him.

"I called the office from a pay phone at the marina to check on the status of my tickets to London and Sydney."

Nara set her wine glass down on the broad arm of her deck chair. Nomis sensed she was a bit miffed.

"And?"

His reply was tired and drawn.

"They want me back in Boulder a day or two early."

Nara began to nervously tap her fingers on the arm of the deck chair.

"A day or two. I hope they aren't expecting you to fly. It's a good thing that Herbert and Liz were out of town this week. If they had been in Ottawa, flying would have left me to drive halfway across the continent alone. A good three days' drive."

Nomis got up and began to massage Nara's shoulders and back.

"That's what they wanted, but I talked them out of it. It's your holiday as well as mine. You had to juggle commitments as well as me. Cutting it short and burdening you with the drive back to Boulder is out of the question. They agreed to delay the Sunday meeting until early . . ."

Nara finished his sentence. Her voice became animated as she reached for his hand.

"Monday morning. Nomis. It's a good two days' drive."

"We can do it in one long, fifteen-hour day," Nomis replied coolly. "We can take turns."

As it turned out, Nara drove most of the way while Nomis worked in the back seat. He wasn't too talkative, either. He had a lot on his mind. On Monday there was that hastily called meeting, and he was on the road by the end of the week—a lecture in London or Cambridge, and then one in Australia.

Even without his laptop, he was preoccupied with his ever-present yellow pad. Nara even felt at one point that he was on the phone. All the files he needed were back at the office, but these days you were able to work anywhere with a wireless laptop or cell phone. It was easy with Solarnet. That was why Nara had insisted he leave all his wireless paraphernalia in Boulder, otherwise he would have been glued to it all week.

When they arrived home, waiting for Nomis was an urgent, secure message from the National Security Agency, in Washington, D.C. Nara was familiar with the drill. It usually entailed a round of meetings, with his contacts at the FBI, the CIA and the DEA. Nomis often joked about his role in the process, claiming he was the breath of fresh air the process needed to stay afloat in the quagmire into which Solarnet security sometimes fell. As far as Nomis was concerned, when it came to his involvement, there was no stovepiping. Lots of cross-ventilation was the name of the game when things got hot.

After he read the message, Nomis confessed to Nara that the sunset they had enjoyed the night before began to blaze away in his head again, and this time it was neither glorious, beautiful nor pleasant. It seemed laden with a lot more than her whimsical calculation regarding CO_2 had suggested.

"What's up, Nomis?" Nara asked as they unpacked their things.

"No use unpacking my things; IB needs some help," Nomis snapped. "The Monday morning meeting is canceled. I must leave no later than tomorrow. I'll be giving that lecture in Cambridge a day early, and the one in Sydney a day late. The one in London is also canceled. Not enough time. COP has added Singapore to my itinerary. They have arranged a stopover there for a few days before I head off to Sydney. From Sydney, I'll be moving on to the Antarctic."

"Antarctica?" Nara exclaimed.

"Yes. For a day or two. So it's going to be a hectic trip: London, Singapore, Sydney and the Ross Ice Shelf. I guess I will be coming back via Santiago or Buenos Aires. I don't know yet; I'll call you."

Nara had difficulty hiding her anxiety.

"Antarctica? Isn't that where that prison is located full of those . . . those international terrorists who . . . who have committed electronic crimes?"

Nomis's lips tightened, forming a perfect circle as he took a deep breath. He paused. Then a big smile slowly crept across his face.

"All I can say is 'the Antarctic'. You know the drill. I've got my secrets. I mean, COP has its secrets."

Nara was having some secret thoughts of her own. She had an urge to inform Nomis that she was going as far as London with him. Nomis must have read her mind.

"I feel very bad about our little jaunt to Mille Lacs being cut short. Say, why don't you come along as far as London with me?"

Nara threw her arms around Nomis and kissed him.

"Nomis, I was just going to suggest that very thing."

Nomis's response was firm but welcome.

"As far as London!"

"I'll rent a car, drive to Plymouth and visit Doris Llewellyn the day you're in Cambridge," Nara said. "Not to be rude, but I think you're wasting your time. I doubt there're any infidels in Cambridge of the type COP is worried about, unless you're recruiting. We can go to a show, shop . . . "

Nomis's reply put a damper on Nara's wish list.

"No, I'm not recruiting . . . and when you return from your visit with Doris, we'll meet at the Gloucester Millennium Hotel in Kensington. That's where I'll be staying the night before I leave for Singapore. We'll have a quiet dinner, just the two of us."

28
Nightfall

Rush hour traffic in London was fierce, so shortly after 4:45 P.M., Nomis and Nara caught a cab to Heathrow.

"Dinner was lovely last night, Nomis," Nara remarked.

Nomis responded slowly and deliberately. Nara knew the drill. She folded her hands and settled back in her seat, resigned to playing the brother and sister role of her youth.

"Nara, when I was up in Cambridge, there was a fellow from Oxford who attended my lecture, a lexicographer by profession. Oxford has just acquired a gift of an old dictionary. Well, it isn't exactly a gift. They're going to pay a substantial sum of money for it. It's only half-finished and follows the common usage format of the *Oxford English Dictionary*. The origin appears to be the high plateau of Tibet. It's very strange. My grandpa told me a story once; I used some of the elements of it in a book report for . . . "

Nomis's voice had an esoteric quality that trailed off before he had finished his thought.

"Nomis, I found . . . " Nara began, but Nomis paid no heed.

"Tomorrow he might courier a few examples to the hotel, some pages. He wants me to look at them. With all the rush since Mille Lacs Lakes, I mixed up the dates. Forgot to update my Palm, I suppose. I told him my plane left tomorrow night for Singapore, not tonight."

Nara distanced herself from what appeared to be yet another demand on Nomis's time.

"Nomis, you aren't going to take on the job of deciphering those pages for him, are you?"

Nara tugged on his arm, pulling him toward her. Nomis's reply was firm.

"No, don't worry! I just thought I might give him some ideas about how to proceed. When the material arrives, just tuck it away and I'll deal with it when I get back to Boulder. Put this with it. It's my lunchtime doodling on the subject."

"Doodling," Nara replied. "Was it that boring up in Cambridge?"

"Here, take my cell phone, too. Tuck it away in your purse for safekeeping. I won't be able to get it through customs in Singapore."

As Nara tucked them away, Nomis's mind seemed to follow her hand into her purse, burrowing down right beside his doodles.

∞ ∞ ∞

The taxi driver turned onto the M1; there was quite a traffic snarl up ahead. Nara hoped her chitchat about the trip to Plymouth might divert his preoccupation from his lexicographer friend at Oxford and those doodles in her purse.

"Nomis, when I was in Plymouth, Doris told me she might be moving in the next few weeks, to a place just outside London, much closer to her children, I suspect. I'm going to stay over a day or two, meet her in Windsor and take a look."

"Are they in the same boat as we were—big house and no kids?"

Nara was pleased. Her strategy seemed to be working.

"I think so. We also took a little jaunt across the moors to Tintagel. On the way we stopped at Princetown, where a prison is located, built by the British after the Napoleonic Wars."

"Unlike my knowledge of U.S. history, my familiarity with U.K. geography is next to nil. Princeton," Nomis replied. "Is there a Princeton in Wales?"

"Prince-*town*," Nara said. "And Doris doesn't live in Wales. She was born in Wales!"

Nara paused. Nomis eyes appeared glazed.

"Have you . . . "

"No, Nara, I haven't retreated to my cloud world."

"The prison was built by the French prisoners of war themselves," Nara continued. "The British even considered incarcerating Napoleon there."

"No doubt penance for the help the French provided George Washington during his Christmas raid on Trenton," Nomis replied.

"The mist on the moors was thick and boiling, like I always imagined your cloud world to be. That prison had walls of stone and brick, but it also had natural barriers. There was no chance for escape because of the moors and the mist."

The taxi driver couldn't resist commenting.

"The moors are like a prehistoric beast. They can devour you."

Nara was delighted: a confederate with little interest in the contents of her purse, except for his fare.

"So you know the story about the apparition?" Nara replied.

"The old-timers say that it has appeared from time to time," the taxi driver replied. "When it does, you can hear a primordial moan mingling with the mist."

"They say it conjures up in your mind what Wellington must have heard as the English cannons ripped the French flank to shreds at the battle of Waterloo, causing Napoleon's elite guard to flee in all directions," Nara said.

"That apparition flickers like a will-o'-the-wisp, too, barely visible to the eye," the taxi driver added.

"Is it true that once an escaped convict, who had become utterly mired in the moor, was led back to his proper reward by what the guard at the main gate claimed was the languid and docile image of a French soldier, dressed in the uniform of the army of Napoleon? Supposedly the guard was terrified."

"Not nearly as terrified as the convict. He dropped dead of fright a few minutes later," the taxi driver added.

Nomis turned to Nara.

"Out there on the moors, it seems the prison was ringed by a certain truth, the truth of conquest. The French had lost, and to some of them who understood that fact, Princetown was their reward; to others it was their duty to escape, even if they became mired in the moor, joining the will-o'-the-wisp and the mist."

The intensity of Nomis's remark was unsettling. Nara, like Napoleon, decided to retreat to safer ground.

"Tintagel reminded me of Black Creek," Nara replied. "It was the legendary birthplace of King Arthur. Like the Princetown prison, it had its barriers too, but they kept people out, not in. The path up to the castle on the cliff narrowed at one point, and then crossed a deep gorge. It was very difficult climbing. A bridge spanned the gorge, like the one at Black Creek where we met the man shoveling snow."

"You're right. One man was able to defend against an army of a thousand, picking them off one by one as they filed through," replied the taxi driver.

As Nara babbled on, she began to realize the taxi driver was the only one listening. Nomis's mind was roaming, like a cell phone looking for a stronger signal. Nara pleaded for his attention, using a skill she had acquired during thirty years of marriage. She was gentle but deliberate.

"Nomis, knock knock. Are you there, Nomis?"

Nomis began slowly, but wasn't as sure of foot as Nara. Nara followed. The taxi driver didn't.

"Remember the summer after we were married, we visited Osaka Castle before going on to Kyoto? As we climbed from level to level, the stairway got narrower and narrower. At the highest level, there was barely enough room to wriggle through. There at the top, one man was able to defend the treasures of the warlord, or his secrets."

Nara's eye caught a glimpse of the traffic snarl up ahead. She wondered if the driver had enough room on the left to wriggle through himself.

"Yes," she replied. "All of those castles were built that way."

Nomis interrupted.

"And today, at the top, there is always a big ceremonial sword, the one used to defend the treasures and secrets of the warlord. Even the Zen Temple at Kyoto—Nanzen-ji—has that design. Remember?"

"Now that you mention it, I do," Nara responded. "Also . . . "

Nomis abruptly cut her off.

"In Fermanagh, Northern Ireland, you and I once visited an Augustinian Abbey. Remember? It was a ruin located on Devenish Island in Lough Erne, near Enniskillin."

"Yes, we had to take a boat to get there," Nara replied.

Nomis's composure became one of an old-fashioned toy soldier. His unruffled manner was only surface-deep. Inside he was wound up as tight as a top.

"On that island was a round tower of stone which still stood. The stairs at the top narrowed; only one man at a time was able to wriggle through and there, also, one man could defend the treasures and secrets of the day with ease."

"Yes, I remember," Nara replied. "But you spent your time chasing that sheep around the old cemetery."

Nara's attempt to unwind him failed. His voice seemed to be in metamorphosis as it throbbed with pain. Something vile was struggling to get out.

"I know. But the technology of secret-keeping in the twelfth and thirteenth centuries at Tintagel, Osaka, Kyoto and Enniskillin were all similar, and today they are all useless, made obsolete by advances in the enemies' technology. However, the principle of our photon filters is the same. We look at one photon at a time as they squeeze through a narrow passage."

Nomis's tone became dispirited and thin.

"You know, Nara, the same technology seems to spring up all over the world at about the same time. Our photon filters now guard trillions of secrets that travel the Solarnet daily. How long will it be until our enemies find some way to render that technology useless?"

Nara replied firmly but softly.

"That's part of your job! To guard the pass with your photon light filters and, if they fail, if the enemy finds the cracks, to search for ways to keep one step ahead while never, never giving any ground."

Nomis didn't reply.

Nara whispered.

"Knock, knock."

"Sorry, I was thinking again of the ruins at Tintagel and Enniskillen, and the fact that the Osaka Castle was still standing, but in a field of cell phone antennae . . . It gives me the willies. They're like a field of ears and eyes, listening and looking for cracks in the walls of the castle," Nomis replied.

Nomis paused for a moment as the traffic suddenly slowed and then sped up. His words sounded metallic and out of sync with the stop-and-go tempo of the traffic.

"Princetown and Princeton, each had their walls, moors, and mist, circled by the truth of conquest. Had Einstein at Princeton become a prisoner of his own truth, or is it I who now is a prisoner of his conquest, of his truth?"

Nomis's tremulous, halting, frantic monologue made little sense to Nara. His tone became sullen as he glanced and then motioned toward her purse. The tall, thin surgeon's words: *perhaps never . . .* rung in his ears.

"This newer technology between my ears makes me feel like a prisoner of my own head, a monster, like some sort of Jekyll and Hyde character. A scholar, yes, a scholar. In the morning, running down . . . ah . . . criminals in the afternoon, and God knows what the hell might happen when night falls!"

Nara hardly knew this Nomis—this sullen, spring-loaded, metallic toy soldier, wound up tight as a drum, spouting off about criminals and God knows what after dark. It was clear that Nara's chitchat about

Princetown, Tintagel, Enniskillin, Osaka and Kyoto had hit upon something vile lurking within her purse. Her plan of distraction, which she hoped might extract Nomis, had instead unhinged Pandora. She wasn't sure what was going to happen next, or in which direction he might go off.

As quickly as Nomis's voice had become metallic and taut, his deliberate, more familiar, reasoned tone reappeared. The ill will he had for himself dissipated. He smiled, settled back into the seat beside Nara and began to chuckle. The Nomis that Nara knew was back. Whatever it was had passed, or perhaps snuggled down once again next to those doodles in her purse, where it belonged.

"You know, Nara, I'm a regular Frankenstein. Some bad hacker could probably break into my head and see using my eyes, or read my thoughts, or worse."

Nara replied, half-laughing. She felt the after-shock within herself over what seemed to be, for Nomis, a touch of acute self-doubt.

"You aren't wireless yet, are you?" Nara said. "Maybe you ought to click off your new eyes, just before you go to sleep tonight. I am sure that you might enjoy drifting back into your little cloud world. After all, not everybody has such a high-tech retreat from today's stress. It even might do you some good to chase those sheep around on Devenish Island in your dreams. And, remember, the glare of the morning sun."

"Remember, there is no clicker. These new implants are truly part of me now, powered by the low voltage of my brain," Nomis replied.

"Then at least put down your window shade. You will be flying southeast."

"The glare of the morning sun?" Nomis said.

"Yes!" Nara replied.

Just then, the taxi pulled up to Terminal 2. Nomis checked in and they both headed for the United World Airlines executive lounge. Nomis was fumbling with the tickets that would take him round the world, when Nara gently took his hand in hers.

"Nomis, I started to tell you something when we first got into the cab, but you cut me off. I have a little present for you. I slipped them into your carry-on luggage back at the hotel."

"Them?" Nomis replied.

Nomis unzipped the side pocket of his carry-on. It didn't take him long to rustle the book by Winchester from the bag.

"I thought you might want to finish what you started last week," Nara said. "And there's a bonus."

That coy little smile crept across Nara's face.

"Hudson," Nomis replied. "You managed to locate *Green Mansions*!"

"No, but I did find something called *Footprints of the Gods* by none other than Nomis Chester."

Nomis sat there, looking at Nara, shaking his head ever so slightly from side to side.

"Footprints of the Gods."

Nomis began again to paw through the side pocket of the carry-on.

"It's between the pages of the Winchester book, honey."

Neatly folded between the pages was something Nomis hadn't seen in thirty-five years. It was that book report he had done for "Plots with Potts".

A big, broad smile filled Nomis's face.

"Well, I'll be damned," Nomis declared.

"I hope not," Nara replied. "Say, did your grandpa ever tell you a story like the one the old medicine man tells the young boy on the bluff?"

Nomis puckered his lips, furrowed his brow and rubbed the shiny top of his balding head.

"Yes, now that you mention it. But only sort of like it. Perhaps only . . . "

Nomis paused as he carefully thumbed through the yellowing, dog-eared manuscript.

"Yes, I did use parts of one of Grandpa's stories," Nomis replied sheepishly. "One he told me in confidence."

"In confidence? Is that why you never told me about it?" Nara asked.

"Well, I must confess, now that I remember, when I showed *Footprints* to Grandpa, he wasn't too happy. He said I ought not to have used any part of his story in that book report. I was supposed to repeat the story to someone young, in full, only when I was old, in the same manner he had done when he was old and I was young."

"Which parts upset him?" Nara asked. "The dictionary and god-counting parts seem to be only a clever rehash of the Clarke and Winchester books."

"Yes, with some of my own thoughts about the battle between words and numbers, and my little rendition on the birth of the Solarnet," Nomis added.

"You mean art and science," Nara replied.

"Well, at the time, as I recollect, it was my internal battle, you know, English and Math," Nomis added.

"Which part upset him?" Nara asked again.

"It's so long ago," Nomis began. "But, as I recollect, what upset him most was the part about the old medicine man vanishing at the end of the story, when he chanted," Nomis replied.

"Why did that upset him?" Nara asked.

"He never explained why," Nomis replied. "He said someday I might understand, if I had a good heart."

"If you had a good heart," Nara replied.

"Oh, I told you he was always harping on about 'good heart' this and 'good heart' that. It was just Grandpa. We finally came to an understanding about the good heart thing and the nature of truth, after that plane ride with the crazy crop duster. You know, which way is down and the *ifs*, *ands* and *buts* problem, remember?"

"I remember the part about you getting airsick," Nara added.

Nomis couldn't help laughing.

"You would!"

Nomis's explanation seemed to satisfy Nara and her little present seemed to have done exactly what she hoped for—it unwound him. As he collected his laptop Nomis mentioned that a pre-season game of the NFL was scheduled for the following week between the Denver Broncos and the Houston Texans.

"Would you like me to pick up two tickets?" Nara asked. "The game might be a good way to relax after such a strenuous trip."

Nomis agreed.

When he left for the gate, she gave him a big hug and kiss. She was amazed. Those eyes of his looked like they had tears in them.

A mathematician with electric eyes that cried—impossible; but one can always hope, Nara thought.

∞ ∞ ∞

He had not mentioned it to Nara at the time. He must have written it, the little bit of math, in the back seat of the car on their return from

Minnesota. Nara found it on his desk when she returned to Boulder. She had a feeling that it was for his eyes only, just like that secure message from NSA.

Nightfall

The lake was calm that day
In the presence of the sun
For what wind could be gay
If day would soon be done

Not a ripple could be seen
No treetop dared to sway
How could the sky seem so keen
And yet so far away

Now the sun grows heavy
Now a cloud appears
Now the lake grows restless
Now the trees show fear

Now I see a ripple
Now I hear the wind
Now the day is over
Now the night begins

Nomis must have been very rattled by that message as he didn't properly shred it. That wasn't like him. She found a piece of it with the poem, and on it was written two or perhaps three words in a very strange language: ♌♋♑♒♎♋♎. Beside it, he had written ♌[a]♑♒♎[a]♎.

When Nara put the material sent to the hotel by the fellow from Oxford and Nomis's lunchtime doodling on his desk, she noticed those doodles of his were identical to the scribbles contained on the scrap of paper: ♌♋♑♒♎♋♎, and beside them was written ♌[a]♑♒♎[a]♎. Nara knew a little bit about how Nomis worked, and it did appear he was more than just giving advice on how to proceed. It looked like ♋ = [a] was some sort of crib.

What is Crazy Eyes up to now that I'm not aware of? Nara thought.

29
Turn-About-Unfair-Play

Before Nomis took his seat, he retrieved that book on dictionaries from his briefcase and stuffed his case in the overhead bin. He placed the book in the seat back pouch, quickly surveyed first class and then settled down, making himself comfortable.

"Wonder what's for dinner," he mumbled.

The auto attendant gave him quite a fright as it popped out of the ceiling.

"Pardon me, Dr. Chester. Dinner will be served forty-five minutes after the flight departs. You can choose between two entrées tonight, Chicken Kiev or Beef Wellington, both garnished with . . . "

Apparently, the 797 was fully automated. Only two human attendants were on board. First class passengers had their own personal auto attendant—a computer. Dinner was ordered by touching the items desired, which were displayed on a flat screen. The selection was excellent. The personal touch was part of the service; a human being delivered Nomis's order to his seat.

In economy class, dinner was prepackaged and delivered by a mini vending machine, located in a compartment in the back of each seat, behind the fold-down tray. A supply of coins, currency or pre-purchased tokens was needed to eat. What goes around comes around. United World Airlines must have copied the idea from Horn & Hardart. One hundred years ago, H&H had been famous for its automats. Unlike H&H's, there was no selection in economy class, and the food wasn't hot—usually sandwiches, fruit and boxed juices. That was why Nomis always insisted on a first class seat.

Nomis grumbled as he pushed the auto attendant back into the ceiling.

"My head and the auto attendant ought to get along just fine tonight."

Once more the flat screen dropped down in front of him. It was the auto attendant again.

"Pardon me, sir. You called."

Nomis surmised that it not only responded to touch but also was voice activated and the words "auto attendant" and "dinner" were fatal. The thing kept babbling away, so he asked it to display the menu. As he touched the image of Chicken Kiev on the screen, he got the urge to take Nara's advice and turn down his eyes.

If a good night's sleep is the result, turning down my eyes might be worth the trouble, he thought.

But turning down his eyes was a thing of the past. It wasn't like ordering dinner—a matter of pushing buttons.

As he pushed the flat screen up into the ceiling, he caught a glimpse of Nara standing at the window of the United World Airlines lounge. Drawing her attention wasn't as easy as summoning the auto attendant from its roost in the ceiling, either. He failed.

For the moment, Nara, you're the one who must live in the past while I explore the future, Nomis thought.

The syringe for booting-up was in his checked luggage. It was impossible to put that sort of thing in a carry-on. The ion sniffers might root it out. Anyway, he didn't know how to turn the implant off, except for looking straight into the sun or a bright light and that, he had been warned, might cause serious damage. He only knew how to reboot the implant if it went down. So he scrapped the idea of retreating into his cloud world.

"What a life," he muttered.

Images popped into his head of the trial of the three-fingered man and the manner in which he had described to the prosecutor the onboards' functionality.

What I get to see depends on the outcome of a democratic vote between my three onboards, he thought. *As long as two of those little buggers agree, everything is OK, but if three different images pop up, a slugfest might develop between the nanos. Under those circumstances, pulling the plug on them and then rebooting might just be the best route to take. But how to do it?*

When the plane left the gate, Nara finally found Nomis's window. Their eyes met. The short time Nomis had her in view was dreamlike. She waved. Her lips moved, but only the bustle in the cabin was audible to Nomis. As his hand touched the window glass, he became anxious.

What will her reaction be as the future unfolds? he thought. *Has she any inkling as to what went on in the back seat of the car during our long drive back to Boulder?*

His neck craned as the angle of the plane cramped his view. His bald head brushed the ceiling. Down came the auto attendant a third time.

"Pardon me, sir. Did you . . . ?"

Nomis reached up and flipped the switch, turning it off altogether.

"It's either me or you, Nara. I mean, madam. Pardon me for pulling your plug."

As Nara faded from view, the words of the tall surgeon—*perhaps never*—replayed in Nomis's head.

No doubt it will be a revelation if and when Nara finds out about the cell in my head, he thought. *She'll be dumbfounded if she ever learns why there wasn't a meeting on that Monday morning before we left for London. Secrets between husband and wife. Not good, not good at all!*

Nomis, the director, and IB personnel did their business by conference call on Saturday while Nara was driving. It took place right under her nose, between Minneapolis and Albert Lea on Interstate 35. He rang up someone on the way to Heathrow, too, in the middle of their conversation about Tintagel. Cell phones usually bring people closer together. The one in his head seemed poised to pull them apart.

The phone was only a small part of their future. There was *much, much more* to those third-generation implants than meets the eye, but one thing at a time. Well, one thing needs to be said now. As time passed, Nara began to feel that Nomis's maxim was becoming a family affair. As for Nomis, he became more and more annoyed with that phrase *perhaps never.*

The engines made a big whooshing sound as the plane took off, and sprayed out very little heat. Its only footprint was the sound of the wind and rushing air. As night fell, with that as *his* footprint, the sound of the wind, Nomis was on his way to Southeast Asia.

It was going to be a long night. Singapore was ten hours away to the southeast. Once airborne, he did remember to take Nara's advice. Lowering the window shade seemed to narrow the distance between them. It made him feel good.

His activities in Singapore would delay his arrival in Sydney by a day. They would also take him to the Antarctic, down near the Ross Ice Shelf—or what was left of it; global warming had taken its toll. It was Tuesday, July 1, 2053. That meant the dead of winter in the Antarctic, with long, cold nights. The plane was comfortable enough, but the prospect of fifty-five degrees below zero Celsius at noon bothered him. For those reasons—a long flight and long, cold nights—he had access to lots of reading material, and, if needed, to Solarnet.

When COP was formed and took over the Net back in 2011, the name was changed, as well as a host of other things. For Nomis, replacing *Inter* with *Solar* seemed the logical thing to do even though he was only ten and a prisoner of his cloud world. Later, under Nomis's guidance, the whole system went to light speed. Fiber optics and photon filters were what did it; that and a systems approach to computer connectivity, not to mention Nomis's brain child, Quantum II. There was a move to change the name from *Solarnet* to *Solarsys* to defuse all of those in-jokes about Quantum I's successor, Quantum II, catching an individual's health care records, or an unsuspecting person's e-mail. Nomis was dead set against it, so it never happened—the name change, that is.

Any files he might need in the next few days were back at his office in Boulder. Light would transport them to him, safe, sound and secure, no matter what the temperature. Any others Quantum II was able to easily hack, although "supply" might be the more politically correct word.

Onboard pilots were a thing of the past, and on Nomis's flight to Singapore that night, all but two of the flight attendants. The pilot was back in London, guiding the plane by messaging—Einstein's spinning photons. There was a brief period, after photon crypto came into use, when the ban on cell and laptop use by passengers had been lifted. But, thanks to Mr. Monger, cell phone use was permanently banned on planes, as was the use of wireless laptops.

Back in the early 1990s, Einstein's spinning photons had created a false sense of security within NSA, the CIA and the FBI. When Nomis wasn't even a twinkle in his father's eye, those agencies thought that technology was the answer to most, if not all, of the problems they faced. The human touch became a thing of the past—a Cold War relic. Smart bombs were a big improvement over dumb bombs, but a spotter on the ground, mingling silently and secretly among the enemy with a good pair of eyes and ears, produced an immense improvement in efficiency. Those terrorists had their spotters on the ground, mingling for years with the innocent and the naive before they hit the Twin Towers in New York City. Nomis's birthday had seen a rebirth of the old-fashioned Cold War notion that the human element, the human touch, was an undeniably important component of both security and freedom.

The problem in Singapore, part of that *much, much more* issue mentioned earlier, was one that needed the personal touch. Technology did have its limitations, and the Investigative Branch periodically chose to rely on people to get the job done. For COP, it was simply a game of *turn-about-fair-play*. For the IB, which had the technological advantage of machine-assisted intelligence and human-enabled matériel, it was more like *turn-about-unfair-play*.

∞ ∞ ∞

When Nomis was on a plane, it was like a little nirvana where there was no Solarnet, and time and everything else wasn't compressed by Quantum's mechanics. Planes didn't do the light speed thing yet. He had time to read, the old-fashioned way, without the aid of Solarnet—a gift of the three-fingered man.

Rereading *Footprints of the Gods* did bring back a lot of pleasant memories, but the similarities between his grandpa's story about that ancient kingdom's strange language and what he had heard at the session with the lexicographer at Oxford left him with an eerie feeling. He soon found himself flipping through Simon Winchester's book, *The Professor and the Mad Man*.

I've never noticed it before, but Winchester's first name spelled backwards is Nomis. Hmm. And without the "Win," Chester pops up, Nomis thought. *The cipher in me seems to be on the prowl.*

It turned out that the chicken Kiev, the soft ice cream for dessert and the brandy had made their mark.

A touch of stomach acid, Nomis thought.

As he reached into his pocket for some Rolaids, his money clip fell onto the floor, beneath the seat of the passenger in front of him. Some of the bills came loose from the clip and became scattered about, along with a few white tablets. The passenger in front of him was kind enough to pick up the bills that Nomis wasn't able to reach. When he handed the fistful of bills to Nomis, he quipped about how valuable the little cache was, especially the two-dollar bill, which seldom circulated.

"It's a long flight tonight. I was about to get a little shut-eye. Mind if I move my seat back?" the passenger asked.

Nomis pointed to the two-dollar bill.

"If I spend that one, it might bring bad luck. You're supposed to give it away."

The passenger thrust his hand over the seat back offering to accommodate him but Nomis declined to do so. A woman was sitting across the aisle with a small child, about eight or nine years old. The child kept making eyes at Nomis, peeking at him from behind her seat back. Her mother seemed to be encouraging the child.

"Go ahead, honey," Nomis heard the woman say.

"Give it to the little girl," the passenger said as he withdrew his hand.

"My little girl is a real go-getter. What she wants she usually gets," the mother said.

The little girl marched over to Nomis and pulled some Vietnamese coins from her pocket.

"I have a coin collection; I have too many of these. I'll trade you eight of my coins for that two-dollar bill of yours."

I have no use for those coins. It's like giving the two-dollar bill away, he thought.

Nomis made the trade. The little girl's mother threw in a bonus—a handful of those antacid tablets had rolled across the aisle and landed under the child's seat.

"Better put these in a safe place; they're more valuable than those coins."

The power of suggestion soon engulfed Nomis. When the passenger in front of Nomis put his seat back, Nomis also began to feel very drowsy. He decided to put the book on dictionaries aside and catch the movie later.

Nomis and Nara had a little thing they always did before they dozed off at night. In fact, his grandpa used to say the same thing to him when he was little. "Sweet dreams, Nomis."

It was 11 P.M. London time. When Nara was fighting with her body clock, sleep habits weren't always predictable. With probably twelve hundred miles between them, Nomis whispered, "Sweet dreams, Nara." He hoped at that very moment she had whispered the same.

30
CIHPAR

When the movie began, the cabin lights dimmed. Nomis was slipping into a world devoid of sound, smell, texture, or color. Its tenants are numerous but nameless shapes and forms—the hieroglyphs of the mind. In such places, the subliminal nature of thought has no warranties, no guarantees. It is a world that harbored emotive forces, which might either explode or implode, depending on their fancy.

Dreams, like poetry or the message of a cipher, aren't upfront about their subject matter. They take strange twists and turns as they grope their way through the debris of a life and emerge just below the limit of consciousness. They are full of codes. Elements don't manifest themselves in an orderly fashion.

Latent elements may explode, causing a return to conscious thought, or implode, hiding among displaced allusions. But the allusions of a dream are unrestricted, sometimes even magical, like the steganography of a code-maker, where anything goes. Unlike the allusions of a comedian's jokes, they are displaced and far removed. The punch lines are purposely ciphered in the rubble of one's life. They are many times too painful to laugh at openly. An unconscious snicker suffices.

A broken marriage becomes a broken leg; a man whose management won't take his advice becomes a prisoner in a room with walls covered with egg cartons; a conversation about borderline political fund-raising becomes a swimming party in the dust bag of a vacuum cleaner; indecision about the choice of wallpaper becomes a hall with many doors.

An ocean appears . . .
Melting ice wells up from a steaming cup of coffee
A high plateau floats by
A mountain roams
Noodles ooze from a purse

An anxious frenzy errupts . . .

A loaf of half-baked bread
Tadpoles copulating in a plastic bag
Son's reflection in a mirror
Dad spinning in an office chair

Strange animals come and go, flaunting their private parts
A room full of men with calculators
Men scurrying after money blowing in the wind
A crooked room with neither up nor down

An anxious frenzy erupts . . .

Mirrors flying forward and backward
Socks inside out in a washing machine
Transparent cell phones
A cockatrice shedding its skin

Then something very strange happened. In the midst of that dream, Nomis heard a voice that called him by name. And it wasn't raspy, but sing-songy, like you might hear in a hospital over the public address system. For a brief second he thought it was the voice of that man shoveling snow by the little bridge over Black Creek. But this voice was frantic.

"Dr. Nomis Chester, Dr. Nomis Chester, Dr. Nomis Chester," the voice sang out.

Then he heard another, more familiar voice say "ON CONNECT," and spit out what he knew to be the number for a secure telephone line that enabled him to communicate with Quantum II, using a secure terminal located in his study at home in Boulder.

"I'm in!" the second voice said. "I'm in Quantum's Demilitarized Zone! But I need to walk in the front door, you know, get past the second firewall legally, so I can figure out what's going on here. Give me your password, quick, before the intrusion detection system shows up. Look, a packet just flew by me. There goes another. I'll try to get a look inside. Impossible, too much encryption, but I did get some of the routing of that second packet hacked. It was cihpar@cop.nomis.dream. Uh oh, I think they're on to me."

"Pardon me, who are you?" the dreaming Nomis thought he either said, or heard someone else say; he wasn't sure.

"I'm Dr. Nomis Chester," the voice replied. "Look, here comes the intrusion detection system. I'm off, out of here, gone!"

∞ ∞ ∞

Nomis suddenly exploded into consciousness. He was shaking; everything was shaking; the plane was pitching and rolling. A second or two later, it suddenly stopped. Nomis looked at his watch. He hardly was able to see the dial, as his eyes seemed to be dim and cloudy. It was 11:02 P.M.. He had been dozing for only two minutes.

"Pardon me, are you Dr. Nomis Chester?" an auto attendant asked the person seated a few seats behind Nomis.

"Over here; I'm Dr. Nomis Chester," Nomis replied.

His personal auto-attendant emerged from the ceiling.

"Where have you been?" it asked.

"Right here in my seat. I guess I was dozing," he replied.

"You must have been sleep-walking. Someone was using your cell phone or a laptop," it replied.

He made a note to himself. As soon as the plane landed in Singapore, he must call Boulder to report. The cellphone business and that pitching and rolling had to be checked out.

Nomis was feeling a little edgy after that dream. Even though one can rarely remember details, dreams can do that to you: make you feel edgy. Like a magician's act, they always leave you wondering where the tiger really went, especially if is a dark night and a long walk home. He finished the book on dictionaries, which he found much more interesting the second time around, and then decided to do a little math with words. With luck, he thought, it might put him to sleep. He retrieved a yellow pad from his case and began to doodle.

Hello there, friend
Where have you been
From what I've seen
You're on the . . .

Nomis wasn't able to concentrate. There seemed to be something else crawling around in his head, wanting to get out into the open, and the little girl who had ended up with his two-dollar bill was at it again, peeking over the back of her seat. He put down his pad and pencil.

"What's your little girl's name?" asked Nomis.

"Cynthia," replied the woman.

"Cynthia," said Nomis. "She certainly is a little go-getter."

Nomis scribbled a little ditty on his pad about Cynthia, but decided against giving it to her. It was his personal impressions and they weren't that flattering.

Cynthia comes,
Cynthia goes,
Cynthia wants,
Cynthia gets.

Rather than return to his poem, he continued to doodle. He changed Cynthia to cipher and reversed the order of the first two lines.

cipher ~~Cynthia~~ goes
cipher ~~Cynthia~~ comes
cipher ~~Cynthia~~ wants
cipher ~~Cynthia~~ gets

He titled it "Cipher Goes and Gets."

Well, what the hell, let's run it all together, Nomis thought; *it's a ditty about ciphers, anyway.*

Ciphergoesandgets

And, of course, like any good cipher, I ought to reverse the order.

stegdnaseogrehpic

OK, now, let's see. What else can I do to hide the meaning? Get rid of the 'd' and the middle 'e' . . . oh, yes, sack its partner, 's', too.

steg [~~d~~][na][~~se~~]ogr[e][hp]ic . . .

Nomis was on a roll. There seemed to be a momentum building in his hand, the origin of which he wasn't aware.

Reverse the 'na' and the 'hp', then . . . yes . . . the last 'e' becomes 'a'.

steg[na → an]ogr[e → a][hp → ph]ic . . .

To his surprise, the word *steganographic* popped up.

steg[an]ogr[a][ph]ic . . .

Nomis sat there, looking at that word for the longest time. A cold chill descended. His feet became icy. He reached for a blanket. The momentum of uncertain origin again welled up.

Now what else can we do here? Nomis thought. *Reverse it again. And break it apart, perhaps.*

cihpar gona gets

Nomis became intrigued by his little exercise in cipher.

Cihpar gona gets who? he thought.

The three-fingered man popped into his head.

Perhaps drop the 's' and add the target—Cihpar gona get Mr. Monger? Yes, this cipher is going to get Mr. Monger, that's for sure, Nomis thought.

His pad was a mess from the doodles. So he turned the page and rewrote the finished product, with a few minor changes.

Cipher goes . . .
Cipher comes . . .
Cipher wants . . .
Cipher gets . . .
Erase the 'd'
the second 'e'
and sack its partner 's'
if 'e' becomes 'a'
'an' prevails
reverse it again along with 'hp'
and break it apart
drop the 's'
add your target
and what have you got
Cihpar gona get Mr. Monger!

He titled his little ditty "Cihpar" and soon turned his attention to the other poem. The edginess stayed with him for a while, but as he wrote it seemed to dissipate.

Goodbye There, Friend

Hello there, friend
Where have you been
From what I've seen
You're on the mend

I've been away
For longer than I care to say
But now I think this is the day
That I'm back for good to stay

I sat in many many seats
In steel towers, in empty streets
But my place was never there
They often gave me quite a scare

I picked a place, so safe and sound
Inside myself I did abound
As I grew I needed space
To show my newly featured face

Now I'm out and it feels good
I think, I should
In my new time
Not think and act as if I'm blind

For this was long my point of view
It really kept me in a stew
But now I know that that's not so
Goodbye there, friend, it's time to go.

When he was finished, he put his yellow pad in his case and then slipped into a deep, deep sleep.

Nomis wasn't aware of it at the time, but in that dream he, or rather his subconscious, had unknowingly stumbled upon COP's biggest secret. CIHPAR stood for *Cop's Integrated High-Powered Automated Robot*. The problem was that the conscious Nomis didn't know anything about CIHPAR. It was a secret to which his conscious mind wasn't a party. His conscious mind was also not aware of the secret contained in that little ditty about Cynthia and her desire for the two-dollar bill. It contained the key that unleashed CIHPAR, MAIHEM's latest gismo. It seemed that Nomis's *maxim* was fast becoming more than a family affair. It was about to get very personal, very personal indeed.

31
Mondo Cane

Palms, cell phones and laptops without an international license for a satellite link were a no-no in Southeast Asia: they were the favorite of drug runners and terrorists. It was impossible to get garden-variety electronics through customs; you had to park them with an agent for pick up when you departed. Luckily, the circuit in Nomis's head, and the modems installed in his laptop and Palm, were satellite compatible. He was counting on his international license to eliminate any problem.

Nomis glanced at his watch.

Well, we're right on time, Nomis thought.

His thoughts became audible as he fumbled through his computer case.

"Now, let's see. The international license . . . Ah, here it is."

Nomis's mind began to roam as he and the other passengers swarmed the customs and immigration area; he got a dial tone.

"Nuts," Nomis muttered to himself as he thought, *off*.

There was a battery of automated sniffers located in front of each agent's booth. Several times a day, airport employees often crossed from secured to unsecured areas. The surveillance equipment was used to keep them honest. A bad egg might be tempted to make a fast buck by passing contraband, or even a bomb, to a mule who was headed for the transit area to board a connecting flight. Those automated sniffers were now the tools of the trade. Unlike dogs, they didn't need any treats, and never registered any false positives or negatives. Unlike the onboards they were always right for the right reasons.

The irony of it all: most were manufactured by MAIHEM. Understandably, Nomis was flummoxed by the thought of confronting MAIHEM's technology. He knew the physics and mathematics of it all.

The old implant had always set off the buzzers of those airport sniffers, a precursor of the search to follow. The hunt for contraband always caused the alarm to buzz a second time. Then out came Nomis's ID card, which explained the situation.

Some security guards gave him the once-over again; others just waved him on; a few always grinned while giving him a second pass; once, after reading his ID card, one eager agent broke out laughing. He suspected Nomis was a mule, and the ID card a nefarious diversion designed to throw him off the trail of a suitcase full of drugs. Nomis was strip-searched. It nearly caused an international incident. He never got over it.

With the new implant, there was nothing to worry about, but those metal detectors always raised the hackles on the back of Nomis's neck. After being strip-searched, they tended to arouse the fight-or-flight response in him, sending his systolic reading into the stratosphere. It was like what some people experience in a doctor's office: "white coat syndrome" it was called; Nomis called it "strip-search syndrome."

The drug laws in Singapore were unforgiving. If his eyes went down and he had to shoot up, the explanation might become tedious. Technically speaking, his head was now part computer, with a licensed wireless satellite link. That was the reason that COP, with the help of NSA, had secured a diplomatic passport for Nomis. If anything did go wrong and aroused suspicion, diplomatic immunity is the easiest way out.

Those syringes in his checked baggage were another matter. They were covered by a letter from Bethesda full of bureaucratic bafflegab about a special study in which Nomis was participating—a new drug for arthritis. Those nubbly fingers of his were proof enough.

Those with diplomatic passports were usually afforded some courtesy. Nomis scanned the immigration area. Two flight attendants had just rounded the corner and were heading for a booth at the far left. Nomis waved his red passport in the air, as did a half-dozen others. The agent, who was a woman, gestured for them to proceed.

He always found women agents to be less menacing. Once, when his old implant set off a buzzer, a woman agent inquired if he had a left or right brain implant. When she found out it was located on the left side, she waved him right through without any further questions.

Nomis was feeling at ease. The line was moving slowly, so he decided to make that call to the Director of COP in Boulder.

On, he thought.

Much to his chagrin, the three passengers in front of him didn't have diplomatic passports. One by one, they were invited by the agent to join one of the other lines. Nomis was up next.

A few seconds later, a call came through. It was Boulder calling Nomis.

"Oh, shit, yes, for God's sake," Nomis said.

The agent was startled by Nomis's unsolicited expletive.

"Pardon me, sir!"

Nomis paused. His face was without expression as he silently reviewed the in-head cell phone's protocol.

Yes, Nomis thought.

His reply to the agent was timid, submissive and barely audible.

"Ah, sorry, madam. I was just going over in my head a list of things I must do today, besides get some sleep. Talking to myself, long flight. Sorry."

Nomis's blank facial expression soon became quite animated as his conversation with the director proceeded. His lips sometimes moved but made no sound, his head bobbed back and forth, and he gestured with his hands periodically.

Look, I'm at customs and immigration, I'll call you back. OK, go ahead. Yes, the cell phone might have been activated by mistake when I was dozing. How did you know I was dreaming?

The agent wasn't amused by the strange behavior unfolding before her. It was quite evident that Nomis was preoccupied, distant and, at times, evasive.

"Passport and disembarkation card, please," the agent requested.

Nomis handed the agent his papers.

What the hell does that have to do with the cell phone? Yes, I was dreaming I was dozing for about two minutes, from 11:00 P.M. to 11:02 P.M. You think that I must have thought the key word to activate the cell while dreaming?

"Anything to declare?" the agent inquired.

Nomis was having trouble keeping track of two conversations at once. Confusion descended upon him.

"Details like that are impossible to remember."

The agent was quite surprised at his response to her question. Nomis was too!

"They are?" the agent said.

Nomis was flustered. He again adopted a deadpan look.

Shit! Nomis thought.

What do you mean "shit"? the director replied.

Hold your horses! Nomis thought.

Nomis's voice became monotone, almost humdrum.

"Sorry. Talking to myself again."

He began to rifle through his briefcase and again turned his attention to the director, who was babbling away in his head. But this time he was careful to maintain eye contact with the agent.

Look, I can't manage two conversations at once—I'm making an ass of myself here and details like that are impossible to remember. I can't even remember the broad details of that dream as it is. That's right, there were only five others sitting in first class. Quantum II ought to have picked them up. It did. No, I don't think they changed their seats. I was sitting behind them.

The agent's tone of voice became testy as she stared at Nomis intently.

"Sir, anything to declare!"

Say, what is this all about? You'll call back? At what time? OK OFF.

"Oh, yes, I have a laptop," Nomis replied.

"Does it have a wireless modem?" the agent asked. "Please, boot it up!"

Nomis extracted the laptop from his case, booted it, and produced his international license. The agent examined the laptop's license and glanced at the screen.

"Three licenses have been issued," the agent replied. "Other devices? A wireless Palm or handheld cell phone?"

"Other devices?" Nomis said. "Oh, yes, I have a Palm with a satellite link, too."

"That's two. And the third?" the agent insisted.

Nomis had never carefully examined the new license agreement that COP had secured for him prior to his departure. He had also left his cell with Nara in London. He knew it had no satellite link. He looked the officer in the eye, knowing full well that one of the three must be for the technology that linked his head to a satellite somewhere in the sky.

"Other devices? I must have left it in my head . . . I mean haste. I mean left it . . . I mean them . . . in London in my haste to leave last night. I was very rushed at the last minute, madam. I didn't bring it. I mean them, with me. I mean I only brought the Palm and the laptop."

"Is it 'them' or 'it'? One or two?" the agent asked firmly.

The agent's stare became a squint. She was certain that he was hiding something. It gave Nomis the shivers. He felt she was strip-searching his mind. Next might come his person, if he wasn't more careful with his answers.

"One! The Palm and the laptop are satellite-compatible and the one that is missing is my head-held . . . I mean hand-held cell, which I left in London with my wife," Nomis replied.

"Left it in your head, and now you left it in London, did you?" the agent said.

"Yes, in London," Nomis replied.

The agent stamped his passport and scanned each license before returning them.

"I'd get some rest, sir. Enjoy your stay," the agent replied.

As it turned out, she had made a notation on the disembarkation card that his luggage was to be searched. They didn't find any electronics, but they did find the injection kit. The letter from Bethesda and those nubbly fingers got him off the hook.

There was a strut to Nomis's gait as he exited the customs area.

Getting past those checkpoints is nothing like what the three-fingered man must have had to go through to breach Quantum II's firewall, Nomis thought. *At least I still have all my fingers. For a moment that agent did make me feel like a criminal, but all I was doing was having a stealth conversation with the Director, right under her nose. Big deal!*

Nomis's pace slowed.

She was looking for the cracks in my armor, Nomis thought.

The personal touch at the border was the most effective way to catch a criminal or a terrorist, but the personal touch had failed. Nomis didn't know whether to laugh or cry.

The strut returned to his stride by the time he reached the taxi depot. He felt good about himself and the technology in his head. He wasn't able to do much else. It was physically part of him now. Inside himself he felt a love brewing for the technology; the kind of love a young man has for a car with a throbbing exhaust, leather seats and a boom-boom stereo. If Nara had been there, she, too, might have felt the sea change in Nomis's attitude for it was Nara, Nomis's other half, who was most at risk in the pecking order that might result.

∞ ∞ ∞

Nomis had sixty minutes to reach the United States Embassy,

where Boulder expected to call him, using a secure channel. When Nomis arrived, a change of plans had occurred. There was a crisis brewing. The ambassador, who had been up all night, was disheveled. He plied Nomis with what he knew, which wasn't much.

"The director is on a plane to Washington, D.C., to attend a hastily called meeting at NSA," the ambassador said. "He will be calling you from the plane, not Boulder."

Nomis was ushered by the ambassador to a windowless room with lead-lined walls, floor and ceiling. There was a table in the center of the room, a single bench-like slatted chair, and a phone at one end of the table by the chair. They chatted for a minute and then the ambassador excused himself. When he left, a red light over the door went on as the door swung shut; it bore the message *Room Secure*.

A few minutes later, a metallic sound filled the room. It bounced from wall to wall, as if it were looking for a way to escape. Nomis opened his case, retrieved his yellow pad, flipped it open to an unused page and picked up the phone. The director's tone of voice was hurried and without punctuation.

"We don't have much time. I'll be in Washington, D.C., at NSA in about an hour. Let me get right to the point, listen carefully. Your implant is more than something which lets you see, makes cell calls or sends e-mail by using thought commands. The circuitry incorporates untested technology that MAIHEM didn't have reason or occasion about which to tell you . . . "

Nomis began to doodle nervously on his yellow pad. His reply was curt.

"What the hell are you talking about?"

What the director said next elicited an acute case of white-coat syndrome.

"The engineers set up a temporary password which activates the new option. They assured me it was failsafe. It was the word Cihpar . . . "

Nomis instinctively flipped the page of his yellow pad backwards. Staring him in the face was his little ditty, "Cihpar."

The director's voice droned away in the background.

"CIHPAR is an abbreviation for Cop's newest gismo. It stands for COP's Integrated High-Powered Automated Robot. The password is the mirror image of the ass end of the word steganographic. Raphic in reverse, or cihpar. The engineers thought it was cute. Thanks to your subconscious, it backfired on them."

Cihpar is gona gets me! Nomis thought.

Nomis flipped to the first page of the pad. His eyes became glued to the name of the little girl who wanted his two-dollar bill—Cynthia. The director's voice became a faint, unpunctuated hum.

" . . . the circuit designers also made a software error. The OFF command used to deactivate the cell circuit also deactivates the new untested option. We think the cell phone and the new option were both activated and then deactivated by your subconscious while you were dreaming."

Nomis didn't answer. The unpunctuated hum intensified in his head and became sing-songy.

"Are you sitting down?" the director asked.

Nomis continued to stare at his yellow pad, concentrating on the name Cynthia. His reply was monotone and robotic.

"What for?"

The director became impatient.

"Sit down, Nomis, for God's sake. We don't have much time!"

The image of the man shoveling snow appeared in Nomis's thoughts, but he was meticulously clearing the snow from the cracks in between the planks, not filling them. Nomis felt himself slipping through into the icy waters of Black Creek. He backed away from the slatted chair while struggling to keep his balance.

"Sit, Nomis, sit," the director barked. "You're in a dog's world now . . . mondo cane!"

Nomis replied in a dutiful and obedient tone of voice.

"Yes, mondo cane, God, Mondo Cane."

The director began to blurt out more of CIHPAR's technical details.

"The new option, when activated, sets up an electrically charged aura, which, which . . . ah . . . when activated, gives your appearance a . . . ah yes, a translucent quality. The aura makes you, your bones, anything you're wearing, anything close to your body . . . well, as I said, translucent. Yes, that pretty much describes what the aura does. Oh, yes—as the aura consumes light, it creates heat. You can't stay in the translucent state for more than an hour or two. The up side is you'll always have a great tan."

Nomis's astonishment reduced his speech to an almost inaudible mutter.

"Translucent, you say? You mean like in, ah, see-through? Diaphanous?"

"I mean translucent like invisible," the director replied.

Nomis began to stutter.

"You mean like . . . like . . . I can see . . . you, but you can't see me?"

The director again responded in an impatient tone.

"A little crude, but that's one way to put it, Nomis."

What the director had just said to Nomis didn't compute. It didn't make any sense. Remnants of that dream began to dart and then rumble through Nomis's skull. He slowly began to understand its meaning. The sing-songy sound became a grinding, ugly, raspy noise, like what occurred when you ran your fingernails over a slate blackboard. The red light over the door caught his eye.

Turn that thing off; I want out of here, now, ground out the raspy voice in his head.

He felt that time was both slowing down, but rushing by him. He became faint. His mouth became dry. His bowels felt like they were going to let go. For a moment, he thought he had returned to the cloud world of his youth. Nomis was slow to reply. When he did, he was candid.

"A little crude. You're joking! No, you're just plain nuts! No, this is the antithesis of my cloud world."

"This is no joke," the director replied. "It's serious business! Those circuits and the software permit you to cloak yourself in a cloud or haze of plasmons. It permits you to acquire personal stealth. The particles absorb your outgoing signal. Light gets in, but not out. It is the reverse of the cloud world you knew as a child. Topsy-turvy is a good way to characterize it. This time, everybody but you is blind. Nobody sees the light reflected from . . . er . . . nobody can see you, but you can see everybody. For CIHPAR, *blind* really does mean *invisible*. But you aren't the one who is blind; everybody around you is!"

Nomis's reply was testy.

"Personal stealth, my aura, plasmons, a topsy-turvy world. Shit!"

He went over to the small washroom that was annexed to the secure room, looked in the mirror and repeated the word CIHPAR out loud.

"Are you still on the line, Nomis?" the director asked.

"Ha! It doesn't work," Nomis replied belligerently.

"Four times, you must think it four times," the director shouted into the phone.

There was silence and then the ears of the director rang with Nomis's reply.

"LUTE SING DAMN, WINTER IS A-COMING IN!"

Shit, OFF, Nomis thought.

"Nomis, what we want . . . Nomis, Are you there?" the director shot back.

Nomis interrupted.

"This is a hell of a time to spring this. My image wasn't there in that fucking mirror until I thought the word OFF."

The director's tone of voice turned upbeat.

"Wonderful. It works!"

Nomis felt both insulted and betrayed.

"Wonderful! Bullshit! I had no idea something like this was in the works. It's a hell of an invasion of my privacy, you know. I ought to have been informed; I ought to have had a choice. I've a lot of questions that need answers."

The director's speech became metronomic.

"There was no time. We are short of time as it is now. Your original contract covered things like this. Boulder has the right to beta-test new options. It is only at the time of a test that they must inform you. Most of it is software. We have programmers back in Boulder, developing new options. You've known that from square one! Or have you been living a life of denial? We have a serious problem that must be dealt with today. You are the only one on the face of the earth who can help out."

Nomis was so angry that he threw the phone down on the table and began to pace about the room. The director was able to hear the metallic echo as Nomis ranted and raved.

"Right. You people need help, you sickos! The whole bunch of you, not me you need, you need a psychiatrist, or maybe two or three."

The director again yelled into the phone, demanding that Nomis pick it up. Nomis's reply was blunt.

"I'm using the speaker."

"I am sure our psychiatrist and your programmers in Boulder will be interested in that dream," the director replied.

Nomis was barely able to conceal his contempt for the director.

"Programmers, psychiatrist . . . What do you mean by?"

"Look, you will receive another call in about five minutes from F. Howard Sourceman, the president's national security adviser. He is the ultimate authority on today's issue," the director replied as he cut Nomis off and then hung up.

Nomis had questions, questions that went unanswered. The fiery sunset he and Nara experienced at Mille Lacs Lake began to glow again. A thunderhead loomed in the far reaches of his mind. His thoughts began to fly in all directions at once. A vortex of raspy words and awkward phases appeared without form or pattern or rhythm or purpose.

Then, as quickly as that cyclone in his mind had overtaken him, a sudden calm prevailed. His mind had found the eye, or perhaps the reverse—his eye had found the mind that had been his best friend. It began to plump up those words, adding both form and rhyme to what, a few seconds ago, had been laced with chaos.

His feelings exploded onto his yellow pad.

Questions

Good God you dope
Is this a soap
Or must we hope
For word of pope

Papal bull
I've had my fill
Of words that seem
To be a dream

You have delayed
A simple choice
The route to take
You now should voice

What has your tongue
What keeps you mum
I think you must
Stop this fuss

Make up your mind
Give me a sign
I've had my fill
Of this drill.

Sadly, his Herculean effort only produced a ditty. It was mechanical, angry, and devoid of any deep feeling. He sensed he was losing the ability to reach down inside himself and hoist to the surface what bothered him. It was frightening.

32
Beltway Razzle-Dazzle

Sourceman was a Rhodes Scholar. He had three Ph.D.s, in history, in applied math and in social psychology. He also spoke five languages. He was the perfect example of the trophy child. His parents were very proud of him. He could do no wrong.

Sourceman's tone of voice was at times patronizing, often sympathetic, but most of the time matter-of-fact. He rarely lost his temper and had a dislike for profanity. He was also a master of the good cop-bad cop game. If he had the right teammates, he more often than not ran you into the ground. He was known as the razzle-dazzle champ of the Beltway.

"This is F. Howard Sourceman, the president's national security adviser," the voice said. "Did you have a pleasant flight out to Singapore?"

Besides anger, there was a touch of paranoia to Nomis's tone of voice.

"Mr. Sourceman," Nomis exclaimed. "Listen up. Let's skip the bull and get to the heart of the matter. Needless to say, that flight was a nightmare for me. My privacy has been invaded by what now appears to be your technology. Your people tricked me. In fact, I suppose that nothing which I am about to say is news to you: no doubt you know what I am thinking right now, even before I articulate it."

"Whoa, whoa, Dr. Chester. Now hold on, son," Sourceman replied. "What happened is the result of an unpardonable screw-up in Boulder. But we didn't trick you. We just didn't fill you in on all of the details. All of us operate not knowing for sure the full details of the plain text. But, that's life, *n'est-ce pas*?"

"*Merde*!" replied Nomis.

"I don't know the details, but as I understand it, the people in Boulder think you hacked into your own head," Sourceman snapped. "I am going to put you on the speaker phone so you can talk to the director of COP, who has just joined me."

“Nomis,” the director said, “your subconscious launched the attack. We think it hacked into our new software, the stuff in your head; it ran an unauthorized beta test, which stumbled onto that untested option. Your dream was the wormhole! I must say, your subconscious was absolutely brilliant.”

Nomis’s face lit up.

“It was?” Nomis remarked.

The director smiled as he continued; Sourceman nodded his approval.

“Yes. It surely demonstrated the weakness in our new technology.”

Nomis’s remarks became analytical.

“I suppose you’re going to tell me that the attack of my subconscious was the psychic equivalent of the ‘T’ cells of my immune system at work targeting their prey, or COP’s beacons on Solarnet, or even those little ‘Ts’ of a bloodhound’s nose.”

Sourceman gave the director the thumbs-up sign.

“You’re right on the money. That attack sniffed out and identified our untested option. It used that dream of yours as a cover. That was brilliant; just brilliant! Quantum II was totally fooled by it.”

“If Quantum II was fooled, that puts me in the same class as the three-fingered man. Are you going to banish me to the Antarctic too?” Nomis replied.

Sourceman shook his head violently.

“Appeal to his sense of patriotism,” Sourceman whispered.

“No, no, no. You’re on our side, Nomis,” the director added. “We think your subconscious might have begun a trace to Quantum II—you know all the details—but you, as one of the foremost experts on the science of secrecy, are well aware of what’s at stake. For you it is now very personal; your unique ability to achieve personal stealth can . . . ”

Sourceman produced a pad, on which he wrote, “Let me give it a go.”

His plan was to gain Nomis’s confidence by appealing to his intellect.

“Look, Nomis, remember Mary Queen of Scots lost her head because her secret code was broken by Sir Francis Walsingham, Queen Elizabeth I’s Principal Secretary. We are in a situation today that is much like that of poor Mary.”

Nomis wasn’t impressed with Sourceman’s knowledge of the dark doings of the English monarchy, as any cipher knew that story. His attitude became belligerent again.

"I am glad to hear that heads will roll as a result of this screw-up. Say, what do you mean by a trace to Quantum II?"

"For sure, rolling heads isn't what he means," the director shot back. "Let me be straightforward. The other side has been working, for some time now, on a way to break into Quantum II which leaves no footprints. If they succeed, chaos might rain down on Solarnet."

Nomis's ambivalence was apparent to Sourceman.

"This has been done only once, by the famous three-fingered man," Nomis replied.

Sourceman again scribbled on his pad.

"He's ambivalent. Let's try a little razzle-dazzle. Pass it back and forth. Make your points count. It'll wear him down. Don't let him get a word in edgewise for a while. Turn the heat up. Make him sweat!"

The director nodded in agreement.

Sourceman: "As I understand it, you are currently on your way to the Antarctic to conduct a final interview before the three-fingered man's sentence is carried out at the end of this week. We now have information that his son was his accomplice."

"His accomplice," Nomis muttered.

The director: "You are also well aware that he never revealed how he did it. Your objectives, during that final interview, are first to determine how he did it, and second, to ascertain if he has informed anyone else, including his son, of his methods."

Sourceman: "His son has been on the run ever since his father was caught in the act on that flight from Rio. Luckily he was apprehended in Singapore one month ago running drugs from Thailand."

The director: "He is now being held by the Singapore authorities. The government is moving swiftly on this one, as his arrest was drug-related. His trial will begin tomorrow. He will no doubt receive the death penalty."

"Death . . . " Nomis mumbled.

Sourceman: "But we now have intelligence that the other side will attempt to set him free sometime during the trial. We don't want his testimony public, nor do we want to deal with the risk that he may fall into the hands of the other side. I, being the final authority on this matter, have made the decision that he must be terminated."

What's the difference, anyway? Either we do it or the Singapore authorities do it, Sourceman thought.

Nomis's tone of voice became hushed.

"Terminated, without a trial?"

Sourceman's tone was resolute.

"Terminated. I'm the judge on this one when the safety of U.S. citizens are at risk. You have the technology in your head to do this and make it look like an accident or suicide."

Nomis was aghast.

"What the hell!"

The director: "Go stealth!"

Sourceman: "Push him down the stairs on the way to the courtroom, hang him in his cell, poison his food, but do it before the trial starts tomorrow. If the code-breakers win this round with the code-makers, we are back to Stone Age messaging. The implications are mind-boggling. Our only recourse is you and that high-tech aura of yours."

"No way," Nomis replied.

The director leapt back into the conversation; he got very personal.

"Forget about Boulder's ability to read your mind. The fact is if we don't take this one little baby step, the entire world might be able to hack into your head, Nomis. Mary Queen of Scots lost hers to the executioner of Elizabeth I; you may lose yours to every bad hacker in the world."

"What do you mean by that?" Nomis replied.

Sourceman: "Use your head on this one, Nomis; don't let those hackers use it. Your secret is, in fact, ours too. Help us keep our secrets secure. If not, we both might end up on the executioner's block."

The director: "Our forefathers expect us to do our duty. Your great-grandfather and mine did what was needed in time of battle. Now it is our turn. You have the power to act. Use it, now, while we have the advantage! We need your personal touch, now, Nomis, now!"

My grandfather, the Code Talker, when he tucked me in at night always said "sweet dreams," Nomis thought. *And I always did what he asked of me. But this is a nightmare, not a sweet dream. They are asking me to let the primitive and vicious part of my brain rule my actions, to let the Mr. Hyde in me run wild and unchecked. I am being asked to wage war, a war of stealth in the most personal way. I am being asked not to kill a bunch of files at arm's length with one of my parallel processing algorithms, but to kill a human being face to face—and this they call the personal touch.*

Nomis's mind began to roam.

"Dr. Sourceman, give me some time to collect my thoughts," Nomis said.

"OK. We'll call back shortly after eleven A.M. your time."

∞ ∞ ∞

Nomis did a little math. Again what resulted was nothing but a ditty. It was depressing.

What Now Is There

Why are we here
Is there anything to fear
Are there other routes
To suit

I am bugged not by fleas
But by things I fail to see
I hope you're not as blind as me
Remember national security

And where is cipher policy
From what I see
It's out to lunch
With a bureaucratic bunch

What a feast
What a beast
Must I eat
To keep my seat

From spring's uprise
To summer's demise
But now I must
With your trust

Utter what I feel

Get off your butts and maybes too
Do something new

What now is there
Gives me a scare

At 11:25 A.M., the phone rang.

"Nomis, can we count on you?" Sourceman asked.

"No, Mr. Sourceman," Nomis replied. "I won't do what you ask."

"Dr. Chester," Sourceman said, "I want the director to explain what you are up against here. I want you to understand that COP isn't engaged in street magic."

"Nomis," the director said. "Let's be honest with each other. Are you sitting down?"

Nomis's reply was sarcastic and surly.

"No, apparently I can float too."

"Quantum II monitored your entire dream," the director responded.

The director and Sourceman heard Nomis mumble something.

"What was that?" Sourceman asked.

Nomis's voice was by now devoid of any bounce or spring. It was flat and bitter, like a good bottle of champagne gone bad in the hot sun.

"I said, winter isn't coming in; it's here in Singapore right now!"

The director of COP continued.

"Nomis, I lied."

Nomis was incensed. The tone of his reply was indignant.

"You lied!"

"Yes," replied the director. "Quantum II has been tracking you for two months, ever since the new implant was installed. Quantum II's Intrusion Detection System zeroed in on that dream a few seconds after eleven P.M. The IDS suspected the dream was a coded hack of your new implant. Eventually the IDS decided the dream was just a bunch of disconnected, goofy subconscious images about things you had been thinking and reading on the plane that night. But Quantum II got so engrossed in that nutty dream that it missed the ongoing search by your subconscious for the password, CIPHAR. It, like you, is a maestro at stealth. The dream was also used as a cover by your subconscious as it fought back and hacked its way into the Demilitarized Zone of Quantum II."

Nomis wasn't too concerned about the manner in which his subconscious had fought back. He was fixated on the invasion of his private space by Quantum II. Nomis began to concentrate. When he did, he was able to block anything and everything out. The phone conversation began to fade away, but the plain text of the message he had just heard remained clear.

The conversation with the director of COP revealed that Quantum II was capable of taking control of Nomis's mind, a mind that had been his best friend when he was blind, a mind that might now lose its free will to a bunch of bouncing packets of light, if he didn't agree to do what they wanted done.

Nomis's tone of voice became subdued.

"Was my dream stored in Quantum II's memory banks?"

The director's reply was matter-of-fact.

"For sure. It's part of the data from your unauthorized beta test. It's invaluable. MAIHEM's programmers are already picking it to pieces. So far we have determined that your subconscious tried to get into Quantum II's memory bank and erase it."

Nomis didn't pick up on that last part about the memory bank, or the attack of his subconscious. He was too angry; "livid" is the best word to describe his mood. It was his privacy that he was most concerned about, right then and there.

To Nomis this was the most vicious privacy attack that he had ever come across. What they had on a CD, or wherever, back in Boulder wasn't his phone number, not his credit card numbers, not his health records, nor his stock portfolio, not his voting record for the past thirty years, not his bank account balances, nor the number of pairs of shoes and socks he had purchased during the last five years; all that was bad enough. The last line of that poem Nomis had written about Toynbee began to ring over and over in his ears.

What they had was my most personal and private thing of all, Nomis thought. *My dreams, the essence of my very being, what Nara called, along with my poetry, her private and personal window to my soul.*

And if they had that, his soul, well, maybe Toynbee was right.

I see only men. I see only men. I see only men. Nomis thought.

But dutiful Nomis had no choice; he was caught up in a real dog show, chain and all around his neck. All he was able to do was trot around the course laid out by Sourceman, keeping that snake of a tail, that cockatrice's tail, between his legs, out of sight, ready to squeeze the life from the enemy.

"OK," Nomis said, "I'll terminate your man in Singapore, today—with only one *if, and* or *but.*"

"One *if, and* or *but?*" Sourceman replied.
"One condition," Nomis said.
"What?" Sourceman asked.
"I will need some treats," Nomis replied.
"Treats?" Sourceman responded quizzically.
"Money!" Nomis replied.
"How much?" Sourceman asked.
"Ten million. In a Swiss Bank!" Nomis replied.
"Done deal," Sourceman indicated.

33
Clocks that Tick

The time Nomis spent in the lead room was psychologically painful. It was the low point of his day. It left him numb. The high point was a luncheon with the ambassador and a few key members of his staff. At the luncheon, he was periodically pumped by the ambassador's staff about his position vis-à-vis the son of the three-fingered man. His answers lacked both concern and urgency. The ambassador also remained mum as he fingered his daily briefing notes and a large Fed Ex envelope which his assistant had just dumped in his lap. Finally, the ambassador's speechwriter, the quintessential word man, whose reputation preceded him, blurted out something totally out of character.

"Give him one of your lectures on the mathematics of secrecy. That ought to bore him to death!"

Nomis's reply was a little testy.

"One of you ought to take the initiative and push the son of a bitch down the stairs on his way to court tomorrow! Any takers?"

Those at the luncheon were stunned. Nomis wasn't.

I have a mind to accommodate that guy. Boring him to death with a summary of the technical material I'm going to present in Sydney might just suit. The technical route is always an effective way to engender in my uninformed critics the urge to flee, Nomis thought.

The ambassador's reaction to the word man's impertinent and rude remark was similar. After lighting up a cigar, he leaned over and cupped his hand to Nomis's ear.

"How about an impromptu briefing on crypto? I'll give you an opening."

Nomis nodded his approval. The ambassador continued to puff on his cigar. When coffee arrived, the word man made his move, beating the ambassador to the punch.

"What's new with the crypto crowd back in Boulder these days, Nomis? If you say the secret word, does a duck come down and give you a hundred-dollar bill?"

Not exactly what I expected, Nomis thought.

That uncontrollable impulse to bend the mind of the word man and all of the others in the room returned. The loose cannon in him was about to go off.

"You bet your life, Groucho," Nomis responded.

"Touché. I don't have any hundreds; will a cigar do?" the word man replied.

Nomis decided to chuck Sydney's mathematical theme, substituting a philosophical one.

"I wrote a little something today, a little ditty, when I was being co-opted this morning into Sourceman's covert pack of twenty-first-century code-talking bloodhounds."

The ambassador lowered his glasses. His head shook ever so slightly from side to side. Nomis paid him no heed.

" 'Do something new, what now is there, gives me a scare.' Now, that's the essence of COP's latest mission statement. It's quite appropriate for an organization full of dreamers, I think," Nomis blurted out.

The word man's brow began to furrow. The faces of those who were waiting patiently for him to continue showed evidence of boredom. Nomis got the urge to trot out CIHPAR as the door crasher.

Here's COP's latest gismo, which MAIHEM dreamt up just last week; now you see me, now you don't, Nomis thought. *No, mine is a secret that must be kept. I'll code up my answer to the word man's original question, unloading my secret to whoever has the ability, patience or desire to decode it.*

As he began to speak, a very strange feeling came over Nomis, a feeling he hadn't experienced since childhood, right after his father's death. At the time he wanted, in a dreadful way, to talk about his dead father, but wasn't able to bring himself to do so. Instead, he talked around and over and under and through his grief, but never directly at it. It was the only way he was able to relieve his pain without losing himself to it. He found himself about to play the same childish game, but this time as a grown man.

"You know, there is just as much art in secrecy as there is mathematics. Hiding things is not just about using prime numbers in a way which makes the result difficult to factor. It is about developing entire systems, systems that mimic the best that nature has to offer. I call it computer connectivity. It is also about physics and biochemistry and philosophy and ethics.

"Most take the point of view that human beings are already the best secret-keepers that nature has to offer. But humans are a relatively new experiment here on earth. If one uses an anthropologist's clock, humans learned to count and assemble dictionaries just a short time ago. If one uses a physicist's clock, well, human beings are the unborn. Regardless, humans live a very cramped intellectual life, feeding on a dangerous formula, composed mainly of their own deadly breath."

That last remark got those bureaucrats sitting on their hands. Some even left the room!

"There is much to be learned from the manner in which the AIDS virus keeps its secrets," Nomis continued. "It leaves no footprints once it has hunkered down and done its damage within the T cells of a host . . . "

Nomis paused. Some of the eyes that remained open were beginning to glaze over.

I'm putting them to sleep, Nomis thought. *Not the best example to use here. Maybe polar bears? Yes, polar bears.*

"Another example is found in the Arctic. To avoid detection when stalking their prey, polar bears hunker down in the snow. The most adept slide on their bellies, behind a block of ice, and cover their black nose with a paw. Without that black nose, the hue of the bear and his environment are identical—whites and grays—and the bear becomes invisible to his prey, the ringed or bearded seal. The light reaching the eye of the seal, coming from both the snow and the bear, is indistinguishable. It is as if no light at all is traveling from the bear to the eye of the seal; one might say that the light is trapped by some magical force lurking within the bear's white furry coat . . . if you aren't aware of the tricks your eyes, or, for that matter, any of your senses, can play on you, no less the tricks of the bear."

Heads bobbed and eyelids grew heavy.

Polar bears seemed to have hit a dead spot too, Nomis thought. *Let's try trains.*

"Take the example of two trains stopped at the same platform. One departs and the other remains stationary. To the person seated in the stationary train, it appears that he or she is moving backward, if that stationary eye teams up with the brain's assumption that the other train is the one that isn't moving. It takes a quick burst of lateral thinking to unclothe the lie of the stationary eye. In a few seconds, one's sense of balance or motion finds the contradiction that sets the brain, and finally the eye, straight. It takes two independent readings, one from the eye and one from the ear, for the brain to decide what is happening. It's the same with depth perception. That's why you have two eyes: one is not enough and three is one too many."

Nomis paused and took a sip of coffee as he surveyed the ripening field of blank stares before him.

I'm not getting through, he thought.

"Can I borrow that FedEx envelope, Mr Ambassador?" Nomis asked.

Nomis held it up above his head.

"Can anybody tell me where the arrow is on this envelope?"

There was no response.

"Toddlers never fail to find it," Nomis added.

There was a renewed effort by all to find the arrow. No success was forthcoming. Nomis finally had to show them where it was.

"It's between the E and the X," Nomis began.

For some, the arrow ought now to leap from the envelope; for others, it might blink on and off, as their brains fight to decode the letters and the arrow simultaneously, Nomis thought.

"Now, a toddler's head is not cluttered up yet with the abstractions of the adult mind, like letters and words; his brain is still looking for images and pictures. To his brain, an arrow is an arrow and an E or X is junk. He quickly discards all the junk and sees only the horizontal center line of the E and the left half of the X. Up pops an arrow in his brain, as the junk sinks into the background."

Nomis paused to survey a room where heads now nodded in agreement.

"When the eye is misled by what's in a picture, we crypto nuts call it steganography. With the increased speed and memory capacity of computers, the old chestnut 'a picture is worth a thousand words' has taken on new meaning for us at COP. It's an old trick of nature, blending your messaging with your surroundings: insects, newts and polar bears have taken it to the extreme. I call their variant 'personal' or 'corpus stealth'. They just look like a leaf or a twig or the snow. FedEx does it in reverse. They buried their arrow in a bunch of words, not their words in an arrow. No need for any fancy algorithms or an advanced degree in number theory, physics or bio-chemistry here for the code-maker. But the code-breaker, a seal, for example, needs something that detects body heat to put his brain straight. He needs tools to rid his mind of the clutter."

Nomis paused for another sip of coffee.

"Now, I don't mean to imply that I'm a tool, but . . . "

Perhaps I am just that, a tool, Nomis thought.

"If a seal had man's gift of numbers and words, it might eventually develop a flipper-held infrared detector or the like to differentiate the heat of the bear from that of the snow and ice. That device would be the seal's sniffer. It would tell him what was lurking in the haze of the ever-present dawn of the Arctic, as the sun traces its elliptical path across the sky during the summer months, or what was prowling beneath the flickering fingers of the Aurora Borealis during the long, dark winter's night. Such a device also might be a gismo capable of upsetting nature's balance, which might take eons to restore, and if that seal was able to think at all about the ethical and moral consequences of that device, it might think twice about its use."

Nomis paused again to collect his thoughts.

"There is a bell at the Temple of Nanzen-ji in Kyoto, Japan, which, when rung, produces a sound with a long tail that fades away to nothingness. Change also has a long tail, which usually fades away to nothing at all. But when you ring change in, once in a while it reverberates and squirms and wriggles its way into places which you never suspected it might. Worse still, change can be a one-way street, which leads to a brave new world of seals and bears, or prey and predator, each world porting a different pecking order than the one before."

Again Nomis paused.

Is the cryptographer in me prey or predator, or both? Nomis thought.

"Are we the seals or the bears? Will technology change the pecking order for better or for worse? Will our technology some day stalk us? Has that day arrived already?"

One of the ambassador's staff reacted like that young colleague of Eiseley. He maintained that Nomis had entangled himself in a labyrinth leading in circles.

Well, at least one of them understands the plain text and sensed the circular route implied by some of my concerns, Nomis thought.

Others at the session were certain that Nomis was off his rocker. They were worried about tomorrow's problem—what the son of the three-fingered man was about to reveal. Nomis knew he would reveal nothing. The SOB would be dead by morning. As far as Nomis was concerned, he really didn't give a damn. His little talk had defused his pain.

They are not strategic thinkers, Nomis thought as he left the dining room with the ambassador. *They think in straight lines which never touch. They have no idea that a monstrous bell will ring tonight. It will make no sound, but will go round and round and where it stops, nobody knows.*

Again, he did not know whether to laugh or cry.

∞ ∞ ∞

Days near the equator were a twenty-four-hour cycle of cool morning breezes, mid-day heat which sticks to you, warm late afternoon rain, and evening haze without variation or variety. The temperature was thirty-four degrees Celsius when Nomis arrived at his hotel. A local rainstorm was lurking offshore. In an hour or two it might move inland, bringing some relief to the heat and humidity. By evening, the sky would clear, but the heat haze would conceal what Nomis was used to back in Boulder—stars. In the morning, the cycle would begin again.

His hotel, the Shangri-La, whose namesake was the hidden valley in Hilton's novel *Lost Horizon,* where water stopped time for those who bathed in it, was a marvel of artistic design. On the way to the complex in which his room was located, one passed by a swimming pool. Its appearance was similar to the clocks found in Salvador Dali's paintings. It was irregular in shape, as if it had melted in the tropical heat of the midday sun. At the bottom of the pool was a large submarine clock encased in a disfigured plastic globe, whose surface mimiced the pool's irregular shape. At one end of the pool was a bar whose countertop did the same. There, one could while away the time, swim and enjoy a cool tropical drink as the second hand of that clock slowly but surely made its way around the dial. It seemed the perfect elixir for Nomis's pain.

The complex that contained Nomis's room was built around an atrium filled with numerous varieties of tropical plants. Large palms and thick vines grew upward, and flowers of all types draped themselves from each level, forming a curtain of blossoms that defused the light coming from an opening to the sky above. Specks of red, orange and light green, with trailing feathery tails, were visible through the dense foliage.

One might easily have mistaken those specks of color for hummingbirds. A closer look revealed its horticultural cousin, the bird of paradise. Their blossoms were a mite bigger than a hummingbird, but from a distance, they seemed just as delicate and colorful. They littered the floor of the atrium just like the dandelions or swamp marigolds found alongside the country roads outside of Princeton and near Concord.

The entrance to his room was adjacent to a balcony, which ringed the atrium. Nomis paused, putting both hands firmly on the railing. He peered down upon the specks of red and orange, leaning over to the point where he was about to fall.

"I am *Dahetihhi* the hummingbird, may I join you?" Nomis bellowed.

There was no answer.

He turned and entered his room, which faced the pool with the submarine clock. He peered out the window at the odd-shaped body of water below.

"Am I *Dahetihhi*, the fighter plane? May I . . . ?" Nomis whispered.

His words were choked and barely audible. Again, there was no answer.

Nomis went to bed early. His head spun with maps and grass and math and words and the fire of a billion sunsets. Insomnia consumed him. Each time he nodded off, a terrible dream awoke him. It was always the same. He was underwater, gasping for breath, in a pool filled with clocks whose hands he was frantically nailing to the clocks' faces.

At about 1 A.M. he got the urge to call Nara, but didn't. Instead he took a few sheets of paper from the desk by his bed and began to write. He found it very difficult. It was 3 A.M. before he had finished.

Best Friends

Where is the nail I need at last
In the rubble of the past?
To look is not what I call fun
For strength to do what must be done

Search a while in lonely heap
For a friend to keep, to keep
Best friends are what one seldom needs
Until one walks in empty streets

I looked and looked with all my might
But could not see a single sight
Myself is now an empty place
With no best friend to guide me safe

Best friend you are
Because your mind
Is simply just a part of mine
Or could it be the other way

Don't break this simple link
A thing so cruel I dare not think
To hide now from my other half
Is, not, I think, my urgent task

In the end I will not fail
A thought that often makes me pale
One last chance of you I ask
For time to fasten past at last.

He tucked the poem into his case, dressed and left his room. He was gone for about an hour. He returned to the hotel and went for a swim. Immersing himself in the pool with the malformed clock was not the elixir he sought. It only heightened his guilt and anxiety.

The following afternoon, while waiting for his flight to depart for Sydney, Nomis used Solarnet to set up an account in a Swiss bank to handle the blood money he had earned during the early morning hours. Shortly afterwards, he received a call from the director, who was noticeably agitated.

"Quantum II just received your account number, but what the hell was that briefing on seals, bears and flipper-held infrared detectors all about?"

Nomis's reply was matter of fact.

"They didn't complain about AIDS, trains or the FedEx arrow, did they?"

"Nomis, you're a loose cannon. I had to clean up after you, set things right. I don't relish the thought of doing it again if you're planning to go off in all directions at once in Sydney."

Nomis's reply was laced with sarcasm.

"I was attempting to stretch the minds of those at the embassy. I needed some practice before I stretched the neck of that . . . "

"Enough said!" the director roared.

34
Nightmares

On the flight from Singapore to Sydney, last-minute preparation for his lecture at the University of Sydney kept Nomis occupied. He had expected a crowd composed of specialists, not bureaucrats, whom he knew might pose lots of interesting questions. He dared not horse around with them. In fact, Nomis was able to field any question thrown at him without much preparation; he was just reluctant to sleep. He had had enough of those deadly encounters with Dali's clocks.

By the time he departed Sydney for the Bay of Whales, located just east of the Ross Ice Shelf, Nomis's anxiety had gone sky-high. Dali's clocks were only a dream from which he was able to awake, but CIHPAR was a living nightmare. Twice the night before he had awoken to find himself in CIHPAR's clutches. He remained awake during the entire flight by occupying himself with a book he had acquired at the University of Sydney's bookstore. It had an ominous title—*Scott's Last Voyage*—and dealt with Robert Falcon Scott's disastrous attempt to beat Roald Amundsen to the South Pole in 1912.

When he arrived at the Bay of Whales, where the little community near the prison was located, he was exhausted. Sydney is about as far from the Bay of Whales as New York is from Los Angeles, and the Antarctic's footprint stretched as far again. Surrounded by the Southern Ocean, which touches the Atlantic, the Pacific and the Indian Oceans as well as the Scotia Sea, the bottom of the world was both sprawling and remote.

In July, it was also barren and desolate, nothing but ice, snow and cold, which penetrates everywhere and everything. At sixty below zero Celsius, flesh freezes in a flash. The instant the door of the plane opened, the cold rushed in and took charge of Nomis's thoughts.

So, this is the snowy desert where one hundred and fifty years ago Scott froze to death during his race with Amundsen to reach the South Pole. It's about as close to a topsy-turvy Hell—a Hell with the heat turned down—as one might get, Nomis pondered.

The Jekyll and Hyde within Nomis was aptly characterized by the attitudes of Scott and Amundsen toward their dogs. It wasn't the little Ts at the end of their snouts that Amundsen had valued; it was their flesh. On the way to the Pole, he reduced his dog pack little by little, feeding the slaughter to the chosen. His was a dog-eat-dog world. Scott wasn't able to contemplate such a murderous adventure with his dogs. He relied on three motorized sledges.

Nomis was equipped with CIHPAR, the homologue of Scott's motorized sledges, but to reach his objective he must play Amundsen's dog-eat-dog game.

Things have not changed much in the world down under, Nomis thought. *Perhaps in this topsy-turvy world, where up is down and down is up, the Antarctic is one's private Hell*!

The day after Nomis arrived, he had the urge to do a little cross-country skiing. He was a great fan of George Plimpton, and, like Plimpton, he was keen to accumulate a list of exploits and conquests. He had chalked up a few already, such as the time he and Nara had hiked the Rideau Trail from Ottawa to Kingston in less than five days with their friends Liz and Herbert, or the time he went skydiving on his fiftieth birthday. The latter he had experimented with near Santa Barbara on the Pacific coast. It had been a near-disaster. Those late morning updrafts near the coast, on which the California Condors glide effortlessly, almost blew Nomis out to sea.

He had brought neither boots nor skis to Antarctica and wasn't able to locate anyone in the community whose boots might accommodate his flat, wide feet. Warned to dress warmly and to follow the prison road if he ventured beyond the perimeter, he set out on a pair of snowshoes. He was careful to avoid the fissures in the ice and snow which often appeared. Falling into one might be the end of him.

The Aurora Australis, as the Van Allen radiation belt was called in the southern hemisphere, was ascending toward the zenith from a dusky line of haze, a few degrees above the horizon to the south. Pale fingers of red, yellow, purple and green light stretched upward, constantly in motion, squirming and wriggling in the night sky as if trying to free themselves from the hand of a giant, or squeeze through an unattended crack in the heavens.

The forces behind nature's strobe lights had been explored using measurements taken from the radiation that they produced. It took the tools of man—space probes like *Explorer, Pioneer, Sputnik, Mechta and*

Lunik—to uncover their natural secrets. They contain streams of charged particles, hurtled by the sun's solar flares into interstellar space toward earth. When they reach the vicinity of earth, those particles are caught by the earth's giant hands, its magnetic field. To humans, those particles are deadly. The radiation from the trapped particles exceeds by many fold the maximum amount humans can endure.

As he tramped along in the snow and ice, Nomis's mind began to roam.

It is the Earth's magnetic field which shields man from the wrath of those solar flares, Nomis thought. *In the Arctic, too much bear might be the death of those seals, as is the case of roentgens and humans. But there are no bears in the Antarctic. Perhaps the seals and the penguins were the victors, with the help of some misunderstood or secret technology of their own. Perhaps they somehow were able to detect the body heat of a bear from a distance.*

Out of the corner of his eye, Nomis caught the twinkling light of a satellite making its way across the sky to the northwest.

Those space probes, with their infrared cameras, are the homologues of my hypothetical heat sensors, he thought. *What are they looking for tonight?*

The force which arched itself from pole to pole, trapping those deadly particles as they streamed outward from the sun, also had a homologue. At his command, a force also cloaked him, trapping the outward-bound light reflected by his body and thus protecting him from the wrath of his enemies.

Those magnetic belts occurred naturally, but his shield was man-made. This bothered Nomis to no end. As he trudged back to the little community, that extraordinary bell at Nanzen-ji began to toll in his head. Where its long tail might lead, Nomis did not know, but at least he heard its swagger.

∞ ∞ ∞

The prison was located on a remote peninsula, the Edward VII Land, protruding into the Ross Sea. On July 6, 2053, one of the coldest days in his life, Nomis took the snow-crawler to the prison. His strategy was to observe the three-fingered man for a day or two, off and on, in his stealth state, like a polar bear with his nose covered by his paw.

As the crawler approached the prison, Nomis put a note on the seat, indicating that he'd call when he was ready to return. He repeated slowly in his mind *CIHPAR, CIHPAR, CIHPAR, CIHPAR . . .*

When the crawler reached the prison entrance, the driver turned to collect his fare.

"What the hell? Where is . . . ?"

The driver circled the crawler, opening each door in turn. When he found Nomis's note on the back seat, he turned toward the prison's lights to read it.

Nomis slipped through the open door and stood beside the crawler, surveying the landscape until the crawler departed. It was barren and desolate.

He made his way toward the prison gate. It wasn't the sound of the wind that left its footprint this time; it was Nomis himself.

"The crib which might give me away. Hmm. No outside work or walking on rugs," Nomis mumbled to himself. "This beta test is not going well."

The remoteness of the prison put it in the same class as the Australian continent during the eighteenth and nineteenth centuries, or Princetown after the Napoleonic Wars. For the former, when a man was sentenced to *the passage*, it meant Australia. Now *the passage* meant the Antarctic. Virtual methods were the only routes of escape open to inmates.

The Ross Ice Shelf prison was fully automated, but the issues at hand needed Nomis's personal touch. CIHPAR was a little more advanced than the paw on the nose routine dreamt up by polar bears. Despite the footprints he had left in the snow, Nomis figured that with CIHPAR's help, the job might not take much time at all.

Why fight it if it can be used to gain an advantage? Nomis thought. *I can be out of here and on my way back to Boulder in time for the NFL game next Monday night. Nara might approve after all. CIHPAR might just be that little box which saves time. Hope she has remembered to buy the tickets.*

Hacker prisons were very liberal. They were equipped with a network of computers that had access to a partition of the Solarnet. It was secured by a firewall, a Demilitarized Zone and photon cryptography that were thought to be impenetrable. It was a strange network; backward, designed to keep users in, not out. Its perimeter was patrolled by software called the Extrusion Detection Systems, which looked for suspicious behavior in the Demilitarized Zone that was outward-bound, not inward-bound. That was the job of the Intrusion Detection Systems. It was all controlled by Quantum II, located in Boulder.

Hackers did not care for the information aspect of the prison network controlled by Quantum II. They were more interested in just messing it up. The first group of prisoners, under the supervision of COP, developed the prison software and protocols. That was a big mistake. Those from COP who managed the spec writing, quality control and beta testing were not up to the job. It was a case of the inmates being more adept than their keepers. They built all sorts of wormholes into the system. It took two years to clean it up.

In the mid-twentieth century, inmates spent their time making knives out of implements they smuggled in secret from the commissary, or dumping large quantities of laxatives into the soup of a fellow prisoner who hadn't paid his dues, or worse. Today, in the twenty-first century, inside this prison, what was passed around in secret was virus-laden computer code.

The talented inmates spent their time writing code whose objective was to break out of the partition allocated for prison use and screw up Quantum II. Some were not experienced enough to attempt that, so they just messed up the files of other inmates.

As long as it was contained, Quantum II let them hack to their hearts' content. Sometimes the prison partition got so messed up that Quantum II had to shut everybody out for a few nano seconds and clean it up. However, someone in Boulder had thought it was a good idea to establish a regular clean-up cycle. This gave the smart ones a crib, a weak point in Quantum II's armor.

The prison had never experienced a breakout until about a month before Nomis arrived. An inmate had entered the global climate control partition by cribbing on the regular clean-up cycle. Quantum II suspected that the three-fingered man was the culprit. Breakouts were not handled the way they had been in the past. No sirens, bells, whistles or cell counts. The idea was not to let the other side know that you knew. That might give them even more information to crib on.

Unlike CIHPAR, the guilty party had covered his tracks so well that the investigative branch wasn't able to make head nor tail of what was going on. MAIHEM knew what the three-fingered man could do, if he put his mind to it. It was incumbent on them to find out exactly if and how he had and what he had screwed up in the climate control partition, if anything.

The sentence of the three-fingered man was to be carried out in a few days, and Nomis's job was to first do a little snooping, although

Nomis was inclined to use the word "spooking," and then interview him one last time. Once the sentence was carried out, hackers usually died of a deep depression or committed suicide.

Some thought the method of execution for hacking was cruel and uncivilized. In spirit, it was the same as that doled out to Mary Queen of Scots. The computer files of the three-fingered man would be hacked to death by Quantum II every few seconds. He would never again be able to write any code, which might mess up the affairs of commerce or state on Solarnet, no less play the games which went on inside the prison partition.

Nomis did manage to uncover the secret of Monger's success before Quantum II systematically hacked his files to death. His technique was nothing more than a topsy turvy honey pot linked to a flaw in the intrusion detection system. Instead of Quantum II setting a trap for the intruder, the intruder set a trap for Quantum II. Monger had cannibalized a bunch of dreamlike screensavers developed by a group who called themselves the Dream Wonks. These screen savers were derived by electronically recording the brain waves of subjects who were actually dreaming at the time the recordings were made, and then adding sound and color to the resulting wave patterns. Subjects were instructed to engage in any and everything prior to their recording session which might leave them anxious or angry. Dream Wonks even petitioned an institution for the criminally insane for permission to use its most deranged inmates as subjects in what they claimed at the time was a scientific study. The resulting package of screen savers was dubbed "The Cuckoo's Nest". Needless to say their objective was to avoid dreams that were boring or humdrum.

At first Monger's technique was mind boggling, but Nomis later realized that his sub-conscious had accidentally stumbled onto something very similar, a situation which almost brought on a set of conditions that might have rendered Quantum II vulnerable for a split second. His sub-conscious never found the flaw because it was focused on prying a password loose from his conscious mind permitting it to get by the firewall legally.

Although unable to dream itself, Quantum II had the ability to analyze the dreams of others. Its parallel processing algorithms were ideally suited for the sort of lateral thinking needed. Nomis himself had even helped develop the software. COP eventually planned to market a website which would permit licensed access to psychologist and psychiatrist. What the criminal had developed was a kaleidoscope of seemingly disconnected dreamy images designed to attract the attention of the IDUs while floating around Quantum II's DMZ. The electrifying nature of the dreamlike images was designed to distract Quantum II's defenses and at the same time whip up Quantum II's curiosity. All that was needed was a way to egg on Quantum II's curious nature. Monger, like Nomis, stumbled by accident on a simulated switch which not only controlled the intensity of the IDU's search but also, by mistake, booted up and subsequently controlled the software which analyzed the dreams of others. If the dreamlike images were crazy enough, this caused a vicious circle to develop which for a second or two consumed all of Quantum II's resources including those devoted to the IDUs. That second was all that was needed for Monger to slip unnoticed into Quantum II's main memory.

During the interview the criminal didn't admit to passing the information on to anyone else. He knew what stealth was all about. Nomis was appalled by this chink in Quantum II's armor. Needless to say, it was his doing. It could be easily fixed with a patch but there was no point in being blindsided by a blunder he himself had committed. It was foolish to assume that the criminal had not passed his secrets on, until proven wrong by events. He informed the director of his quick fix via e-mail but decided to keep the details, especially Quantum II's fascination with the dreams of others to himself.

On the way through Los Angeles Airport, a piece in the paper caught Nomis's eye.

> Singapore. July 8, 2053:
>
> Singapore police admitted that they have no idea who slipped Howard Monger the belt with which he hung himself in his cell the night before he was to testify, on his own behalf, in a trial which might have shed new light on the famous escapade of his late father, Ward Monger, known as the three-fingered man. Ward Monger himself, on word of his son's death disappeared into the Antarctic night and was found frozen to death . . .

Good, they are both dead, Nomis thought.

∞ ∞ ∞

When Nomis arrived in Boulder, it was late. Nara was still awake.

They hugged for the longest time, but Nomis mentioned nothing of what had happened in Singapore or the Bay of Whales. When emptying his pockets, some of those poems he had written fell out onto the floor. He picked them up, placed them in the little brass box on Nara's dressing table, locked it tight, and climbed into bed beside her.

"Sweet dreams, Nomis," Nara said as she kissed him on the lips.

He lay awake for a while, thinking about Nara, his two children, Yazzie, and Manygoats and Redhouse. When he dozed off, he began to dream. Dream Wonks surely missed a whopper.

Princeton

graduate student days
jogging on a hot July day
an ice cream shop
the Baltimore
lining up
a herd of Zebra
waiting to drink
the savannas of Africa
a predator lurking nearby
crocodiles beneath the cool water
a lioness hidden in the green lush grass
a head of white hair
machines making static electricity
white hair sticking up all over the place
green fresh grass of a savanna
white hair again
ice cream cones
Albert Einstein's image
fading to his father's
his grandpa's
his great-grandpa's,
and then to Einstein's again
T shirts
the ZIA on the front
waving at Einstein
T shirts
Hiroshima or Bust on the back

waving again
T shirts
cross hairs on the front
T shirts
COP's logo, ⊣ ⊢, on the back
bolting from the line
running
out of the sky
back in Kyoto
seeing the pure sound of gongs ringing
rings unraveling to nothingness
exploding
ten million tiny florescent particles
chased by the particles
charging up the steps of the temple
a passageway to the top
smaller and smaller
wriggling through
a big iron box
emptying his pockets
pieces of paper
poems
a long sword
waiting
streams of words and numbers
floating up the stairs
riding tiny florescent photons of light
a firm grip on the sword
only three fingers
swinging and hacking
at the photons of light
one by one
his own head
rolling across the floor of the temple . . .

Nomis awoke in a cold sweat; the room felt freezing cold, like the Antarctic winter had followed him to Boulder and suddenly rushed into the bedroom through the chinks in the walls. But it was mid-July in

Boulder. He sat in the half-dark room, head in hand, naked, and did a little math.

Lines of Life

There is nothing more absurd
Than what we call the herd
The line is always there
The end is never fair

From deep we wait our time
To pass the length of line
The price is much the same
No matter what the game

I am a little fearful
Of what is out of sight
I think I should with all my might
Get out of line tonight

The choices I made in Singapore and the Bay of Whales were rooted in duty. But I will go no further. God knows what I or others might do with CIHPAR's power, Nomis thought.

The problem was not whether God knew or, for that matter, anybody else; the problem was that Nomis knew and had already exercised that power twice to his advantage. What disturbed him most of all was that the power of CIHPAR was addictive. The second time he had employed CIHPAR's power was more enjoyable than the first.

It was then that Nomis made his decision. He was going to insist that COP return the technology in his head to what he had bargained for when he first joined up, twenty-eight years ago. He simply wanted to see, and that was all: no more and no less. No cell phones, no e-mail, no CIHPAR, no downloading of software that might violate his free will by taking a hack at his head, and no uploading of his hopes and dreams which might do the same to Quantum II. He had had a taste of what that might lead to, and wanted no more.

35

The Escalation

In early July, the weather in Colorado had turned hot and dry. Going from sixty below zero Celsius to twenty-nine above in two days was no picnic. That, and Nomis's much-maltreated body clock, made getting started on Monday morning a chore, but his sense of duty prevailed. He was certain that the director was counting on a speedy verbal report of the goings-on which had occurred during the flight between London and Singapore, the events in Singapore, and the outcome of his Antarctic adventure with the three-fingered man, just before Quantum II hacked his files to pieces.

He was also eager to raise the delicate issue of the technology in his head. CIHPAR had become a monstrous problem. The screwed-up command circuit, sleepless nights, footprints in the snow at the prison and bullying his subconscious were just a few of its failings. He had to plan his handling of the issue carefully. Nomis was sure that he was no longer tamper-proof. He didn't know who was listening. That alone was enough to produce enormous anxiety. He didn't want his dirty laundry bandied about by anyone or anything.

He was about to phone the director to confirm the time of his debriefing appointment, when Nara entered his study. She seemed troubled and was clutching a piece of paper. It was an e-mail that she had found on his computer a few days after her return from London, dated the day Nomis took that overnight flight to Singapore.

July 1, 2053

from N. Chester

I'm in! I'm in Quantum's Demilitarized Zone! But I need to walk in the front door, you know, get past the second firewall legally, so I can figure out what's going on here. Give me your password, quick, before the intrusion detection system shows up. Look, a packet just flew by me. There goes another. I'll try to get a look inside it. Impossible, too much encryption, but I did get some of the routing of that second packet hacked. It was cihpar@cop.nomis.dream. Uh oh, I think they're on to me.

"Pardon me, who are you?"

"I'm Dr. Nomis Chester. Look, here comes the intrusion detection system. I'm off, out of here, gone!"

satellite 2345667378

"Honey, I didn't mean to pry, and I normally don't look at your e-mail, but as you were away, I thought it best to weed out any stuff from the kids. I know it's none of my concern, but I'm curious. What's this one all about?"

On occasion, Nomis used prose that was poetic, full of double or triple meanings, when he intended to avoid an issue.

"It's just a message sent to me by my subconscious; a message sent from my inner-self to my outer-self in plain text; a piece of evidence which suggests that Quantum II is not tamper-proof."

One more example as to why I just want to see, simply just see, Nomis thought.

Nara felt his insensitivity; she didn't let it pass.

"What do you mean 'by your inner-self'?"

Nomis snatched the e-mail from her hand and stuffed it into his briefcase. His tone became clinical.

"It's evidence that I had a few problems with Quantum II. I will probably have to take a jaunt to Bethesda to get it straightened out. Maybe next month."

"Bethesda? Evidence of what? What problems?" Nara asked.

Bethesda? Why did I mention Bethesda? Nomis thought.

He tried a different tactic and kissed Nara on the forehead, then on the cheek, as he whispered, "Problems, well, Quantum II malfunctioned!"

"What happened? What does Bethesda have to do with Quantum II?" Nara asked.

Nomis's reply was short and quick.

"Crossed circuits! Say, didn't we plan to attend tonight's pre-season football game between the Texans and the Broncos?"

Nara was not impressed with his two-word offering, or with the change in subject.

"How could that be, Nomis?" Nara asked.

"You bought the tickets, didn't you?"

"No, how did your circuits get crossed?" Nara asked.

Before he answered, Nomis turned his back to Nara and looked out the window. His intentions remained, but again his tactics changed. This time his prose wasn't peppered with double meanings or kisses on the cheek; it was embellished with half-truths.

"I had two problems. Now, you didn't hear this from me, Nara. In a fit of boredom, I successfully hacked Quantum II, just for kicks. Things like that COP personnel don't normally tell their wives, ever! And my eyes also gave me a little problem, they need adjustment."

Nara slowly nodded in agreement.

"You poor dear. Enough said. Now, the Broncos-Texans game . . . tickets were scarce. I wasn't able to get any."

Nomis was rushed and eager to get on with his morning.

"Look, I'll hunt down two on the Solarnet before I leave for the office."

The phone rang several times as he searched Solarnet for two reasonably priced tickets. He finally got fed up and paid a small premium. As he was about to rush out the door, the phone rang again.

Nara's third degree, overpriced tickets on the Solarnet, eager-beaver employees . . . now the phone again. Will it ever end? Nomis thought.

"Can you get that, Honey? I'm really running late."

"It's the director."

"I'll take it in my study."

" . . . tired but I managed to weather the Antarctic. Yes, thanks for the quick follow-through on the Swiss francs. Yes, I checked, it's all there. I want to raise another issue. Yes, about the technology in my head. I want the options terminated as soon as possible.

All I want is the basic sight package, that's what we agreed to initially. I have done my duty. There is one other thing. I'm not tamperproof, and neither is Quantum II. I have the evidence . . . you have concluded that also? Then get it out of my head ASAP, as I might become Quantum II's worst nightmare. You know what I mean by it.

You will? Are you sure? Good! Say, has Quantum II got a copy of that dream of mine stored somewhere in a file named cop.nomis.dream? How did I know? You told me in one of those phone conversations we had when I was in Singapore. You only remember telling me Quantum II had downloaded it, not the file name? You have a copy of that other dream too? The nightmare. Which one? All of them! Well, there you are: Quantum II and I, we're each other's worst nightmare. Anyway, I want my dreams destroyed, all of them! No not my hopes, just my dreams. This isn't a time for jokes. OK, good! I feel much better now. I'll see you at the debriefing in about an hour."

Nara overheard the last part of his conversation and felt compelled to offer her two cents.

"It's a topsy-turvy world you live in, Nomis Chester. Did I hear you say that Quantum II was destroying your hopes and dreams? Maybe it's pay-back for that hack of yours!"

"Nara . . . shhhh!" Nomis replied as he flew out the door.

Destroying his hopes and dreams . . . how can he feel good about that? I know I wouldn't, Nara thought.

∞ ∞ ∞

COP's corporate headquarters was a deceptive building. Topsy-turvy, too. It goes down, not up. In fact, it goes down into the earth four times as far as it goes up. It's an architect's answer to the need for very tight security. There are forty floors below grade, as they call it, and only ten above, with nothing at all on the ground floor but banks of elevators and a line of computerized kiosks, used by visitors to contact those on the upper or lower floors if access to the building is required.

Most visitors feel the building harbored an intrusive environment. Mort Stone, the talkshow host, would have been appalled by its meddlesome ways. Nomis often referred to it as a living, breathing organism, because of the way its sniffers follow around those who have appointments. The whole building is designed to mimic Quantum II's defensive and offensive systems. The lobby on the ground floor is just a Demilitarized Zone; those computer kiosks and elevators are the intrusive detection systems, and the visitor's pass, spit out by the kiosks, are a beacon.

The entire layout is designed to discourage the general public from entering the building because of the nature of the work, and, at the same time, to make it a home away from home for those who work in secret there. One item contributed to the home-away-from-home idea more than anything else—the climate control system managed by Quantum II.

Ever since that problem with legionnaires' disease in Philadelphia about seventy-five years ago, climate control in big buildings has been an issue. The anthrax problem after the attack on the World Trade

Center also brought air quality concerns to a head. Quantum II, with the help of Solarnet, solved that problem, too.

In fact, Quantum II, located twenty stories below grade, or "bottom side", as it is called, not only monitors the climate in COP's headquarters, but also that of thousands of other structures located all over the country, including domed sports stadiums, subways, malls, office buildings, post offices and the like.

There are sniffers located throughout each building to detect the presence of microbes, toxins and explosives. The system is even able to predict flu epidemics, biological/chemical attacks, or the presence of a suicide bomber from real-time data, which its sniffers collect from public malls, sports stadiums, post offices and most other public places.

If an employee comes to work with the flu or a bad cold, Quantum II sends an e-mail demanding that he or she go home until they are not contagious. Some employees often complain that Quantum II knows when they have recently made love. Pheromones are a piece of cake for Quantum II and its sniffers.

Above ground there is a large atrium in the center which spans the eighth, ninth, and tenth floors. It resembles a giant greenhouse. Key management personnel all work above ground. Those who do, have "made the grade", are called "green thumbs" and get to work in the greenhouse. When one makes the grade, one acquires a plaque on which is affixed a green rubber thumb, placed in the thumbs-up position.

Nomis is one of them. His office is located on the ninth floor, topside, directly below that of the director. All who work on the three top floors are able to move freely between them, but only the ninth floor has an elevator bank. Escalators carry the traffic down to the eighth floor and up to the tenth floor.

∞ ∞ ∞

It just wasn't Nomis's day. On the way to work, he was ticketed for running a red light. Then, on route to the director's office, rushing up one of those escalators, he slipped and fell. When Nomis came around, he was in a hospital bed at the Boulder Community Hospital. His left hand was bandaged, as was the side of his head. He was very groggy. Nara was by his side. Accidents often bring out the child in a person. Nomis was no exception.

"I'd like a dish of soft ice cream," Nomis said as the grogginess wore off.

Nara was annoyed with his priorities. The distance between them seemed to widen when the health care attendant brought him the ice cream.

"This makes me feel very good; it tasted good, too," Nomis said. *It makes me feel very bad*, Nara thought. *I didn't stay all night to be upstaged by a dish of soft ice cream.*

"What happened?" Nomis asked.

Nara took his bandaged hand in hers.

"Please don't. It hurts," Nomis added.

"You had a little accident, Nomis, but everything is OK now."

"I remember slipping on the escalator. A click-click sound, then nothing," Nomis replied. "My hand. What happened to my hand? It aches! And my head?"

Nara winced. When the muscles of her face relaxed, her expression was one Nomis had seen only a few times before, like when she had come to his office to tell him that Manygoats had died.

"Well, Nomis, when you fell, you were near the top of the escalator, juggling your office keycard, building pass, your laptop, a couple of files, and a cup of coffee. Your keycard slipped through your fingers and became lodged in the crevice where the moving stairs disappear beneath the floor at the top. I guess that was the click-click sound you heard. When you tried to retrieve the card, your index finger also got caught in the crevice. Anyway, they were not able to stop the escalator in time. The paramedics weren't able to free your finger. They finally had . . . "

Despite his weakened condition, Nomis became animated and then angry. It was all he was able to do to raise his bandaged hand into the air. His tone of voice became a mixture of a snarl and a growl.

" . . . to cut off my finger. Did they take a hack at my head, too?"

Nara felt partly to blame. Her trembling voice revealed her guilt. It was all she could do to hold back her tears.

"Your finger couldn't be saved. I shouldn't have held you up with my questions about that e-mail."

"Did they tamper with my head, too?" Nomis demanded.

Nara took his other hand in hers. He pushed her away.

Perhaps the brother-sister route is the better approach, Nara thought.

"Well, I wouldn't say 'tamper', but they did fix whatever had gone wrong with your implant. They even flew in a special team of surgeons from Bethesda."

"Bethesda! Did the director explain any of the details to you?" Nomis asked.

"No, but he said that you and he had discussed the matter early yesterday morning over the phone. And, remember, you had also mentioned some sort of a problem to me. So I signed the consent form. They assured me it was routine."

Nomis began to finger his scalp with his good hand. He came upon a huge bump, as big as an egg.

"And they wanted to check out that bump," Nara added. "They were concerned about the possibility of pressure on your brain and your eyes from what they called a subdural hematoma."

"And," Nomis barked.

"It's not a problem," Nara said. "The director will be calling today or tomorrow."

Nomis wasn't able to take his eyes off his bandaged hand. His throat tightened. His mood became volcanic. The fire of that Minnesota sunset began to burn in his head like a humongous solar flare. The words in his head went round and round but seemed unable to reach his tongue. It was as if they were defending against an intruder, the way the magnetic field does high above the earth. His voice became a low rumble. Nara felt the earth was about to move.

"Perhaps I'll have that finger pickled. No, I ought to mount it on a plaque and hang it next to my green thumb, pointing to the director's office one floor up."

A kaleidoscope of his life rushed by him like an old film in fast-forward. He hid his three-fingered hand beneath the extra pillow on his bed and glanced out the window. In the distance, the Rocky Mountains had lost their magnificent snowcaps. He felt he was melting away too. A horrible void formed within him, which Nara's love seemed unable to fill.

He thought about the sense of loss the three-fingered man must have felt when he, Nomis, had ordered Quantum II to systematically wreck his files. The midnight walk in the Antarctic that Monger had taken came to mind, as did an image of his son, slowly swinging back and forth like the pendulum of a diabolical clock as he hung by his neck from the belt in his cell in Singapore. He again looked at his bandaged hand.

"The son's revenge," Nomis mumbled.

He asked Nara to leave. He wanted to be alone. Nara knew what was going to happen and produced a pencil and a single sheet of paper from her purse.

Old Films

One can make corrections
To well-maintained directions
If there are affections
One must have reflections

To wear a hood? To look aside?
At times like this without a guide
But times of change, views so plain
Why are they strange to those in pain?

As simple as this is to say
Can one claim it true today?
Some at the start are very smart
Others laugh and stand apart

It could depend on those who care
To keep one's spirits free and fair
This could bring one to the view
That change could come without ado

Those who choose to view old films
Could find their sight transposed as fright
Those who choose to see old films
Could find their fright transposed as sight

The pain would cease to be obese
The heart might start to play its part
The choice to make, not hard at all
The end result could be a ball

Poetry always made Nomis feel better. It was a coded message sent from his inner-self to his outer-self, like that e-mail.

36
The Sun's Revenge

Later that Tuesday, Nomis reluctantly broke the "perhaps . . . never" pledge he had made to Orin Sedgewick. He informed Nara in confidence about the cell phone which had just been removed from his head.

"It was a last-minute addition to the new implant," Nomis added. "It turned out to be a big problem on the plane to Singapore."

Well . . . not exactly, Nomis thought.

"Why didn't you tell me?" Nara asked. "One of COP's little secrets I suppose. Well, Nomis, many of the loose ends that I had been unable to piece together of late are cut loose by what you just said."

"What loose ends?" Nomis asked.

"Oh . . . those uneasy feelings I had on the way back from Mille Lacs Lake, and those I experienced during that taxi ride to Heathrow, they all fall into place now. Say, did you use it to make that call to your office from the marina at Mille Lacs Lake too?" Nara asked.

The marina. I forgot about the marina. Perhaps it wasn't wise to tell her, Nomis thought as he reached for the arm of the TV. *Better watch what I say from now on.*

"Could you sit in the other chair, Nara? You're in the way of the arm," Nomis suddenly demanded.

Trimming those loose ends now seems to have widened the gap between us, Nara thought.

Despite Nara's attempts to pursue the details of his confession, Nomis remained tight lipped. Finally a smile crept across Nara's face.

"I guess all that ringing in your ears ought to go away; it wasn't tinnitus after all," Nara joked in an effort to lubricate his jaw.

Nomis wasn't amused and remained silent. As seconds became minutes any tenderness which remained between the two of them melted slowly away. He remained aloof and unconcerned. She felt unconnected, unappreciated and anxious when Nomis abruptly pushed the TV aside and headed for the washroom, slamming the door behind him. A few minutes later Nara heard him babbling away. It sounded like gibberish to her.

"On, hmm, good! Connect, ahh, excellent! Ci . . . gar, ci . . . gar, ci . . . gar, off. Off. Off ci . . . gar. Are you there? Calling ci . . . gar" was all she was able to make out.

"Are you all right?" Nara asked.

Nomis's gruff reply only increased her anxiety.

"Yes, yes. I don't need any help. I'll be out in a minute," Nomis grunted.

When he emerged from the washroom, he seemed to be in a better mood, but now Nara was the one about to burst into a fit of gibberish. After all, she loved him, and his antics worried her. She even thought that perhaps his speech had been affected by his fall or he had had a stroke, as those noises from the washroom sounded like he was stuttering.

∞ ∞ ∞

On Wednesday, the director came to visit Nomis.

"Well, Nomis. I hope that you're feeling better. You have been through a lot," he began.

Nomis was as curt with the director as he had been with Nara the day before. He was quick to put him to the test.

"Is the download option out?" Nomis snapped.

The director closed the door. He spoke slowly and deliberately.

"Sedgewick removed the cell phone, the e-mail option, and the download facility. It was mostly software, anyway. But you might still be able to do your disappearing act. There was no way he could have removed CIHPAR without a lot of collateral damage."

He asked Nomis to accompany him to a more secure room where three others were waiting, one of whom was Orin Sedgewick.

Sedgewick began in earnest.

"Hello, Dr. Chester. How are you today? I headed the surgical team that . . ."

"How am I? That depends on what you have to say," Nomis interrupted.

Sedgewick's tone of voice became icy-cold.

"Well, Nomis, we are all grown men. Let me get right to the heart of the matter. When I was instructed to remove the cell, e-mail and download option, I advised the director that the surgical procedure wouldn't be a problem. Most of it was software, anyway, except for the communication circuits, and those weren't difficult to extract. But your disappearing act was, and still is, a concern. It seems that what I originally put in place has become part of you."

"Jeeesssussss . . . part of me!" Nomis exclaimed.

"It was a very advanced piece of circuitry and in fact designed especially for you, for your brain structure, electro-chemistry, personality, and the fact that you dreamt a lot when you were young and were blind prior to its installation."

"But I tried to activate CIHPAR and it didn't . . . " Nomis replied.

" . . . work. Are you certain of that?" Sedgewick interrupted.

"Yes, it didn't respond to the thought commands," Nomis said. "I even repeated the commands out loud. It didn't work then either. I think my poor wife thought I had gone mad."

The director was clearly shaken by Nomis's last remark about Nara's state of mind.

"Nomis, I sure as hell hope Nara wasn't in the room with you when you tried to activate CIHPAR."

"No, no, no! I was in the washroom with the door closed," Nomis replied.

"It might be something simple, like that bump on your head from the fall," Sedgewick said. "We aren't sure. The circuitry was part of the sight-restoring implant, but it seems to have vanished."

"Jeeesssusss . . . first it's part of me, now it's vanished!" Nomis shrieked again.

"It was made of a new, experimental material and might have been absorbed by your body," Sedgewick said. "If that's the case it's gone, probably excreted by your kidneys or chemically changed by your liver and then metabolized."

Or maybe it screwed up my DNA, Nomis thought.

"You mean I pissed it out," Nomis replied grinning.

"Crude, but accurate," Sedgewick said.

"Was it toxic?" Nomis asked.

"No, you aren't in any danger," Sedgewick said.

Nomis remained concerned.

"No danger at all," Nomis added.

"No danger at all. Now. You must report back to us if anything strange happens in the future."

"Yes, yes, I understand. But why not take out the entire implant and replace it with a new one?"

"What now is there shouldn't scare you; it's just like new; it seems to be in perfect working order," Sedgewick replied.

Nomis sensed a familiar ring to Sedgewick's words but wasn't able to place them in context.

"Except for the disappearing circuits," Nomis remarked. "Well, I guess if that's the only part of me that has disappeared, I'm satisfied."

"There is one thing I want to check. It's only a remote possibility," Sedgewick said. "Were you exposed to a radiation source during the last few weeks?"

"No. Well, maybe. I went snow-shoeing the night of an extraordinary display of the Aurora Australis," Nomis replied.

"That might be a factor, but it's remote. A hyper-mutation of your genes from over-exposure to charged particles might have occurred. Oh, and one last thing. During that two-minute dream of yours on the flight from London to Singapore, after you had gone stealth by accident, Quantum II has determined that you kept fading in and out. Did your vision also become clouded?"

"Yes, it did," Nomis replied.

"We traced both problems to the level of oxygen in your blood. That plane is now out of service for a refit of its ventilators."

"You mean to tell me if that cabin had de-pressurized, I might have gone blind, as the implant would have shut down," Nomis added.

"It's a possibility," Sedgwick replied.

That night Nomis had another one of his nightmares. He seemed unable to catch his breath and was tormented by his missing index finger.

a finger
continually floating above his head
pointing upward
its hue changing color
a supple pink
a blood red
a bruised yellow-purple
a gangrenous green
the bloody stump end
periodically caressed his forehead
a white coat floats by
on the back a sign that reads
Team Aurora Fingeralis

∞ ∞ ∞

Relationships are like hardwood floors. During hot, dry spells, the cracks begin to show. On Thursday, Nomis gave Nara that last poem he had written. He hoped his little gift might put a damper on their emotional dry spell. Losing that index finger had thwarted their plans to go to the Monday night pre-season football game between the Broncos and the Texans. Nomis suggested flying down to San Diego in two weeks' time to attend the Broncos' season opener with the Chargers. By then, he was assured by his doctors, he would be on the mend. They both hoped the Broncos-Chargers game wouldn't be a replay of that preseason game they had missed. The Broncos had been hacked to death by the Texans.

"Their domination of the game was just a brute force attack, just a lot of muscle power, probably revenge aimed at Quantum II for its ability to control the price of oil and oil substitutes," Nomis quipped. "You know, what Quantum II has done in the area of energy conservation is quite astounding."

"Now, don't sell me short," Nara replied. "If you recall, some of us at the National Center for Atmospheric Research were involved in setting up the information feed. Data from a network of weather satellites circling the globe, ocean buoys strung across the Pacific to monitor El Niño and La Niña, sunspot activity, tidal flows . . . "

"Yes, yes. I remember," Nomis interrupted.

"Don't 'yes, yes' me, Nomis Chester," Nara replied.

Nomis began to laugh sympathetically.

"Nara, my bad humor must be catching!"

For the first time in a week, Nara smiled.

"Well, that data was fed to Quantum II. With its help, we produced forecasts over four to six months, which were quite accurate. Quantum II now processes that data continuously, as we speak."

Nomis leaned over and gave Nara a peck on the cheek.

"You're absolutely right. But given enough data, Quantum II can master anything. Look at what it did to the business cycle with the help of chaos theory and those physicists, mathematicians and economists working in White Sands, New Mexico."

Nomis paused. Nara sensed the old Nomis lurking about the hospital room. His tone became pedantic.

"But it was the National Security Agency that put the two together—weather and economic forecasting—suggesting that Quantum

II play the futures market for energy types in Chicago. With Quantum II's help, NSA is now able to insure that the future market price for fuels is nearly perfect. No cycles at all."

He was off and running again, lecturing to his favorite audience of one. Nara smiled for the second time in a week. It made her feel much better.

"As a result, most other players dropped out. With such accurate forecasts of both the weather and the business cycle, no one is willing to challenge Quantum II. It's now able to set the price of all energy types in ways that avoid the ups and downs of the past."

A week's worth of tension began to scatter about the room. Nara's eyelids began to flutter and then her head drooped.

"As I remember," Nomis continued, "the Middle Eastern oil suppliers were very upset at the onset of this activity by Quantum II. One could well understand why. After the collapse of OPEC, many wanted to partner with Quantum II. NSA would have none of it, but you know NSA. Who knows what goes on under the table? Nowadays, fuel substitution, futures prices, demand and supply correlate only with population growth and inflation, both in the short and long run. It makes things a lot simpler when you can bet for sure on the future. Nara, Nara, are you asleep?"

"No, no," Nara replied. "Not yet."

"What did I just say?"

"You wanted to bet for sure on the future," Nara said.

"Right! Well, almost right," continued Nomis. "You know, I often wonder what might happen if someone developed a method for predicting the outcome of NFL-AFL games with the same accuracy with which Quantum II predicts the weather and energy consumption. I suspect the betting pool might come to an end, like OPEC, as the person with the method would quickly drive excess profits and gambling rents to zero."

"Like OPEC, they might try to bar any such person from participating if he ruins all the fun," Nara replied.

"A more sinister approach might be to partner with the betting pool, keeping such a system under wraps in return for a cut in the winnings," Nomis mused. "If you were in it to continuously win, buying into a money machine like a casino is more attractive than patronizing it."

That coy little smile spread across Nara's face.

"You might want to consider my little casino," Nara said. "I put those tickets you bought up for sale on the Solarnet the afternoon of your accident. I made a fifty-dollar profit on a pair of one-hundred-and-sixty-five dollar tickets, or a little less than thirty percent in one day. Can you beat that?"

"That afternoon the tickets were probably in even higher demand than during the morning, when I bought them," Nomis replied. "Like oil prices, the key is to know for sure both demand and supply in the future, before you place your bet. You have to know the score in advance to win big."

You mean one must have an advantage to play against the house, Nara thought.

"And if and when they find out you have a system, the house will, no doubt, quietly tell you to take a walk, no questions asked," Nomis added.

"But if the system is foolproof, it might be more advantageous for the house to make a deal with you and keep it a secret," Nara replied.

That's what happened with OPEC. Saudi Arabia had made a secret deal with the U.S. when it became aware that Quantum II was about to become a method player in the Chicago futures market for crude oil. The NSA offered the Saudis a cut in the take. It wasn't long after that deal was struck that OPEC went the way of all flesh.

∞ ∞ ∞

Nomis was out of hospital by Friday. He spent a few days loafing around the house, reading for pleasure, answering mail and setting up a number of appointments for the week in which he was due back at work.

One of the books he dusted off was Eiseley's *The Immense Journey*. One chapter got him thinking about what Sedgewick had said concerning hyper-mutations. Anthropological evidence indicates that flowering plants had exploded on the face of the earth in a very short period of time, some eighty million years ago. It was a case of CIHPAR's horticultural topsy-turvy homologue: "now you don't see them, now you do!"

As Nomis pondered what Eiseley had to say, he found himself mumbling out loud.

"I wonder if the sudden appearance of flowering plants was preceded by a period of immense solar flare activity? Perhaps the reprieve of the sun after one of those ice ages? When will the next such explosion take place?"

His questions went unanswered. It didn't seem to matter. Working in his study felt good, even working on problems that had no solution, yet. One that he wanted very badly to solve was the source of that emotional dry spell between him and Nara.

He followed through on his own suggestion and bought two tickets to the Broncos-Chargers game for the following weekend in San Diego, surprising Nara with the tickets. He even suggested taking a short hop over to Albuquerque for a day or two on their way back to Boulder.

∞ ∞ ∞

It was a lovely starry night for a walk, like the ones he remembered when he was a child. Nomis and Nara even decided to sit cross-legged, as he had done with Yazzie and Manygoats and Redhouse, and count stars. They picked a spot on the high bluff on the edge of Tijeras Arroyo. They got to talking about how he had picked Navajo names for himself, his father, his grandpa and his great-grandpa.

"As a child, I even dreamt that I was able to spin around on the rings of Saturn," Nomis remarked.

Nara knew the stories well, as Nomis had told them to her many times before.

"How about that time you thought your blindness had also made you invisible," Nara said.

"You mean *blind means invisible*," Nomis replied.

"What an uncluttered child's mind will do to avoid the truth," Nara added.

Nara got up and walked toward the edge of the bluff.

"What about the stories you never told me, the one Manygoats told you in confidence?"

"You mean *Footprints of the Gods*," Nomis replied.

"You used Manygoats' title too!"

"Well . . . yes," Nomis admitted.

"Nomis, you little thief."

Nomis began to chant *Dahetihhi, Neasjah, Taschizzie, Jaysho* over and over again. Nara stopped a short distance from the edge and turned toward Nomis.

"Nomis, where are you, silly! It's too dark to play hide and seek. We're too old for that, anyway," Nara said.

Winter is a-coming in, this two-headed newt is singing damn . . . it's happening . . . CIHPAR you little bugger, you're back, OFF, Nomis thought nervously to himself.

Nothing happened. Absolutely nothing happened—not a flicker, nothing!

Strangely enough, his panic was short lived and only skin-deep. Deep down inside, it didn't bother him; he actually liked it, perhaps even loved it. Nomis decided then and there that he wasn't reporting what had just happened to the director or Sedgewick. He had done his duty, and if they took a knife to him again, he had no idea what the collateral damage might be.

"Where are you, Nomis?" Nara repeated frantically as she returned to where they had been sitting.

OFF, OFF, OFF, Nomis repeated again and again in his head.

Nothing happened. His mind began to roam deep within himself. It analyzed, reanalyzed, computed, distilled, re-computed, deciphered, differentiated and integrated. The words of Manygoats rung in his ears: "Someday you will understand." Suddenly, the words he needed surfaced from his heart, not his head.

"Backwards, it's got to be backwards," Nomis finally blurted out.

"Honey, where are you and what's got to be backwards?" Nara replied.

He positioned himself directly behind Nara near an outcropping of rock.

"*Jaysho, Taschizzie, Neasjah, Dahetihhi*," Nomis chanted ever so softly, over and over again.

"Over here by the big rock," Nomis shouted once he was certain he was no longer in CIHPAR's clutches.

He walked slowly toward her, pointing toward the sky.

"You know, each one of those stars is a footprint of a god," Nomis said.

Nara kissed him softly on the lips.

"And how many billions of those do you think I can . . . ?" Nara asked.

Nomis interrupted her.

" . . . count. Enough to make a very big dictionary, I suppose," he whispered.

"No, kisses, silly. I can give you a billion kisses," Nara replied.

As they drove back to their hotel, Nomis was uncharacteristically quiet. He had a fleeting notion that perhaps Sedgewick might have looked in his heart, not his head, for that missing circuit. That's where he had found it. Maybe Sedgewick or the director did know, as they said at one point, that they *wanted to get to the heart of the matter . . . but there might be too much collateral damage.*

It also occurred to Nomis that Sedgewick might have tried a little harder to stitch his finger back onto his left hand.

A three-fingered man with such a heart as mine. Impossible; or, perhaps, incredibly dangerous, Nomis thought.

Stealth can be heartless at times. It was like giving a holy man a gun! You never knew why, when or in what direction it might go off.

∞ ∞ ∞

The day after they arrived home, Nomis announced to Nara that he had some work to do in his study. He closed the door and sat down at his computer. The link to the betting pool for the NFL-AFL was quick. The next Broncos-Texans game was in three weeks.

He brought up the web page that displayed the odds for the manner in which touchdowns might be scored—for pass versus run, for yards gained by quarter, for number of field goal attempts, and so on. He concluded that none of those worked to his advantage.

He looked up the win-loss records of the Texans and the Broncos, and there it was. The Broncos had never won in Houston. Whatever it was—heat, humidity, what they ate the night before the game—they never had won in Houston.

He brought up the page permitting him to interact with the betting pool's electronic odds maker.

"What are the odds for a win by the Broncos by a point spread of four touchdowns?" Nomis keyed in.

"247 to one," the machine spat back.

"I want to place a bet on the Broncos' next game in Houston; the Broncos will win over the Texans by four touchdowns," he keyed in.

"How much?" the machine spat back.

"9,000,000 Swiss francs," Nomis keyed in.

It was a little difficult without that index finger, but he managed.

"CHF 8,000,000 at 247 to one, for a point spread of four touchdowns, Broncos over the Texans, Saturday August seven, 2053. Do you wish to go short or deposit now?" the machine responded.

I must have made a mistake, Nomis thought.

"Not 8,000,000 but 9,000,000 Swiss francs," Nomis keyed in, using his good hand.

"CHF 9,000,000 at 247 to one for a point spread of four touchdowns, Broncos over the Texans, Saturday August seven, 2053. Do you wish to go short or deposit now?" the machine returned.

"Deposit now," Nomis keyed in.

"Please make the transfer," the machine spat back.

The banking system was a wonder. Nomis gave it his one-time public-use key to facilitate the transfer of the Swiss francs from his account. Once this key had been used, the codes were changed. Only Nomis knew the details of the humpty-dumpty algorithm that produced the next key, so there was no danger.

But the few seconds that passed always bothered Nomis. During that tiny interlude, a timing hack was always possible. Monger had used such a tiny interlude to his advantage to defeat Quantum II's firewall. Those few seconds might also be exploited by Quantum II, if it were sniffing around the betting pool. That was also a source of anxiety for Nomis as some years back he had found and fixed the flaw which had foiled Quantum II's desire to access the records of the betting pool when searching for background information on both Stephan Rinkey and Ward Monger.

"An electronic signature authorization is needed to make the transfer and to place your bet. Please transmit. Where do you want the proceeds deposited in the event you are successful?" the machine queried.

Nomis sent it a one-time-use electronic signature key for his Swiss account and told the betting pool to place the winnings in the same Swiss account if he was successful.

Bad money after bad money . . . my revenge, Nomis thought.

If he were successful, nearly two billion Swiss francs would be dumped in that account next Saturday, and the betting pool might go bust to boot. If he lost, he would be out some change that he had come by in Singapore for slipping that poor sod a belt and driving him mad in his cell with CIHPAR's invisible antics. He had kept flicking himself on and off. The guy had thought he was hallucinating.

In the privacy of his study, just to be sure, Nomis called upon CIHPAR, flicking himself on and off a few times. It felt good. In fact, it loved it, and so did he!

Nomis bought one ticket to the August seventh Broncos-Texans game. He told Nara that he had to go to the Johnson Space Center in Houston on business the Friday before the game, and had made plans to stay over to attend the Broncos-Texans game with some of his NASA buddies.

37

Nomis, King of Quantum's Mechanics

Nomis arrived at COP's headquarters very early on the Monday after the game between the Texans and the Broncos. His e-mail inbox contained a note from the director, dated late the previous Saturday. A meeting was scheduled for Monday at 9 A.M. sharp, in COP's Secure Compartmentalized Information Facility, or SCIF, as it was called.

There were a number of other items. One of them was from a NASA buddy and was entitled, "Nomis, King of Quantum's Mechanics." Nomis chuckled when he opened the e-mail. On his computer screen appeared an animated stick figure, kneeling before what appeared to be a hooded executioner clutching a large, crescent-shaped blade. The figure's index finger was resting on a large wooden block. A few seconds after Nomis opened the e-mail, the blade came down and severed the stick figure's index finger. Almost instantaneously, a bogus news clipping appeared on the screen.

> Boulder, July, 2053.
>
> Then Nomis, the King of Quantum's Mechanics, laide his finger upon the blocke most quietlie, & stretching out his armes & legges cryed out in manus tuas domine three or foure times, & at the laste while one of the executioners held him slightlie with one of his handes, the other gave two strokes with the blade before he cutt his finger, & yet lefte a little gristle behinde at which time he made verie small noyse & stirred not any part of himself from the place where he laye . . .

The old English used in the phony clipping gave its source away. His NASA buddy, to suit the needs of his prank, had pilfered Richard Wingfield's original text in the *Narration of the Last Days of the Queen of Scots*, which dealt with what happened to Mary, Queen of Scots, after her secrets had been exposed.

Nomis entitled his reply "In Manus Tuas Nomis." It was short and to the point.

"Thanks. At least it wasn't my head. Illegitimati non carborundum. Cheers!"

He printed out the original e-mail, along with his reply, and stuffed it in his briefcase to share with Nara that evening.

The SCIF was located around the corner from the director's office on the tenth floor. It was used to discuss top-secret issues only, and was similar to the room in Singapore with the slatted chair, the red phone and the big red light, which lit up with the words "Room Secure" when the door clanked shut. COP's was courtlier than the one in Singapore: there was a second red light which blinked when someone wanted to enter, deliver a message, or retrieve material from those inside. Nomis preferred to call it the "lead room." Like the one in Singapore, it was shielded with lead, and when you were led into it something sinister was either underway or about to happen.

That animated stick figure came to mind as the escalator passed by the spot where he had lost his index finger. The next stop was a room similar to the one where he had first been introduced to his sidekick, CIHPAR. Both were unsettling. To reduce his anxiety, he employed a trick that never failed him. By the time he passed the director's office, he was deep in thought, cluttering his mind with all sorts of irrelevant tidbits.

Those airtight rooms are a world unto themselves, Nomis thought. *Not even the natural radiation from my body—that little bit of radiation from carbon fourteen I inhale every day of my life can escape from the SCIF's clutches. Carbon fourteen is nature's beacon or smart card, which Albert Einstein and Hans Geiger helped hack. There is a lot riding on those little bits of radiation. A thousand years from now those little bits could reveal my birthday and probably a lot more about me. Man's brain, given enough time and resources, can hack almost any code, even the secrets of nature found in the double helix.*

"Ooops," Nomis exclaimed.

To his surprise, as Nomis turned the corner, he ran headlong into Orin Sedgewick, almost knocking him off his feet. The impact dissolved the tidbits. Nomis's mind instinctively pigeonholed their essence for safekeeping. As always, Sedgewick's tone of voice was warm and personable.

"Well, how are you, Nomis? Good to see you!"

His presence caught Nomis off-guard.

What's he doing here? Nomis thought.

"Just fine," Nomis replied. "What brings you to COP so early on a Monday morning?"

"Late Saturday the director e-mailed me," he replied. "Wanted me to attend an early Monday morning meeting, so here I am. Maintenance is working on the air conditioning system. The director told me to wait outside."

"Did you fly in early today from Bethesda?" Nomis asked.

"No, yesterday morning. Took a drive up into the Rocky Mountain National Park . . . beautiful country up there," he said. "Didn't I catch a glimpse of you in the baggage area at the airport on Sunday?"

Just then, the director turned the corner. Hastily Nomis decided to ignore Sedgewick's observation about his whereabouts on Sunday morning. When the maintenance man left the room they seated themselves around the large table in the center of the SCIF. Nomis plunked his briefcase down on the floor beside his chair. The director began rifling through a sheaf of papers.

Orin looked intently at Nomis.

"Was that you I spotted at the Denver Airport yesterday morning?" he again asked Nomis.

Oh, shit, I guess I'll have to answer him, Nomis thought.

Nomis's tone was antiseptic. He hoped his mention of NASA might leave him squeaky clean.

"Yes," he replied. "I was at NASA on business last Friday."

"And you stayed over?" Sedgewick replied.

What a bitch, Nomis thought.

"Well, because of that accident on the escalator, Nara and I missed that preseason Monday night football game in Denver a few weeks ago, and you know how I love football. So, I stayed over and went to the Broncos-Texans game. Boy was it hot. The air-conditioning . . . "

Nomis' mention of the Broncos-Texans game caught the director's interest. He shoved aside his sheaf of papers, turned toward Nomis and began to rattle away like a Gatling gun.

"So, you experienced the heat firsthand? That climate control failure was a hack. We have big problems—Quantum II seems to think the origin of the hack was somewhere in Asia, perhaps the high plateau of Tibet."

Beads of sweat began to form on Nomis's brow.

"A hack? Tibet? I thought it was just a blown compressor or the like! What else have you got?" Nomis replied.

"Very little as of now. Quantum II is doing a scan of all related activity on Solarnet in the past three weeks."

"A big job?" Sedgewick asked.

"Hope to have something in the next fifteen minutes," the director replied.

The red light began to blink politely. The director left the room. When he returned, his hand was clutching a piece of paper. He handed it to Nomis.

"The scan has turned up two items. There was a lot of activity by someone between Denver and London via a server in Lhasa, Tibet, about two weeks prior to your visit to the Antarctic. Quantum II thinks that the electronic profile matches that of the three-fingered man or his son."

"Monger did freeze to death in the snow and ice, didn't he?" Sedgewick asked.

That remark cranked up Nomis's anxiety a few more notches.

How does this guy know these sorts of details about my trip? Nomis thought.

"This doesn't make any sense," Nomis replied. "Both Monger and his son were incarcerated at the time, unless that breakout from the Antarctic prison was worse than we suspected."

"Did you see the bodies?" the director asked.

Nomis glanced nervously at the second item. It seemed that Quantum II also had something to say about the win of the Broncos over the Texans.

"The son's, yes. The father's, no. But the traffic was two weeks prior to my trip," Nomis replied. "As for the breakout, I saw no evidence of anything about which I haven't already reported to you in that e-mail."

"Did the intrusion detection system apprehend any attempted hacks? Did it contain him within the prison's Demilitarized Zone once you implemented that quick fix of yours?" the director asked.

"Yes, as far as I was able to determine!" Nomis replied. "As for that activity from Tibet, it looks to me like its origin is an observatory located in Lhasa. Not very useful, or even related to the problem in Houston. Just scientific data, and a garden-variety picture of the planet Saturn."

Nomis's mind began to roam.

"Take a look at that second item; it is very strange," the director continued.

Nomis glanced again at the second item. The palms of his hands became damp with perspiration. His response was evasive.

"Was Quantum II monitoring me when I was inside the prison? Was any downloading to Quantum II underway at the time I was inside the prison?"

Sedgewick joined in.

"This is problematic. It looks like Quantum II only hacked or latched onto your dreams. It was only interested in brain activity that was deep in your subconscious. It reported nothing about your conscious activities."

He paused. A faint smile crossed his lips. He began to laugh.

"Perhaps your conscious mind is too boring," Sedgewick said.

Perhaps Quantum II's fascination with my dreams is rooted in its own inability to dream. Perhaps it was trying to discover how to do it, Nomis thought. *Or maybe Quantum II is a voyeur and just likes to watch.*

Sedgewick continued.

"That was a big disappointment to us; our new software did many things we had not expected it to do. I am convinced we don't understand how to program the interface. The two systems aren't compatible—your brain and our nanos."

"You mean my brain and CIHPAR," Nomis blurted out.

"That's one of the reasons we agreed to remove the software quickly. It's also the reason why you must report back to us anything strange which happens to you."

Does this guy already know what happened on the bluff? Nomis thought.

Sedgewick paused, and then continued. "Overall, your subconscious ran an excellent beta test and I . . . "

Now Nomis was the one who couldn't help but laugh. As he did, he searched his briefcase for the e-mail which Nara had found.

"My e-mail didn't go into detail, but I suspect that my subconscious mind discovered the three-fingered man's original wormhole, the one he used to hack Rinkey's preflight recordings of his method and technique, during that dream I had on the flight from London to Singapore, the wormhole my conscious mind uncovered while at the prison in the Antarctica. Here . . . here's the evidence that my subconscious breached the first firewall of Solarnet prior to my arrival at the prison and got into the DMZ; not the prison DMZ, but the big one here in Boulder, located twenty floors below us," Nomis said.

He handed Sedgewick the e-mail.

"What's this? 'Nomis, King of Quantum's Mechanics'?" he replied.

Nomis snatched it back. The director began to laugh.

"Sorry, the bottom one's an item for my wife."

Nomis returned the top one to Sedgewick.

"Look at this. Whoever sent this e-mail seemed to know how to breach the prison firewall and get into the DMZ here at Boulder," Sedgewick said.

"The 'whoever' you're referring to was 'my subconscious,'' Nomis replied.

"The e-mail was sent on . . . " the director asked.

"The first of July," Sedgewick replied. "Before Nomis arrived at thc prison."

"And when I finally discovered how the three-fingered man originally did it, I experienced a feeling of déjà vu, like I had known Monger's secret all along. My conclusion: my subconscious figured it out before my conscious mind came upon Monger's secret."

"Not surprising; you were the architect of the code," Sedgewick replied.

"True," Nomis said.

The director's tone of voice turned suspicious.

"This wasn't included with the material you e-mailed to me concerning your quick fix," the director said.

"No," Nomis replied.

"OK. Why was it, I mean, was your subconscious frantically asking for your password?" the director asked. "It seemed to want or need to get past the second firewall legally. Why?"

"It appears that it did not have enough time to hack it; it suddenly disappeared just as the IDS showed up," Nomis said.

"Right," the director replied. "That's when you woke up to all that shaking on the plane, which abruptly stopped about five seconds afterward."

"You may be right about figuring it out before you arrived at the prison. That dream occurred just before your visit to the Antarctic prison, and we had no other evidence of subconscious activity prior to your visit, except for those Dali clock nightmares you had in Singapore," the director continued.

How much does this guy know about what goes on in my subconscious mind? Nomis thought.

"And you were nowhere near the prison at the time of that second nightmare, the one in which you lopped off your own head," Sedgewick added. "You were back in Boulder—right?"

He knows I lopped my own head off; I've got no secrets at all, Nomis thought.

Nomis's tone turned sarcastic.

"At the prison I take it that Quantum II was listening, and there must have been a lot of telemetry. Was it checking to see if I was dreaming? It was your software, not mine! I had no control."

Orin Sedgewick's reply was unapologetic.

"Yes, it was checking every couple of seconds."

No wonder this guy knows the details; the goings-on of my subconscious must be his favorite soap opera, Nomis thought.

Nomis began to chuckle to himself.

"Was the cycle regular or random? You know, white noise—like static—or were the cycles predictable? And did the telemetry have to authenticate itself, or did Quantum II just assume it was me?"

"If it was on a regular cycle, and if Quantum II assumed the return telemetry was from Nomis and it was not, that might be Monger's most recent wormhole, the one which seems to have materialized after your quick fix," the director said.

"I did take a nap the afternoon of my second day at the prison. I was tired. I found an empty room and locked the door. But I don't recall any dreaming that went on, and as I understand it, neither does Quantum II. Anyway I'm sure my patch blocked Monger's screen saver antics," Nomis remarked.

"Screensaver antics?" the director queried.

"I'll explain later. I think Sedgewick is on to something," Nomis replied.

"So you didn't use the SCIF at the prison for your nap?" Sedgewick asked.

"No," Nomis replied, "I used the SCIF only when I wanted to gain access to Quantum II on my laptop over a secure scrambled channel. There is nothing in the regulations that says I had to sleep in the damn thing."

Nomis's mind was now roaming at full bore. When that happened, he was able to break the most insidious puzzles thrown at him. Suddenly he shouted right into the face of Sedgewick.

"THAT'S IT! THAT BETA TEST SET ME UP AS A SLEEPING, WALKING SIDE CHANNEL RIGHT INTO THE HEART OF QUANTUM II! WE'VE GOT A TEMPEST SITUATION ON OUR HANDS HERE. RADIATION FROM YOUR LITTLE BLOB OF SYNTHETIC BRAIN TISSUE MUST HAVE BEEN LEAKING OUT ALL OVER THAT PRISON. THIS TIME AROUND THE THREE-FINGERED MAN PICKED IT UP AND USED THAT UNSECURED CHANNEL TO WORM HIS WAY RIGHT INTO THE HEART OF QUANTUM II! DID YOU CHECK FOR VAN ECK RADIATION WHEN YOU INSTALLED THAT THING IN MY HEAD?"

"No," Sedgewick mumbled.

38
Illegitimati Non-Carborundum

Orin Sedgewick's Monday morning quarterbacking had come to nothing. It was Sedgewick's flawed software that had let the play breaker slip through Quantum II's well-thought-out offense.

It looks like events suggest that Monger did reveal his secrets to a third party, Nomis thought. *Whoever was responsible for the playbook the day of the climate control hack was very clever. Once the code-breaker got hold of my telemetry, he just piggybacked a ride right into the heart of Quantum II.*

Nomis seemed relieved. The director wasn't. He asked Nomis for the piece of paper, studied it and then began to rattle away with his own analysis of the play-by-play which occurred that Saturday in Houston.

"Let's see, the second item indicates Quantum II found that a three-fingered man appears to have made a bet which broke the NFL-AFL betting pool."

The heel of Sedgewick's shoe began to tap the floor.

"Have they shut it down?" he asked.

"Yes!" the director replied.

"There goes my beer and chips," Sedgewick mumbled.

Whoa! Nomis thought. *He was on the losing end of the stick*!

Even though his palms began to sweat again, Nomis couldn't help smiling.

"It first looked like the same man who initiated all that traffic from Lhasa was responsible for the wager. But, Quantum II suspected that the bet might have been set up in a manner that caused the trace to circle halfway around the world and back again. The circle turned out to be a fluke of the international communications switching system. The guy who made the bet got routed all over the place before he finally made a connection with the betting pool. It sometimes happens when loads are up. Also Quantum II decided the guy in Lhasa had four fingers, as his method and technique were a bit different from that of a man with three fingers."

The director paused as he lowered his glasses.

"The fact that the trace circled back on itself suggested that the three-fingered man had to be located right here in Boulder!"

Nomis tried to shepherd the discussion back to the first item.

"Look, I might have been infected by a virus at that prison. Whoever it was might have ridden in on the telemetry and planted some code in my subconscious which just became part of that second dream, you know, like sticking a message in a picture of a pair of giraffes and then sending that picture on to a buddy."

Nomis glanced nervously at the director and then continued.

"When deciphered, it's really child porn, an order to buy some cocaine or a signal to commit a terrorist act. With the power of these machines, this goes on all the time. Remember the Twin Towers, and those steganographic messages!"

Nomis's imagination began to run wild. Whenever it did that, it was capable of conjuring up the incredible.

"Dreams are like going to the movies before the talkies. They are only a picture show. In those disjointed images of my dream, a message might have been hidden anywhere."

His arms flailed the air as he continued.

"For example, at one point I remember I picked up a sword, to defend my poems or perhaps my very being—who knows. Quantum II might have got so engrossed in that dream that it missed what was really happening again, just like it did in the first dream or with those crazy screensavers of Mongers. That e-mail shows that my subconscious was almost into Quantum II, undetected the first time."

"Screen savers?" the director mumbled.

Nomis almost punched Sedgewick in the jaw as he thrust his left hand toward the director.

"In that second dream, when I picked up the sword, my hand had only three fingers."

His eyes shifted to Sedgewick as he continued.

"Either your implant has made me clairvoyant, or the early arrival of my three-fingered left hand was some sort of planted signal or signature that was totally missed by Quantum II."

"You're right; you didn't lose the finger on your left hand until the following day," the director added.

"Right!" replied Nomis. "Maybe Quantum II is just a very fast copy of those who wrote the code which made it tick. We have tried our best to make it super-intelligent, but maybe, just maybe, it has our faults. It can get distracted by a good tale, only sees what it wants to see or perhaps even harbors our likes and dislikes.

"Maybe that whole dream was a coded message, with many levels," Nomis continued. "Maybe the light packets chasing me up those stairs were nothing but code. As I remember, they were composed of words and numbers. There might have been a pattern to them, even simple Morse code—dots and dashes running after me up those stairs. Who knows, it might have been the code needed to break the climate control system in Houston. Worse still, maybe it was a monster virus, timed to go off on a regular schedule, aimed at all of the buildings that the climate control system monitors. This guy is smart, and the three-fingered man was probably his mentor. Have you erased that dream yet?"

What a pile of do-do, Sedgewick thought. *This guy can spin a yarn a mile long.*

"Yes," the director replied.

"Well, that's that," Nomis replied. "We'll never know."

The red light began to blink again. This time Sedgewick went to the door to retrieve the material. When he returned, he began to stare intently at Nomis's left hand. His mocking reply only increased Nomis's anxiety.

"Nomis, your reputation has preceded you. You are without doubt the biggest dreamer on the face of the earth."

Those were your requirements, you asshole, Nomis thought.

"Your explanation is the biggest pile of bullshit I have ever heard, and I might add those silent films usually had a pianist who played his heart out, dreams don't," Sedgewick continued. "No matter, you crypto nuts are full of coded messages, and that one takes the cake. You think your math always puts you ahead of us scientists. To you, we are just your humble sidekicks, along for the ride. Nomis, we look at hard evidence."

He thrust the piece of paper in his hand into Nomis's face.

"Have you had any indication that those missing circuits are still viable, still working?" Sedgewick demanded. "Quantum II has also determined that a win over the Texans by the Broncos was next to impossible last Saturday, something like ten thousand to one. It predicts that a twelfth man was on the field each time the Texans punted the ball. It also predicts that the officials couldn't have missed the infraction four times in a row, unless the twelfth man was invisible. The original odds of two hundred and forty-seven to one changed at game time, when the temperature reached ninety-nine degrees. The Broncos had been working out in Denver all week in sixty-eight-degree weather. They had arrived late Friday night, and because of the heat decided to skip the pregame warm up. Three of their linemen were playing with the throw ups. Nomis, do you want me to continue?"

Sedgewick grabbed the piece of paper from Nomis and handed it to the director, who continued to riddle Nomis's incredible theory with Quantum II's findings of fact.

"Quantum II also took a look at financial transactions following the game. A very large sum of money was transferred to a Swiss bank right after the game, just before the betting pool went bust," the director said. "Was it you who screwed up the climate control system and placed that bet? Did you use the cover of a screwed-up climate control system to mess with the odds after you made your bet, just before the game began? Did you block those punts with CIHPAR's help?"

What Nomis did next was the knee-jerk reaction of a child caught with his hand in the candy jar, who was determined to hide from the truth. He began to chant slowly *Dahetihhi, Neasjah, Taschizzie, Jaysho* over and over again.

His image began to fade.

"Turn on the gas," Nomis heard the director say.

Sedgewick produced from his breast pocket what looked like a clicker and proceeded to push its one button. A hissing sound emerged from the air conditioning vent. Both the Director and Sedgewick pulled masks from their pockets and put them on.

Shit, he has got his own version of my old clicker. I've been set up, Nomis thought.

Soon Nomis found it difficult to catch his breath. It was like being in very thin air on a mountaintop. His breath seemed to be escaping from between his ribs, wherever they were. He felt that he was suspended on some sort of middle ground. He caught a glimpse of his reflection in Sedgewick's eyeglasses. Only his head was visible.

A nasty scene developed: two grown men chasing a head around a big table. At one point, Nomis—or Nomis's head—ducked under the table. Sedgewick had to get down on his hands and knees to locate him, as Nomis's arms, body and legs were nowhere to be seen. All that was needed to complete the scene was a pianist frantically playing his heart out!

"Look, we have just reduced the oxygen content of the air in this room by flooding it with an inert gas to the borderline needed for consciousness. The atmosphere in this room is approaching the equivalent of fourteen thousand feet above sea level. Your implant won't work above that height. In fact, if we reduce the oxygen any further, your implant will shut down. You will go blind," the director yelled.

That remark cut Nomis deeply. What followed was the coup de grâce.

"You will have to shoot up to reboot your sight system. And we have control over all but one of those syringes. As I remember, you have only one in your possession," Sedgewick shouted.

"What a tale! I tell you, you're the one full of bullshit," Nomis's head replied as it bobbed from one end of the table to the other.

It's a good thing CIHPAR is still around, Nomis thought.

"We need your help and you need ours. Do as we ask! You don't have any choice!" Sedgewick yelled.

Nomis climbed out from under the table and sat down, putting his forehead on the table top. His eyes did seem a little cloudy, similar to when he had awoken from the first dream on the plane to Singapore. Orin Sedgewick put his hand on Nomis's head, the way an executioner might.

Choice under the threat of authority isn't the exercise of free will; it's a second best solution, but many times it's the best that men can offer, Nomis thought.

He sat there like that for a minute of two. The scene at Fartheringay Castle, when Mary Queen of Scots had had her head hacked off, came to mind. It seemed to fit his current situation to a T. Nomis, the king of Quantum II's mechanics, had been done in by his own brainchild.

A shower of sparks appeared in his field of vision, followed by a sensation of curtains moving across his eyes. That second dream, that horrible nightmare, flickered through his mind. An image of those swirling packets of light, boiling up around him into his secret place in the temple in Kyoto, rushed into his head. The lead room got very cold. He felt like he was being sucked down a hole in the ice, by a swift frigid current.

"What's your answer?" Sedgewick demanded.

The features of the lead room, the table, the chairs, the director, Sedgewick and the lead walls, began to take on the characteristics of a post-impressionist painting. The images of mass and receding space reaching his brain seemed to be composed of tiny packets of pigment, varying in intensity. Soon the images degenerated to a tangled mass of photo-like dots without shape or form or color. He wasn't there in his secret place in Kyoto, or circling Nara's Loop, but trapped in their secret place—their SCIF. Nomis was going blind and they had the advantage.

"In manus tuas domine," Nomis repeated. *"IN MANUS TUAS DOMINE!"*

"What did he say?" Sedgewick asked the director.

"Restore the oxygen level in the room," the director replied.

"No, what did he . . . ?" Sedgewick asked again.

"Do it, now!" the director demanded.

Soon Nomis was back, all of him.

"Look, it was me who placed the bet. Bad money running after bad money is my excuse. If winning that wager has put the NFL-AFL betting pool out of business for a while, all the better. I don't have much respect for those who profit from the innocence of others. I have always been sympathetic to those who play such games blind to the fact that the tables are tilted in favor of the house. I planned to keep only some of the winnings and give the rest to a charity for the blind. It was the way I wanted to deal with Singapore and my guilt. I am dutiful, but I have my boundaries. I also have souls to worry about, you know. Your use of my gift of stealth resulted in a man's death without a fair trial; my use won a football game. All I did was change the tilt of the table a bit in favor of the blind and the innocent. I do think there is a difference!"

The director was astounded at his confession, but less so at his defense.

"So you had nothing to do with the climate control system hack?" the director asked.

The red light began to blink again, and another note was passed to the director. Again he began to rattle away.

"Let's see. Quantum II has determined that it was probably an accomplice of the three-fingered man, located in Tibet, who hacked the climate control system. There was a lot of traffic between Singapore and Lhasa about a year ago. A trace has also been uncovered: a lot of cross-talk that originated in Tibet, made its way to Iraq and then London, finally ending in Boulder. There was also some traffic the day before the Texans-Broncos game. Strange. It was outbound traffic directly from Quantum II to Lhasa. It was a graphics initiation file again—a GIF.

Quantum II analyzed it; this report says it was just another picture of the Rings of Saturn, but Quantum II wasn't able to match it with any known photo of Saturn. It was sent to that same observatory in Lhasa which previously sent the scientific data. It wasn't encrypted, so Quantum II didn't think it was of any value. Also, there wasn't one, but two large transfers made the day of the Texans-Broncos game to banks in Switzerland. One from Iraq, and it had nothing to do with the betting pool."

"Do you have the image from that GIF?" Nomis asked.

There was a shuffle of papers as the director looked for the image associated with the GIF.

"Here," the director replied.

The minute Nomis saw it he laughed, one of those belly laughs. It felt good.

"This looks to be more than an isolated hack," Nomis said as he continued laughing. "These are the florescent particles that chased me up the stairs at Nanzen-ji Temple in Kyoto in my dream. This is clever, perhaps the most clever thing I have ever seen or dreamt. I was the mule who carried the message or whatever it was. Perhaps a monstrous virus. Whoever did this didn't even have to encrypt the message; that dream of mine did it for him and Quantum II's curiosity provided the wormhole. Then it just became a picture of the Rings of Saturn, probably sent to that same phoney observatory in Lhasa to validate that the mule had delivered the goods into the heart of Quantum II. God knows what else those rings might port. We now have to assume that Monger did tell someone about his newest gismo and via my head that someone also got into Quantum II's climate control system. There might be some server in Lhasa or Baghdad or London clicking away with a surprise a week. The only thing to do is track the accomplice down. But stealth is the secret here. We can't let the other side know what we know. It is an old principle. It gives us the advantage."

Nomis then turned to Sedgewick who, during the last two hours, he had grown to dislike immensely.

"You can well see how one can lose the advantage to anyone who knows how to play this cat-and-mouse game. You had the code right under your nose, encrypted in my second dream, and you erased it. That lousy beta test permitted whoever is responsible for this mess to set up a side channel into the heart and soul of both me and Quantum II.

Because of this, we have now got a war on our hands—a cyber war; a war of mathematicians."

Orin Sedgewick became defensive and he flaunted the clicker in Nomis's face.

"There remains the issue of your continued ability to go stealth. You didn't keep your end of the bargain and report any abnormalities to us."

The director looked at Nomis, then at Orin, and then at Nomis again.

"*In manus tuas* Nomis," the director mumbled to Sedgewick.

"What was that?" Sedgewick asked.

"Forget it! Nomis and his disappearing act can be very useful to COP, given the current situation."

"*Illegitimati non carborundum,*" Nomis mumbled to himself.

"*Illegitimati non carborundum?*" Sedgewick queried.

This is definitely cyber war. And as such it has restored my advantage, Nomis thought as he walked toward the door.

"*Nolite te bastardes carborundorum,*" was Nomis's reply as the door clanked shut.

"What did he say?" Sedgewick again asked the director.

"You're an M.D. And you don't know any Latin?"

Orin Sedgewick shrugged his shoulders.

"We are in Nomis's hands. Don't let the bastards get you down," the director replied.

"I don't intend to," Sedgewick declared.

You ignorant, egotistical son of a bitch, the director thought as he departed the SCIF.

39
Button Pushing

Since their return from San Diego, the emotional dry spell that Nara felt had been laid to rest seemed to be up and about again. Nomis's demeanor soon rivaled that of those first few days in the hospital. He seemed uncommunicative, reserved and indifferent toward her. On Monday when Nara arrived home from work she discovered Nomis had spent the afternoon sequestered in his study on the phone with the lexicographer from Oxford. Shortly before dinner a courier delivered an envelope addressed to Nomis. At dinner the phone rang several times. Nomis only revealed to her that a problem had cropped up somewhere in Asia which needed, as he put it, his personal touch. Nara questioned him repeatedly about the particulars, but he remained quite taciturn. After dinner, she wasn't able to pry much of anything out of him, except the vaguest of details. It wasn't until she was drifting off to sleep that Nomis's reticence subsided.

I guess I ought to throw her a few bones, Nomis thought.

"I'll be stopping in London before going on to Iraq, Hong Kong, and Tibet. I'll probably be coming home by way of Tokyo," Nomis whispered in her ear.

"Around the world?" Nara mumbled.

"Yes, you might say that," Nomis replied.

"I'll remain home on Tuesday to help you pack," Nara was quick to add as she sat bolt upright in bed.

Not good, Nomis thought.

"Pack!" Nomis hastily snapped. "I suspect your motives are partly selfish. What's your second agenda?"

Now that was completely out of character. The more information I'm able to wring from you before you depart, the less I'll have to pump out of you upon your return, Nara thought. *If I bare my soul, it might loosen your jaw . . .*

"Well. The aftermath of the trip to Antarctica was full of surprises. Your quiet manner has produced an intuitive feeling within me. Is the potential for more of the same lurking in the background?"

"Come on, Nara, how many times must I . . . "

"OK, OK," Nara mumbled as her imagination ran wild.

∞ ∞ ∞

On Tuesday morning, at every opportunity, Nara continued to press Nomis for information, but to no avail. He remained evasive and tight-lipped. Out of desperation, Nara went online and took a peek at his Visa statement on the off chance it might be revealing. At lunch, Nara was brimming with unanswered questions.

"Nomis, I confess. I was checking our Visa statements and found an item that might be fraudulent," Nara said.

"Fraudulent?" Nomis replied.

"Yes, fraudulent! An item purchased at the Mountain Outfitters."

You nosy little . . . Now, where did I put that stuff? Yes, in the carriage house, Nomis thought.

He made a joke of the whole thing.

"They don't call me Heinrich Harrer for nothing," Nomis said. "But let me tell you, I don't plan to spend seven years . . . "

Nara was incensed at his flippant attitude.

"Who's Heinrich Harrer?" Nara asked.

"Oh, a German prisoner of war who escaped over the Himalayas."

"Nomis, for the second time this summer I am feeling very uneasy," Nara interrupted.

"Come on, Nara. This trip is no different from the one I took to Antarctica," Nomis replied.

"That's why I feel so uneasy. Who knows what will get into you this time?" Nara said.

Nara's response was thoughtless, driven by emotive forces that had been building prior to Nomis's sojourn in Houston. Nomis, although clearly angered by her remark, concealed his displeasure.

"Now that was unkind, terribly unkind," Nomis said. "I'm not . . . "

"Well, so far I can only see bits and pieces, vague shadows. The substance of your trip is lacking. You have never been so close-mouthed," Nara replied.

Nomis was taken aback by her unexpected choice of words.

Bits and pieces, vague shadows. Does she suspect? Did I accidentally activate CIHPAR in my sleep again? Nomis thought. *No, impossible, it would have freaked her out!*

"I get the feeling that a lot is going on that I'm not privy to," Nara added. "Why won't you confide in me? I'm your wife. What's this *personal touch* business all about, anyway?"

Women can be incredibly perceptive at times, Nomis thought. *Their sixth sense is scary, really scary. Or maybe I'm just paranoid!*

Men can be so dense at times, Nara thought. *Maybe Nomis is having an affair. Sometimes men leave coded confessions. It's the way they deal with their guilt!*

"You know what the personal touch is all about," Nomis replied. "What's bothering you, honey? You know the rules. I can't . . . "

"What rules?" Nara asked disparagingly.

Nomis shook his head in disbelief.

"COP has its secrets. You know."

"I've heard that one before and know what it means. It's the brick wall I and everybody else hit when institutions decide it's time to clam up. Nomis, this is my house as much as yours. I make some of the rules here. What goes on here is my concern. I have a right to know what's happening inside these four walls."

Touché, Nomis thought. *She's really trying to push my buttons. Better throw her a few more bones.*

"OK, OK," Nomis replied.

The backwash from Nara's headfull of questions swirled around Nomis like the waters from the Bay of Fundy. At times he thought he might be sucked under.

"How about all that telephone and courier traffic, which began late yesterday just after I arrived home!"

"All I can say is that it will probably continue off and on until early tonight. This trip is short notice. I have much to do."

Nomis paused.

"And don't get upset when you see the phone bill. I was on the phone with that chap from Oxford all . . . " Nomis replied.

"You and your funny dictionary. Didn't you tell me that project was of little interest to you? You were going to . . . " Nara replied.

"No, I said that . . . " Nomis began.

"The director called you right in the middle of dinner last night! What was that all about?" Nara asked.

"There's nothing new there. He instructed me to make plane reservations to leave for London on . . . " Nomis replied.

"Early this morning I overheard you arranging for a courier!" Nara said.

"The office is sending me a supply of reboot cylinders, and I confirmed my plans with the director; I leave on Wednesday morning. I also indicated to him that I'd be working at home today," Nomis replied.

After lunch a courier arrived with a package for Nomis.

He decided to gamble on its contents.

"Here, Nara, you open it. I've nothing to hide," Nomis said.

Some of Nara's tension dissipated as she unwrapped the package and found it contained nothing but ten reboot cylinders.

"You see, nothing but the antidote. All this activity is just routine preparation for my trip. Maybe the rush is getting to you. Relax, honey," Nomis added.

Nomis also began to loosen up a little after the antidote arrived.

"Now these are slick. A new and improved design. Much easier to use and more versatile," Nomis remarked.

"More versatile? What do you mean?" Nara asked.

"Be careful! Those little cylinders are driven by compressed air," Nomis said.

"They're color-coded, too. Some are red and some are white," Nara replied. "They remind me of those things dentists use to inject pain killers."

"They look more like an Epinephrine auto injector. You know, for bee stings," Nomis added.

Nomis carefully examined one of the cylinders.

I'll add a bit more information to the unwrapping, just enough to quell her anxiety and her neverending stream of questions, Nomis thought.

"Quantum's focus on the suspected source of the problem is definitely located in Tibet," Nomis said. "I'll need more than the usual two doses on this trip, because of the high altitude and thin oxygen. I guess that's what is meant by more versatile, suited for high-altitude use."

Nara flashed that coy little smile at Nomis. It made him feel he had finally struck a balance between what he knew and what he was willing to tell her.

"And the item you purchased at the Mountain Outfitters?" Nara asked.

Nomis had been fooled by that coy little smile before. He had no choice but to come clean.

"An oxygen mask with a variable flow rate adjustment used by rock climbers to provide a periodic hands-free burst of oxygen, an assortment of rock climber's pulleys and a tube of shoe goo used for temporary boot repairs when in a place like Lhasa," Nomis replied.

"Lhasa," Nara replied. "The chance of a lifetime. I'll carry your bags!"

"Oh, is that what this is all about?" Nomis added. "Sorry, not this time."

His reply was too quick, and without any sympathy for denying me the chance of a lifetime, Nara thought.

"Shoe goo, a rock climbers mask, pulleys . . . what . . . "

"I plan to do a little hiking, maybe even a little rock climbing," Nomis replied.

∞ ∞ ∞

Those ten doses of the reboot chemical got Nomis thinking. In the early afternoon he headed straight for the old carriage house. As he exited the kitchen he told Nara he needed a break and wanted to work with his hands for a while. He asked her not to disturb him for a few hours. He locked the doors, turned on the lights and put some old sheets across the side windows. He placed the oxygen mask, four of those cylinders, his digital memory stick camera, the pulleys, and a mirror on the workbench. He used the tube of shoe goo to seal shut the little vents on either side of the mask which permitted fresh air to mix with the flow of oxygen.

His mind became a centrifuge of activity. It wasn't long before he too was brimming with a slew of unanswered questions. It spun off question after question as he went about making the preparations needed to answer them. They pecked away at him like a flock of hungry starlings that had just come upon a tomato patch full of slugs. His questions, like Nara's, were hungry for answers.

Is the circuitry which controls CIHPAR separate from that which controls my sight? Nomis pondered. *With car radios these days, buttons are multi-function; the same buttons control the tuner, the chip player, the plasma screens and the GPS system. Is the same true for what is left of the technology in my head? The OFF command for the cell and the e-mail had been entangled with the OFF command for the stealth sequence by MAIHEM's engineers. The OFF command ended up serving both options by mistake. CIHPAR has mysteriously reprogrammed itself once the cell and e-mail option were removed.*

For the transition to stealth, the four-word chant is now the energizing cue, not simply CIHPAR *repeated four times. And why is the* OFF *command now useless? Is my stealth state influenced by the reboot chemical, or is it only responsive to the chant* Dahetihhi, Neasjah, Taschizzie, Jaysho? *How are the reboot chemical and the four-word chant related, if at all? I always feel a little faint when I chant . . . it seems that the transition to stealth might be a big consumer of oxygen.*

Is going stealth like taking off in a big jet, where fifteen percent of the fuel load is used to get airborne? Once in that state, less fuel might be needed. In view of such mechanics, a reboot might or might not affect me when in stealth state.

Nomis paused. He heard footsteps. It was Nara. His pulse quickened. He lay down on the garage floor, near the front of the car.

That's strange, it's locked, Nara thought as she tried to push the door open.

"Nomis, are you in there?" Nara yelled.

"Yes," Nomis replied.

"Open the door. The director's on the phone again."

"I'm sorry; he'll have to call back. I'm under the car."

"Under the car? What are . . . ?" Nara asked.

"Found a loose hose, fixing it for you," Nomis replied.

As Nara's footsteps receded, Nomis sprang to his feet and checked the doors and windows again. As he did, his mind began to roam.

Pure mathematics is no help here, he thought. *Need to reverse engineer myself, take myself apart. Impossible, I'm flesh and bones, hate to admit it. Mathematics' poor relation, experimental science, the only route.*

Nomis shook his head.

Experimental science in an old carriage house without proper controls or instruments? he thought.

But that's exactly what Nomis planned to do with the equipage he had brought with him, if experimental science, and pushing one's own buttons and watching what happened might be regarded as one and the same.

Pretty crude, thought Nomis. *Sedgewick might regard what I'm about to do as self-diagnosis. Something that any sane person ought to avoid. But I really have no choice in the matter.*

Nomis's head began to spin again as the muscles in the back of his neck tightened.

I feel much like a piece of complicated electronics without an easy-to-read and easy-to-understand manual, Nomis thought. *Have no idea what will happen when I push this or that button in this or that sequence.*

He took the towrope from the trunk of his car and fashioned one end of it into a harness that fit under his arms and between his legs, like what might support a man or woman in a parachute. He attached the end of the rope with the harness to a ceiling hook located in the back, off to one side. That old hook had probably been used to hang the carcass of a deer or steer after the kill, or truss up the hoof of a horse when being shod. It was big enough to support a team of horses. To relieve the tension he began to fill his mind with bits of trivia.

Must have been how Chadwick felt, back in the 1940s. Ended up searching for those neutrons in a POW camp—the converted stables of a cold and windy Potsdam racecourse. Feel a bit like I'm off to the races myself. This time I intend to keep the winnings.

To attach the rope he used a slipknot, which could be unraveled by tugging on the loose end, which he left dangling. He moved an old blacksmith's stool over, climbed into the harness and kicked the stool out from under himself.

. . . had no easy-to-read manual either, Nomis thought. *Wanted to know what the interior of an atom's nucleus looked like, how the mechanics were organized. Took him fifteen years to crack that egg. Managed to sustain his search for those elusive little buggers by bribing his guards. Needed a compound that the Berlin Auer Company used in toothpaste to make teeth glow in the dark—thorium. Boy, could I use some aspirin right now, or a cold beer.*

He was left suspended in the harness, but was firmly supported by the hook. He tugged on the loose end of the rope and dropped to the floor. He reset the height of the harness so his feet just touched the floor. He was now sure it would keep him from cracking his head when he blacked out.

Nomis felt something like a POW, too, in a war between a dead man's code, whoever the dead man's accomplice was, and COP. To COP he was a trusted agent. He would do his duty. But he was in that war, now, partly for his own salvation. Like Nara's, his motives were partly selfish too. He also had a second agenda.

Unlike Chadwick, who had bribed his keepers to secure the constant supply of thorium needed in his experiments, Nomis didn't know how many extra cylinders he might cajole from the director to replace those he intended to use that afternoon. And he didn't have fifteen years; he had only one short afternoon before he left for London. At least it wasn't cold and windy that Tuesday. It was the dog days of August, hot and humid.

Nomis worked for another half-hour to organize the pulleys, digital camera, mirror and oxygen mask into a system that permitted him to answer most of his questions. He intended to rig the mask to simulate various altitudes for a given number of minutes and record what happened when he was out cold, using the digital camera.

The director had warned Nomis not to mess with the implant shutdown mechanism. It was a very tricky business, as Nomis had learned the day before in the SCIF. But pushing his own buttons and watching what happened was much more attractive than having someone else push his buttons, especially someone at COP.

After putting a few cylinders in his pocket, he carefully reviewed what had happened in the SCIF on Monday morning.

As I chanted, the oxygen content in the SCIF dropped, Nomis thought. *My image began to fade, didn't black out. Implant didn't shut down. Vision became clouded, ended up in an in-between state, half-blind and half-invisible. The director restored the oxygen, didn't have to chant. All of me came right back, including my failing vision.*

He began to pace to and fro. Sweat rolled from his forehead. As he passed the window with the old sheet over it, he peeked out. Nara was nowhere to be seen. He was clearly on edge.

I could suffocate and duplicating Monday morning's outcome might be a waste of a cylinder, he thought. *Let's see . . . the chant and the reduction of oxygen were simultaneous, in Monday's case. I tried to go stealth the instant the inert gas was released, but I never achieved full stealth or blacked out—never lost my sight. So why should I? Perhaps to complete that cycle. In what state might I be if I had blacked out in the lead room and full stealth hadn't been achieved by the time my eyes shut down?*

Nomis began to laugh. It reduced his tension.

Perhaps a bodiless, blind head lying motionless on the floor? Nomis thought. *Maybe a blind and stealth-less body in the same predicament? And in what state might I be when I came to: a bodiless, blind head or a blind, stealth-less body? Yes; it's worth it to complete the cycle which the director initiated in the SCIF, to be sure of the outcome!*

Again Nomis heard footsteps and again it was Nara.

"I need the car," Nara yelled. "Want to mail a package and go grocery shopping."

Nomis had to scramble to dismantle the paraphernalia dangling from the hook in the ceiling and hide the motley assortment of items he had placed on the bench.

"OK, OK," Nomis replied as he unlocked the carriage house door.

"You're clean as a whistle, Hose Man," Nara remarked.

"Hose Man?" Nomis replied.

Nara smiled.

"Dr. Hose Man, then," Nara said.

"I was very careful," Nomis replied.

As she closed the car door, her eye caught the old sheet draped over the window.

More bits and pieces; more like Dr. Slick Tool, Nara thought as she backed the car from the carriage house.

Nomis closed the door, reassembled his contraption, climbed into the harness, turned on the digital camera, donned the mask and set the oxygen flow at its lowest level. Several bursts of oxygen were to follow at the three-minute mark. He hoped the setting would simulate the atmosphere at fourteen thousand feet and then revive him. Once he began to feel light-headed, he also began to chant: *Dahetihhi, Neasjah, Taschizzie, Jaysho.* The chanting accelerated his light-headedness. It also produced an urge to rip the mask from his face. It was all his iron will was able to do to resist his instinct for self preservation.

When he came to, he was blind. He administered the reboot chemical and regained his sight. His stealth was gone. He reset the camera and reviewed his handiwork. It was worth a good belly laugh. While unconscious, there was his head, floating above the harness, helpless as could be. When he regained consciousness, but before he administered the reboot chemical, he was back, all of him.

Never try to go stealth when losing consciousness at the same time, Nomis thought. *A shortage of oxygen screws things up. The draw of oxygen when making the transition to a stealth state seems to be very, very great. If I pass out, half-in and half-out, during the transition to stealth, that's the way I remain: half-in and half-out. The transition to stealth probably shuts down of its own accord.*

Nomis chuckled to himself.

The eyes have it, so to speak, Nomis thought. *When I regain consciousness, the process also reverses itself without chanting. Without enough fuel being pumped into those jet engines, I never get airborne, a delicate state to be in, as one approaches the end of the runway.*

In fact, that was exactly what might have happened in the lead room if the director hadn't demanded that Sedgewick turn off the gas. If Nomis had blacked out, he'd have been a bodiless head, prone on the floor; a very precarious position to be in if someone had wanted to take a hack or two.

Let's see, Nomis thought. *The difference between the next case and yesterday's is no simultaneity. Events occur one after the other. If I'm in a state of stealth and then black out, is stealth retained after I black out? And when I regain consciousness—if I reboot—will I retain my stealth? If yes to both, then once in the stealth state, that state is independent of a black out-sight loss-reboot cycle!*

Nomis removed the mask, turned on the digital camera again and began to chant *Dahetihhi, Neasjah, Taschizzie, Jaysho*. In about a minute he had achieved full stealth. He reset the oxygen flow and donned the mask. Within one minute he blacked out. When he came to, he was blind. He administered the antidote and regained his sight. As he did, Nomis noticed a faint image of himself flickering in the mirror and a slight touch of light-headedness.

He played back what the digital camera had recorded to establish his state when he was either unconscious or conscious, but blind. Then Nomis chanted to restore his image. The transition appeared to be normal, with no evidence of flickering. He was back, all of him.

It seemed that stealth is independent of my loss of sight, caused by a blackout, and the subsequent reboot cycle, except for the flickering image at reboot time. When in a stealth state, this suggested that the draw of oxygen by my brain at reboot is so great that the ongoing need for oxygen required to maintain my aura of Plasmons is compromised.

This time it was like going into a steep climb in a fighter jet with its after-burners fully deployed, or a house full of appliances with not enough amps to get them up and running all at once. Every bit of power was needed to both approach and maintain the angle of ascent, or the plane might stall. When vacuuming, if the fridge went on, the lights might dim. If the air conditioner was also drawing power at the time, the fridge might just blow a fuse.

Even when making the transition to a stealth state, he felt a little faint—no doubt his metabolism was going through the roof. Once in a stealth state he remained invisible regardless of the need for a reboot cycle, provided there was no shortage of oxygen.

He toyed with the idea of returning to the first case and testing one of its variants, but the idea of rebooting to regain his sight and chanting at the same time, given the huge draw of oxygen which resulted, appeared very risky.

Nomis paused. His brow furrowed as he scratched his head.

I sure as hell don't want to get stuck in a stealth state for the rest of my life, regardless of how much I like it, Nomis thought. *Pushing my own buttons in the wrong sequence might send me right back to Bethesda.*

No doubt Nara would understand. She often had to return her laptop to the dealer after she screwed up the operating system or the bios by hitting the wrong key, or not understanding what she was doing when fooling around with various options. But having to explain to Sedgewick or the director how his implant had got all messed up wasn't a happy thought. He decided against it. He didn't want any blown fuses in his head from an overload.

He did try fiddling with the amount of the antidote needed to get rid of the faint image of himself at reboot time if he was also in stealth state, but a double dosage produced such a rush that he gave up trying to establish a more suitable dosage. What he was planning was risky enough. He had used up four of the ten doses, anyway, and there was Nara to worry about. She might return at any time. As Nomis went about dismantling his little laboratory, he was compelled to ponder a third case.

40

Mirror, Mirror on the Wall

Let's see, Nomis thought. *The topsy-turvy case—a variant of the first case . . . already toyed around with it; rejected it.* No, *no, the reverse of the second case: blind, then invisible, in sequence with three parts, first variant: no reboot cylinder on hand to regain my sight when invisible; second variant, chanting restores both sight and image; third variant . . .*

He paused. A smile crept across his face. He found himself mumbling out loud.

"Might I be able to see with my heart? When I was blind as a young boy, in my dreams I was able to see!"

He toyed in his mind with his grandpa's explanation.

Had to be a good man to see with my heart, Nomis thought. *Worked in my dreams . . . but with this new technology, don't know the outcome . . . only in my dreams did it happen; only there was I able to see!*

Nomis walked over to the workbench, propped up the mirror on an old tin of nails and began lecturing his image.

"In a topsy-turvy world you might be forever blind when visible if you weren't able to get your hands on a constant supply of those cylinders. Worse still, life might become a one-way window. You could see out, but no one could see in? Such a situation wouldn't clash with your personal make-up. The implant had been designed to interface with your personality. Ordinarily you don't let people in on what you've thinking in a straightforward manner. Your output, especially when it comes from deep within you, is always coded. That is your image or perhaps the better word is footprint!"

His image turned an ashen white. This particular outcome of the third variant was unthinkable.

Was already one screw-up, OFF command's crossed circuits, might be other screw-ups, he thought. *Fooling with this technology might bring on a horrific result; might trap myself in a world of blindness when visible, and one of stealth with sight!*

The mechanics of this outcome came a little too close to home. Nomis began to chide his mirror image. Anyone within earshot might have thought the heat of the day had rendered him silly.

"In cryptography there is what one calls one-way functions. The math is quite peculiar. Some people call these mathematical constructs 'humpty dumpty functions'. Once they take a great fall, it is hard to put them back together again. They are the foundation of secret-keeping on Solarnet. You have to have very special software and very fast computers to undo a hash function, as one-way functions are sometimes called."

While on the university circuit, Nomis had often used the word *hysteresis* to describe a hash function's one-way window property. Words like 'hash' had repeatedly confused the naive latecomers to his lectures on Solarnet security. Most thought they had mistakenly stumbled upon a talk on culinary science rather than cryptography. Nomis's antics didn't help. He often illustrated the concept using an egg as the only prop, which he hard-boiled during the course of the lecture, eating it at the end.

From somewhere deep inside, Nomis felt something struggling to gain his attention.

You know how to make it solid, just apply heat, it whispered. *But you don't know how to return it to its original state—yet.*

Nomis paused. The hair on the back of his neck bristled.

Those are the very words I tossed out at the end of my Solarnet security lectures, prior to gulping down the egg, Nomis thought.

Usually dusted with a little salt and pepper, the voice from deep inside replied.

He began to feel cold and anxious. The phrase Sedgewick had used the day Nomis was briefed on the workings of the cell and the e-mail option rang in his ears.

"Or perhaps, never," Nomis shrieked. "SHIT . . . was that son-of-a-bitch aware of the risks, BUT . . . BUT DIDN'T TELL ME?"

The one-way window aspect of a hash function married to the technology in his head horrified him. Nomis thought for a moment he was hallucinating. His mirror image seemed to be struggling to gain his attention. He reached out and touched the mirror's surface. To his astonishment, his image spoke to him.

"I am your silent partner in this war of yours. I have come up with my own insidious defense—a place that will insulate both you and me from this increasingly cruel world of terrorists. A place, where light can get in but not out. The director has said that I am a powerful maestro of stealth. Your crazy dreams are my proof. It was I who reprogrammed the stealth option to respond to your childhood code names for you, Yazzie, Manygoats and Redhouse."

Nomis was both fearful and flabbergasted. His heart pounded. A torrent of perspiration formed a damp circle between his shoulderblades. Finally his fist came crashing down, breaking the mirror into a jumble of little pieces which lay scattered about the bench. He scolded them as he swept them into a pile, which he deposited in the garbage can by the door. The side of his hand bore its revenge. A small gash bled profusely for a minute until he blotted it with a clean paper towel.

"You want to entrap me in your crazy up becomes down world," Nomis bellowed. "I have encountered those worlds before and want nothing to do with them."

He had a horrible feeling that the blind-to-invisible sequence might permanently shut down the technology in his head. The key to undoing that process mightn't be a simple antidote or chant. The password might be much more difficult to come by; a complicated balance between feeling and reason, managed by his subconscious. If one didn't strike the right balance, one might be blind in this world, but have one's sight in a world of stealth.

What a choice you offer! Nomis thought. *God damn, what a choice!*

His thoughts roamed back to the SCIF.

Choice under the threat of authority isn't the exercise of free will, but it's the best that men can come up with; the second best, he thought. *The threat . . . the authority of the unknown or of ignorance, not the director or Sedgewick. Not appealing at all. Know neither the outcome nor the way back with certainty.*

A blank stare consumed Nomis's face.

"And I don't know if I'm a good man," Nomis muttered. "Or, worse still, how many players there are in this game of cyber war! I have my own agenda; I am not only COP's agent, but also I have become my own agent—a double agent of sorts. That makes two. I am also the custodian of a dead man's code. That makes three. For whom is my subconscious working? That makes four. Maybe Quantum has left some code that is able to take control of CIHPAR ticking away inside my head, ready to go off at COP's command. After all, the director had felt its power. That makes five, and the three-fingered man makes six. Before his death, he might have planted more code in my head, other than those florescent particles which chased me up the steps at Nanzen-ji in that dream of mine."

As he dismantled the harness, his thoughts went back to the New Mexico desert and that other dream he once had, and what his grandpa had said to him one starry night:

> In my eyes, there was a tiny camera that takes a picture using magic paper. Inside my head was a little darkroom, to make that magic paper work, but very, very small. There is always some truth in your dreams, but only you can know that truth. Will my eyes ever run out of that magic paper? If they did, a Navajo can see with his heart, if he is a good man . . .

His head sank slowly into his hands.

If the circuitry related to stealth has already migrated to my heart or become part of the pneumogastric or vagus nerve, then it might function at a higher altitude in thinner air, thought Nomis. *The brain is the biggest consumer of oxygen . . . it would go first. That's what fainting is all about: it's the body's way of rendering me horizontal on the floor to insure the blood flow to the brain is increased, and thus the oxygen. The transition to stealth many times made me feel faint. Perhaps it was the competition between heart and brain, between feeling and reason, which caused light-headedness during the transition. Perhaps there is some part of me, some other half, which doesn't quite know if it should lay me horizontal, giving me time to reconsider what I might be about to do. Perhaps it is my love for Nara.*

∞ ∞ ∞

By late Tuesday afternoon, Nomis's outlook had noticeably improved. Getting all of that intellectual bile out in the open was the perfect elixir. He dismantled and disposed of the apparatus in the garage. Wrecking the digital camera's memory stick was next, but as he was searching for a hammer to do the deed, Nara returned from her errands. Helping her carrying in a week's groceries for one person wasn't a big job, but that, and the urgent need to phone MAIHEM to obtain four extra cylinders to replace the ones he had used that afternoon, distracted him. He got the run-around from the supply clerk. MAIHEM needed the director's OK for the release of more than one cylinder. This upset him. He fretted over the possibility that he might end up with only seven cylinders, or eleven minus the four he had used that afternoon.

The casualty was the memory stick. It remained in the digital camera on the bench in the garage.

Tuesday evening at dinner, Nara sensed that he was much less relaxed than at lunch. She tried to defuse his tension with small talk.

"Well, I went to the post office today to mail a package to the kids and I had to wait ten minutes at the service window. There was no one around."

Nomis's reply was sullen.

"I returned the director's call just before dinner."

At one point during the to and fro between Nomis and Nara, the number seven surfaced. It made no sense to Nara; she insisted by her count he had eleven cylinders. Again the bits and pieces didn't seem to add up. Nomis didn't dare divulge to Nara the choicest tidbit of his conversation with the director. She might have walked out on him, right then and there.

Nomis and the director had also finalized an agreement whereby Quantum would anonymously return Nomis' winnings to the betting pool, no questions asked. Rumor had it that the bookies were now under investigation for rigging the Texans-Broncos game. COP hoped the no-questions-asked return of the winnings would quell the rumors. The director didn't want Nomis's name, or that of the investigative branch, COP's, Quantum II's, or MAIHEM's, to surface during any future investigation. If it did, COP planned to blame it on a software glitch.

After dinner, Nomis retired to his study to attend to a few last-minute details. He was fiddling with his e-mail when Nara appeared at the door, holding the digital camera. She had the strangest look on her face. She couldn't help laughing.

"You must have left the digital camera in the garage. I found it on the workbench when I put the garbage out. What are these funny pictures of you hanging from the ceiling of the garage in . . . in what looks like a parachute harness, with that mask over your face, Nomis?"

Nomis was dumbstruck. Nara's laughter soon became a guffaw as she cycled through the pictures.

"Nomis, there must be something wrong with the camera. In some shots, only your head is visible; in one case, you keep fading in and out," Nara said. "Oh! Here's one where you look like you're sound asleep."

Stupid, stupid, stupid, Nomis thought.

He nuzzled Nara gently on the cheek as he peeled her fingers from the digital camera. Nara let out a little giggle as she slowly released her grip. As he was about to offer an explanation, Nomis's jaw snapped shut, clamping down on his tongue. His straight-faced explanation was incredible.

"Nara, I am planning to do a little hang-gliding in Tibet. Remember when we took that short course with the Denver Club a few years back, on vacation in Acapulco on my 49th birthday? Well, I was just getting the hang of it, so to speak."

"Very funny. But that wasn't really hang-gliding," Nara replied. "Weren't you tethered to a rope and pulled by a power boat?'

Nara paused.

"Hey, aren't lakes in Tibet icy cold?" she added.

Or is this another one of those bits and pieces? Nara thought.

Again Nara paused.

"Nomis, did you break a mirror in the garage today?" Nara said without thinking. "I found a lot of bits and pieces in the garbage."

Nomis's face remained expressionless as he nodded.

"It was the following year in California, now that was hang gliding," Nara continued. "You almost got blown out to sea. Anyway, Tibet hasn't any warm bodies of water in which you might end up, does it? They're all glacier-fed, aren't they?"

Nomis's reply was flippant.

"OK, think what you want. I wore the mask to see how it might feel when I jump from Everest. It's some thirty thousand feet high. I'll call you from Tibet, if I can, as I'm floating down; fill you in on the details of my adventure, OK?"

Nara's reply was sassy.

"Anyway, I'd like to send the memory stick to the kids as proof you're still human—except for your eyes, OK?"

Nomis's response was quick, but he was careful to be solicitous.

"Please don't. I need . . . " Nomis pleaded.

"Then, I'll send it by e-mail!" Nara interrupted.

There was no answer from Nomis. He just put the digital camera in its case and tucked it away in the bottom drawer of his desk. Nara didn't press the point. Later he found her sound asleep in the back room. He retrieved the digital camera, reset it, pointed it at her and let it roll.

When Nara awoke, he told her that he had taken a few shots of her with the digital camera. Nara suggested he take them with him to show her good friend Doris who was now living just outside London. He agreed and took a few more shots of their new house.

That's the end of those funny pictures, he thought as they trundled off to bed.

"Nomis, those silly pictures—they are so ridiculous. I still think the kids might like to see what their humanoid dad does in his spare time. So I hope you don't mind; I still want to send a copy to the kids," Nara said.

"What do you mean by 'humanoid'?" Nomis asked.

"Well, your eyes, Honey. Don't they tip the scales in the direction of a machine?" Nara joked.

"I confess. Without thinking I used the stick to take those shots of you and the house, Nara," Nomis replied. "I think I erased them by accident."

Nara seemed to expect as much. Her silence was evidence enough that Nomis was living up to both the letter and spirt of his maxim.

Stupid of me to leave that memory stick in the digital camera, but my plan won't unravel now, Nomis thought. *It is very interesting how* CIHPAR *gives me the confidence to bluff my way through almost anything . . . the little crisis of the funny pictures didn't bother me that much. It was so incredible—Nara didn't see it exactly for what it was, but rather saw it as an error of the camera's eye, just like the error the human eye often makes as it sits idle in a train when another departs. We are seldom willing to take giant steps in the way we look at things, and this gives the advantage to those who have done so already. I have already taken my giant step. I wonder if, and when, Nara will take hers.*

41
Lawn Mowing

After landing at Heathrow, Nomis headed for the Millennium Gloucester Hotel. It was early, about 8:30 A.M. Rather than hang around the lobby for two and a half hours until check-in time, he paid for the extra day. He hadn't slept during the flight and intended to nap for an hour or two. On the way to his room, he asked the concierge to find the address and telephone number of Nara's friend, Doris Witherby (nee: Lewellyn), who had recently moved from Plymouth to Windsor. He wanted to follow through on his promise to Nara and post the digital memory stick to Doris. He was puzzled when the concierge presented him with the information that he requested. Doris had made a last-minute decision and bought a property in Henley-on-Thames, the little town where the famous rowing regatta—The Henley—is held each year.

Henley. Often drew on the analogy of Alfred's seamless machine in my attempts to cut out the stove-piping within COP, and, later on, elsewhere, at NSA, CIA *and* FBI, Nomis thought as he stuffed the piece of paper with the address on it in his breast pocket.

He set the alarm on the clock radio for noon, pulled the curtains closed, flopped down onto the bed and promptly began to doze. The phone rang a couple of times, but in his torpid state it was easy to ignore. By 11:30 A.M., he felt refreshed. He showered, shaved and dressed, after which he retrieved his messages: one from Nara and one from the U.S. ambassador. A briefing had been scheduled later that afternoon at the embassy. He returned the ambassador's call, indicating that he would be there at 3:30 P.M., as requested. Then he called Nara.

"You're up early, honey," Nomis said.

"Couldn't sleep," Nara replied.

"Me neither. I was napping when you called. Had one of my crazy dreams."

"Uneventful flight, I hope?"

"Yes," Nomis replied.

"Is the Millennium the same old place?"

"More Arabs than ever."

"Did you post my package to Doris?" Nara asked.

"Not yet," Nomis replied. "I wanted to check with you on the address. It seems she moved to Henley-on-Thames, not Windsor."

"Henley is up the Thames from Windsor, isn't it?" Nara asked.

"I think so," Nomis replied.

"It must be that house at the end of the cul-de-sac, down by the river? The garden was so ill-kept. I was sure she was going to take the house in Windsor," Nara said.

Nomis didn't answer.

"Nomis, are you there?" Nara asked. "Was it the one on the cul-de-sac?"

"I think the issue is definitely at a dead end. How would I know? All I have is an address!" Nomis replied.

"Very funny. I guess she changed her mind. So what else is new?" Nara asked.

"Henley brought to mind Alfred's seamless machine argument," Nomis replied.

"Alfred's seamless machine argument?" Nara asked.

"You know, the analogy I often use when dealing with my colleagues," Nomis replied.

"Who's Alfred?" Nara queried.

Nomis was surprised.

"Alfred, my freshman roommate at MIT," Nomis replied. "How could you ever forget Alfred?"

"Oh, yes, Alfred!" Nara mused. "That guy with the gorgeous physique."

"Who claimed those high-tech skiffs or shells, when combined with eight oarsmen and a coxswain, were a unique combination of brains and brawn," Nomis added.

"As I remember, he was a very good student, and very argumentative," Nara replied.

"The brainy part wasn't only one of those nine heads," Nomis continued, "but also the high-tech nature of the shell itself—carbon-fiber composite, sliding seats, and long oars braced by titanium outriggers."

"Nomis, you're at a dead end too; it's too early in the morning for Rowing 101," Nara complained. "Can you give me her new address and phone?"

"Yes, but first hear me out," Nomis replied. "To be considered more than just a many-headed beast, as Alfred referred to the Harvard heavyweights, those nine heads and the technology embodied in a shell have to be a seamless machine."

"Something, I suppose, that many an engineer at MIT worships?" Nara scolded.

"You're an engineer, honey," Nomis replied.

"And I suppose you think you're a seamless machine," Nara said.

More recently I have begun to apply the same logic to myself, as I feel more and more like I'm a many-headed beast, Nomis thought.

"Far from it," Nomis replied. "I had a dream when I was napping. I was in a double—you know, a shell for two people. And the other person in the boat was also a double, my double, it was me and myself!"

"They were both you? Are you sure it wasn't a scull?"

"Yes, and the other guy was constantly catching crabs," Nomis added.

"Catching crabs?"

"You know, digging into the surface of the water with his oar and upsetting the balance of the boat," Nomis replied.

There was another long pause. Nara broke the silence with a little giggle.

"So, when you were shaving, did you give your mirror image the seamless machine lecture too?"

There was no reply.

"Nomis, are you there?"

Nara's lack of interest in Rowing 101 hadn't been appreciated. When Nomis did reply, he was rather abrupt.

"I've got some time to kill," Nomis said. "I'd better ring off."

"I love you, honey."

"Ditto," was all that Nomis was able to muster as he rhymed off Doris's new address and phone number.

"Honey, why not spend it at the National Gallery?"

"I think I'll do just that," Nomis said.

∞ ∞ ∞

A special exhibit of the nineteenth century American realist, Thomas Eakins, was showing at the National Gallery. Nomis took Nara's advice and hopped a bus to Trafalgar Square and headed for the basement of the Sainsbury Wing. He picked up one of those audio guides as he entered the exhibit. The overview was quite enlightening.

"Eakins was a close friend of Walt Whitman, and, as was Whitman, Eakins was quintessentially democratic in his outlook," the voice of the audio guide began. "Eakins, like Whitman, sought out and celebrated truly American scenes—baseball fields, boxing matches, rowing races, swimming holes, and surgical theaters, to name only a few. Eakins's works offered ringside seats to all of them."

"Surgical theaters," Nomis mumbled to himself. "Let's see, the '*Gross Clinic*', one of Eakins's most celebrated paintings. Must give that one a look-see right away."

As he rounded the corner, Eakins's masterpiece loomed in the distance. At first it was difficult to find a spot where bobbing heads didn't block his view. He politely worked his way to a place directly in front of the huge canvas, activating the audio guide once again when he had the work in full view.

"Painted by Eakins in the mid-1870s, the '*Gross Clinic*' is a powerful and realistic statement of the true character and nature of a post-American Civil War surgeon," the audio guide voice continued. "The surgeon of Eakins's amphitheater strikes a professorial, even God-like pose . . . "

He is obviously a man of wisdom, skill and compassion, endowed by Eakins' brush with absolute power, authority and confidence, Nomis thought. *But God-like . . .*

"As he leans back, bracing himself on the railing of the amphitheater's bottom row of seats, his disciples are obviously engaged by his good works," the audio voice continued.

Good works? He's got blood on his hands, Nomis thought.

"Many others, with their heads cocked every which way, are seated above in various states of concentration," the voice continued. "His patient lies prone on a table with a deep gash in his thigh. The mother of the patient is seated off to one side, weeping. Prior to Eakins, such scenes rarely depicted a surgeon, a man with absolute advantage over those in his care, with his patient's blood on his hands."

I suppose what stands between the surgeon and the covert evil he might do with his knife is his oath, the Hippocratic Oath, Nomis thought. *The guiding principle of which—to ensure professional behavior—points to the life and health of those in his care as his first priority.*

After examining every detail of the Eakins canvas, Nomis felt that he had consumed a spiritual meal. The painting was overpowering; even infectious. Perhaps "contagious" is a more appropriate word to use.

Nomis concluded that the surgeon of the "*Gross Clinic*," although bloodied, was fully aware of his duty to his oath. Nomis came away with a feeling that he must replicate the spirit of goodness he saw in Eakins's musings with pigment and brush.

As Nomis rambled about the gallery, taking in Eakins' oarsmen, boxers, baseball players and swimming holes, his thoughts returned again and again to the *Gross Clinic*.

Perhaps I am naïve, he thought. *Perhaps Eakins' message isn't about caring or duty or the professional behavior of those with absolute power and advantage. Perhaps the surgeon's patient is a corpse, dead as a doornail by the surgeon's covert knife. Perhaps the woman in the shadows is mourning the murder of a husband or a child. Perhaps his disciples are also learning the covert skills of murder. Perhaps the oil on that canvas codes up a message about the dark side of man. Perhaps those images of Eakins are necromantic. Perhaps its prediction describes an outcome where an oath has become an evil covert knife. Perhaps that professorial God-like pose is only a ruse, a stratagem designed to conceal the surgeon's true intentions.*

Perhaps Nomis had forgotten all about the poem he had written after he had attended that lecture on Toynbee at Harvard many years ago.

Nomis stopped at the bookshop of the National Gallery before he returned to the Millennium, hoping to find something interesting to read during the long flights he faced in the next few days. He found just the thing—a paperback copy of a book he had been looking for prior to his departure from Boulder entitled *Seven Years in Tibet* by Heinrich Harrer, the escaped German prisoner of war who had spent seven years in Tibet and ended up as one of the teachers of the fourteenth Dalai Lama.

∞ ∞ ∞

As the taxi made its way back to the Millennium, a few lines from the "Song of the Open Road" in Walt Whitman's *Leaves of Grass* crept from Nomis's subconscious into plain sight.

Still here I carry my old delicious burdens,
I carry them, men and women,
I carry them with me wherever I go,
I swear it is impossible for me to get rid of them,
I am fill'd with them; and I will fill them in return.

It's odd that in what is really the humblest of great books, Leaves of Grass, *Whitman began—in its very first edition—with the startling egotistical statement 'I celebrate myself',* Nomis thought. *Perhaps my musing about the dark side of Eakins is wrong. Perhaps those lines from the humblest of books captures my intentions too, to celebrate, to pour out, the best of myself. Perhaps old George Wordhel was right!*

When he reached the Millennium Gloucester, there was another message awaiting him from the ambassador. He seemed upset, even frantic. He insisted Nomis come to the embassy as soon as possible. Nomis left the hotel by taxi at 3:10 P.M. Those London taxi drivers are usually not very talkative, but this one was.

"That was some power failure in the U.S," the cabby said, "just like the blackout of 2015 . . . have a brother who lives in Hoboken, on the Jersey side, across the Hudson from Manhattan. People stuck in elevators, Holland tunnel lights out, cell networks dead, the computerized call system failed . . . hell for us cabbies when the technology we depend on poops out. That call system can be a many-headed beast, even when up and running."

42
The Gross Clinic

Upon his arrival at the embassy, he was escorted to their SCIF. To his surprise, Orin Sedgewick was there with the ambassador.

"I didn't see you on the flight out of New York last night," Nomis said.

"I flew from Dulles. How are you feeling?" he began in earnest.

The fact that he said *feeling* and not *doing* was a bad omen; so was the fact that he was there in the SCIF with Nomis again. On the table in front of him lay a diplomatic pouch that hadn't been opened. As the ambassador broke the seal, opened it and took out a piece of paper, the big red light over the door went on; apparently there was something else cooking. The ambassador was called away to deal with it. He handed Sedgewick the slip of paper as he left the room.

"Quantum II has completed its trace on the perpetrator in Tibet who is wreaking havoc with the power grid in the U.S.," Sedgewick said. "Have you heard? He did the East coast early this morning."

I was right—a surprise a week. Should I crow a bit? Nomis thought.

"If we don't quickly put an end to this business, there might be a surprise a week," Sedgewick continued.

Really! Nomis thought.

"The probability is about eighty-seven percent that Quantum II is also right about Middle East involvement," Sedgewick added. "The ring leaders appear to be located in Iraq and are using contract hackers located in Southeast Asia and the whacko in Tibet. Their organization and technology resembles a many-headed beast."

"So is Baghdad my first stop?" Nomis asked.

"There is no need for you there," Sedgewick replied. "We need your personal touch elsewhere. This hack of the power grid is a real invasion of our privacy, and it has got to be stopped at the source."

Ditto, thought Nomis.

Sedgewick continued.

"We want you to proceed directly to Lhasa, go to the address on this slip, check it out, then terminate the man and destroy his equipment."

"I'm hardly a trained assassin," Nomis asserted.

From the pouch, Sedgewick retrieved a picture from the *Straits Times* of Monger's son hanging from that belt in his cell.

"Your stealth gives you the power to do anything you want. This picture is proof enough," Sedgewick shot back. "Take a look!"

"I'd rather not. Anyway, I didn't lay a hand on him. I only harassed his mind to the point where he took his own life," Nomis replied. "It was his choice!"

"No matter. This time it must look like a rival group has done the job. Get them fighting among themselves," Sedgewick added.

"You mean those renegade hackers scrambling for contracts with foreign powers who don't see eye to eye with us?" Nomis asked.

"Yes! It must look like one criminal mind has done in another, jealousy among thieves," Sedgewick replied.

And murderers! Nomis thought.

"Have we got a plan?" Nomis asked.

"Yes!" Sedgewick replied. "It is simple, quick, clean and foolproof. We have made arrangements for you to join a terrorist—I mean, tourist group that will arrive at Narita Airport north of Tokyo the day after tomorrow. These terrorists are all members of a club, the Skydivers Club of greater Denver, Colorado."

The fool is playing right into my hands, Nomis thought.

"You mean tourists," Nomis added.

"Yes. They are on their way to Lhasa to attend the World Skydivers' Conference. The director indicated that you were once a member of that club, and he has taken the liberty to ask Nara to call and reinstate your membership."

Which one? Terrorists or tourists? Nomis thought.

"The director has done what?" Nomis queried with surprise.

"Yes. We decided that it is best if you enter Tibet as a tourist," he replied.

"You mean terrorist," Nomis added.

"Call it what you may," Sedgewick replied.

Orin Sedgewick reached into the pouch, retrieving a flash card, a single cylinder—identical, except for its bright blue color, to those that Nomis used for the reboot process—and what looked like a server's communication or networking card. He chuckled to himself as he placed them on the table. Nomis began to feel like one of Eakins' disciples as he leaned forward to get a better look at the strange assortment.

"This flash card contains a deadly computer virus called 'Hiroshima or Bust.' We cribbed the name from that nightmare of yours, Nomis. Clever, don't you think?" Sedgewick said.

Nara's and my privacy are without doubt at great risk here. Before long I will find that COP has sold the movie rights to my dreams and nightmares to some Hollywood producer, Nomis thought as Sedgewick droned on.

"When activated it gives you thirty seconds to kill it, then it kills you."

"Me!? Kills me!" Nomis replied. "I'm no suicide bomber."

Orin Sedgewick didn't reply. He was on his way to some sort of a high. It was quite a sight. He became manic, and at one point began to salivate. A bit of saliva dripped from the left side of his mouth, which he quickly wiped clean with a handkerchief.

"It also kills your storage device, disks, memory sticks, light boxes, chips and any storage device connected to a site that has recently sent an e-mail to you," Sedgewick continued.

"An e-mail to me?" Nomis added with surprise.

"This virus is highly contagious, like the black plague," Sedgewick added.

"You must mean it's set to activate when that hacker in Lhasa opens any e-mail sent from Baghdad."

Sedgewick finally nodded and then continued.

"Built into the card are eight slots. Now, listen carefully! You must remove those red-and-white-striped cylinders from seven of the eleven reboot kits we supplied you with in Boulder and place them in the slots marked O."

Sedgewick very carefully picked up that blue cylinder.

"Place this cylinder, which I brought from Bethesda, in the slot marked *FOB*, located on the top left hand side of the card."

Nomis's response mocked Orin by imitating his manic tone of voice.

"FOB . . . free on board? Do I get the guy in Tibet to sign for it, or what?"

Sedgewick replied in a gloating tone, almost spitting into Nomis's face.

"No, fuel oxygen bomb! It's a miniaturized version of what is called a 'daisy cutter' or a fuel air bomb . . . or FAB. FABs were used on the Afghanistan-Pakistan border to root out those who ordered the take-down of the Twin Towers at the turn of the century. But let me continue. Then very carefully substitute this card for the com card in the main server and then load the software. Finally, throw the little switch located below the cylinder in the *FOB* slot, using a ballpoint pen, and leave the premises. Look, it's all here in this easy-to-understand instruction manual. Memorize it and then shred it!"

"What am I dealing with here?" Nomis demanded. "What's the bottom line? Why use the antidote? What's in that extra blue cylinder?"

"As the criminal is scrambling to deal with the virus on his server, the eighth cylinder, the blue one, will release a very explosive gaseous material that is harmless and odorless in an environment that contains less than fifty percent oxygen," replied Sedgewick. "Your reboot cylinders will then release the antidote, which is a chemical that concentrates and absorbs oxygen, like your red blood cells, but one hundred times more efficient."

So that's what those reboot cylinders of mine do. They supercharge my red blood cells, Nomis thought. *Very, very interesting.*

"Once this happens, the oxygen content of that gaseous material begins to climb," Sedgewick continued. "When it hits fifty percent—boom, you're dead."

"I'm dead?" Nomis shot back. "I'm dead! Me?"

An insincere smile crept across Sedgewick's face.

"Did I say *you're* dead?" Sedgewick replied. "I meant the hacker's dead. It's not all that bad. We make the victim feel good during his last fleeting moments of life. The concentration of oxygen gives him a big rush as he tries to save his files. And that rush distracts him from what is really going on around him. It's an old trick."

An old trick, thought Nomis. *Tricks are something that have never sat well with me.*

Sedgewick continued his diabolical monologue.

"The virus comes with a few other little delicacies. It flashes the final scene from that classic old film, *Dr. Strangelove,* on the server's monitor—the one with Slim Pickens riding the A-Bomb down to the target, waving his cowboy hat. The target takes the form of a circle, which gets bigger and bigger with the tick of each second. During the last sixteen seconds, the program adds one cross-hair to the target circle each second. Right before it goes off, it looks like a modern bomb site, or perhaps a big sunburst, like you see when you look directly into the sun for a second or two."

That's what an H-Bomb is, a big sunburst, Nomis thought.

Nomis's tone of voice turned cynical.

"Does the virus have audio and play, 'Until We Meet Again,' sung by Vera Lynn?"

The Zia, the blinding sunset at Mille Lacs Lake and the Balt nightmare all rushed to the edge of Nomis's conscious mind. They clambered to get out, but then fell back, retreating into the dark corners of his mind.

"It's all for the enjoyment of our friend in Lhasa, who is about to get blown to smithereens," Sedgewick said. "The nation, I am sure, will applaud FOB's mafiaesque and surgical nature. It isn't at all like what we had to do at Hiroshima or Nagasaki."

Those first two A-bombs, very, very messy. So many killed. Infected a lot of other nations with a very bad bug, Nomis thought.

"With this one we are going back to basics—we call it the quintessential human touch," Sedgewick added, "and with your help, we will be using some of the terrorist's own medicine on him to effect the cure: stealth. As we used to say when we were young and naive, as kids playing cops and robbers or war games, turn about, fair play."

Nomis's mind drifted back to his early afternoon encounter with the work of Eakins.

The man in the SCIF with me is the antithesis of the surgeon in that painting, the Gross Clinic, Nomis thought.

The final comments on the audio guide rang in his ears.

"Eakins' treatment of a boy's bare, diseased thigh, exposed to the knife in the unsanitary conditions of a surgical theater in the late nineteenth century, so disturbed the jury of Philadelphia's 1876 Centennial Exhibition that they insisted it be hung in a dim corner among the army medical exhibits."

Perhaps that jury was right at the time; surgery was as brutal as war before the world of microbes had been fully understood, Nomis thought. *Maybe Eakins's masterpiece still deserves to be hung in some dim corner, out of sight. Maybe the jury did understand its dark side.*

"Nomis, do you understand what must be done?" Sedgewick asked.

Is this surgeon before me in the SCIF, with his cylinderized scalpel, a manifestation of the dark side of Eakins's genius? Is he no better than a terrorist with a box cutter? Is he an evildoer? Must I apply the same low standard to myself to insure my personal survival?

Nomis's voice became computer-like.

"How many cylinder slots for the antidote are there?"

"Seven plus the one for the fuel oxygen bomb," Sedgewick replied.

Boom, my plan is dead. I have only seven cylinders left, Nomis thought.

"You were given eleven, as I remember. That leaves you with four. More than enough to cover the risk of a shut-down in the next little while, even in the thin air of Lhasa. So you're all set," Sedgewick replied.

If it works as advertised, it sure will look like one criminal mind did in another criminal mind. There is more than some truth in that, Nomis thought.

Orin gave Nomis the thumbs-up sign.

"Boom, you're dead . . . er, I mean . . . boom, he's dead," Sedgewick remarked as he left the room.

As Nomis was packing up, the ambassador entered the SCIF. He provided Nomis with a new set of airline tickets. With them was a note saying he had also canceled the old routing to Baghdad via Dubai, and had prepaid his hotel in Lhasa.

43
Two-headed Newts

The SCIF always imposed its authority in ways that left some room for choice, but as always, there was a threat lurking in the background. Regardless, Nomis was determined to follow through with a personal plan for survival. On the way back to the Millennium, he shut his eyes and sank down in the taxi's back seat, imagining himself to be in a skiff, gliding across the early morning glass-still waters of the Thames. He began to sort through his options. Shortly those many-headed feelings were clamoring at the edge of his subconscious again.

Killing the hacker some other way, wrecking his equipment and pocketing the seven cylinders, might permit me to continue with the original plan I hatched in my garage, he thought.

But going that route wouldn't get to the other servers, as *Hiroshima or Bust* was programmed to do, his self replied.

It would also give the director a heads-up, and maybe the same to other contract hackers, that COP was on the prowl in a very personal way.

No doubt! Until recently, it was the hackers' files that COP killed, not the hackers themselves.

Resetting the com card in a way that didn't involve the FOB cycle is another option.

You're no hardware engineer—just a theoretical mathematician. The likelihood of screwing it up is high.

The com card might also be a smart card.

Possibly! Once installed, it might report back to Quantum II the minute you flip that little switch and again when the card detects that an e-mail from Baghdad has been opened.

Worse still, the card might be programmed to report back to Quantum II that I tampered with it.

Anyway, if you circumvent the FOB mechanism, you'd have to throw the hacker out a window or drown him in his bathtub. The surgeon did say that the plan was foolproof. You'd be the fool if you didn't follow it exactly.

There is the unthinkable. I might simply disappear.

Aside from the pain this would bring to your family, which I think you may not be able to bear, you might be hunted down and terminated by COP if the hacker wasn't dead by the end of the week.

During the button-pushing exercise, I wondered if sitting somewhere in my head were a few lines of diabolical code, waiting for their cue to do just that.

I've another ugly thought. Stealth in any venue is a weapon and you don't have a monopoly on it. Unknown to you, COP might have left that cell in your head to carry out a daily reporting cycle on your activities.

I placed that Texans-Broncos bet after the director told me the cell had been removed, having no reason to doubt him. If the director had known about the bet in advance, he could have confronted me before the game.

But he didn't. Standard operating procedure is to never let the other side know what you know.

You're right!

And the surgeon seemed to know more of the details related to your little escapade in Houston than revealed by the analysis of Solarnet traffic. You might be bugged after all!

To proceed with any plan, even the one hatched in my garage, I have to assume that the cell is out.

Until and unless you find a contradiction.

At this point, I'm sure of only one thing. Those cylinders aren't flesh and blood. My original plan was to reverse-engineer them once I had determined the outcome of the third sequence.

You mean the first-you-go-blind-and-then-activate-CIHPAR thing?

Yes. I figure I need a dozen or more cylinders to complete my analysis.

No way! You already used up four conducting your initial experiments . . . and *Hiroshima or Bust* leaves you empty-handed. So the plan you hatched in your garage isn't feasible. Give it up, at least for the moment.

And I suppose my own personal stealth is at risk if I do something that is uncharacteristic or reckless, like trying to steal a few cylinders.

Better to take the route of accountability with no further uncharacteristic actions on your part . . . and also continue to look carefully for evidence of a contradiction.

I dread those contradictions.

Like any good mathematician, you ought to.

Yeh, you're right!

You're better off taking the *if and only if* route of a mathematician. You must be, and be seen to be, dutiful.

Then my only option is to use all seven cylinders as required, risk the return trip to Boulder with no antidote, and implement my original plan at some later date when I can come by more of those reboot cylinders.

Right. Reconstitute your garage lab, run all of your experiments over again, but breathe pure oxygen as a substitute for those cylinders.

Good idea. If pure oxygen does restore my sight, that will set me free from those little cylinders. I could then accumulate for experimentation any extras I might be given. If pure oxygen didn't restore my sight, I would reboot with a standard-issue cylinder to regain my sight and go the reverse-engineering route when the time was right.

Nara's the biochemist, not you. That route would take resources, a knowledge base and much, much more time.

But it might move me closer to understanding the outcome of the third sequence. Part of the one-way window problem will be solved if I could restore my sight without those cylinders.

But that's the easy part. What happens during the hard part is as worrisome a question as finding a contradiction . . .

Correct!

. . . and you might run into an engineering screw-up.

You mean a crossed circuit or two.

Yes. When blind, will your sight return when you summon CIHPAR by chanting? Will it be like being in your dreams? And if you chant to restore your image, will your sight remain, or must you reboot by raising the oxygen content of your blood?

If not without those cylinders, or a successful outcome of the alternative which uses pure oxygen, life might turn out to be what I fear most of all: a living nightmare, a humpty dumpty process, a life of blindness when visible and the opposite when invisible. That would be hell!

∞ ∞ ∞

Nomis phoned Nara upon his return to the Gloucester Millennium.

"It looks like I am going skydiving in Tibet after all," Nomis said at one point.

"I know and I don't much like it," Nara replied.

Nara proceeded to babble on about the conversation she had had with the director.

"Nomis, it seemed rather odd when the director asked me to reinstate your old membership in the Denver club. I did mention to him how preoccupied you seemed to be, but making those funny pictures in the garage the day before you left and forgetting about the membership . . . unlike me, he didn't think it odd at all. He just said you'd forgotten to attend to the membership."

"He didn't think what odd?" Nomis asked.

"Forgetting to attend to the membership. And I guess the funny pictures, although my comment about them seemed to pass him by," Nara replied. "He just asked me to attend to the membership as soon as possible. Say, on your way back, why don't you take a day or two and visit my friend in Kobe?"

"I might just do that. My routing takes me through Japan. I will call him when I get into Narita on my way to Lhasa. If it works out, I will have the routing changed to Osaka/Los Angeles/Boulder, rather than Narita/Los Angeles/Boulder. When I get into Osaka, I can hop a train to Kobe. I'll call you from Narita if it all works out, and again from Lhasa when I arrive there," Nomis replied.

A few minutes later, another call came through. It was Doris. She suggested that Nomis pop over to Henley-on-Thames for dinner that evening. Time was tight, but Kensington Station, where he could catch a train to Slough, was a short hop from the Millennium. Doris even volunteered to meet him at Slough around 6:30 P.M.

The back country route from Slough to Henley followed the Thames as it meandered through the countryside, passing by the playing fields of Eton and a little town called Marlow. The same was true of the conversation. It meandered too, and so did Nomis's mind. As Doris droned on, Nomis tried his best to appear interested. Doris's new house *was* the one located on the cul-de-sac, with a grassy spot and garden that backed onto the Thames. Soon the conversation took a turn to more personal matters—her children, then their children, and then a rehash of the trip across the moors she and Nara had taken. Finally she got around to Nomis and his strange desire to jump from airplanes.

"Nara called me shortly after lunch," Doris said. "I'm concerned, and she is too! What's a grown man like you doing jumping out of airplanes in Tibet? I must say, it's a bit odd."

Nomis's reply was as empty of content as Doris's remark was unsettling.

"Odd—you know me better than that. Tibet is an adventure I've always wanted to experience," Nomis replied.

Why do Doris and Nara both regard what I'm going to do as odd, while the director seems unconcerned? Nomis thought. *Nara seems to think her comment about the funny pictures made no impression on the director. Was that the case? Or was the response of the director a contradiction? Did he already know about those funny pictures before Nara had mentioned them to him? And if so, how did he know?*

The dinner was quite relaxing, until Doris started talking about her garden. She was in the throes of bringing order to it. In its day, it must have been quite stunning, but the former owner had let it get out of hand. It was a mess, with everything growing every which way, and the tangle of vegetation wasn't the only problem. That afternoon she had also found a number of deformed frogs, some with extra legs poking out of their heads, and a two-headed newt. One of the newt's heads was deformed and had no eyes. Doris said it was the strangest thing she had ever seen. She had kept it in a bottle to show Nomis.

The head with no eyes was also able to take on the hue of its surroundings much more effectively than the one with eyes, even though they were both attached to the same body. It was as if that head were endowed with a stealth that protected it from that which it couldn't see. But of course it could, if you considered the little creature as one not two. It disturbed Doris to no end; Nomis was horrified!

As they strolled down to the river's edge, a rowing shell with two men in it, each with one oar, and no coxswain, glided by. In that pair, as they were called, two heads had to work as one to win. Doris set the little creature down on the riverbank.

"I doubt if a many-headed living thing can survive. Sure it will get along until it is eaten by some predator, like a snake, a bird, or the larva of a dragonfly," Doris remarked.

"Yes, I agree, it's not nature's way. It's too complicated; it's unnatural," Nomis replied. "There are much simpler systems. Some mistake in its genome occurred, which violated the KIS principle."

"The kiss principle?" Doris queried.

"You know—keep it simple," Nomis replied. "Newts, or, for that matter, humans, just don't need two nervous systems."

But isn't that what Quantum II's network is? Nomis thought. *A parallel-processed super-cooled CPU driving a humongous backbone, and a horrendously intrusive spinal cord? With all of those clients and their PCs connected to Quantum II, isn't the number of heads in the millions?*

Nomis studied the perfectly balanced pair intently as it glided by.

"I just spent the afternoon in COP's version of a skiff," Nomis mumbled.

"Pardon?" replied Doris. "I thought you spent the day working in London."

Nomis pointed toward the pair as it rounded a bend in the Thames, passing out of sight. His reply was metallic in tone.

"I did. Ears and eyes count a lot with that twosome."

"Always the Code Talker! Really! Give it up!" replied Doris.

Doris drove Nomis back to Slough to catch the late evening train to Kensington Station. As the road wound through the English countryside, Nomis's horror subsided. He began to feel a strange kinship to that two-headed newt. He often thought of himself as two people: the one who could see and the one who couldn't.

44
Teddy Bears

It was during the descent into Narita Airport, north of Tokyo, that the opportunity presented itself. It began with a number of bangs and popping noises, followed by the sound of roaring air and a lot of yelling and screaming. The commotion and confusion, which had originated on the upper deck, soon spread to the entire plane. It was quite unnerving when an oxygen mask dropped down in front of Nomis and a man's voice was heard, issuing instructions over the plane's auto attendant system.

"Place the mask over your face; pull it toward you to start the flow of oxygen."

Nomis's seatmate, who had been quite talkative, even intrusive, quietly and efficiently donned his mask. Nomis did the same.

Escorted by one of the two human attendants, those in the upper deck began an unruly and disorganized exit down the narrow stairs to the lower deck, taking seats wherever they were able to find them. Confusion on the lower deck increased as a shortage of seats quickly materialized. The dry, raspy tone of the voice coming from the auto attendant, that continued to provide information and direction, didn't help matters.

"I'm a retired pilot," the voice crackled. "The one flying the plane is located at Narita Airport."

Nomis's mouth went dry as any spare fluid in his lymphatic system made a beeline for his armpits.

OK, Quantum II, it's your call. Where the hell are you? Nomis thought.

In mid-sentence, the soft, soothing, reassuring tone of a woman's voice suddenly replaced the man's. Nomis's comfort level rose.

Quantum II has taken control and is obviously modulating the voice of the retired pilot, Nomis thought.

"Must have been an instantaneous electronic sex change," his seatmate whispered.

Nomis couldn't help but laugh at this politically incorrect remark, even though it was about a bunch of microchips. It momentarily relieved his tension.

"The seal on the port-side upper deck door has come loose," the auto attendant said. "The door is partially open. No one has been injured, but the plane has decompressed. The two onboard airline employees have secured the door as best they can, but you must continue to use your oxygen masks until the plane descends to below eight thousand feet."

As the last of the passengers filed down from the upper deck, Nomis noticed that the cabin lights were beginning to dim.

Normal precautions to prevent an explosion when oxygen is in use, Nomis thought.

Shortly afterwards, he started to feel faint. Suddenly, sparks began to fly, just like in the SCIF in Boulder. He yanked on his mask so hard that the tubing came loose from the ceiling.

"There's no flow. I'm going to faint," Nomis yelled at the flat screen.

"Pardon me, Dr. Chester," the auto-attendant replied.

By the time it had answered, Nomis's head was flopping from side to side. It finally landed in his seatmate's lap. He was out cold. His seatmate struggled to bring Nomis to an upright position. The human attendant produced some smelling salts. One whiff and Nomis's eyes popped open. He became bloated with fear. He was as blind as a bat.

I dare not say a thing, Nomis thought.

He didn't have to. The human attendant thrust an oxygen canister into his face, placing the cup over his nose and mouth. She had a hard time turning the valve. The auto attendant added to the confusion by constantly asking if it might help! Finally his seatmate had the sense to turn the thing off, while the retired pilot wrestled with the valve. A hissing sound signaled success.

"Breathe. Deep breaths. It's pure oxygen. Breathe."

After a few deep breaths, Nomis felt a rush and then again became light-headed. Slowly the faces of those bending over him began to appear in his field of vision. He felt a second rush as the rhythm of his heart became irregular. His pulse quickly doubled and then fell back to a more normal range.

As Nomis began to collect his thoughts, the oxygen bottle took on the persona of a toddler's favorite teddy bear. No one was going to take it from him. It was then that Nomis realized that he had in his clutches the wherewithal to reveal the outcome of the third sequence. Pure oxygen was a good substitute for the reboot cylinders!

He switched the auto attendant back on. Its calm voice again filled his ears.

"We will be below eight thousand feet in a few minutes, but the masks must be worn until the plane begins its final descent into Narita, at which time, for safety reasons, the oxygen will be turned off and passengers will be asked to remove their masks."

The magic of its sugary tone was depleted by the pandemonium which gripped the cabin. Nomis became crazed with fear. Above the uproar, he thought he heard a passenger a few seats in front of him claim that he had smuggled aboard a parachute and was prepared to jump out the open door if worst came to worst. As the engines spooled down, Nomis had a fleeting thought.

Was the time ripe to take the plunge? I ought to get up and go to the washroom, carrying the canister of oxygen. I will cut off the flow and hopefully pass out. When the plane drops below eight thousand feet, I will come to and hopefully be blind. I will go stealth, and afterwards use the oxygen canister to regain my sight and image, whatever the case may be.

Nomis's fear turned to euphoria.

I have a choice here, he thought. *If it all works out, I can implement my personal plan, my last and final disappearing act, in Lhasa.*

Suddenly there was another loud thump, the sound of roaring air as before, and an abrupt lurch of the plane to the left, followed by lots of vibration, a sense that the plane was fishtailing like a giant sea creature, and more screaming and yelling.

In the uproar that followed, Nomis's thoughts became even more erratic.

Why wait any longer? If it looks like we're going down, I'll implement my personal plan here and now. What have I got to lose? Nomis thought. *I'll go stealth, use the turmoil to swipe that guy's parachute, make my way to the upper deck and jump.*

Despite his ebullience, a look of desperation soon crept across Nomis's face. The outlandish nature of his plan stemmed from a knee-jerk reaction to a now-pulsating anxiety that verged on panic. He began to walk, zombie-like, toward one of the toilets, carting the oxygen cylinder along with him. As he opened the door to the lavatory, the auto attendant's voice took on the timbre of an undertaker.

"The door on the upper deck has departed us," the auto attendant said.

Its somber tone brought him to his senses.

How could that guy have smuggled a parachute aboard? Impossible with all the security. Probably wishful thinking on his part, Nomis thought.

He left the door half-open and started back to his seat.

"The plane's tail has been slightly damaged," the auto attendant added. "We've been cleared for an emergency landing at Narita and will be making a much faster descent and possibly a hard landing."

As the plane rocked back and forth, a white-knuckled Nomis made a one-handed lunge for his seat's armrest. With the other hand, he steadied the canister as he savored its contents.

In cases like this, I hope Quantum II remains in command, Nomis thought.

The auto attendant's punctual reply astonished Nomis. It was as if the thing were reading his mind.

"The pilot who guided us across the Pacific will be on the tarmac to greet us when we land at Narita."

The poor sod, thought Nomis. *Quantum II has demoted him, thank God*!

"A demonstration will appear on the flat screen above your seat just prior to landing," the auto attendant added. "No one must leave their seats for any reason. As was the case when we departed London, a few minutes before our final approach, your seat will automatically turn one hundred and eighty degrees. Upon completing its rotation, you will then be facing the rear of the plane. Your back and head will be firmly supported by the seat back during descent and deceleration. Be sure your seat harness is securely fastened."

Well, that's that, inasmuch as the third sequence is concerned. With my rubbery legs I'm unable to make it to the washroom again, anyway, Nomis thought. *My immediate problem is getting back on the ground in one piece, and I pray that Quantum II can do that.*

What Nomis's seatmate had to say about getting back on the ground wasn't at all comforting.

"It's not easy landing a plane with a damaged stabilizer."

"Stabilizer? I thought it was the tail," Nomis replied.

"Tail, stabilizer, same difference. To keep the plane from fishtailing and to make the turns needed on approach, the pilot must compute the drag caused by the hole where the door used to be located and then individually vary the thrust of each engine to keep the plane from rolling over onto its back as he executes the necessary turns."

Nomis's disapproving glance revealed the source of his seatmate's expertise.

"I fly for pleasure. Certified on a Cessna 190 center thrust," he said. "I know what this plane . . . "

"Quantum II is now in command," Nomis blurted out.

His seatmate just smiled.

"The situation will become more delicate for Captain Quantum at touchdown," his seatmate retorted.

Nomis couldn't help but laugh.

"Captain Quantum is a computer," Nomis replied.

His seatmate looked askance at Nomis.

"And my name's Orville Wright! Regardless, we won't be floating onto the runway. One of those cushy landings for which United World Airlines is so famous is out of the question. This landing will be more like squatting onto an aircraft carrier at half-throttle. And we will be coming in much faster. You know what I mean—a controlled crash, like landing at Salt Lake City."

Nomis knew exactly what Orville was talking about.

When landing at Salt Lake City, once you have cleared the Rocky Mountains and start your descent, it's like an express ride in an elevator ten thousand feet down, with the spoilers flapping in the wind all the way, Nomis thought.

Nomis's voice began to tremble.

"A controlled crash?"

"Yes, on the way down you might just become weightless for a few seconds and then your weight will double," Orville replied. "You might even end up with black eyes."

"Black eyes?" Nomis queried.

"Yes, caused by the sudden change in pressure in your eye sockets as the plane both rapidly descends and then decelerates. You'll see. It's going to be an abnormally hard landing and quick stop. I suggest you fill your lungs with air, put your thumbs in your ears, pinch your nostrils shut with your fingers, close your mouth tight, squeeze your eyes shut, puff up your cheeks and blow."

"What in God's name for?" Nomis replied.

Orville smiled again.

"To keep your eyes from rattling around in their sockets."

My eyes from rattling around! What does this guy care or know about my eyes? Nomis thought.

A few minutes later, much to Nomis's surprise, the auto attendant indicated that all passengers were to undertake the same crazy exercise. Nomis wondered how he might manage that as well as keep a tight grip on the oxygen canister. His solution was to place it between his knees and lean over to take a whiff every minute or two. When he wasn't sniffing oxygen, his excellent peripheral vision made it easy to see the faces around him, including that of his seatmate.

The entire cabin looks like a class of second graders making faces at each other, Nomis thought. *I suppose the comedy of it all might be a stratagem of Quantum II, designed to disperse the tension that will gush from a panic-ridden last few minutes. No doubt it knows exactly what it is doing . . . I pray,* Nomis thought.

Just prior to touchdown, one of the human attendants removed the oxygen canister from between Nomis's knees. As she did, she blushed.

"Anything that isn't bolted, strapped down or stowed will fly forward when we brake and it might end up in your . . . "

Nomis's prayers were answered. Quantum II performed flawlessly, even though at the moment of touchdown, the landing gear felt like it was coming through the floor.

The human attendant was right, too. Everything not bolted down or stowed away ended up in the front of the plane, including one passenger, who broke his arm. At the last minute, he had tried to take a picture of those bloated cheeks with thumbs and fingers doubling for ear and nose plugs.

If Captain Quantum could muster a giggle or two, the moment of touchdown would have been the impetus, Nomis thought as he deplaned.

When he passed by one of the human attendants, he asked if United World Airlines might supply him with an oxygen canister. He was quite argumentative.

"I'm on route to Lhasa, Tibet, and given what happened on the plane, I'd feel more comfortable if I was able to get my clutches on one."

"Unfortunately passengers aren't permitted to carry on explosive devices such as an oxygen canister," she replied. "But perhaps your hotel in Lhasa might supply one."

Nomis felt a momentary sense of rejection, as if the human attendant had denied him a favorite toy.

∞ ∞ ∞

At Narita, despite his rattled state of mind, Nomis had no problem joining up with the Denver group. There was also plenty of time to think; perhaps too much time. The connecting flight to Lhasa via Hong Kong didn't depart until late afternoon. His only problem: the anxiety producing ordeal of decompression, along with the accompanying fatigue, had resulted in a proclivity to promptly forget the names of those to whom he had just been introduced. The converse wasn't true.

Some remembered Nomis from his participation at one of their orientation meetings some years back; others from Nomis's first jump on his forty-ninth birthday. With that second implant, which had been battery-powered, he had been told by those at Bethesda never to jump again. But he jumped anyway the following year, south of Santa Barbara, and hadn't experienced any problems. One member of the Denver group who had jumped with him both times asked if he was going to jump a third time in Tibet. Nomis didn't answer, but it got him thinking.

When the third implant was installed, I was told to avoid very bright sunlight and thin air. Today that delicate power system in my head proved jumping might be a risky business. But I was prepared to fly out the door of that plane. God. Panic and impatience can drive you to do almost anything, Nomis thought.

When Nomis had jumped that second time south of Santa Barbara, the person in charge had been a woman, but there was a man in charge now. Zackery Gimley was his name. He was a real organizer, and quite pushy. He must have been new on the job. Nomis wasn't able to place him. He insisted that Nomis take charge of his own jump gear which he, Zackery, had personally lugged all the way from Denver.

As Nomis sorted through the various items, including boots, knee and elbow pads, an insulated suit, socks and gloves, a utility belt and a helmet with sun visor his mind began to churn.

The primary and secondary chute has the appearance of a back pack, he thought, *and the utility belt has a number of niches, one of which contained an unlabeled canister.*

He began to think seriously about having another go.

"What's in the canister?" Nomis asked.

"It's for oxygen. It's empty," Zackery replied. "A local supplier in Lhasa will fill it. It's impossible to transport explosive material."

Later Nomis surreptitiously removed the canister and the pack with the chutes. He checked the remainder of the jump gear as baggage and slipped the canister into his carry-on luggage.

Despite the risk, a jump might be manageable now that a simple canister of oxygen can be used to reboot, he thought.

It didn't take much time for Nomis to become personally attached to that empty canister. Having it in his grasp was a calming influence. Fiddling with the valve and expecting, as if by magic, that it might somehow begin to hiss, was relaxing. Even cradling it in his lap while he browsed through Harrer's book about Tibet produced a sense of security. However, by early afternoon, his anxiety, driven by the thought of jumping with an empty canister and his desire to know the outcome of the third sequence, got the better of him.

He decided to use the canister as a prop. At the United World Airlines ticket counter, he indicated that it was empty and for health reasons he needed either a replacement or a refill. His ploy was one big mistake. The canister was examined by security. A personal search ensued and was followed by the recall of his checked baggage. Eventually Zackery had to intervene on Nomis's behalf when what he claimed was a backpack turned out to be the chutes. He was finally told to check it all. He received little consolation from United World Airlines' promise to supply a canister if needed on the flight. For the second time that day, he had been stripped of the one item to which he had become personally attached. Nomis began to have belated second thoughts.

Maybe the risk was too great, Nomis thought. *Maybe I ought to just deal with the hacker and be done with it.*

The flight from London, the incident on the plane, his ordeal with security, and his obsession with the empty canister had worn him down. By mid-afternoon, he was running on nervous energy. By boarding time, he had worked himself into another snit, determined to be first in line at the gate for the transit bus to the plane. A profiler singled out his behavior as suspicious. He was questioned and searched a second time. Again Zackery had to intervene.

As a result, they both missed the first transit bus and had to take the second. Once on the bus Nomis sat in the back, nervously doodling on the inside cover of Harrer's book with a ballpoint pen, while the remaining latecomers boarded. He wasn't able to relax. His mind just kept going, with that ballpoint pen as its slave. As the last few passengers boarded the transit bus, the pen's clicker jammed. Nomis's eyes quickly assumed the pen's role. They nervously scanned up and then down the aisle, going from person to person, as he tried to recollect the names of those he had been introduced to earlier in the day.

Once on the plane, much to Nomis's surprise, he found Orville seated in the front of the cabin. Nomis's fatigue gave way to a feeling of uneasiness.

Was he on his way to Lhasa or only going as far as Hong Kong? Nomis wondered.

As Nomis passed by, their eyes met. Nomis nodded. His uneasiness turned to paranoia when Zackery sat down beside Orville.

Maybe, just maybe, I'm looking for the wrong sort of contradiction. If Quantum II is out of the loop, the director and Sedgewick have no way of gaining any feedback, save for the old-fashioned way. A second agent, or, as Sedgewick recently put it, the definitive personal touch.

As the plane made its final turn onto the runway, Nomis's eyes made several loops of the cabin. They paused for a few seconds each time they passed by the back of Orville's head and that of Zackery. The third time around they fluttered once or twice and slowly slid shut.

A contradiction or just a weekend pilot and a guy who jumps out of airplanes? Nomis pondered as he dozed off.

45
Charm Boxes

Thanks to Zackery, check-in at Lhasa's Holiday Inn was well-coordinated, right down to the room assignments and baggage handling. The advance payment arranged by the ambassador was also a godsend. All the Holiday Inn needed was an imprint of Nomis's credit card to cover his incidentals. The Denver group was assigned rooms on the lower floors. The upper floors were reserved for business travelers willing to pay the shot, and for wealthy Chinese awaiting treatment at a nearby medical center.

The conference was also well-attended. The hustle and bustle of the hotel lobby was proof enough. The ground floor shops and restaurants were already overflowing with delegates. Most claimed it was due to the location. There were also lots of extras, including a tour of the ancient city scheduled for the following morning. Nomis signed up for what he expected might be a quick overview of Lhasa. He got more than he bargained for. The tour guide was a Tibetan national, an anthropology student who had attended Hsiamen University in Fukien Province, China.

Her choppy, monosyllabic, modulated pattern of speech was fascinating. She had turned English into a language of one-syllable sounds with letters like *n* which weren't even pronounced.

"Good morn-ing, my name is Yangchenla and your dri-ver name is Khünpela," she said. "I hope you have set-tle into your ho-tel by now. Those of you with coat may want to place them in the ov-er-head rack. There is on-board rest-room for your com-fort loc-ate to the rear. The bus is also e-quip with an ox-y-gen sys-tem for your com-fort and con-ven-i-ence. Lha-sa is some twelve thou-sand feet a-bove sea level . . ."

Nomis found her use of the English language novel, but the choppy mode of speech was irksome. Soon he discovered himself unconsciously correcting her phonetic and grammatical errors.

"With the thin air of Lhasa and for-ty people on-board it is quite ne-ces-sary; if you feel faint at any time, twist the little vents on the panel located above your seat to start the flow."

Nomis reached up and turned on the flow of oxygen.

Have me in mind, Nomis thought.

"I have placed an information sheet and a map of Lhasa on each of your seats. Please, have a look at them. The map shows the route the bus will be taking. We will be viewing some of the noteworthy historical sites of Lhasa, but won't be visiting them. You can use the map to locate places that you might want to return to later, during the week, for a more detailed look."

Nomis used the map to reconnoiter as he scanned the cityscape from the bus window.

Location of the Holiday Inn is here, and the British consulate—a short walk—excellent, Nomis thought.

"If you have any questions, just spin the little prayer wheel by your seat; it makes a pleasant chirping sound," Yangchenla rambled on. "I will take note and personally answer each of your questions at the end of the tour. OK, everybody ready?"

Khünpela pulled away from the hotel, slowly making his way to one of the few wide thoroughfares.

Information sheet contains both propaganda and history, Nomis thought. *Let's see, prior to Chinese arrival in the 1950s, Lhasa a maze of narrow dirt roads, anything but clean. Littered with the dead bodies of animals, food for ravens and dogs, atmosphere malodorous, often had to hold a scented handkerchief to your nose.*

Nomis found himself searching for his own handkerchief as he scanned the sparkling clean streets for rotting carcasses. There were none to be seen.

Disease not a problem. Thin air and climate discouraged breeding of flies and most other insects, a missing link in the food chain, not a frog or newt in all of Tibet.

"No newts," Nomis mumbled. "*Je m'en doute.*"

"The Forbidden City, as Lhasa used to be called, is situated in the Tsangpo valley along the banks of the river Kyichu, which is over there to your left," Yangchenla began.

Most of those in the bus began to rubberneck to the left. Nomis was in the minority. He chose to leaf through Harrer's book.

"The Kyichu runs clear and cold from the glaciers and is a tributary of the Tsangpo which, after finding its way to Bangladesh, becomes the Brahmaputra. It finally empties into the Bay of Bengal, along with the Ganges, which lies to the west of it," Yangchenla added.

River Kyichu, let's see, Nomis thought. *Harrer reports springs dried up, fourteenth Dalai Lama summoned the Oracle of Gadong, hmm. To do his magic. Most famous rainmaker in Tibet fell into a trance, gyrations reached a poetic frenzy, words taken down by ministers. Body sinks to the ground, carried out, astonishing thing happened: it always rained. Harrer's friend Peter Aufschnaiter installed a water gauge on the Kyichu, found level rose on almost the same day every year. Never seized opportunity to become successful oracle, too bad!*

Nomis's magical chant and those circuits in his head that seemed to have vanished came to mind as he visualized that warm, late spring day when the Oracle's gyrations reached a poetic frenzy, the same day that Aufschnaiter's scientific method recorded the level of the Kyichu at its highest.

Feel more of a kinship to Oracle of Gadong than Aufschnaiter's gauge, thought Nomis. *Haven't the faintest idea why the river in me rises and falls . . . just know that it will when I summon CIHPAR.*

"On or near its frontiers to the west, north and south are located the world's most massive mountain barriers, whose snow-packed slopes are the rivers' source," Yangchenla said. "Everest and K2 are the tallest among them, located to the south, toward Nepal and Kashmir. Only in the east are such natural barriers lacking. There the mountains of the west, north and south gradually undulate down into the Chinese provinces of Szechwan and Yhnnan."

Our flight to Lhasa followed east to west route from Hong Kong, Nomis thought. *Lack of natural barriers must be the reason.*

The bus engine moaned as it rounded a corner. A sudden tenseness developed in Yangchenla's voice.

"This historical gateway has left Tibet and its history open to the influence of China and vice versa. Tibet, and especially Lhasa, is a mixture of the very new and the very old. There always has been a certain tension between them, too."

New and old, Nomis thought. *New part probably traces origin to China's participation in globalization. Some spin-off landed in Tibet.*

"Tibet isn't wired; it's wireless. Its geography of massive mountains, open to the sky, couldn't shield it from the onslaught of the cell phone and communication satellite. In Tibet there is an ancient saying: the sky talks . . . and it still does," Yangchenla said.

The sky talks, thought Nomis.

"Strangely enough, the old part is the endemic contribution of a culture shielded from the outside world for centuries by the very same thing, its geography," Yangchenla added.

The sky talks. The sky talks, Nomis thought. *Line from Footprints? Line from Footprints! Strange! Truth in Great-Grandpa's stories? Impossible!*

"There are many stories and historical events that illustrate the tension between the old and the new. Some of them are quite tragic," Yangchenla said. "For example, between 1903 and 1904, a British expeditionary . . . "

Computers and god-counting . . . the old and the new, Nomis thought.

" . . . force led by a Lieutenant Colonel Francis E. Younghusband entered Tibet from northern Kashmir, not from the east. After several battles, the expedition made its way to Lhasa. The last of those battles is representative of the contrast between the old and the new, which today is still the essence of Tibet."

Tibetan counterpart. Perhaps the battle of Waterloo, Nomis thought.

"The elite of Tibet were armed with muskets equipped with wicks, which had to be lit to ignite the explosive charge that forced the ball from the gun's barrel," Yangchenla continued. "The British were armed with modern rifles, machine guns and breech-loaded artillery, using modern ammunition and shells."

No doubt tension high and nerves taut, Nomis thought.

"The English gentleman that he was, Younghusband begged the Tibetans to put down their arms," Yangchenla explained. "A single shot rang out, fired in error amidst all the unease. What ensued was mayhem; pure mayhem. During the five-minute hail of rifle, machine gun and artillery fire which followed that erroneous shot, the Tibetans were devastated."

I was right. The elite guard ended up slaughtered by Brits, Nomis thought.

"Younghusband discovered later that each Tibetan also had a prayer box attached to a cord slung around his neck. Its role was to stop the bullets from piercing his body," Yangchenla added. "He also found that the Tibetans had extinguished their wicks as a sign of good faith shortly before the confusion began. In doing so, a musket might have accidentally been discharged."

The tour guide droned on. Nomis fell deep into thought.

Technology in my head far more advanced. Personal stealth the ultimate weapon. Hackers armed with packets of light. Capable of bringing down a power grid. Personal stealth a haze of undulating plasmons. Boom, You're dead. MAIHEM's surgical masterpiece of instant death. No wick-driven muskets, no little charm boxes nor gentlemanly-like conduct. Odds are overwhelmingly in my favor. Assault won't be like what took place near outskirts of Lhasa, no hail of lead and steel. A methodical, surgical process. Must look like thieves falling out, not massacre championed by superior numbers or technology.

Nomis grew cold when he learned from the fact sheet that a very high percentage of those in Lhasa were holy men.

Holy men supported by any kind of technology are dangerous combination, Nomis thought. *Younghusband and Brits saw the carnage a holy man's charm box inflicts when mated with inferior technology . . . suicide, pure suicide.*

Nomis began to fidget with that little prayer wheel. It kept chirping, so much so that the tour guide chose to digress from her monologue.

"Sir, please hold your questions until the end of the tour. I will answer them then!" she remarked.

She placed the emphasis on the word "will" but gave no time for Nomis's reply, save for a nod of his head, as she quickly returned to her history lesson.

"Three other great rivers flow from the east of Tibet—the Yangtse, the Mekong and the Salween—toward China and Southeast Asia. There a chain of parallel mountains runs north and south. The region is favored by an excellent climate. It was through this gateway in eastern Tibet that the first Mongolian emperor, Kublai Khan, entered China, making his presence felt during the mid-thirteenth century. It was also through this gateway, in 1950, that the Chinese Communists entered Tibet with the same result, and it was through this gateway that, in 2005, the Qinghai-Tibet railway first linked Golmud City in China with Lhasa permitting the Chinese to flood into Tibet."

46
Forbidden Places

Yangchenla began to list the contributions the Chinese had made to Tibet and its people. Nomis sank back into his seat. His eyes closed. His thoughts drifted back to his early childhood. As a young boy, his blindness had denied him the benefit of observing body language, the expression on a person's face or the movement of their hands. But his blindness had taught him how to dissect a person's voice, and Nomis had never lost his ability to detect a voice that held commitment, or the lack thereof.

. . . commitment . . . swift, warm and fluid . . . the run-off from a spring rain . . . lack of it . . . moves at turtle's pace . . . a glacier . . . hard and icy cold, Nomis thought.

The tour guide's pattern of speech began to slow down. As she continued, her voice turned hard and cold.

"The 1950s brought a massive influx of Chinese," Yangchenla said, "and the deportation of many young Tibetans to China for training, which continues to this day."

With his eyes still shut, Nomis felt the coldness and pain of her words. Then, as quickly as her voice had turned icy cold, it regained its warm, supple tone.

"Finally, in March of 1959, a revolt broke out in Lhasa, provoked by an attempt to sequester the Dalai Lama, who, contrary to the wishes of the Chinese, later fled across the Himalayas to India, never to return to Tibet again," Yangchenla said. "The Dalai Lama was the fourteenth in a line that can trace its origins back as far as the thirteenth century, to one of the most celebrated men in Tibetan history, Gan-den Trup-pa."

Again her voice turned painfully icy.

"Subsequent to the flight of the fourteenth Dalai Lama, the Panchen Lama became the nominal head of what was called at the time the preparatory committee."

At least honesty prevails, no matter how painful, Nomis thought. *Certainly put Brits in bad light. No mention of the massacre by Chinese.*

Nomis opened his eyes just in time to catch his first glimpse of the Dalai Lama's winter palace. There was a renewed sense of commitment in Yangchenla's voice.

"In the 7th century A.D., the indigenous, animistic Bon cult, a form of Shamanism that was considered by some to be a decadent form of Chinese Taoism, abounding in demon worship, sorcery, magic, dream interpretation and even human sacrifice, fused with the Buddhist faith to form Lamaism. The sinister elements of Bon have long since disappeared under the influence of the nobler doctrine of Buddha."

Dream interpretation, thought Nomis. *Can use some of that.*

"The Dalai Lama, whose winter palace, the Potala, we are now passing, is an incarnation of Chen-re-zi, the patron deity of Tibet," Yangchenla continued. "Incarnation lamas are saintly sages who have achieved Buddhahood or enlightenment and, with this, the right to escape into nirvana from the circle or Wheel of Existence."

Wheel of Existence . . . let's see what Harrer had to say, Nomis thought. *Ah "saw with my own eyes workers going through each spadefull of earth, removing anything living." Think I'd rather come back as a hummingbird.*

"But these saintly sages deliberately postpone the state of bliss by being reincarnated on earth, committing themselves to remain until the time when all living things attain nirvana," Yangchenla added. "The Potala, one of the most amazing examples of architecture in all of Asia, with its thousand rooms, rises some nine hundred feet above the city. Built in the middle of the last millennium by the fifth Dalai Lama, its stone walls, story by story, slope inward."

Hundreds of windows, Nomis thought. *Wider at bottom than top. Balance, grace and symmetry.*

"The central block contains the chapels and is a deep crimson color, while the outer wall surfaces are whitewashed. The roof glitters with the tombs of former Dalai Lamas, and is also dotted with evidence of our widening wireless world."

Satellite dishes and cell phone antennae, sprouting from Potala, Nomis thought. *Quite a sight . . . the old and the new.*

"We won't be stopping, but inside the Polata itself are council and audience chambers, storerooms, two treasuries, a Great Library, many chapels and apartments for three hundred monks, as well as the winter quarters of the Dalai Lama and some of his ministers," Yangchenla added.

A library, Nomis thought. *Must see before I depart.*

"Until the seventh century A.D., the Tibetan story is mantled in legend," Yangchenla continued. "But the Great Library does contain a few documents related to the history of Tibet prior to the seventh century. Until just recently, the earliest known reference to Tibet is contained in an ancient Chinese document dealing with the banishment of San Miao tribes to San Wei by the Emperor Shun in 2255 B.C. San Wei is thought to be an ancient name for the Tibetan Plateau."

Tibetans might be of Chinese origin after all. Another "lost tribe of Israel" story, Nomis thought.

"You have probably noticed that my spoken English is very choppy," Yangchenla explained. "The Tibetan language belongs to the Indo-Chinese family and is similar to Burmese; it is monosyllabic and uses intonation and stress instead of inflection. For me, a Tibetan national, it is hard to give up the old. I make no apologies. The Tibetan alphabet was borrowed from the Sanskrit. With thirty consonants and five vowels, it came by way of Kashmir in the seventh century A.D., at about the same time as King Song-tsan Gam-po unified the country, made Lhasa the capital, and built the Jokhand, a great Buddhist temple, which we are now passing to your right on the central square. The Jokhand is considered the holiest structure in Tibet."

The old prevails. No cell phone antennae or satellite dishes . . . yet, Nomis thought.

"By the way, the original spelling of the language has been retained while the spoken language has changed over the centuries," Yangchenla said. "So for you language experts, today's orthography is far from phonetic."

Nomis again detected a coolness to her voice.

"In addition, there are three dialectal differences. The speech of the upper classes was distinct from that of the lower classes until the latter half of the last century, when the Chinese put in place a program of universal education and training for all," Yangchenla added.

"Located on that nearby mountain top to your left is the medical college, where students were once taught to cure illness by using herbs, plants, sorcery, magic, incantation and dreams."

Redhouse and Manygoats could have shown them a thing or two, Nomis thought.

"Thanks to the Chinese, it now has some of the most modern equipment in the world, and is a center for organ donation and transplantation. There have been many new advances made in the area of artificial limbs, stemming from the land mine problem in Southeast Asia in the last century. Some of their work there even involves computer-regulated organ systems, especially in the area of hearing and speech. However, they haven't solved the problem of eyes yet, but they are working on it."

My eyes might fall prey to organ thievery, have to pry them out of my head, or worse, CIHPAR, too. No good without vanishing circuits, Nomis thought.

"In fact, foreign ideas and practices were avoided for centuries, and visitors like you, except for religious pilgrims and traders, weren't welcome in Tibet until just recently. They once believed that Western conveniences and even medical practice implied an irreligious devotion to material things rather than their belief in the healing power of an extensive pharmacopeia of plants."

Wow, just like Redhouse, thought Nomis.

"They feared that technology might undermine their beliefs, one of which is the transmigration of the soul. Their place in the Wheel of Existence—the cycle of rebirths—depended on their conduct. It's impossible to escape from that circle until one achieves perfection."

Perfection, Nomis thought. *Impossible to escape until one achieves perfection.*

"Today, in the twenty-first century, these ideas still exist and are practiced daily by some three hundred holy men who live in the Polata. Their beliefs haven't been shaken by this wireless world we now live in. If you recall, the western side of the Polata bristles with satellite dishes and cell phone antennae."

The motor droned on as Khünpela inched the bus up one of the more narrow grades to the west of the Polata. So did the monologue of the tour guide. Nomis's mind again plunged into deep, unstructured thought.

Perfection, he thought. *Perfection to an expert in number theory. The mathematician's mathematician. What Andrew Wiles had searched for, a timeless solution to Fermat's Enigma. Fermat's challenge and its solution, no corpulent structure for thousands of years, both had been there all along, in their own anemic, invisible state, waiting. Fermat tossed the challenge into the laps of his mathematician friends, Wiles added the necessary intellectual bulk required for a solution . . . his solution now timeless . . . entombed in the algorithms which locked up the secrets embedded in those packets of light that travel the Solarnet.*

Nomis found himself mumbling out loud as a structured series of questions emerged in his mind.

"Had Wiles arrived in his nirvana? Why did he continue to teach his students, tossing out new puzzles and then offering encouragement to those who groped for a solution? Did he expect every living thing to achieve perfection?"

"Did I miss something? Who's Wiles?" the person in front of him remarked.

Embarrassment drove Nomis to sink down into his seat again. His thoughts went with him.

My invisible state, Nomis thought, *to me what the solution to that enigmatic challenge of Fermat's was to Wiles.* CIHPAR, *my perfect state. The essence of my being, without reference to material things, its nothingness, like what I experienced when a child with no eyes, when invisible only mind could see. Only in my dreams. Able only to imagine, with the uncluttered mind of my childhood.*

The images of that dream he had had long, long ago, while a student at MIT, seeped from his subconscious mind.

in the beginning
the universe had no eyes
and there was darkness everywhere
a cloud, a ring, and numbers
were the sum total
of what filled the void . . .

Reboot cylinders, like the massive mountain barriers to the south, west and north of Tibet, Nomis thought. *Not geological but technological boundaries. Must discard or overcome to progress further in quest for personal perfection. Want to be able to imagine in a pure state, again nothing but mind . . . want even more. The ability to return at will to the world of the material, depends on outcome of third sequence. Will outcome reveal one-way mirror, a hash function, a humpty-dumpty process?*

Want gateway like that to east of Tibet, no geographical barriers, mountains of the south, west and north gradually undulate down to the Chinese provinces of Szechwan and Yhnnan, permitted those who have had inclination or curiosity to come and go into and out of what had been considered a forbidden place for centuries.

Nomis's lips moved but he made no sound as his thoughts again became more structured.

Will I be able to pass back and forth between my two worlds with ease and see with my heart in one and with my mind in the other? Do I have within my grasp the key to a door, a wormhole, to and from nirvana, which swings both ways, inward toward the bosom of reason and outward toward that of feeling? Is it possible, or will it, in my special case, be forbidden, as it was for centuries in Tibet? Is there a contradiction somewhere that I have missed in my quest for the many-headed, seamless machine of my dreams?

Just then, the tour bus came to a stop in front of the hotel.

"I hope you have enjoyed the tour," said Yangchenla. "For those of you who are interested in having a closer look at the Polata, there is a second tour scheduled for tomorrow, early in the morning. There are still some seats left. Please see the concierge for more information."

As he stepped from the bus, Yangchenla made her way toward Nomis.

"You had some questions, sir?" she began.

"Yes," Nomis replied. "Can you tell me if the Great Library in the Potala is computerized, you know, with the latest equipment for information retrieval, perhaps even from Solarnet?"

"Yes, it is," she said. "During the last ten years the younger monks have taken it upon themselves to bring the Great Library into the modern world. But I'm not sure about access to Solarnet."

"Thank you, thank you very much. A wonderful tour," replied Nomis as he turned and headed for the British Consulate down the street.

When he returned from the consulate, he asked the concierge if the hotel might supply canisters of pure oxygen to guests who had health problems.

"Sign here. Charge is on your room," the concierge said.

The canister was bright red with large white lettering that read *Property of the Lhasa Holiday Inn.*

47

Oxygenarius Erectus

Nomis tossed the canister onto the bed, walked into the bathroom, flicked on the light, positioned himself squarely in front of the mirror and chanted. As he did he saw the reflection of his Adam's apple slithering up and down. His ears began to ring. He began to feel faint. His chin slowly sank toward his chest as he staggered backward and fell toward the bathtub. The shower curtain broke his fall, but the impact forced his head back, slamming it into the tile wall with a thud.

"Ah, shit," Nomis grunted.

Sparks began to fly as he struggled to free himself from the hammock-like swing created by what was left of the shower curtain. His vision blurred. The bathroom light began to dim. He managed to chant again. The fireworks in his eyes subsided, but a raging torrent of thought erupted in his head.

Big trouble. Boot-up phase to stealth an incredible consumption of oxygen. More oxygen needed than the thin air of Lhasa can provide. Implant in my head begins to shut down worse than the descent into Narita.

The dizziness persisted. He made his way to the side of the bed on all fours, hoisting himself up high enough to bat the oxygen canister to the floor. He held the cup to his nose and mouth and turned the valve. It hissed. He lay there on his back, clutching the canister, feasting on the flow. The dizziness slowly melted away. He pulled himself up with the help of the chair by the desk, turning his head every which way as he fingered the welt on the back of his head.

Two systems, eyes and stealth, huge amounts of oxygen needed at boot-up. What to do? First gorge on oxygen, then chant.

He sat bolt upright before the bedroom mirror, firmly grasping the canister. A mixture of curiosity, circumstance and opportunity compelled him to give it another try. After half a dozen huge whiffs, he chanted again. He became giddy. A beefy sexual urge quickly followed. The tremendous quantity of oxygen that he had inhaled began to do its magic; his image slowly vanished from the bedroom mirror. No sparks or fireworks appeared, but within seconds he was flabbergasted to find that his penis, too, was bolt upright. His left hand made its way to his crotch. It was as bulbous and hard as the oxygen canister his right hand was clutching.

What next, oxygenarius erectus? What a monster! COP's engineers will laugh themselves silly. Their boner, not mine, biggest one they ever made. And Nara's opinion on this button? She'd be pushing it every chance she got. Whoa!

He reluctantly chanted again. Immediately his luminescent image began to flicker in the mirror. The lump in his pants slowly receded. Soon he was back, all of him, exhausted and as limp as a dishrag.

Nomis's tone of voice turned orgiastic.

"Yes! Yes!" Nomis blurted out.

By trial and error he confirmed his theory about the unexpected side effect. Four huge whiffs were enough to stave off the onset of dizziness, but not stiffen him up. He was jubilant. He was one step closer to a thorough understanding of the third sequence and its nuances.

Take the plunge, a voice from deep within him said. *Run the one-way mirror test . . . defect to a life of stealth, now!*

His mind raced.

No more unwanted boners. Must deal with dynamic effect of altitude on dosage and certainty of proper sequence. Stealth's boot-up, an extraordinary need for oxygen, implant might shut down at same time—not what I need—penis problem suggests another crossed circuit. No—now not the time!

Nomis's reluctance to take the plunge was understandable. He needed time to think. Denial quickly became an obstacle. He chose instead to sort through the stuff Sedgewick had issued to him in London, and the jump gear he had picked up from Zackery at Narita. He had collected the communication card and that eighth cylinder from the British consulate shortly after the orientation tour had returned to the hotel. It had come in with a bunch of other communication cards for their computers, shipped by the Brits in a diplomatic pouch to avoid detection.

"The gentleman warrior Younghusband might have rolled over in his grave had it not been for the truly unique and surgical ability of my asymmetric advantage in technology," Nomis mumbled.

A smile crept across his face as a fleeting image of he and Nara rolling around in bed percolated into his conscious mind.

And there's my unique advantage also, Nomis thought as he laid out his deadly cache of seven reboot cylinders.

They looked like little candy canes. Nothing was further from the truth when combined with the insidious, sinister content of the eighth cylinder. The fine print on its side revealed its true nature. Some joker had misspelled the abbreviation MAIHEM. It read: *MAYHEM a subsidiary of COP.* If that eighth cylinder itself wasn't destroyed when the detonation occurred, a calling card was the last thing Nomis wanted to leave. He used his aftershave lotion to remove the joker's comments.

The last two items were the address of the hacker and the jumpsuit's canister. The latter Zackery had returned to him late that afternoon, charged and ready to go. So was Nomis. He used Yangchenla's map to reconnoitre. He concluded that the location of the hacker was in the same district as the Holiday Inn. He phoned the front desk to inquire if the hotel complex had a business centre or rented commercial space other than on the first floor.

"Yes, sir, but it's not open now. Hours are eight A.M. to seven P.M. No access for tourist groups such as yours; for the exclusive use of those staying on the upper floors, and those awaiting treatment at the medical college," the concierge replied.

"I need a cell phone and also a wireless modem. Mine's on the blink. Is there a wireless store in or near the hotel complex?" Nomis asked.

"In the adjoining building; the 'wireless something or other warehouse,' . . . branches throughout the region and in China also," he replied.

"The only one?" Nomis asked.

"In this district of the city. They service what they sell and I'm told they enjoy it. Owned by a group of young men who found a life of solitude and contemplation a little too rewarding," the concierge replied.

"You mean Buddhist monks?" Nomis asked.

"Well, former Buddhist monks. Rumor had it they were Chinese sympathizers."

"Sympathizers?"

"Caught running a prostitution ring in the Potala," the concierge added.

"It's quarter past ten. Are they open now?" Nomis asked.

"You looking for a little action?" the concierge asked.

"No, no. For a cell phone and modem," Nomis replied.

"Doubt it. Like the business center, most shops in this district open at eight in the morning, close early in the evening."

Nomis was eager to take a look-see anyway. As he chanted and inhaled from the canister to regain his stealth, he couldn't help thinking of Nara. The state change was quite pleasant, even addictive, with no unnecessary side effects.

∞ ∞ ∞

An underground pedestrian walkway led to the adjoining complex. At the end of the walkway sat a security guard with his feet up, reading a sci-fi comic book about invisible men who occupied another dimension. When old technology was used to protect a perimeter, stealth was a wonderful thing. Little did the guard know that one of those invisible men was looking over his shoulder at the business directory.

An outfit called the Wireless World's Warehouse was located one floor up. An escalator led to the second floor. It was shut down for the night. Nomis used it anyway. At the top, directly facing the escalator, were a number of shops, one of which was the WWW. It was well-secured with a heavy plate glass door.

What looked like a service counter spanned the back wall of the shop, which had been painted in the French style of *trompe l'oeil.* To the eye the wall looked like part of the massive facade of the Potala, but to the touch it was a fake—a painted wall. On the counter was a sign that read: REPAIRS. Behind the counter was a door. Like the windows of the Potala, it was narrower at the top than the bottom. It had a sign affixed to it, which read MONKEY BUSINESS.

Some joker's idea of a life of solitude and contemplation. Technology changes so fast—don't repair it; throw it out, Nomis thought.

From under the door behind the counter, a faint light was visible. Someone was working late in the back. Nomis remained by the glass door for a few more minutes, studying the layout of the shop. A lump formed in his throat when he noticed a faint image of himself. His anxiety rocketed. He had left the canister in his room. Expending as little energy as possible, he turned, walked to the escalator, descended to the ground floor and passed by the security guard without arousing suspicion. He had had enough of CIHPAR's antics for one evening.

48
Monkey Business

For Nomis, jogging had to be both invigorating and educational. On the second morning, he was out the door of his hotel by 6:15 A.M., determined to do three to five miles before breakfast. He used Yangchen-la's map to get his bearing. The temperature was perfect, sixty-seven degrees Fahrenheit, and the air was dry. It reminded him of the weather in February he and George had experienced as kids in Albuquerque. There were only two drawbacks—the possible need to stop every few minutes to inhale a bit of pure oxygen; and too much inhaling might be disastrous, as his jogging shorts were skimpy and tight. The jump suit utility belt solved the former problem. Its niche held the oxygen canister snugly in place when not needed. The latter never became an issue. He suspected it was evidence of another crossed circuit. It was quite nerve-wracking—too little and he went blind; too much and he went stiff.

Today I'll follow the Linkhor to the east, Nomis thought as he limbered up.

The Pilgrim's Road followed the canal constructed by Peter Aufschnaiter, Harrer's friend with the river gauge who had missed his calling as a rainmaker. When Nomis reached the canal, he stopped to test the temperature of the water, wetting a towel that he used to cool down the back of his neck.

Feels good on the neck, but too cold for a swim, Nomis thought, wringing the excess water from the towel.

From the canal, the view of the Potala was spectacular but deceptive. Its massive facade of ten floors was dwarfed by the mile-high mountains jutting from the Kyi River plain, which was already more than two miles above sea level.

Without other references, eyes can easily be deceived, Nomis thought.

As he pressed on toward the Shrine of a Thousand Buddhas, Nomis heard the moans of deep-throated trumpets coming from the direction of Chagpori Hill, where the Medical School was located. The gongs of Nanzen-ji Temple in Kyoto came to mind as the moan of the trumpets trailed off to nothingness.

Must remember to call Shuji Matsubara when I get to Osaka, Nomis thought.

As he retraced his steps, he came upon a zealous Lamaist on hands and knees, inching his way around the five-mile loop. Nomis slowed to a walk to avoid kicking up any dust.

Prefer to jog my way to a happier life, Nomis thought.

In the past, wooden gloves and a leather apron were all that protected hands and knees as a pilgrim crawled. This one still preferred the old ways. He even carried with him a sack of parched barley flour for sustenance.

On his return to the hotel, Nomis checked the daily program of events organized by the Denver Club, posted at the entrance to the group's breakfast room. There was an early morning trip to the Potala, as well as one departing after lunch, and a nine-A.M. showing of a skydiving documentary made a few years ago in Tibet by Zackery. Two other showings were scheduled later in the day. At the last minute, Nomis decided to skip the nine-A.M. showing and catch it instead during the afternoon.

Nomis was anxious to lay his eyes on the Potala's library in his search for a crib that might help him decipher the symbols ♌, ♑, ♒, and ♎, about which the lexicographer from Oxford and the NSA had been so concerned. That late-night foray to the WWW with its *trompe l'oeil* also compelled him to adhere to COP's agenda rather than his own. Deceiving the eye was at worst an innocent joke; the sarcastic nature of the sign, MONKEY BUSINESS was worse; but making a mockery of Quantum II was something altogether different.

COP's god-king mustn't sit idle, Nomis thought.

Breakfast was typical tourist fare, so he grabbed a boxed juice, some goat cheese, and an apple, and headed for the concierge. On his way through the hotel lobby, he ran into Yangchenla.

"Good morning," her staccato voice rang out. "The early tour of the Potala has been delayed thirty minutes due to a mechanical problem with the bus. I noticed you didn't sign up. It's not too late. We will be leaving shortly!"

"Sure!" he replied. "Do I have time to shower? Just returned from my early morning jog."

The tour bus pulled up in front of the hotel entrance adjacent to a small group that had already gathered.

"Hurry. Please, excuse me!" she said.

Nomis dashed off toward the elevators, but found them jammed with breakfast traffic. He took the stairwell to the third floor, munching on his apple. He quickly showered, grabbed the larger canister of oxygen and retraced his steps.

∞ ∞ ∞

Groans were heard from those who had been on yesterday's tour, as Yangchenla began to recite her little blurb.

"Hello again. Many of you met me yesterday and have already heard my little spiel, but I am afraid that I must do it again. It's company policy. My name is Yangchenla and your driver's name . . . "

As Yangchenla babbled away, Nomis took the opportunity to study the fact sheet on the Potala.

Traces out the route after entering the complex, Nomis observed. *Library on itinerary, also a great room with a solid gold statue . . . One of the thirty-five richly carved and painted chapels. A cell used for meditation. One of the seven mausoleums where Dalai Lamas are interred . . . Illustrated volumes of the scriptures, written in inks made of powdered gold, silver, iron, copper, conch shell, turquoise and coral . . . colors of choice found infused in elaborate murals, motifs, doors, walls . . . yellow, red, blue and green.*

Richly colored, round-faced guardian deities glower with popping eyes. Prayer wheels continuously turn, crammed to the brim with supplications and appeals. Monks . . . elaborate yellow hats called the tagdroma, typical of the Gelugpa sect. Shaped like a punk rocker haircut. Frequenting the meditation cells and chapels, centuries of history. An office, temple, school and living quarters, all rolled into one. An enormous storehouse. Priceless scrolls, golden regalia, armor and armament and seven thousand enormous volumes, some weighing nearly eighty pounds.

The fact sheet went on for another three pages. By the time Nomis had finished reading it, his mind was spinning like one of those prayer wheels. He hunkered down in his seat, turning his attention to what he might see out of the window. Yangchenla provided the play-by-play. What she had to say added to his mind's angular velocity.

"On the way to the Potala, we will pass by the Barknor or inner Holy Walk. It encircles the Jokhang, the holiest shrine of all Tibet, which I pointed out to some of you yesterday. We will then follow The Pilgrim's Path or Linkhor to the west. This path is much longer than the Holy Walk, about five miles, and follows the perimeter of the ancient city of Lhasa. It will take us past the Ra Mo Che Monastery and finally to the north side of the Potala."

Must try jogging west around the Linkhor tomorrow, perhaps the entire perimeter, Nomis thought.

"The Potala's center block of pale red, a holy color of Lamaism, is flanked by two white wings facing south. On the roof are the tombs of the Lamaist saints."

As Nomis craned his neck, someone poked him in the shoulder from behind.

"Want to get a better look?" a voice said.

A little blue-haired English lady, her face laden with rouge, thrust her opera glasses over his shoulder.

"Sure," Nomis replied.

Jutting from the corners of the tombs, golden gargoyles, Nomis thought. *Atop the roofs of the tombs, winged angels, and beaked and horned monsters, all of gold. Affixed to the roofs, hammered golden tiles.*

"The most magnificent of these tombs is that of the thirteenth Dalai Lama. Jewels and a ton of gold encrust his mausoleum, and three gilded spires represent baskets holding Buddhist scriptures," Yangchenla said.

Nomis returned the opera glasses as the bus came to a stop. It parked nowhere near the entrance to the Potala, as the climb was much too steep for the bus. One had to ascend a huge number of steps on foot to reach its great gateway, which, when closed, became an ethereal but massive barrier.

Climbing those steps took a great deal of energy. It drew blood away from Nomis's head to the muscles of his legs. Nomis's oxygen canister came in handy. On the way up he had to take a whiff every time the sparks began to fly. One poor woman, also sporting a canister, asked Nomis if he had come to the medical center on Chagpori Hill to undergo a heart transplant.

"Ma'am, a change of heart is something I have just recently begun to contemplate," Nomis replied with tongue in cheek.

Nomis began to understand why "Tibet" and "forbidden" had been synonymous for so long. One glance south at the mountains framed by that ethereal gateway provided a clue. As it opened, it revealed a clear and unobstructed path to the Potala's dark, dingy interior. And those mountainous barriers, with their angular slopes and great gorges, were about as inviting as the interior of the Potala. The group formed a half-circle around Yangchenla at the entrance as she continued her play-by-play.

"The architects of the Potala, like the American architect Frank Lloyd Wright, must have taken their design cues from the lay of the land," Yangchenla began. "Wright incorporated into the design of his Prairie House the lines of the steppes of the mid-western American prairie. As you can plainly see, the persona of the Potala is that of an Everest or a K2–solid, permanent and impenetrable."

Nomis was impressed with her knowledge of Western architecture.

The Polata. A miniature Tibet, Nomis thought, *complete with angular ascents. Just climbed one, reached that door. Conceals a great gorge. Penetrates deep into the Potala's mountainous interior. Sure hope that library isn't impenetrable.*

"Note the richly colored, round-faced guardian deities with unblinking eyes that glare," added Yangchenla.

Eyes. Crazy eyes that don't blink, Nomis thought.

"As you can see, religious art adorns the walls, and in one of the great rooms you will find an immense image of the fifth Dalai Lama, made of solid gold," Yangchenla said.

"Splendid and imposing as it is, it seems miserably dark and uncomfortable as a dwelling place. Is that why it's called the God-King's Golden Prison?" one member of the group asked.

"Perhaps, but the Norbulingka palaces and its summer gardens, which also deserve a visit, are located some two miles from here. They were begun by the fifth and completed by the thirteenth Dalai Lama," Yangchenla replied. "They are usually used rather than the Potala, once summer arrives. They are very beautiful. Now, if you will all follow me to one of the great rooms, where . . . "

∞ ∞ ∞

Nomis strayed from the group and headed for the Great Library, which contained over six-thousand scrolls. When he entered, he sensed an innocence about the young monks as they scurried to and fro. In their orange silk robes and matching, plate-shaped papier-mâché headdresses, they seemed free from moral wrong and unacquainted with evil. Nomis managed to strike up a conversation with one whose English was superb. He was wrestling with a massive fiberoptics cable. In fact, the buds of a computerized information system were sprouting everywhere.

"Yes, the library itself is a magnificent depository of historical facts and odd myths, with a memory that stretches backward in time some four or five millennia," the young monk said.

Four or five thousand years . . . clearly must know its purpose by now. Maybe not, perhaps still a work in progress, Nomis thought.

"It must live and breathe Tibet's historical past," Nomis replied.

"The propulsion plant moving it forward into the future is its momentous memory," the young monk added.

"Forward?" Nomis queried

The young monk waved his hand in the air, pointing every which way.

"Much is inaccessible here. But this labyrinth of cables, modems, servers, monitors, printers and CPUs will fix that," the young monk boasted.

"Impressive!" replied Nomis.

"It will also provide foolproof security for some of our most valuable manuscripts," the young monk added.

"You mean they'll be available virtually," Nomis replied.

"Yes," the young monk replied. "Eventually, our goal is to make all six thousand of them available virtually."

"Any problems?" Nomis asked.

The young monk hesitated. When Nomis heard his answer, he was surprised, as his query had referred to the information retrieval system.

"Yes. A valuable manuscript disappeared about five months ago. Part of a dictionary."

An opening I hadn't expected, Nomis thought.

"Was it very old?" Nomis asked.

"We think it pre-dates the ancient Chinese document that deals with the banishment of the San Miao tribes to San Wei by the Emperor Shun in 2255 B.C."

"Of course you've copies," Nomis said.

"Luckily, yes. An original and two copies, along with a number of etched copper plates."

"Copper plates?"

"Yes, evidence that Asia was far ahead of Europe in the years before your Christ."

"In good condition?" Nomis asked.

"Very good condition. They were recently discovered at a construction site just south of the Potala, deep in a cave. The opening was most probably covered by a landslide or earthquake long ago."

"Very dry conditions probably helped to preserve them," Nomis added.

"Yes, we get only twenty inches of rainfall a year in Lhasa," the young monk replied.

Like the Rosetta stone or the Dead Sea Scrolls: a factual bridge to Tibet's ancient past. Expected to fill many gaps in the library's memory. Maybe COP's too, Nomis thought.

He paused. His crazy eyes began to blink.

And maybe mine, too.

"Can the public still view the copies of what was taken?" Nomis asked.

"No! They will be available virtually in a few months. Three Ws is doing the work for us," replied the young monk.

"Three Ws?" Nomis asked.

"Wireless World's Warehouse," the young monk replied.

Nomis's attention sharpened. A closer look revealed the stickers of WWW were all over the servers and routers.

"What kind of work?" Nomis asked.

"Custom software, very speedy, efficient, high volume access to the Solarnet."

"Any dedicated lines?" Nomis asked.

"One dedicated, high-speed, secure optical fiber line which goes direct to the library. It will permit WWW to maintain their custom software."

"Almost all links in Tibet are wireless, aren't they?" Nomis asked.

"Correct," the young monk replied. "Theirs is one of the few ground links in Tibet."

A ground link. Seems unnecessary and odd, Nomis thought.

As Nomis made his way down the steps to the bus, his thoughts pulsed, much like an algorithm searching for the encrypted key to a locked box that harbored many, many secrets. That dedicated, high-speed secure landline was a second gateway to the Potala's interior. The labyrinth of cables, modems, servers, monitors, printers and CPUs might be a design taking its cue from a topography that was the antithesis of that found in Tibet and certainly within the Potala—a landscape imbued with chaos, steeped in mayhem, flawed in its historical perspective and focused on the imperfect.

A frightening thought. Not impenetrable. A second gateway, worming its way into the propulsion plant of the Potala, poised to drive the innocent off course, Nomis pondered as the bus pulled away.

49

Lama⊣ ⊢Ocean.Net

Nomis, along with three others who had visited the Potala that morning, didn't want a Western lunch. They were looking for something exotic, something genuinely Tibetan.

"Let the waiter choose," one of them suggested.

"No alcohol for me," replied Nomis.

"Not even a beer?" replied another.

"Tea will do me just fine," replied Nomis.

The waiter recommended tsamba, a thick paste of ground, parched barley and buttered tea, along with a mild beer also made from barley. When the tsamba arrived, it looked like the Tibetan version of hummus, but smelled like rank, stale fat; the beer had the hue of dark Guinness Stout with legs. Nomis was glad he had stuck to tea. He might have taken a second cup, but was paged by the concierge.

"Dr. Nomis Chester?" the concierge asked.

"Yes," replied Nomis.

He handed Nomis an envelope. The note inside was short and sweet. It was from the Brits.

"Urgent encrypted message from Boulder. For your eyes only. Pick up ASAP," the note read.

Nomis excused himself and trundled off to his room to pick up his laptop. The consulate was only a short distance from the hotel, so he walked. At the consulate, he used his public key to decipher the note after he had copied it to his laptop. It took the better part of an hour. On his way back to his hotel room, he mulled over its contents.

Another power-grid attack. The Chicago area targeted, preceded by deluge of virus-laden e-mail. Quantum II foiled both. Attack on grid began about 10 P.M. *Lhasa time, yesterday.*

He took a match to the note he was handed at the restaurant, and then flushed the ashes down the toilet.

Hmm . . . attack occurred short time before observing someone working late at the WWW, Nomis thought.

There was more. Quantum II had traced the origin of both attacks to a server in Lhasa. However, it wasn't the same server responsible for the failure of the climate control system at the Houston Superdome during the Texans-Broncos game. The origin was a newly established address. Quantum II suspected it was a slave address, also responsible for the e-mails sent the day before, containing material infected with a virus called *Asian Graffiti*. The virus had the potential to destroy the guts of Quantum II's operating system, leaving only a shell, and stranding tens of millions of messages on Solarnet's highway of light. The e-mails associated with the virus attack had been sent from *lama⊣ ⊢ocean.net*.

Nomis could not help laughing as he erased the file he had copied onto his laptop at the consulate. With science, in the best of times and sometimes the worst, luck prevails. The fact sheet handed out by Yangchenla prior to the start of the previous day's orientation tour had contained a bit more history than was reported in her monologue, with regard to the line of some fifteen Dalai Lamas stretching back as far as the thirteenth century. The word "Dalai" is a Mongolian word meaning *ocean*. It had been bestowed on the third Lama in that succession of fifteen after he extended the religion of Tibet to Mongolia. He was, in fact, the "Ocean Lama", having engulfed Mongolia with the religion of Tibet.

Although the route by which he had unraveled that puzzle was roundabout, the address *lama⊣ ⊢ocean.net* raised some very straightforward but delicate questions in Nomis's mind.

Attacks might be originating from within the Potala. Monks certainly had the equipment . . . high-speed connection between WWW *and the library also worrisome. Tonight's the night,* Nomis thought.

For the remainder of the afternoon, Nomis's activities focused on his personal agenda. Nomis caught the tail end of the late afternoon showing of the skydiving documentary. Apparently there are fierce updrafts on the Kyi River flood plain, like the Santa Ana winds that come in from the Pacific Ocean near Santa Barbara in California, or the chinooks that often scream in from the eastern face of the Rocky Mountains, onto the Alberta plains.

In California, the condors have used the heat-driven updrafts of those Pacific winds for eons to effortlessly float or glide in the sky all day long. The wind builds in the late morning and early afternoon, when the sun is highest and brightest in the sky. A few years ago, Nomis learned about those updrafts the hard way! Caught in one, he was almost blown out to sea. In Tibet there was little danger of getting blown out to sea, but the high peaks rising from the Kyi River flood plain did pose a problem.

That evening, at about 6:30 P.M., he made plans to visit the WWW in stealth state. However, Nomis soon realized he had another problem. How might he get the communication card and eight little cylinders into the shop? Any clothing he wore also became stealth, but it did not work with hats, or, more precisely, hats on his head. The same was true for the cylinders and the communication card. When the aura of plasmons was boiling around him, both seemed to float in the air like hats on his head. But hats, gloves or any other type of clothing held close to any other part of his body did become stealth.

Unfortunately, this was not the case with large metal objects. On his head or elsewhere, chanting had no effect on them. With regard to hats, he suspected it had something to do with the range of his body's aura. The atmospheric diffusion was always strongest around the head, caused by the extraordinary draw of oxygen by the brain. There was that time in the SCIF when the oxygen content of the room had been reduced, and all but Nomis's head became stealth. For large metal objects, he had no idea. It was time for another round of button-pushing.

As an adult, he had to chuck out a lot of accumulated baggage in order to push his own buttons. He felt like a six-month-old infant watching, then discovering, and finally exploring what turned out to be his toes when beginning to investigate things other than the oral impulse to suckle. Later in life, it was his dreams about which he began to wonder, much, much more complicated than his toes, but the principle was the same. Such investigations—of toes or dreams—were the budding of a different kind of hunger, one that focused on understanding self-image.

Nomis began this round of button-pushing by donning a hat and going stealth with the aid of four measured whiffs. However, once stealth had overcome his image, he then gorged himself on oxygen from the canister. The hat finally disappeared, only to reappear a few minutes after he stopped inhaling. There was only one problem. Subsequent to chanting, as long as he saturated his system with oxygen, the hat became toast, but his penis ended up hard as nails. Although Nomis was slowly building a manual for himself, a little book of rules to live by, this particular section was not exactly useful, at least in the current situation.

Experimentation proved fruitless. There was nothing he was able to do but put up with the discomfort.

He packed the communication card, the cylinders and, for peace of mind, the canister in his coat close to his body and bingo, all went stealth but the outer shell of the canister, parts of the communication card and five of the seven cylinders. He huffed and puffed a bit on the oxygen canister and they soon disappeared too. So off he went, hatless and unseen, head, cylinders, communication card, canister and all, with his private parts hard as a nail, huffing and puffing on the oxygen canister once in a while to maintain the integrity of the haze of plasmons that boiled around him.

At the WWW, the plate glass door was wide open, but the door behind the service counter was only ajar. Only one customer was being served near the front of the store. To be on the safe side, he gorged himself with more oxygen, then carefully slipped through the plate glass door, made his way to the door behind the counter on which "Monkey Business" was affixed, and squeezed through it. Once inside he picked an out-of-the-way spot to wait for the proprietor to lock up and leave.

His plan was to determine whether the proprietor was acting alone or conspiring with someone in the Potala. Regardless, Nomis intended to install the "FOB" package, without setting the little switch. He wanted to observe his target for a few more days to ascertain when might be the most opportune time to arm *Boom You're Dead*. If the shopkeeper was his man, Nomis wanted him, but he also wanted as little collateral damage as possible. Those were the rules of engagement that he was bound by.

Nomis remained for some time, hunkered down like a polar bear, behind his high-tech block of ice, scanning the horizon for seals. At one point he removed the communication card, cylinders and canister from beneath his coat and hid them inside a loose air vent. Feeling a lot less anxious about any unexpected flickering, his body was at rest now in a torpid state, demanding little oxygen. In addition it provided some relief from those unwanted side effects—it gave his private parts a well-deserved rest. Shortly after Nomis had squirreled away his treasures, the proprietor locked up and left the shop.

One aspect of the room intrigued Nomis. At the back was another door. Affixed to it was a sign reading NIRVANA.

First Monkey Business, then Nirvana, Nomis thought. *What a life.*

50

Uptight, Upright and Pumped

Nomis was quick to exit from hibernation. He was eager to play his hunch. *Nirvana* had to be an important piece of the puzzle. Much to his chagrin, he found the door locked, and under such circumstances, his stealth state was unavailing. Whatever that door concealed, it was inaccessible.

Monkey Business was another matter. The WWW had marshaled quite an elaborate array of computer power, communication gear and light speed feeds. However, Nomis quickly concluded it was only capable of initiating feeble, perhaps even inconsequential cyber attacks, nothing like those vicious widespread assaults that had recently occurred.

Bit of a surprise, Nomis thought. *Expected to find much more equipment, traffic analysis of Quantum pointed in that direction.*

To take on Quantum II, you had to have more than a couple of PCs and servers. More important were the scraps of printed material, found by one server, employing the strange language he had been working on with the lexicographer from Oxford and, before that, with the NSA.

But to kill a man, Nomis needed more evidence than a couple of PCs and snippets of paper with funny-looking squiggles scrawled all over them. He needed something that linked the proprietor directly to the recent Solarnet attacks. He had to be absolutely certain, but he had only a scant chance of breaking the coded material, or whatever it was, without a direct feed to Quantum II.

Set one up, Nomis thought. *Use the shopkeeper's equipment. No. Too risky. It will take too much time.*

Once confirmed, NSA will get its surgical strike, pronto. But certainty for Nomis was always a trial. After all, his was the *if and only if* world of the mathematician.

His predicament reminded him of the situation the Japanese must have faced in WWII. Navajo was such a strange language that the Japanese weren't able to break the code derived from it. It had left the

Japanese speechless. It left Nomis speechless too, in all ways but one. For the second time that day, a voice from deep within him argued its point of view.

Take the plunge. Run the one-way mirror test. Do it now.

Nomis again chose to ignore its carping request. Instead, as planned, he installed *Boom You're Dead,* but held off activating it until harder evidence was in hand.

Into the wee small hours of the morning, messages and e-mails continued to arrive. All were encrypted. It was three A.M. before Nomis decided to call it quits. Prior to his departure, he copied the proprietor's custom communication software and a number of e-mails sent from the WWW to the chief IT monk at the library in the Potala. He then abandoned *Monkey Business* for the comfort of his hotel room. Exhausted, he napped for an hour. By four thirty A.M. he was at it again, picking the proprietor's communication code to pieces.

In any effort, there are always spin-offs. The effort of the WWW to bring the Potala's IT system up to date was no exception. Nomis found that the communication software had linked together all of the computers in the Potala in parallel, including the three hundred or so located in the apartments of the monks. In itself, this was not unusual, but that was not all! Nomis suspected that when the Potala's network was hooked to Solarnet, the WWW had the wherewithal to turn Solarnet loose on itself by using COP's technology as its delivery system.

A *parallel-processed brute of a system,* Nomis thought. *Rivals Quantum in technical abilities, and speed.*

As a prime contractor in the undertaking to bring the Potala's library into the modern world of information storage and retrieval, it had buried, in its custom communication software, code that was able to *hijack* the Potala's IT system from almost anywhere in the world via Solarnet.

As Nomis sifted through the various files he had pinched from WWW, he came upon a disturbing e-mail, which contained a telltale recommendation the WWW had made to the chief IT monk at the library in the Potala. It was dated the morning after the Chicago attack had been foiled by Quantum II.

Unsuccessful Chicago attack might be dry run, Nomis thought.

It argued that one hundred more PCs would be required to ensure that service was available in all locations throughout the Potala's one thousand rooms.

Nomis reckoned that the addition of those extra one hundred machines would bring this labyrinth, this medusa of a computer network, to the point where the tentacles of the beast could reach out to any point on the planet. Like a primitive hydrozoan or scyphozoan, it would be in a position to feast on the guts of Solarnet and then poop them out. Nomis's anxiety spiked at the prospect of such a primordial but effective scheme laying waste to the Solarnet.

Prior to his morning jog, Nomis's anxiety peaked again. He discovered that the smaller canister that had come with the jump suit was nearly depleted, and in his haste, he had failed to retrieve the larger canister from its hiding place in *Monkey Business.* His carelessness meant he was dependent on the smaller one until he returned to the WWW, and that would be six to seven hours away. The dithers descended upon Nomis with a vengeance.

More button-pushing ensued. With only himself to converse with, waiting in the isolation of his room affected his good judgment. He toyed around with a number of exotic, even perverted, solutions, one of which was sheer fantasy.

Perhaps safest way to travel stealth . . . nude . . . oxygen requirements might be much less . . . good only for round trip to WWW . . . chilly . . . Wish I could make love while stealth with Nara . . . one of my humongous boners . . . see if it or anything else lights up with all those plasmons boiling around me, Nomis thought.

Both would have caused Nara to doubt his sobriety, the latter his sanity.

He opted for something much less exotic, but just as strenuous as lovemaking. He went stealth with no clothes on, and did twenty-five push-ups, raising his heart rate to one hundred and thirty-five beats per minute. Not a single part of him flickered. But soon twenty-five became thirty, and thirty became thirty-five. He lay exhausted on the floor between fifty and fifty-five. Debilitated and fatigued, he fell asleep for the first time in twenty-four hours, but with little consequence.

By late morning, his anxiety peaked a third time. His pulse pounding, driven by panic, he took a tepid shower. His foray that evening to WWW was almost certain to produce the death of a man. To make matters worse, just before lunch some of his childhood bogeymen showed up.

Phantom of the arc . . . my nemeses, Nomis thought. *On the loose . . . stomach hurts . . . not hungry.*

He tried doing a little math with words, without success. Nothing seemed to provide relief. Depression clawed at him.

Push-ups gave way to a tonic that teetered on the limit of sanity. He considered undertaking a five-mile run nearly nude, but in stealth state.

Follow the Lingkhor . . . circle the ancient city of Lhasa, Nomis thought.

Reason was wanting. The smaller canister might not be worth a damn after a mile or two. He went ahead anyway. He wore only a jock strap and the jump suit's utility belt. The jock was more comfortable, and his perverted logic thought it safer to always be within reach of the oxygen canister, even though it was nearly depleted.

He remained uptight, upright and pumped, yet no light escaped from the boiling haze of plasmons that engulfed his nearly nude body as he circled the ancient city of Lhasa. In fact, his mild depression intensified. His thoughts of Nara did not help. He concluded that if Nara had been there with him in Lhasa that afternoon, pushing his buttons, even she too might not have been able to induce any part of him to light up, not even his private parts. He could neither laugh nor cry at the prospect. By late afternoon, waiting had simply worn him down. He again napped for an hour. When it was time to pay the WWW another visit, he took off his clothes, rather than putting them on. It made him feel like a prostitute.

51

Knowns Versus Unknowns

By six forty-five P.M., the waiting was over. Nomis was on the move again and in a much better frame of mind. It was short-lived, however. In his stealth state, Nomis visited the WWW twice following his nude romp along the Pilgrim's Road—first naked to retrieve the canister from its hiding place, and then fully clothed to finish what he had set out to do the night before.

The second time he had been hunkered down in *Monkey Business* for the better part of an hour when the proprietor entered, sat down at one of the servers and opened his e-mail. It was in that language or code that thus far had been the proprietor's bluff! The proprietor unlocked the door to *Nirvana*, retrieved an old book or binder, and quickly returned. After consulting the book, he became agitated, then angry, and finally frantic.

"*Merde*!" the proprietor exclaimed.

French, Nomis thought.

The proprietor dug a cell phone from his pocket, dialed and left the room. Shortly afterward, the lock on the door to *Monkey Business* went click, as did the toggle switches in the fuse box located near the plate glass door. One by one, the lights went out. Only the screensavers of the servers were left flickering. Something was up. The proprietor had left the shop without deleting the message from the screen, nor locking up the old book in *Nirvana*, nor securing the door to *Nirvana*.

Anger, Nomis thought. *Causes acute bouts of forgetfulness . . . bedfellows.*

To Nomis the proprietor's hasty departure was welcome but troublesome.

Will he be back shortly? Nomis thought.

Quickly and quietly, the snooping began. *Nirvana* had little of interest to offer except that book. It was a storage room with a secure lock and that was it. The book must have been very valuable, a one-of-a-kind treasure that might be worth hundreds of thousands of dollars if auctioned at Christie's. No wonder he kept it locked up.

A *strange language, for sure,* Nomis thought. *If I have anything to do with it, a dead one too. Better off in a museum.*

Yangchenla's comments on the origin of the Tibetan language came to mind.

Lots of notes in the margin, French. All sorts of letters weren't pronounced, Nomis thought. *When pronounced, crazy rules of punctuation and word position prevalent, speaking and writing like night and day, perhaps its predecessor.*

Nomis searched frantically for the word ♌♋♑♒♎♋♎ or whatever it was. The pages containing it were gone, ripped out.

Perhaps the pages that turned up in the hands of the lexicographer from Oxford, Nomis mused as he turned his attention to the jumble of thirty-three symbols and squiggles left on the screen by the proprietor, and the scribblings of the proprietor on a yellow pad by the monitor.

♌⌘⌘♌⍓⌘◆♐❖❍♎❍♋♎♓⬧⌘♈⧫♒❍●⌘⌘⬧❍♌♋♑♒♎♋♎

Nomis's proclivity for serendipitous puzzle-solving was well-known. The most recent example was the enigmatic word "ocean" in *lama⊣ ⊢ ocean.net.* He began to doodle on the yellow pad, writing the one deciphered symbol given to him by the lexicographer over and over again:

♋=[a], ♋=[a], ♋=[a], ♋=[a], ♋=[a].

Unlike a schooner whose sails were set to catch the slightest breeze, he quickly found himself in irons going nowhere. He was becalmed. Like flotsam and jetsam, a jumble of thoughts drifted aimlessly through his mind.

The balt . . . Walden Pond . . . the bluff in Albuquerque . . . soft ice cream . . . the rings of Saturn . . . George . . . the three-fingered man . . . the last time he and Nara had made love.

His private parts began to stiffen. Again he began to aimlessly doodle as his mind's eye floated haphazardly.

[♋] = [a] Nines on their side, sixes on their side, perverted sexual behavior. Tadpoles copulating.

Snippets of that dream he had had on the way home from the Antarctic began to seep into his conscious mind.

An ocean appears . . . a high plateau floats by . . . tadpoles copulating in a plastic bag . . . son's reflection in a mirror . . . dad spinning in an office chair.

One by one, vague images and feelings from the rubble of that dream appeared, vanished and then reappeared. He scratched down what he saw and felt on the yellow pad—one by one. The pointed tip of his pencil passed along the length of each.

An ocean appears: What was it? The Southern Ocean circumvents the Antarctic. Also, Dalai in Mongolian means ocean, an ocean appears maybe a coincidence. Son's reflection in a mirror, Nomis pondered.

For the third time that day the voice from deep within him welled up.

Abandon your image in the mirror . . . take the plunge, it silently whined.

He dutifully returned to the line beginning with *son's,* and crossed it out.

When he did, all hell broke loose. It was like nailing a scratch-and-win lottery or similar to what happened to those who attended his luncheon talk in Singapore. When the clutter of the letters F E D E X was discarded, out popped the little arrow from the rubble of the E and the X . On that return flight from Singapore, his subconscious had deciphered that string of strange characters, ♌♋♑♒♎♋♎, but then encrypted their meaning in a string of dream-driven images, to which the nagging voice from deep within him seemed to have the key—*discard his image.* Nomis's sorting process was abruptly punctuated by an expletive.

"Shit . . . plastic bag . . . dad spinning . . . eureka . . . Baghdad!" Nomis blurted out.

On the pad, he carefully wrote ♌♋♑♒♎♋♎ and beside it he wrote *Baghdad.* He now had five cribs: [b] = ♌, [d] = ♎, [g] = ♑ and [h] = ♒ and [a] = ♋. His pulse quickened as his pencil moved from character to character along the string. A nearly inaudible mumble came from his lips.

"No access to Quantum II's cipher . . . let's see. Not much time, want to be parsimonious, as little effort as possible. Let's try splitting the string up into groups that include what I know and what I don't know," Nomis mumbled.

Group	#	Known	Unknown	Known to Unknown Ratio
♌⌘⌘♌	1	♌	⌘	1 to 1
⍓⌘◆♐❖	2	—	⍓⌘◆♐❖	0 to 5
○♎○♋♎	3	♎♋	○	2 to 1
♓♦⌘♈♦♒○●⌘⌘♦○	4	♒	♓♦⌘♈♦○●	1 to 7
♌♋♑♒♎	5	♌♋♑♒♎	—	5 to 0
♋♎	6	♋♎	—	2 to 0

From ♌⌘⌘♌⍓⌘◆♐❖○♎○♋♎♓♦⌘♈♦♒○●⌘⌘♦○♌♋♑♒♎♋♎, Nomis constructed six groups of varying sizes, arranging them on the pad in a crude table. He was careful not to disturb the order.

Last two groups contain no unknowns. Combined result means "Baghdad" First and third groups contain two unknowns, second and fourth groups contain eleven unknowns.

He concluded that expending his effort on the first and third group might be far more efficient than focusing his effort on the second and fourth group.

As for knowns . . . last two contained five, first and third groups contain three, second and fourth groups contain one.

Again he concluded that the biggest bang for the buck might result from a focus on groups one and three. It was an easy choice. Clearly the ratio of knowns to unknowns was far greater there.

Which to attack first—one or three?

Unfortunately, Nomis's ability to properly weigh alternatives whose differences were not large had been degraded by stress and the pressure of time.

Doesn't matter if I go for the first or the third group. The latter has a higher ratio of knowns to unknowns: two to one. Former has same first and last letter, b . . . Both have only one unknown. Down to two groups with two unknowns. OK, like simple algebra . . . two equations and two unknowns. Doesn't matter which one I start with.

He even let the dictionary sidetrack him.

Let's try the dictionary first.

Nomis's sorting process was again abruptly punctuated by an expletive. He found that ♌ and another one, ☾· were interchangeable in common usage if preceded by two characters that were identical. That first group might be either ♌⌘⌘☾· or ♌⌘⌘♌, depending on the context, and he didn't know the context! A third expletive rolled from his lips and a rush of adrenaline again elevated his pulse. Now there were three unknowns—⌘, ❍ and ☾·—in the first group, not two. The ratio was really one to two, not one to one. He had wasted valuable time.

Ought to have begun with the group with the ratio 2 to 1.

Dropping the first character of the third group produced ♎❍♋♎ or d[?]ad.

"First and last letter are the same . . . fuck all . . . same as group one . . . going in circles," Nomis groaned.

His pencil went to work again. Another expletive rung out.

"Balls, it's got to be *edead*; the third group has to be *edead*."

Again the pencil, and again an expletive.

"Shit, in the first group, if the second character is an *o*, then it might be *boo* something-or-other *edead* . . . whoa . . . add an *m* and drop an *e* and it's . . . *boom* something or other *dead* . . . They're on to me! It's got to be *boom you're dead* something-or-other *baghdad*!"

Nomis quickly jotted down the string that he had come up with, filling in and underlining the characters as decyphered:

BOOM ⌂ O ◆ ♐ ❖E DEAD ♓⬩ O ♈◆ HE ● OO ⬩ E BAGHDAD.

What he had not deciphered, he left untouched. He ripped several additional sheets from the pad, glancing at his handiwork as he stuffed it into his pocket. The combination of BOOM, DEAD, and BAGHDAD was enough to send shivers up his spine. Whoever his adversaries were, he could only conclude that they knew about the FOB. He was invisible, but what he was up to was not. A cardinal sin in the spook business. Time was of the essence. The proprietor might return any minute.

He fixed the trigger by reprogramming the communications card to look for the word ♌♋♑♒♎♋♎. After cutting and pasting the word from the string on the screen to the card's software, he flipped the little switch that armed FOB. Nomis also made the decision to pinch the dictionary. It was no doubt the one missing from the library of the Potala. In its new life as a codebook, it might be a valuable asset to COP. It might even play a key role in Nomis's personal agenda. Unfortunately, it was bulky, and when he managed to position it under his left arm, its image persisted. He took a few big whiffs. He was home free—almost. He was now hard as nails and the hotel canister was too big to fit into the utility belt's niche. Under the circumstance, the condition was unavoidable. He tucked the canister under his right arm and left the WWW to *Boom You're Dead.*

On the way through the hotel lobby, Nomis caught a glimpse of his prey off in a corner with another chap whose back was turned. Their conversation was animated. Arms flailed and feet tapped nervously. Nomis stood nearby, hoping to catch the gist of their remarks, but to no avail. Their tongue was as jumbled as that string on the screen. Nomis took the stairwell to reach his room. As he bounded up the stairs, the canister slipped from his grip and bounced partway down. He retraced his steps, picked it up and bounded up the stairs again. As he reached the top, the image of the book began to flicker and so did he. He sprinted to his room. Stealthing did have its drawbacks. Any prolonged exertion was risky with your clothes on.

Shortly after he shed both his stealth and his clothes, an explosion rocked the hotel complex.

The shopkeeper returned to tidy up, tripped Boom You're Dead . . . it's over. As Sedgewick said, boom, he's dead, Nomis thought.

Wracked with fatigue, he threw himself onto the bed. A feeling of paranoia oozed from within him—his psyche became iced with doubt.

But is he dead? Nomis thought. *And if he isn't, what to do? Shit . . . what if something has gone wrong?*

He heard the wail of sirens in the distance. He returned to the lobby by way of the stairwell. By the time he arrived, it was in an uproar, as was the lobby of the complex. Police and firemen were everywhere. A truckload of soldiers had taken over the tour bus's spot. His angst dissipated.

The guy must be dead . . . didn't even get a chance to see what Nirvana was like, Nomis thought. *Maybe never will, unless blowing people up is perfection, which I doubt.*

52
The Abyss

Early the next morning, Nomis flipped on the TV. There was a piece on the local news about the explosion, but nothing about anyone being killed. He decided to go stealth again and take a look at the shop. He had had his fill of stealthing in the nude. It was easier for him to pace the oxygen needs of his special systems than risk a citation for streaking in Lhasa if he began to flicker.

The WWW was heavily guarded. The door to *Monkey Business* was no more, as was most of the *trompe l'oeil*. Nothing was left but a ball of twisted plastic and metal. There was shattered glass everywhere. FOB had done its job. Everything had been sucked toward that server with crushing force. But there was no blood, and no body. Only what looked like a finger was protruding from the ball.

The morgue, Check the morgue, Nomis thought.

He returned to his room to retrieve the map of the old city. The medical center was quite a distance away, situated on Chagpori Hill on the north side of the Linghor. Jogging had taken only fifteen minutes; walking might take more than a half hour or so and he did not want to take a bus. He shed his stealth and took a cab.

It was quite a climb to the top of the hill where the medical center was located. The road was narrow and without a guardrail. Looking southwest toward the Potala, Nomis was able to see both the hamlet of Shö and the road to the center of Lhasa. To the northeast was the Kyi River, and further to the east was Norbulingka, the summer residences and gardens of the Dalai Lama. Between Chagpori Hill and the Potala was situated the tomb with three spires, which marked the ancient city's western gate. The components of the gate, the *chorten,* symbolized the five elements of the universe. Its square base represented the earth; the dome, water; the golden spire, fire; the crescent moon, water; and the crowning circle, ether. The jagged ellipse of the Lingkhor traced the boundaries of the ancient city.

A world of squares, circles and ellipses, Nomis thought.

Near the summit, a bus approached from the other direction forcing the cabbie to drive dangerously close to the road's edge. The engine of the cab labored. The drop must have been more than 1,500 feet to the floor of the Tsangpo Valley. As he scooted from the cab, in the distance Nomis heard the drone of a piston-driven airplane. It was a party of skydivers. One by one they exited and eventually floated back to earth.

The new and the old, Nomis thought.

Nomis entered the little coffee shop located off to one side of the lobby of the medical center. He bought some juice and then went to the restroom. There was no one there, so he chanted. It did not work; in his haste, he had left the canister on the floor of the cab. Most probably, the thin air of Lhasa was even thinner some 1,500 feet above the valley floor. He retrieved one of his plastic credit cards from his wallet and used it to make a paper-thin cut in the soft tissue between the finger and thumb of his right hand. When he emerged from the restroom, his hand was bleeding profusely. As he turned the corner and entered the waiting room of the emergency unit, he almost upset one of those crash carts used for resuscitation. Much to his horror, there sat the proprietor by the discharge desk. Only his left hand was bandaged!

"That was a close call. You were lucky to get away with only a slight concussion and the loss of your index finger when the glass shattered. If you had arrived a minute earlier . . . " Nomis overheard the attendant say.

. . . *You might now be dead,* Nomis thought.

It took a minute or two to sink in.

Good God, another three-fingered man! Nomis thought. *Technology seems to be a breeding ground.*

Nomis began to feel flushed, and the cause was not the sight of his own blood dripping from his hand, nor was it the lack of oxygen. It was that bandage on the shopkeeper's hand.

Shit. The personal touch failed. Left the server on auto receive-open. Or FOB malfunctioned, Nomis thought.

Just then, an intern summoned the shopkeeper to an examination cubicle for one last look at the shopkeeper's hand. The next thing Nomis knew, a second attendant had led him to another.

"The doctor will be along in a minute," he said to Nomis as he shut the door.

Nomis grabbed the tube labeled "oxygen" from the wall, started the flow and chanted, gorging himself. There was a small mirror on the table—stealth! The cut continued to bleed and peppered the floor with droplets. The little red dots slowly lost their stealth. He put a tourniquet on his hand. The paper-thin cut sealed quickly. In fact, the bleeding stopped just as an intern entered the cubicle. Nomis slipped by him as he stood there, staring at the blood on the floor with a confused look on his face.

As Nomis exited the emergency unit, he carefully retrieved a small oxygen canister from the crash cart and immediately took a couple of whiffs. He quickened his pace, following the shopkeeper down the hall and out into the main lobby. The shopkeeper exited through the lobby door where Nomis had entered. There were no cabs or buses to be seen. The shopkeeper took his cell phone from his belt and placed a call.

To the left of the main entrance, adjacent to the parking lot, one enjoyed that spectacular view of the Tsangpo Valley. Beyond the earthen mound which ringed the lot was an abyss, with rocks so jagged they looked like the teeth of a prehistoric dragon who had thrust his jaws up from the bowels of the good earth for one last breath of fresh air.

On the other side of the earthen mound, the ground sloped off at an angle to the edge of the abyss. While holding his cell phone to his ear, the shopkeeper carefully climbed the berm and descended for a look-see, as the view of the Potala, once over the berm, was truly magnificent.

Nomis followed him to the edge, leaving the canister behind at the top of the berm. The tilt of the land gave Nomis the high ground. He was in an excellent position to push him over. All Nomis had to do was nudge him a bit; it would look like an accident.

Just as Nomis was about to poke him in the small of the back, the shopkeeper turned away from the abyss, bumping Nomis's elbow and knocking the tourniquet from Nomis' right hand. Nomis saw his own image flickering in the lenses of the shopkeeper's glasses. Either the air was too thin or the exertion was too much, or both, and the canister was some fifty feet away. His hand began to bleed again.

Nomis knew what he had to do. It was his duty! He felt faint but stood his ground, as his flickering image danced to and fro in the now-terrified eyes of the shopkeeper. They were nearly nose-to-nose. The features of the proprietor's face filled Nomis's field of vision. The proprietor's left eye twitched. Nomis began to hyperventilate as his pulse raced. The blood, oozing from his right hand, continued to drip to the ground. He clasped his left hand in his right, hoping to stop the bleeding. Both hands became covered with his own blood.

High cheekbones and hair like black straw . . . one of my ancient ancestors . . . crossed over on the ice bridge long, long ago, perhaps, Nomis thought.

Nomis instinctively gave some ground, backing up the berm a few feet. He felt like he was about to pass out. The criminal backed away from Nomis's bloody-handed, flickering image toward the abyss and knelt down, shielding his head with his hands and arms, terrified and in awe at the sight of Nomis's technologically driven appearance.

Nomis stretched his bloody hands skyward, gesturing to the proprietor to stand up and move away from the edge. The proprietor's entire body stiffened. When it did, he lost his footing. As he fell, his arms and legs unfurled from their crouching position and became outstretched. For a minute he seemed to silently float like a condor searching for its prey, or looking for an updraft to carry it to his desert origins, or perhaps to his *Nirvana*. Then he disappeared into the jaws of the mountain. From below, Nomis heard the echo of a primordial moan, as if the good earth realized it had just devoured one of its own. And then silence again. It was over.

"I didn't push him. It wasn't me. He had a choice. He might have walked away. I gave ground. I gestured to him to move away from the edge," Nomis mumbled to himself as he gazed out onto the majestic Tsangpo Valley.

Within minutes his head had cleared and heart rate had lessened. He hoped his flickering image, which had so threatened and terrified the shopkeeper, had vanished. He picked up the tourniquet, carefully scraped up any blood-stained soil and stuffed both into his pocket. He scaled the berm ever so slowly, retrieved the canister and immediately gorged himself with oxygen. He descended into the parking lot, tucking the canister under his right arm. When he crossed the lot, he glanced in the side mirror of a parked car—no image, no flickering and no canister. He took a position at the bus stop, which permitted him to board the next bus through the rear door, undetected.

Must leave this dreadful state, this criminal life . . . this life of criminals . . . nature of the third sequence must be fully understood, Nomis thought.

∞ ∞ ∞

It wasn't easy, traveling stealth on public transportation with a canister of oxygen. In fact, he exited the first chance he had, found a washroom, shed his stealth, washed the blood from his hands, discarded the canister, flushed the tourniquet down the toilet and hailed a cab. It was mid-afternoon when he arrived at the hotel. There were a couple of phone messages—one from Nara and one from someone associated with the Denver Skydiving Club, who was organizing a jump the following morning.

Nomis called Nara in the early evening. She was just getting up.

"Nara, I haven't had a chance to call and didn't call our friends in Kobe on my way through Narita," Nomis said.

"Nomis, were you on that plane that lost the door? I was very worried and called the director right away when I heard the report on CNN. I was very—" Nara blurted out.

"Not to worry. Everybody was OK. But at Narita, when the plane finally landed, I was a little rushed as a result of the confusion. And Lhasa has been a nightmare."

"A nightmare," Nara replied.

"Not to worry, I said! I'm going to re-route through Osaka, anyway, and take the chance that I might catch Shuji. I'm also thinking of taking a side trip to Kyoto, to visit that temple, Nanzen-ji. Remember, the one we explored in the early morning when we visited your parents, just after we were married. I'll call you when I get to Osaka. Tomorrow there's a jump. I might take part. I haven't made up my mind yet," Nomis replied.

"You're too old for that sort of thing, aren't you?" Nara quipped.

"Well, then I might go along for the ride," Nomis mused.

"I saved an interesting piece from the newspaper for you—a letter to the editor published yesterday. Had fallen down an old heating vent and was over one hundred and fifty years old. It dealt with the recent developments in physics at the turn of the nineteenth century. It was very interesting. It focused on all the good that might come from the new technology of the time. Being the old newspaper buff that you are, I cut it out so you can add it to your collection. I'll save it for you," Nara said.

Nomis didn't answer Nara. He was somewhere else—perhaps in his cloud world, perhaps a speck of dust floating around Saturn, perhaps somewhere halfway, in-between, but not there with Nara as they said their goodbyes.

53
Puff the Magic Dragon

Nomis was floating on his back at the shallow end of the hotel pool with his eyes closed, enjoying the peace of the moment, when he heard footsteps and then a watery plunk. Someone had plunged into the deep end. Ripples radiated outward from the splash. The undulating surface of the water stretched and strained, as if trying to leap the pool's perimeter. Some water did, landing on the turquoise tiles that lined the pool's edge.

In the dry air of Lhasa, it would soon be gone. It, like Nomis, could go stealth and then return as a gentle warm rain or a torrential downpour. Or perhaps just float away, molecule by molecule, clumped together in droplets so small the eye couldn't detect them save for the angle of the sun.

When it did, the radiance of a rainbow was magnetic, but its treasure elusive. The point where the rainbow came to earth always seemed to float just out of reach, but Nomis had learned the secret of those shy little droplets early in life. Such pots of gold weren't real but imaginary, like the square root of minus one. Tricks had to be used to transform such obstacles into a workable paradigm.

The same was true with Nomis when he lost his sight. That world, too, wasn't real but imaginary. To survive in a dreamlike state he, too, had to be inventive. The rings of Saturn became his personal rainbow, and sight, its trove. He found he could become part of the illusion himself by floating on those rings. The pain of his blindness evaporated when he did. He could see, but nobody could see him. It was his personal best, but he didn't know it at the time.

As he floated, Nomis surveyed his options.

I'm leaving Tibet by the end of the week. Time is getting short. I've done my duty. No reboot cylinders . . . canisters a good substitute, bulky. Outcome of the third sequence still unknown. What little trove awaits me there? Should I make my exit now? In Japan? Later? Nomis thought.

"Have you made up your mind yet?" the voice said.

Nomis opened one eye, then the other. It was Zackery.

"No," Nomis replied.

Nomis rolled over on his stomach and slowly floated toward Zackery, realizing that he, Nomis, might have just answered his own questions, too.

Zackery ignored Nomis's quick reply. He was hell-bent on making his third pitch in as many days.

Got to make jumping out of an airplane five thousand feet above the Kyi River and landing in a circle thirty feet in diameter, sound like a piece of cake, Zackery thought.

Zackery's cocksure attitude was more than persuasive. However, Nomis really didn't need convincing. He had already jumped twice before.

"Like I said yesterday, I've done it before, but always accompanied by an instructor, unless . . . " Nomis replied.

"I've got just the thing for you," Zackery interrupted. "A tethered harness and a double chute. We'll jump face to face, float for a while, then I'll set my chute, hit the release . . . you'll drop away, but remain tethered to the main chute's harness."

A tether . . . not what I'm looking for; been on a leash for years at COP, Nomis thought.

"Drop away tethered? Wouldn't I have my own chute too?" Nomis replied.

Nomis rolled over on his back, closed his eyes, gently kicked his feet and soon found himself in the deep end of the pool with Zackery.

"Of course," Zackery added. "Two chutes, in fact, but at the end of the tether is a second harness in which you would be strapped . . . we'd float down in tandem. Your chutes would be for back-up only."

"Strapped . . . tandem . . . back-up . . . You could land on my head," Nomis replied.

"OK. The tricky part is the landing," Zackery admitted. "It'll take some coordination between you and me during the last fifteen seconds. We'll always be in contact: the protective headgear we use has a built-in transceiver, which works like a wireless phone. The conversation is always two-way. We'll both come in at an angle—as you touch down I'll release the tether; as the load lightens, I'll pitch up a bit. The idea will be to float over you, in the clear in front of you."

The tricky part caused Nomis's eyes to squint, his nose to wrinkle up and his head to move ever so slightly from side to side.

Total dependence on Zackery until the moment of touch-down. Given the angle of descent, like running out of the sky. Jumping from a plane at five thousand feet, totally dependent on someone you hardly know. A leap of faith, Nomis thought.

"Did you take in that demo session the other day?" Zackery asked.

"Only the tail end."

Zackery sensed that Nomis remained reluctant to take the plunge.

"I'll leave the demo at the front desk. Have a look at the part dealing with the tandem jump using the experimental learner's harness, especially the part about the landing. Then give me a ring tonight if you think you are up to it tomorrow," he replied.

Nomis cleared his throat.

"Experimental learner's harness. Tomorrow?"

"You needn't worry. I've done this before," Zackery added. "I mean- . . . been to Tibet and jumped several times, with a novice along for the ride. Once I popped an ear drum. That medical center up on the big hill fixed me up like new and then some. Call me tonight to confirm."

Nomis replied in a manner that left Zackery guessing.

That evening, Nomis went to the front desk to pick up the demo material. He also rented a movie. It was nearly midnight before he finally got around to watching the demo. He only had time to review the beginning—the jump. That part looked easy enough, so he quickly called Zackery.

"Sorry to call so late."

"Not to worry," Zackery replied. "Still have a few things to do before turning in."

"About that tandem jump," Nomis said. "Looks easy enough to me, but I have some reservations about the thin air up there and the cold at five thousand feet . . . , which is really seventeen thousand. I could black out or freeze to death."

"Oh, don't worry about that," Zackery interrupted. "The harness is equipped with an oxygen canister, and we all don masks at jump time anyway."

"Ah, mine's nearly depleted. I've been using it. Thin air gets to me when jogging," Nomis replied.

"Me, too," Zackery said. "Anyway, that demo was made in New Mexico, and there's no mention of the need for oxygen. Much higher here. We modified the equipment to account for the difference. Those canisters are easy to recharge."

"And the cold?" Nomis asked.

"No problem. An undergarment made of a high-tech reflective fabric solves that one. Didn't include it in your bundle of gear. Never suit up until just before take-off, anyway. Metallic lining reflects your body heat inward. On the ground your blood would boil, but I guarantee, at five thousand feet you'll be toasty warm."

"OK, count me in! What time?" Nomis asked.

Zackery's tone of voice turned business-like.

"Out front at nine forty-five A.M.," he replied. "By the way, I plan to market the tandem jump equipment some day. If you're game, I'd like to bring along a local expert in skydive photography. He'll be taking pictures of our jump using a helmet camera; might use them in a sales promotion at a later date. Review it afterwards . . . might pick up some pointers if you want to try it again."

The next morning, fifteen members of the Denver club headed for the airport by bus, the one with the little prayer wheels that chirped when spun around. Those little wheels were an object of curiosity: almost everyone on the bus fidgeted with them at one time or another. Nomis wasn't sure if they were praying or what.

For Nomis, all that chirping brought back memories of visiting the ornithological gardens at the Franklin Park Zoo in Boston on Sunday afternoons as a student at MIT. The first few lines of the poem he had written while enjoying the peace and quiet of those gardens came to mind.

I am a man, not unlike a bird in flight. Birds and men are much the same, except for what we call the brain.

As the bus drove onto the tarmac, it hit a large bump, jolting Nomis from his reflective mood and putting an end to the chirping. It stopped a short distance from an ancient, but air-worthy, DC-3.

The workhorse of commercial air traffic in the 1940s and early 1950s, Nomis thought. *Done its duty in Vietnam in the 1960s and 1970s as the platform for Puff the Magic Dragon, the thundering, cluster-barreled killing machine invented by Mr. Gatling. Could put a chunk of lead in every square inch of a football field in thirty seconds . . . not very surgical. How many killed on its tour of duty? Now a platform for jumpers in Tibet. Big doors, slow and lumbering and easy to control, but still a piece of technology.*

More recently, Nomis had begun to think of himself as just a piece of technology—a magic little two-headed dragon of sorts.

Will I end up doing a job, but not the one initially intended? Nomis thought.

The pile of rocks Nara's Loop passed by came to mind.

Once the walls of a state-of-the-art sawmill, now a perch for skiers eating their lunch, Nomis thought.

Nomis had never really mastered the icy slope just before the little bridge that spanned the swirling waters of Black Creek. As he suited up for the jump, he remembered what the man shoveling snow had to say about the approach to that little bridge.

It's dangerous to go against the clock, Nomis thought.

54
The Target Zone

Zackery hadn't been kidding. Once suited up, you began to sweat. No wonder! First came the high-tech thermal undergarment and a pair of socks, both made of what looked like aluminum thread: the material glistened in the sun and reflected Nomis's body heat inward; next came the jump suit, which had all sorts of pockets; then came the helmet, boots and gloves, all lined with the same reflective material; last came the chutes.

After he was suited up, Nomis took Zackery's advice and used one of the bus's monitors to review that part of the demo that dealt with the landing. The tricky parts, for sure, were first getting his legs churning at the right speed just before the touchdown and second hitting the target. Scenes from that horrible nightmare in which Nomis had run out of the sky flashed before him.

As Zackery walked away from the bus toward the DC-3, he was quite specific about Nomis's role.

"Remember, you're just baggage on this go-around. As dead weight, your job is to stay out of my way; just do as I ask. We don't want this to turn into mayhem."

Nomis found himself mumbling in a voice that was barely audible.

"Baggage! Do my job by staying out of his way; MAIHEM!"

Zackery apparently had very sharp ears. Even though he was now next to the big door of the DC-3, some forty feet away from Nomis he heard every word.

"Yes! Up there is no place for mayhem," Zackery replied.

Nomis finally got his point when Zackery waved his arms frantically in the air and pointed toward the sky.

"Oh, mayhem," replied Nomis. "Yes, no place for mayhem! Right!"

But the comment about baggage didn't sit right with Nomis.

Nobody ever called me baggage, Nomis thought. *The crème de la crème of my profession, at its pinnacle. Baggage! People like the director or the tall surgeon. Yes, results men, short-term thinkers. In the long run, a dead weight loss.*

A good ten minutes went by before the cameraman finally arrived in an old pick-up truck. Nomis and the rest of the group were introduced to him by Zackery. He was a native Tibetan. Tagtra was his name. He could have been the twin brother of that shopkeeper, with his high cheekbones and black hair like straw.

∞ ∞ ∞

As the plane rumbled down the runway, Nomis's anxiety prompted him to don his mask and helmet, and start the flow of oxygen. It took the edge off an otherwise tense situation. The rest of the group followed suit at three thousand feet, when Zackery gave the signal. As the plane approached five thousand feet, Nomis decided to run a little test. He flipped up his visor and moved the mask to one side. Within a few minutes, sparks began to fly. The air was thinning out. In fact, the plane was actually seventeen thousand feet above sea level. The Tibetan plateau accounted for the lion's share—some twelve thousand of it. Nomis placed the mask firmly over his nose and mouth again. All systems were go. He was ready for his leap of faith.

As the DC-3 made a wide left turn, Zackery began barking instructions.

"Time to hook-up, face to face, and turn on the transceiver in your helmet."

Zackery paused to adjust something located inside his own helmet and then opened the big door. The roar of the air and engines was deafening. The lips and mouth of Zackery opened and closed; what he said was almost inaudible.

"Remember, you're just baggage, my bombload. My smart bomb. I'll get you to the target, don't worry."

The words flew right by Nomis. He missed all of them. It was like a silent film before the *talkies*, or a coded message that one needs time to decipher. There was no time for that now. Shortly, every second would count. A feeling of anxiety again welled up inside Nomis.

Tumbling into the wake of a slow-moving airplane is both thrilling and frightening. The wallop of the turbulent air, like a prizefighter's upper-cut, sent Nomis and Zackery flying. Instantaneously their two bodies became human brake shoes, slowing their forward momentum. Gravity quickly intervened. They fell for about ten seconds. Nomis's adrenaline rush seemed to reduce his anxiety to tolerable levels. Zackery positioned himself facing the earth, spreading his arms and legs like that shopkeeper had done the day before as he floated into the abyss. Nomis had no choice but to remain riveted to Zackery's body, face to face, arm to arm and leg to leg. As they fell toward earth, for a moment Nomis thought the face before him *was* that of the shopkeeper.

"This is how he must have felt," Nomis mumbled.

"Pardon?" Zackery replied.

"Nothing," Nomis said as he realized he wasn't alone.

"We're flying," Zackery added.

Nomis couldn't deny it. They were flying, or more like floating. All Nomis could see was the sky and the sun, big and bright as never before. It was like a giant ZIA. He had no sense of distance or depth. His view was of a vast universe of pale blue with no beginning and no end.

At the twenty-second mark, Zackery again bellowed something. It sounded like "bombs away" to Nomis. Zackery set the chutes and then released the catch that held them face-to-face. Nomis and the harness fell away about thirty feet as the tether unraveled and the double chute of Zackery unfurled, slowing his descent. As the tether drew taut, it became tangled in the feed to Nomis's oxygen mask.

It ripped the mask from his face, loosened the canister from its niche, jammed his sun visor back into his helmet and stripped the glove from his left hand. He began to see sparks, then a dark gray film consumed his sight, and finally, darkness. The implant had shut down. His transceiver was his only hope. He yelled into the pea-sized microphone at the top of his lungs.

"I've lost my mask and a glove, and . . . my eyes. I mean, er, the canister."

"Turn the volume down," Zackery replied. "Forget about the glove; your mask, it's right in front of your face. We're below three thousand feet anyway. Plenty of air. What was that about your eyes?"

"My . . . " Nomis began.

Just then, Tagtra bumped Nomis, twirling him around, whacking him at least twice as he spun.

"You were drawing oxygen right from the take-off, weren't you?" Zackery remarked.

Nomis's voice crackled with fear.

"It seemed to calm me down," Nomis replied.

"You've likely run out or are low," Zackery continued.

"No, the canister has come loose from its niche," Nomis replied.

"I am going to lower an emergency canister and mask to you, anyway. And calm down. Look into the camera and smile the next time Tagtra bumps you. And pull your sun visor down or you'll damage your eyes."

Too late for that . . . it's more like "suck on an oxygen canister to restore my sight," Nomis thought.

Down the new canister came. But where was it? Nomis hung there, blind, stabbing, grabbing and punching at the icy-cold air, accidentally whacking Tagtra several times. Nomis became frantic and disoriented, and the wind chill factor was getting to his glove-less left hand. It was freezing cold. Without thinking, Nomis pulled his knees up into his chest and placed his glove-less hand between his midriff and his thighs to warm it up.

As he curled into a ball, he chanted *Neasjah, Taschizzie, Dahetihhi, Jaysho,* and then suckled the old oxygen canister, which he held between his knees. His right hand was now free. He used it in a desperate attempt to snag the new canister. As he chanted, his field of vision cleared up, but his awkward position caused the old canister to slip away. His left hand was now sweaty and warm. Both hands reached out to catch the new canister; both missed.

"What the hell are you doing?" Zackery yelled. "That cannonball position is reducing the drag. Straighten up!"

He obeyed, then again focused his attention on the new canister. Nomis was flailing around at the end of his tether when he realized it too was gone—that is, his three-fingered hand was invisible. To be frank, he freaked out. He even punched Tagtra in the face several more times with his invisible left hand as he groped for the new canister. Hand-eye coordination was very difficult; there was no hand!

Somehow the three fingers on Nomis's hand had got jammed in between Tagtra's visor and helmet, almost poking the poor man's eye out. Much to Nomis's surprise, Tagtra accidentally punched him again as he pulled Nomis's hand free from the visor. That punch almost knocked Nomis's helmet off. In spite of this, Nomis managed to snag the new canister.

"Tell Tagtra to give me some ground or we may both come a cropper," Nomis replied.

"He's only doing his job," Zackery replied. "We need to record exactly what's going on up here."

Nomis realized he had a serious problem with his hand, the one with the missing finger; the other fingers had become frozen to the new canister on contact.

"Am I still below you?" Nomis yelled.

"Yes," Zackery replied. "Not to worry. Hey, what was that you said during those cannonball antics of yours? It sounded like 'chimpanzee' or some such thing."

"I sneezed," Nomis yelled back.

Too many things had happened at once. Nomis had little time to think. His gut reaction was to chant again. Slowly his blindness returned as he wondered if his fingers, frozen to the oxygen canister, would reappear.

Chanting and blindness have never been linked before, Nomis thought.

Nomis turned the valve of the new canister to high and took deep breaths, gorging his system on its contents. Nothing! He chanted. His sight returned, but his fingers disappeared.

I might have entered a bifurcated world, Nomis thought as his anxiety rose to a new high.

In his frightened and confused state, he wasn't sure whether he was dreaming or awake. But the pain in his left hand didn't lie. It was burning with frostbite. He was wide-awake, and smack in the midst of a nightmare to boot.

Suddenly, the air around him grew warm and moist. He and Zackery began to rise.

"We've hit one of those big balmy updrafts," Zackery barked. "Be sure that your mask is secure, as we might end up at five thousand feet again, or maybe even ten."

Bits and pieces from Nomis's poems rushed into his head . . . *sight transposed as fright . . . fright transposed as sight . . . I see only men . . . -time to fasten past at last . . . the pain would cease to be obese . . . the mind would start to play its part.*

Nomis thought about when he was a child and his father claimed he couldn't float upon the rings of Saturn, but Nomis's dreams and that bow-legged crop duster had proven him wrong, just as his grandpa had been wrong about the manner in which conditional truth can cause pain. Nomis realized he, too, had been wrong; it was his *heart,* not his *mind,* which had to *play its part.* Soon unfamiliar words and phrases began to swirl around him, howling and roaring and shrieking and wailing. He found himself struggling to catch them.

As he rose higher and higher into the sky, he began to hear colors. His ears—or was it his eyes?—began to buzz and then ring, producing a musical version of what he saw as his field of vision shifted from the Kyi River valley, to the mountains framing the Potala, to the sky and back. D'Indy must have experienced the same feeling when infused with the spirit that led him to compose his *Symphony on a French Mountain Air.*

Nomis managed to free his sun visor, which had jammed open when the tether had unraveled. The warmer air also freed the fingers of his frost-bitten hand from the new canister. He passed the canister to his gloved hand and rammed his bare hand into one of the pockets in his jumpsuit. He chanted again. Blindness descended upon him! He again gorged himself with oxygen. Nothing!

As he floated upward, he felt he was drifting backward in time into his dream world. He became calm as his balmy ascent continued, lifting him higher and higher into the sky. Those words that had seemed out of reach were now close at hand. They glowed in the sky like balled lightning, crackling and hissing with immense energy. He could feel their power.

Feel like a speck of dust floating through time . . . A deafening silence envelops my path in the sky . . . Time is consuming my mind . . . Seems like I'm on a giant wheel, turning in the sky . . . The centrifugal force is unbearable. Everything is fusing. I'm going to explode into a trillion florescent packets of light, Nomis thought.

The air turned cold. He was falling once again.

"We're on target. Get ready for the touch-down," Zackery yelled.

Nomis chanted again. As his vision returned, it was like awakening from a dream and none too soon, as the earth was coming up at him very quickly. It was then that Nomis saw it. The target zone looked like a ZIA, a sunburst, a bombsite.

Nomis literally ran out of the sky, as the angle of descent was perfect, just like in that demo video . . . and in that nightmare where he had run and run and run to Kyoto. Standing there in the midst of the giant sunburst, he could not bear the sight. He chanted again. His blindness consumed the target zone.

55

To Be but Not to See

Symptoms of hypothermia soon appeared. His speech became slurred and his coordination clumsy. To combat his frosty malady, Zackery offered Nomis the glove from his own left hand and suggested Nomis not shed his jumpsuit until his bout with the shivers had vanished.

When Nomis boarded the bus, those in the group attributed his oafish behavior to his chilly condition. His chattering teeth confirmed his predicament. But there was more. Nomis was also blind as a bat. A full bladder soon prompted him to head for the toilet in the back of the bus. While washing his hands, he chanted *Neasjah, Taschizzie, Dahetihhi, Jaysho,* ever so softly. His sight returned and strangely enough, he was still all there! With his metamorphosis complete, he returned to his seat. It took some time, but he soon became warm and cozy in his cocoon of aluminum thread.

When the bus reached the hotel, Nomis asked Zackery if he might review the pictures that Tagtra had taken. With camera in hand Nomis made his way to the stairwell rather than using the elevator. The jumpsuit was by then hot and steamy. Halfway up the stairs, he shed both the helmet and his stealth, using his head as a radiator, like a cross-country skier. His blindness returned, forcing him to grope his way to his room. Once there, he changed his state again to stealth.

The camera's screen was so tiny he could hardly see a thing. He fed the picture to the TV in his room. There was his head, in his helmet, but it wasn't fading in and out. And most of the time his hand, the one without the glove on it, wasn't there at all; the canister seemed to be floating, but always directly in front of the end of his wrist.

A casual observer might miss the antics of that hand, but Nomis knew what was going on, and so would anyone else who took a closer look. Nomis put the phone on top of the camera and called the concierge, indicating that he had missed several calls while in his room and suspected the ringer on his phone wasn't working. He asked him to call back. When he did, Nomis let the phone ring several times before answering, hoping the electromagnetic field caused by the ring of the buzzer would mess up the memory stick. He viewed the jump again. The stick had been compromised. He called the concierge again and arranged for the camera to be returned to Zackery.

There was no doubt in his mind. His fall had reduced the sight-restoring technology in his head to rubble. He peeled off the outer layer of the jumpsuit. Next came the undergarment and the socks made of aluminum thread. As he pulled his legs, arms and feet free, they went stealth. He turned to look in the mirror. There was no image. It was button-pushing time again.

The undergarment again became his cocoon; his hands remained stealth, as did his head and feet. But his body, arms and legs—or, more precisely, his bulky outline clothed in the reflective attire—remained visible. As he put on the helmet, his head reappeared. He removed it. Bingo! It was gone. He stood in front of the dressing mirror as a headless, handless, footless figure. He reached for the helmet again and put on the gloves lined with that reflective material. He was back. He looked like the *Man from Glad* in a hockey helmet with no feet. For a short time, he was appalled and aghast, but his mood soon turned pensive as the outcome of the third sequence, the one he had feared all along, stared him in the face.

To see but not to be. The reflective property of the undergarment annuls the effect of my supercharged aura in stealth state. Might give me some flexibility, coupled with a hat and a pair of those socks. Perhaps a standard reboot cylinder might correct the problem, Nomis pondered.

Questions begged more questions.

Can COP put me back together again? Perhaps a new implant . . . Am I now only baggage? Perhaps just a high-tech delivery system—a platform for the personal touch? Nomis thought.

Once again, choice wasn't without a threat. His plan had been to disappear, but not into the bifurcated state in which he now found himself.

"I might have to exist in a world of two states, one blind but visible; the other invisible but with my sight. This isn't what I planned," Nomis mumbled.

The phone rang. It was Zackery.

"Over the shivers yet?" Zackery asked.

"Yes!"

"Good!"

"Please bring the helmet, jumpsuit and camera to the evening debriefing. The reflective undergarment you can keep as a souvenir," Zackery said.

"I'm exhausted and have a lot to do before I leave for Japan tomorrow. I think I'll pass on the debriefing. As for the jumpsuit, I'll have a porter bring it around. Say, there must have been something wrong with the camera—all I could see was a lot of colored squiggles," Nomis replied.

The second time I viewed the jump, Nomis thought to himself.

Zackery expressed his disbelief. The to and fro between Nomis and Zackery went on for another two or three minutes.

"I'll come around to collect the camera," Zackery finally said.

Nomis was quick to reply.

"I've already sent it back to you. The concierge must have it."

∞ ∞ ∞

After a well-deserved nap, Nomis lay on the bed, making mental notes of things he had to do before leaving for Japan in the morning.

Get that old book out of the country . . . grand larceny . . . no . . . a casualty of the spook business. British Consulate . . . slip that old book into a diplomatic pouch—one full of personal items the embassy staff sends back to the UK weekly—address it to Doris in Henley-on-Thames. Attach a note to the outside of the package. Ask Doris not to unwrap it, forward it to Nara in Boulder . . . Explain it was a little surprise for Nara. Plan is to give it to her on my return from Tibet. Need a cane or stick to navigate, just in case; pinch a telescoping pointer from one of those conference rooms reserved for business use. When collapsed will neatly fit in my breast pocket. Call the airline, change my routing to Osaka. Return jumpsuit. Include note with my apologies re: the memory stick. My strategy re: COP . . . Call Nara.

By early evening, he had attended to everything except his strategy regarding COP and the call to Nara. For the first time in years, he did a little math. He shaped his feelings and words into a poem, the ones that had swirled around him when he was caught in the giant updraft—howling and roaring and shrieking and wailing as they went by. He titled it "The Rings of Saturn."

Nomis's strategy, his final disappearing act, was simple. There would be no encores. He intended to put it into play once he reached Osaka.

Got to leave a trail with a dead end, Nomis thought. *Call Nara from Osaka—alert her I'm going to stay awhile in Kyoto . . . Next call her friend Shuji in Kobe, just to chat. Difficult to meet Shuji face-to-face in a blind state. Travel from Osaka to Kyoto by Bullet train and check bags at station. My high-tech cocoon will come in handy.*

But first he had to get there. Traveling blind would be an obstacle. He must be seen leaving Lhasa. He planned on using the metallic undergarment to avoid his predicament. It would permit him to both see and be seen. It too had its drawbacks, though; it was unbearably hot. There was also the problem of his head. He would have to wear a cap all the time. There would be no way to dissipate his body heat. After an hour in that suit, the perspiration would be pouring from his brow. He would have to carry it with him to use only when necessary.

When he finally phoned Nara, the phone rang twenty times. There was no answer.

56
Attention Getters

Nomis was sound asleep when the telephone rang. Half-awake and blind as a bat, he shoved one hand toward the bed's commode in search of the phone. The other groped for the lamp by the bed. The phone fell behind the commode making a dull thud as it hit the floor. It was only when Nomis flicked on the light that he realized he had chosen to sleep in his blind state. He got down on his hands and knees and managed to locate the phone by using the almost inaudible voice coming from the receiver. The cord had become tangled in the wire to the lamp. Without his sight, it was impossible to untangle. Sitting slouched and round-shouldered on the floor by the commode, his drowsy response was in stark contrast to Zackery's peppy reply.

"Fall out of bed?" Zackery asked.

"No, the phone fell," Nomis replied sluggishly.

"About the undergarment. On the way to Lhasa, they were all packed in one of my bags. That aluminum fabric screwed up the metal detectors giving the security people in Denver quite a scare. I just checked with Dragon Air. They have advised me that on the way out of Tibet, any bag containing a metal or metal-like object will be searched. I suggest you put the suit in a carry-on bag if you want to keep it as a souvenir; otherwise chuck it. It's up to you."

"Given I'm blind, a search would only complicate matters," was Nomis's slurred and somnolent reply.

"Did you say 'blind'?" Zackery asked.

Nomis's slumberous eyes opened wide and his hunched position became ramrod straight.

Daft of me. What to do? Diversion . . . need some diversion, Nomis thought.

Down went the lamp onto the floor with a crash.

"What the hell was that?" Zackery asked.

"Sorry. The lamp just fell," Nomis replied.

"Did you say you were blind?" Zackery asked a second time.

Nomis racked his brain for an answer that would shut him up.

How to deal with my reckless remark. What rhymes with blind? Kind, dine, fine, line, mind, mine . . . mine . . . that's it.

"No! Given mine, that would complicate matters for me at the airport."

"Sure will," Zackery replied.

Nomis hadn't planned to carry on anything to avoid just that—a search.

"Say, I've been thinking of returning by way of the Qinghai-Tibet railway," Nomis said.

"Better take an oxygen bottle. That rail line crosses a pass that is more than sixteen thousand feet, and those cars aren't pressurized," Zachery added.

"Aren't pressurized . . . I guess I'll stuff the suit in the waste can," Nomis mumbled as he hung up the phone.

Almost got into another mess. Asinine! Half-awake response while fumbling for that phone. What I must avoid, like before . . . too many things happening at once. Can't let my guard down again, Nomis thought.

His little slip suggested that traveling stealth could easily put into play too many variables. Drifting in and out of his stealth state would be dangerous, he concluded. If he kept turning up in this place or that place in China or anywhere else with no apparent explanation as to how he got there, it might be used as a crib. He had no choice but to return by Dragon Air. He must be seen but not see. He would only use his gift of stealth in situations where it was absolutely necessary. This wasn't the preferred choice in his bifurcated world, but there was really no other way he could get to Osaka. It meant re-learning many of the skills he had acquired as a child, living in his cloud world once again for a while.

No time like the present to begin this adventure, Nomis thought.

To avoid the desk clerk, he called ahead and had the movie, and a few other items he had purchased, charged to his credit card. He bypassed the elevator, as by now he was quite familiar with the stairwell. It was just as well. Going that route avoided the early morning breakfast crowd. That wasn't the case when he reached the lobby, however. It was packed with members of the Denver group.

∞ ∞ ∞

Nomis made his way to what he thought was the center of the

lobby. He drew a map of the lobby in his mind to orient himself, using as his guide familiar sounds and smells—the voices of the desk clerk, the concierge and the porters, the elevator chimes, the rumble of cars and the odd motorcycle as they came and went at the front entrance, the draft from the revolving door, and the aroma of the breakfast buffet including the rancid smell of tsamba. He hadn't forgotten how to do that, even though it brought back some painful childhood memories. Word was circulating that the bus would be delayed—mechanical trouble again. There would be a wait of about thirty minutes. Thirty minutes was a long time to just stand around. He began to feel a little conspicuous, and this was to be avoided. Nomis decided to go stealth and watch.

He made his way back to the stairwell and climbed the stairs to the third floor where his room was located, only to find that the electronic combination lock had already been changed. He ducked into a room near the elevators where the soft drink machine and icemaker were located, put his foot firmly against the door and chanted. Now he could see, but he couldn't be seen. He made his way back to the lobby by way of the stairwell, choosing an out-of-the-way spot as his vantage point.

Shortly afterward, that old pick-up truck arrived at the entrance to the lobby. This time there were two of them: Tagtra and another. Tagtra unloaded two large bags and a number of small, irregularly shaped ones.

Photography equipment, Nomis thought. *Tagtra . . . the one traveling today.*

Twenty minutes later, the bus arrived. It was the same one that had been used for the tours a few days before.

Only forty seats, Nomis thought, *and over sixty-five people flying out today.*

Yangchenla stepped from the bus and entered the lobby, waving her arms to get the group's attention.

"Some people might have to stand on the way to the airport. It's against company regulations, but it's all that can be done."

She distributed a sheet and asked everyone to read it quickly. Nomis walked over to Tagtra, who was off to one side near the revolving door, and looked over his shoulder. He had to be careful not to bump into anyone on the way. The sheet just contained that spiel about safety and the restroom in the back of the bus.

Yangchenla announced a short while later that the bus would be loading in about five minutes. Nomis returned to the stairwell, waited until it was empty, shed his stealth and made his way back to the lobby as best he could.

So far so good, Nomis thought.

Given the position in which Nomis had seen him last, Tagtra would probably be at the head of the line, which, according to Yangchenla, was forming to enter the bus. Nomis had had enough of him yesterday, so he worked his way into the crowd to what he reconnoitered was the middle of the lobby, innocently asking if those around him were taking the bus to the airport to catch Dragon Air 27 to Hong Kong.

"I hope so," a voice replied. "But you're in the wrong line. I haven't checked out yet and they forgot to pick up my bags. Did they get yours?"

A lump formed in Nomis's throat.

"Yes," he replied, feeling conspicuous again.

Just then the air brakes of the bus let out a hiss. The sound came from behind him and to the left. He turned, moved to his right and went with what seemed to be the flow. He was one of the last people in line. As it turned out, the crowded bus was to Nomis's advantage. There were four who couldn't squeeze onto the bus, and Nomis was one of them.

Yangchenla was very apologetic. She hailed two cabs. The drivers were told to follow the bus to the airport. It was a wild ride, very fast and very bumpy. When they arrived, Nomis learned from one of his taximates that the driver was having difficulty opening the doors of the bus. Nomis had no alternative but to tag along with the three others, joining the hustle and bustle of what was already a lengthy check-in line. He engaged in small talk and followed their voices.

"My wife's on that bus; I should have insisted she come with me," a voice said.

"Pardon?" Nomis replied.

"My wife, she's on it . . . look . . . the driver's cranking open the door by hand now," the voice responded with amazement.

Nomis was soon peppered with voices coming from every-which-way.

"Honey, once we began to exit the bus," another voice said, "an animated discussion erupted between Yangchenla and the driver."

"Yeah, he was really in a huff . . . lots of hand-waving. All the bags got piled helter-skelter at the curb," a voice on the right said.

"A porter will be standing by to help you," Nomis heard Yangchenla yelling.

"Driver had no time to move the bags to the check-in area . . . Something about running forty-five minutes late," a voice on the left said.

"You coming with us to Akan?" asked another voice.

"Me?" Nomis replied.

"A group of us are going up to Sapporo on the Isle of Hokkaido. Then it's over to Akan National Park for a three-day hike," the voice replied.

"I hadn't planned . . . " Nomis began as another voice interrupted him.

"You're next, sir, move ahead to number five."

I'll have to say I've misplaced my glasses, Nomis thought.

"Number five," Nomis replied as his anxiety peaked. "I've misplaced my glasses and can't read a thing without them."

He felt the voice take his arm and nudge him to his left a bit.

"Straight ahead," the voice said.

As he bumped into the check-in counter, Nomis thrust his ticket into the air, hitting something hard.

"Please, sir, be careful," another voice said.

The hard thing turned out to be the agent's computer terminal, which Nomis had almost dislodged from its mountings.

"Any luggage, sir?" the agent asked.

"Over there," Nomis said, even though by then he had no idea where "over there" was.

"On the scale, please," the agent replied.

Nomis paused.

Now what?

"Where's that porter?" a voice asked.

"Over there," another replied.

Heads turned as Nomis nervously raised his voice above the noisy hustle and bustle of the check-in line.

"Porter, it's the bag with the big yellow letters NC on it."

The porter quickly retrieved the bag, placing it on the weigh scale. Nomis tipped him and the man seemed extremely grateful. Nomis later realized he had given him a U.S. five-dollar bill.

"Your seat has been pre-selected—21 B . . . is that satisfactory?" the agent asked.

"As long as it's an aisle seat."

After all of those questions relating to who had packed his bag and whether it contained any of the contraband items no longer permitted on airplanes, Nomis was handed his boarding card and tickets, which he promptly dropped. Luckily the porter was standing right there and retrieved them. As Nomis stepped away, he realized that the agent had failed to indicate the number of the boarding gate.

"What gate?" Nomis asked.

By that time, the agent had cleared his computer screen of Nomis's file.

"Dragon Air 27 will begin boarding at seven A.M.," the agent replied. "The gate number is on your boarding pass."

He had to get a stranger to read him the gate number on his boarding pass. He again fibbed to a woman, saying that he had misplaced his glasses and couldn't read anything without them, another little incident that made him stand out in the crowd.

A bifurcated world isn't exactly a piece of cake, Nomis thought. *Very difficult not to draw attention to oneself.*

∞ ∞ ∞

After that string of little episodes of near panic, Nomis decided to go stealth again. It was 6:15 A.M., and forty-five minutes was a long time to wait until boarding. He also decided, when the time came, that he would make his way past the security check to Gate 7 in stealth state, as the Denver group had dispersed. With his group scattered all over the airport, and people going every-which-way in the terminal, it would be next to impossible to find Gate 7 without looking conspicuous.

Evidence of this was soon apparent. It took him fifteen minutes to find a restroom, using only his nose and ears as a guide, and again fibbing about his glasses. It had a row of those little closets for privacy—Asian toilets with just a hole in the floor. He put his foot in the hole when he entered and almost went in up to his knee. He had quite a time getting his foot out. If he had had to call for help that would really have been an attention-getter. He finally did get to chant.

The area near the ticket counters was a busy place. He headed for an out-of-the-way spot to one side. Tagtra again caught his eye. He must have been the last one in line. He was just handing his ticket to the agent at the counter, and only two large bags, plus those irregularly shaped ones, remained.

Nomis's curiosity got the better of him. He changed his position to an area directly behind the ticket counter. At one point he almost fell onto one of those moving belts, which might have dragged him into the chute where the checked baggage enters on its way to the loading dock. That remark by Zackery slipped into his conscience mind.

You're only baggage.

It was a minute or two before Tagtra's bags passed by. In order to see the baggage tickets, Nomis had to flip the bag onto its side, which momentarily caught the eye of the agent. It eventually jammed at the entrance to the chute. Nomis had to move quickly out of the area, as the agent walked over to place the bag in an upright position again. Nomis's trouble was hardly worth the effort. Tagtra was also on Dragon Air 27 to Hong Kong. From Hong Kong he was going on to Narita, not Osaka, so they would be parting company soon.

However, Nomis's curiosity soon changed to a feeling of uneasiness, and then to anxiety. He hung around Tagtra for a good half-hour, looking over his shoulder every chance he had. He caught Tagtra reviewing what looked like a contract. He had been hired by a commercial studio, located in Hollywood, to undertake some sort of air photography in Baja, California.

Strange, Nomis thought. *His bags were checked only as far as Narita.*

Once in the boarding area, Nomis decided to follow the same route he had taken during check-in. He shed his stealth. It was the only way to get his boarding pass through one of those automated machines that compared the passenger manifest, compiled at check-in time, with those boarding. If there were a discrepancy, the plane would be delayed until the difference was resolved. And he would be the object of a search. That he didn't want.

When he could see, finding a place to chant was a lot easier. There was a restroom adjacent to the boarding area. Once in his blind state, he tagged along with those headed for Dragon Air 27 when the flight was called. There was a final checkpoint just before he boarded the plane. The buzzer went off when Nomis passed through. After fumbling around, he produced the telescopic pointer and admitted he was partially blind without his glasses, which he had misplaced. The security people determined that the pointer, minus its rubber tip, could be used as a weapon and confiscated it, giving him a receipt. He would have to reclaim it in Hong Kong. He was told to move on. Little did they know that he, Nomis Chester, was himself a weapons platform more sophisticated than he cared to think about, or those security people could ever imagine.

Once on the plane and in his seat, he was feeling a lot better. Dragon Air 27 wasn't automated. No babbling screens. It actually had a pilot, a first officer and real, live stewards on board.

When he was a child, without his sight, he had had all sorts of help. Now he had only his wits, but his wits could only take him so far.

So far, he thought, *I have ended up in the wrong line, almost missed the airport bus, almost knocked the agent's monitor off its mounting, announced my initials to anyone in earshot, over-tipped a porter, lied numerous times about having misplaced a non-existent pair of glasses, got my foot stuck in a toilet, almost became a piece of baggage, lost my stick to a security guard. To an astute observer, cribs to my personal secret . . . What next?*

In fact, he could have been sitting right beside Tagtra as he couldn't recall what seat number was recorded on Tagtra's boarding card. Paranoia got the better of him again. He moved his elbow over to determine whether the seat next to him was occupied. Whatever it was, it was quite soft.

"Pardon me, sir," a woman said as she shoved his elbow back toward the aisle.

"Sorry," Nomis replied, realizing he had just elbowed her in her right breast.

He was making too many faux pas. He got up and moved to the back of the plane, counting the seats as he walked down the aisle. He arrived at what felt like a curtain. It was the galley. He assumed the restrooms were located along the back wall of the galley. They were. He entered one and went stealth, remaining by the rear exit door, which wasn't open. He located Tagtra sitting a few rows in front of him, to the left, by a window.

"This is the pilot speaking. Please take your seats and buckle up. We will be leaving the gate in about five minutes," blared the intercom.

Nomis returned to the restroom area. All were locked but one, and it was occupied. There was a steward standing nearby. The steward waited for the occupant to exit, quickly inspected it and then locked it up. Nomis was stuck. It was only luck that the steward moved to the front of the plane and began to check that all had fastened their seat belts. Nomis had to risk it. He ducked into the galley. It was empty. He chanted. Once blind and rid of his stealth, he exited the galley. By that time, the steward must have been halfway down the aisle. Nomis had no way of knowing where he was. He accidentally groped him on the way back to his seat. As he did, the steward gave Nomis the once-over.

"Can I help you, sir?" the steward asked.

Again Nomis had drawn attention to himself in the worst way possible.

"No, thank you."

The steward gave him a little pat on his bum as he slipped by.

This is no way to live, Nomis thought as he settled into his seat. He began to review the rest of his plan.

The matter of living couldn't be dismissed. Under cover of stealth, he would go to the Nanzen-ji Temple. At the temple in Kyoto, he would assess the likelihood of living there, undetected.

Must be less complicated than what I have just gone through to simply check in and board a plane, he thought. *Sure glad I didn't take that train to Golmud City. In the last five minutes, fondled a breast with my elbow, groped the steward, got patted on the bum in return . . .*

Nanzen-ji was a place of teaching, a seminary, young men in training, dormitories with lofts, a commissary and a large kitchen. But that undergarment wasn't part of his plan now. He would have to make his assessment at Nanzen-ji under cover of stealth. Once complete, he would return to the train station, collect only those things that he intended to take to the temple, and return there to hide them.

What I could take wouldn't be much; it would be a simple life, no worldly possessions, not even my image, Nomis thought.

He would become a student in training, invisible to his teachers. His first task would be to learn Japanese. After that, perhaps a mentor of poetry who remained invisible and unknown to his students.

It's impossible to really teach poetry; it's very personal—an implosion of reason and feeling, compressed and refined to a point where what emerges is a jewel that both reflects and refracts! Nomis thought.

His desperate situation soon consumed his every thought. Yet his mind drew a blank as to the manner in which he would disappear. His thoughts were generic at most: it had to be public and it had to be final—no encores.

"Hi," said a voice directly behind him. "You had quite a time at check-in, but I see you made it. What about Akan?"

It was one of his fellow taximates. He tossed a map forward. It landed in Nomis's lap. Nomis sat there, faking an examination of it.

Could go off to Sapporo on the Isle of Hokkaido, traveling blind, reverse my strategy, make a special effort to stand out and be seen. Head for the Akan National Park in my blind state, employ a guide, or perhaps join a group of hikers. Maybe even the Denver group themselves, he pondered.

He wasn't sure of the exact outcome of such an undertaking. He had quickly learned never to be sure of anything in his bifurcated world.

Once familiar with the terrain, return alone under cover of stealth, fall over a cliff, drown in a lake, fall into the sea. Leave behind only my camping gear, he thought. *No body would ever be found, would seal the doubt of the director. Count on both Nara's love and Nara's grief to validate my death. At some later date, reveal myself to her. Not sure she would ever forgive me.*

"I might just join you in Hokkaido," replied Nomis as he returned the map.

57

A Perfect Fit

When Nomis arrived in Osaka, he phoned Nara in Boulder. There was no answer. He left a message that he would call back later and then phoned Shuji in Kobe.

"Just a minute, Nomis," replied the voice that answered the phone.

"Hi, Nomis. Surprise! This is Nara."

Nomis was speechless.

"How was your trip to Tibet?" Nara asked. "You must be tired. I would have rented a car and picked you up at the airport, but you know, they drive on the left side of the road here and I don't feel comfortable in that situation. If you hurry you can catch the Bullet to Kobe. I can't wait to hear . . . "

Nomis didn't want to go to Kobe; he just wanted to leave a credible trail that could be followed to a dead end. A phone call to Shuji in Kobe would have been the beginning of that trail. With Nara in Japan, his plan was that much more difficult to implement, maybe even impossible.

What to do? Meet in Kyoto, Nomis thought.

The bifurcated world that he was living in complicated everything. He now needed all his fingers and toes to count the screw-ups that had occurred since he had left Lhasa.

"I'd rather meet at that hotel on the hillside near your parents' old house in Kyoto," Nomis interrupted, in a manner that was uncharacteristic. In fact, he was quite curt.

"The Miyako," Nara replied.

"I'll call for reservations," Nomis snapped.

"It's short notice," Nara said.

"It may work out," Nomis replied. "I'll take anything."

"But . . . "

"You take the Bullet train to Kyoto."

"OK . . . "

"We'll meet there this evening."

"Should I call . . . "

"Let me call the Miyako."

"How will I . . . "

"I'll call you back."

Within the hour Nomis called Nara back to confirm his plan, caught the monorail from the airport to the Osaka train station and hopped the Bullet train to Kyoto.

When not around a lot of people, blindness is not all that bad, Nomis thought as the Bullet train sped toward Kyoto.

It was a challenge, but there was a certain freedom that he had first begun to feel on the plane from Lhasa. It wasn't what he expected. He couldn't put his finger on why. It did feel good. Lots of time to think and drift, just like when he was a child in Albuquerque. Strange as it seemed, his stealth state gave him the same feeling. To all around him, he wasn't there. The result was the same—lots of time to think.

Not so simple to disappear these days, nor make your world disappear, Nomis pondered. *Stealth seems a simple and attractive solution, as does blindness. Bit flabbergasted at my notions about the latter. Used blindness to my advantage in my youth, but later rejected it. Even traded on my talents to avoid it. But technology in its primitive or beta test stage often fails, reaching into the blind spots of the world around you or those of yourself . . . victimizing you.*

He was about to once again trade on a special talent, his stealth, to avoid blindness. This was his weakness. This time the choice would be fundamental, as he would have to give up much that he loved. Perhaps he wasn't the victim, but the criminal, and his punishment would be self-incarceration in his world of stealth, that one-way window where he could see out but no one could see in.

Faking his death appeared to be the best plan. There were only a couple of people in Boulder who might call his bluff. Once he turned COP's technology against them, he would have to assume that he would be a hunted three-fingered man. That was the culture of COP, whether it was a virus, buried in a packet of light, or a hacker.

Might stealth be my prison, my Princetown; I had been its architect in my youth—in my dreams.

And he was sure that only he knew its flaws, the problems uncovered in Lhasa that had produced a bifurcation of his sight, and for that matter, his person.

Unless the director had a heart-to-heart talk with Nara, she might never suspect the truth. Love might cloud Nara's vision. But would it? If my resolve weakens and I decide to reveal myself at some later date, her love might consume her anger, but, in the end she might have to become my accomplice. But would she? And why not now?

Nomis had done his duty; the criminal in Lhasa had been terminated; in fact, he had made his sacrifice twice. And twice that sacrifice had begged the question—was he a good man? He preferred to believe that he was; as long as he maintained his stealth, he saw with his heart, not his head. Feelings ruled; reason played second fiddle. This was the good that he had found in himself. He might be tempted to enter that other world where he could be seen, but he was sure now that the good in him ruled the evil.

∞ ∞ ∞

Nomis arrived at the Miyako at about four thirty P.M. All they had had available on short notice was a bungalow on a wooded hillside to the rear of the hotel complex. It was very Japanese and very simple, but beautifully appointed. He expected Nara to arrive at about six thirty P.M., so he decided to take a look around Nanzen-ji before she arrived. The concierge was nowhere to be seen, so he left a note asking Nara to meet him at the top of the pagoda near the iron box.

"Please have the concierge deliver the note I left on his desk to Mrs. Chester when she arrives," the thin air rang out as he made his way past the front desk.

The clerk seemed puzzled. Nomis had forgotten that he was stealth. As he made his way to the lobby door, the desk clerk and the porter broke into an animated conversation. One kept motioning with his hand, scooping the air toward his ears, as if wafting through the lobby was a breeze bearing a message. The incident again reminded Nomis how difficult it would be to live in his bifurcated world. His error was a crib which could easily be used to decipher his encrypted state and reveal the truth about the demise of Nomis Chester.

On the way to the temple, Nomis followed the path by the canal, which he and Nara had explored in the summer of 2025, shortly after they were married. It was familiar and unchanged. As he passed by what had once been the house of Nara's parents, he began to think about how he would deal with her, face to face.

My original plan was desperate at best, Nomis thought. *No corpus delicti, no witnesses. Would be hunted down by the director. No doubt terminated, maybe even by the other side. Nara would be deceived to the last. Not a good man's doing. Live up to the gift of my one-way mirror. Must begin now and confess all.*

When he arrived at the Son Mon Gate, the last few lines of his poem, "Go back a ways", came to mind.

Go back a ways on road of time
To see what you now miss
There are some sights to keep in mind
Before you . . .

His plan began to fade as he rambled about the grounds of the temple. In fact, the compound would offer little opportunity to live in his bifurcated state. Once he learned to speak Japanese, if he chose to reveal himself and discard his stealth, even though he had Navajo features, his outward appearance was not Japanese and he was getting old. Except for a few, most of the students seemed very young. Reason was pushing feeling aside.

A short time later, in the distance, he saw Nara walking along the path by the canal. He watched her from the cover of stealth as she followed the path by the little pond, with its lily pads and giant goldfish, to the right of the gate. She entered the pagoda and began to climb the steps. Nomis followed. She sensed someone was behind her. She turned. Nomis stopped. He felt she knew he was there. Like an antelope she bounded up the remaining steps and quickly wriggled through the little opening at the top. Nomis waited until she was through before he again began his ascent.

When he reached the top, Nara was over near the iron box, into which Nomis had placed all of his poems in that horrible nightmare he'd had.

"Nomis, come out, wherever you are," Nara begged. "I know that you're here. It's Nara, your other half."

My other half, Nomis thought. *Plato's words, thousands of years ago, characterizes the essence of one's search for love, search which ends when one finds a perfect fit. Ended my search standing among the foundations of Thoreau's little cabin on a snowy Sunday morning, some twenty-eight years ago. Or did that Sunday mark the beginning of love?*

He stumbled to the railing on the other side of the pagoda and softly chanted.

"I'm over here," Nomis beckoned, "by the railing."

The sun was just setting. It was a big red ball of fire on the horizon. Nomis could feel the heat on his face. In a second Nara was by his side. They embraced.

"Nomis, you're staring right into the sun. Don't you remember? That's a no-no. It might cause permanent damage to your eyes," Nara said. "You might be blinded."

They embraced again. Nomis denied his blindness. He looked deep into Nara's eyes, but could see nothing.

That's it, Nomis thought. *For less than a minute facing the noonday sun, I have already fallen into the abyss.*

A moan welled up from deep within Nomis as his blindness stalked his denial. They embraced again. His denial persisted, but he could see nothing.

Damage already been done, Nomis thought.

"Face away from the sun! Give some ground; quickly, Nomis, quickly!" Nara pleaded.

Give some ground, to my enemy the sun, Nomis thought.

"It's too late," Nomis answered bluntly. "It happened in Tibet when I went skydiving. I forgot about the risk of the sun. I'm blind!"

Nara's voice became choked.

"You will have to get a new implant. We can return home together."

"But I am home!"

"You . . . " Nara began.

She was interrupted by the sound of one of those gongs, the sound with long tails that melts away into nothingness. One is never sure when they really stop ringing—when nothing is really nothing. Perhaps somewhere in the universe, those gongs were always faintly ringing, there before the universe had eyes . . . heard for the very first time at the beginning—of Eiseley's time. Tears flowed from Nara's eyes as she turned her head away, looking for the source.

Nomis's voice became soft and gentle.

"I, too, am like that gong. I can melt away into nothingness, too. But I am still here, and I can see. Otherwise it is like being in my dreams in my youth. I know, now, that I am a good man, despite all of my crimes. I can see with my heart!"

"Crimes!"

Nara took his hands in hers and pulled him close to her breast.

"You're not making any sense."

Nomis asked her to sit down on the iron chest. When the gong rang again, he softly chanted. As the sound faded to nothingness, Nara appeared in his field of vision, but he disappeared from hers as he receded into his dreams. Just as his image disappeared a faint moan could be heard, like the universe had just devoured one of its own.

Nara gasped in disbelief. Nomis's voice began to quiver.

"Not a word," the thin air whispered. "I'll explain all to you. It will take much of the night."

He told Nara of his crimes, the plan that would have meant the end of them, and about all of those faux pas that had occurred on his journey from Lhasa to Osaka. Nomis asked for Nara's forgiveness and then for her complicity. She realized how desperate he was and vowed to help pull him out.

Nomis and Nara remained a few more days in Kyoto at the Miyako. They were more intimate and loving than they had been for a long time, sharing their feelings and thoughts about the past and the future. It was difficult leaving the Miyako, but Nomis insisted and Nara reluctantly agreed not to accompany him to Sapporo. She returned for another short visit with Shuji in Kobe while Nomis went on to Tokyo. Nara was at the market when Nomis called from Tokyo station. He left a message that, as they had agreed in Kyoto, he was off to the north of Japan with a few members of the Denver group for four days of hiking.

58
Blind Man's Bluff

It was during one of those cool early September nights when the gruesome attack occurred. Nomis had asked the guide if he could borrow a woolen cap to keep his balding head warm. What happened to Nomis later that night has always been very painful for Nara to discuss. An item which appeared in a Tokyo newspaper gave this account:

> Sapporo, Japan,
> September 5, 2053:
>
> The Japanese government reported today that Dr. Nomis Chester, the world famous American cryptologist, while on a guided hiking vacation in the Akan National Park with a number of others and sleeping alone in his tent, was murdered by a ghoulish attacker wielding a sacrificial sword. The authorities are looking into the possibility that Dr. Chester was the victim of an international ring of Solarnet terrorist hackers . . .

After Nomis failed to turn up for breakfast, the guide went to his tent. According to the guide the only sign of Nomis was a blood-soaked pillow and one of his credit cards. A bloodied sacrificial samurai sword was later found a few hundred feet away, as was evidence that a body had been lugged through the brush to the edge of a nearby cliff by the sea. A bloody woolen cap was also found at the edge of the cliff, where, it was thought, Nomis's body had been thrown into the sea. DNA tests revealed that it was Nomis's blood on the sword, credit card and cap. Because of the quantity of blood found at the scene the police suspected that the sword had been used to sever Nomis's head from his body. One London tabloid reported that his head minus his eyes had turned up in a jar of formaldehyde at that medical college in Lhasa, but this has never been verified.

The guide was held for questioning, as were the other members of the hiking party, but no one was charged. Tagtra was linked to the Akan

National Park tour operation too. Apparently he also had a contract to undertake some photography related to a travel promotion group in Sapporo. He was reported to be in the area at about the same time as Nomis and also had been seen in and around Nanzen-ji in Kyoto, a few days before he turned up at the park. The sword was traced as one reported stolen from that temple in Kyoto at about the same time. Nara had also been a suspect for a while. She had been seen at the temple around the time that the sword had disappeared, but Nara had been in Kobe at the time of the attack.

∞ ∞ ∞

A week after that terrible event, Nara returned to Boulder. Soon afterward, she couriered, to her friend Doris in Windsor and to their friends Herbert and Liz in Ottawa, some material that Nomis had given to her.

Later that same week, the director asked Nara to visit his offices for what he said would be a little chat with F. Howard Sourceman of the National Security Agency and Orin Sedgewick from Bethesda.

Both went right for the jugular. They were certain that Nomis was still alive, that he had faked his own death, that he had gone stealth and that Nara was his accomplice.

Nara reached into her purse and produced a copy of the tape that she and Nomis had made the night they had met at the temple in Kyoto, the night he had confessed all.

"It's all on this tape, everything about your operation, about your forty-two year experiment with Nomis's eyes, about your flawed stealth technology, which ended in Nomis's demise, and about Quantum II's weaknesses. Need I go on?"

"We can charge both you and Nomis with tampering with government property," Sedgewick replied after listening to only a short segment of the tape.

"Government property? I'd like to know where you think that implant ended and Nomis started. It was part of him, not part of COP. You said so yourself!" Nara shot back.

Stakes are getting higher. Will the house tell me to walk with no questions asked? Nara thought.

"There are two other copies of the tape which Nomis and I made. They are by now in the hands of trusted friends. If anything happens to me, or if you pursue the issue any further, those tapes will be released to the press," Nara snapped.

A grin slowly crept across Nara's lips.

"And if he were with us, I am sure that Nomis wouldn't hesitate to give a demo of his talents to the press."

There was silence as both Sourceman's and Sedgewick's eyes darted about the room. Finally they just stared and glared at her. She had the advantage; they were the ones who had to make the choice now.

"We will have you arrested and charged under the National Security Act," Sedgewick warned.

The poker game continued.

"I have a dictionary that Nomis sent to me from Tibet," Nara replied.

"You have a dictionary?" interrupted Sourceman.

Nara reached into her purse and thrust some photocopies toward him.

"He sent it via the Brits before his demise," Nara responded. "If you want the whole dictionary, you're going to have to make a trade. You drop the matter and I keep my tapes. In return, you get the dictionary and my silence."

They asked Nara to wait outside. Once the door closed, she heard a lot of hooting, hollering, yelling and screaming coming from the room. Nomis could have walked right through that battle on the way to his nirvana, and nobody would have known the difference.

Dictionary surely got their attention—now speaking their language, Nara thought. *My silence for that dictionary . . . my words for their word . . . never knew words could be so valuable!*

The offer of the dictionary finally did get both their attention and agreement. They and Nara parted company with no more questions asked.

∞ ∞ ∞

When Nara went through Nomis's effects, she found the little piece of math he had written while in Tibet entitled "The Rings of Saturn."

In the little town of Socorro, New Mexico, there is a cemetery where lie many of the Navajo Code Talkers, who made the stealth of their language so famous during many of the key battles of a war long forgotten. Their language left the enemy speechless. Nomis's own battle is now long-forgotten, too. No one much speaks of it either. There is no grave for Nomis Chester, but there is a large stone which reads:

Doctor Nomis Chester
Dahetihhi
Born 2001—Died 2053

Son of Taschizzie
Grandson of Neasjah
Great-Grandson of Jaysho

For Nara, Wife of Nomis

The Rings of Saturn

I think
I hear a ring
It comes and goes
But makes no sound

As I float
Upon this mote
So close to past
I must not fast

But can I know
The things that make
These rings go round
Without a sound

A silent ring
This thing called time
A blend of many things
A path of yours and mind

Rings, time, path, mind
I think
The same
I think

For Nomis, Husband of Nara

Sweet Dreams, Nomis

The following year, Nara settled in Albuquerque, New Mexico. She has been living there for twelve years now. She often goes to those high bluffs near the Tijeras Arroyo in Montesa Park when her grandson, little Nomis Jr., comes to visit. They sit cross-legged on starry nights, counting stars, and she teaches him what she knows of the Navajo language. When they are finished with the words and have counted enough, they go into town and buy some soft ice cream cones, two of them—one big one and one little one! Nomis says that if they buy three it might be the crib that gives him away. Sometimes they also stop at the observatory and ask the technician to point the telescope at the Rings of Saturn.

∞ ∞ ∞

The Solarnet is now much safer to use. COP hasn't had a successful attack in twelve years, although there have been many attempts. Nara is sure that Nomis is right there in the background as mentor, reminding those who now defend those pathways of light to firmly grasp their mathematics with one hand, but make sure their poetry is always within reach of the other. To do a good job, he claims, you need both.

Much to the displeasure of a few Washington bureaucrats, just last year the State of New Mexico named that bluff Blind Man's Bluff, in honor of Dr. Nomis Chester. The locals say that if you go out to Blind Man's Bluff on dark winter nights when the air is cold and thin, you can see the faintly flickering image of Dr. Nomis Chester and hear him chanting *Neasjah, Taschizzie, Dahetihhi, Jaysho* over and over again. The kids who play there sometimes call this ghostly image the good spirit of Dahetihhi, the hummingbird.

Nara also goes to visit Herbert and Liz every summer at their cottage on a Canadian lake near Ottawa, Ontario. In the fall, after the colors of the maples fade from yellow and brilliant red to brown, and the leaves and seed pods fall to the ground in their circle of life and rebirth, the loons collect on the lake in flocks with their young before they fly south. To some, the loon has always been considered a magical and noble bird. On foggy fall mornings you can hear them cooing in the mist, but you can't see them. Sometimes Nara feels that Nomis has somehow taught them how to dream too. Sometimes Nara thinks it is Nomis himself cooing in the mist.

When the loons leave the lake in the fall, the old-timers say that hummingbirds sometimes hitch rides on the backs of those loons, tucked comfortably within their feathers during the long trip to the Gulf of

Mexico, Texas and New Mexico, where they winter. Nara always departs at about the same time as the loons for the long journey to Albuquerque, where she winters too.

Once a year in the late spring, at the end of the school term, when the cherry blossoms in Japan are full and plump, Nara returns to Kyoto, to Nanzen-ji with Liz, Jessica, and Doris. When one wriggles up through that hole at the top of the pagoda and approaches the iron box, there is always a little group of schoolchildren gathered there.

It is said that if a child places a poem in the iron box, later he or she will find it pinned to the corkboard at the entrance to the pagoda with comments, comments that are always helpful. No one knows how this happens—some say a friendly apparition tacks it there.

Epilogue

In 2004, the international journal, *Physical Review Letters*, published a study that raised long-term hopes for repairing sight and restoring memory. The implications of the research were enormous, potentially leading to the development of a microchip that stimulates brain activity when implanted in the retinas of the visually impaired.

In 2005 the same journal published a study suggesting that a cloaking device which renders objects invisible is closer to reality than one might think. The theory indicates light waves coming from an object can be blocked. When the cloaked object is hit by normal light it produces another kind of light wave called plasmons. Plasmons are waves caused when electrons on the surface of the object vibrate. If the plasmons achieve the right rhythm they scatter the normal light reflected from the cloaked object in a way that renders the eye of the observer selectively blind. Under these circumstances the observer's senses —touch, smell, hearing or taste—might have to do double duty to set the brain, and finally the eye, straight.